Harvest of the Sun

E. V. Thompson was born in London. He spent nine years in the Navy before joining the Bristol police force where he was a founder member of the 'Vice Squad'. Since then he has been an investigator with BOAC, worked with the Hong Kong Police Narcotics Bureau and was Chief Security Officer of Rhodesia's Department of Civil Aviation.

On his return to England he set out to be a full-time writer. A year later, broke but still writing, he swept factory floors, was a hotel detective in London and is now a civil servant in Plymouth Dockyard.

He lives in an old miner's cottage on the moors about which he has written, sharing it with his wife, four dogs, two cats, innumerable kittens, ducks, chickens and goldfish.

Also by E. V. Thompson in Pan Books

Chase The Wind

E. V. Thompson

Harvest of the Sun

Pan Books
in association with Macmillan London

First published 1978 by Macmillan London Ltd
This edition published 1980 by Pan Books Ltd,
Cavaye Place, London SW10 9PG
© E. V. Thompson 1978
ISBN 0 330 26013 8
Printed and bound in Great Britain by
Richard Clay (The Chaucer Press) Ltd, Bungay, Suffolk

BOOK ONE

CHAPTER ONE

Pride of Liverpool, Australia-bound from England, struck a reef off the coast of south-west Africa at 11 p.m. on the twenty-third day of February in the year eighteen hundred and forty-six. The tragedy occurred during the death throes of one of the most violent storms ever experienced in the region.

For three days the captain and his crew had tried to keep the ship bows-on to the hurricane wind that blew from the south and the waves that fought each other and threw themselves angrily upon the creaking ship. The captain had seen three of his ship's five masts snapped off close to the leaking deck by a combination of water and wind. He had watched, helpless, as five of his crew were washed overboard whilst attempting to repair a smashed hatch-cover. The battle to save his ship had been lost long before the sharp teeth of unseen rocks sank into her belly.

Below decks Josh Retallick was squatting on the floor of a cabin when the violent pitching of the ship came to a shudder-ing, timber-splintering stop. He had one arm about an iron stanchion, the other holding Miriam, who lay on a bunk, their three-year-old son Daniel clutched tightly in her arms.

'My God! What's happened?'

Miriam struggled to a sitting position as a thousand-ton wave fell upon the stricken ship and ground it farther on to the jagged rocks of the reef. The screams of the steerage passengers trapped in a holed compartment rose above the thunder of the sea and the shrieking of the wind, and it did not need the cries of a seaman in the passageway outside the cabin to tell Josh the ship was going to sink.

'Quick! We've got to get up top.'

Josh pulled Miriam to her feet and snatched the complaining Daniel from her. He reached for the door and pulled it open. Over his shoulder he called, 'Take hold of my belt – and don't let go. Our lives depend on staying together.'

'Josh, there are some things we need—'

'There's no time. We're going to be hard put to save ourselves.'

Pride of Liverpool added emphasis to his words by writhing on the rocks as they stumbled out into the passageway. The ship was doomed. Even as they cleared the cabin water burst through the bulkhead at the far end of the passageway and swirled knee-deep about them. There was no light to guide Josh to the companionway, and beyond the hatchway to the deck there was only an unknown wild darkness.

A wave attacked the ship and sent Josh and Miriam staggering drunkenly about the passageway, but the rocks did not relinquish their hold. They had the stern of the vessel fast in their teeth and held on with the tenacity of a bull-baiting terrier, pulling the ship down.

The passageway was a scene of panic and confusion. The occupants of the other cabins all had the same instinctive aim — to get up to the deck. To achieve it they clawed and screamed as they fell over fellow-passengers.

Josh could afford to behave no better when he reached the foot of the ladder only to find it jammed with men and women fighting for a place on the steps. Unceremoniously he forced a way through them, flinging aside those who were incapable of climbing up to the deck but would not move forward or back. Once Miriam slipped and Josh had to reach back to grasp her wrist, hauling her up behind him, saved from falling by the others jamming the ladder.

They made the deck and were nearly swept over the side as a wave struck the bow and washed the length of the ship. The water took with it all those passengers and crew who had reached the deck before them.

Now he was here, Josh was uncertain which way to go. All was blackness and confusion, the howling of the wind and the crashing of the sea loud enough to numb the mind.

Another wave poured over the bows of the ship, but this one smashed in a hatch-cover and the water tumbled into a forward hold. It acted as ballast, and the ship righted herself temporarily. Moving out on to the level platform of the deck Josh could hear indistinct voices shouting near the stern. It was here he had seen two of *Pride of Liverpool*'s boats and he cautiously made his way in their direction.

He reached the shattered stump of the mainmast and clung to it while another wave rushed past them, its cold waters swirling waist-high. There were screams in the angry night, and Miriam gasped as the water tore at her, but she never loosened her grip on Josh's belt. Daniel's cries had by now died away to a frightened whimper and his arms gripped tight about his father's neck. Josh could do no more than give him a quick reassuring hug as he listened for sounds in the stormy night.

He heard the voices again – and heard something more. The creaking of a pulley. A boat was being swung out on its davits over the ship's side. Straining his eyes into the night Josh thought he could make out its shape no more than twelve feet away.

He would have to make his move now, before the next wave swept the ship's deck.

'Now, Miriam! With me!'

He lunged towards the outline of the boat, dragging Miriam with him. As *Pride of Liverpool* gave another dying shudder he reached it, his hand gripping its clinkered side.

'Inside. Quickly!'

Handing Daniel to Miriam he heaved them both into the boat.

There was a curse of surprise from inside; but the boat was already slipping outwards away from the ship's side, and Josh barely had time to scramble in himself before it was dangling clear of *Pride of Liverpool*.

'Who's that?' The startled call came from the other end of the boat. 'Are you crewmen or passengers?'

'Passengers.'

'This is a crew boat. We can't take passengers.'

The boat swung inwards, crashing against the side of the ship, and the ropes that held it creaked in protest.

'If you don't keep it away from the side, you'll *have* no boat.' Josh called back.

The wind carried most of his words away, and Josh sensed rather than saw the seaman edging towards him. Then another wave pounded the passenger ship and ground her farther on to the rocks of the reef.

'*Isaiah!* Help me free this rope. If it jams, the boat's lost.'

A voice shouted from the darkness as the bow of the boat swung into the ship's side with considerable force.

The sailor who had been moving towards Josh went back to help his companion.

Pride of Liverpool was breaking up fast now, the rocks tearing great holes below the waterline. The small boat had its troubles too. It was buffeted repeatedly against the side of its mother ship with ever increasing force. While the two seamen struggled with the fall-rope Josh made Miriam and Daniel crouch in the bottom of the boat, then he moved forward to try to keep the bow from smashing to pieces.

A spar and sail from one of the remaining masts were part of the tangled wreckage caught against the davit, and Josh was able to free some of the heavy sodden canvas and stuff it between the boat and the ship.

As he worked he could hear shouts and screams from farther away along the deck of the ship. It was too dark to see, but he gained the impression of activity around another boat on the far side of the deck.

Another wave was thrown up over *Pride of Liverpool*, and a wall of water raced from stem to stern at the very moment that some of the crew were leading a large party of steerage passengers along the deck. More than twenty people were swept off their feet by the sea and carried away into the night, their screams lost in the wind.

Helpless, Josh heard them passing only feet away from him. The same wave lifted the boat up and away from the ship, and as Josh leaned out to hold the canvas in position there was a bump against the clinkered planking not a yard from him.

Josh plunged his hand over the side into the water and as something brushed past he grabbed at it. His fingers took a hold on a thin dress. He held his grip against the pull of the water as two tiny hands clawed their way over his clenched fist and gripped his wrist.

Slowly, his muscles cracking against the relentless pull of the greedy sea, he began to bring the unseen little girl in towards the side of the boat.

Suddenly the whole world went topsy-turvy. The boat tilted dangerously, its stern dropping four feet in a breathtaking fall. Miriam screamed as she and Daniel began sliding uncontrollably down the boat. Then the bow slipped too. For a split second the boat hung level before falling twelve feet to the sea. It landed with a crash that would have burst the seams of a lesser-built vessel.

Josh still had his fist closed, but the girl had gone in the first moment of the fall. As the boat bounced and pitched he crawled to where he had left Miriam and Daniel.

'Miriam . . . ?'

'We're here, Josh. We're here. . . .' Her voice broke. She had thought him lost in the sudden awful plunge to the sea and now she reached out for him.

'Thank God!'

He bruised his shoulder on a thwart as he crawled beneath it to take Miriam and Daniel into his arms. Then they all three crouched huddled together in the bottom of the boat, drenched by the sea and spray but sheltered from the howling wind.

Not until then did Josh open his right hand and release the fragment of calico cloth torn from a small girl's dress. It dropped to the floor of the boat and was washed away by the water that lay inches deep there. Outside in the vastness of the great ocean a ship perished and a little girl went to meet her creator wearing a torn dress.

CHAPTER TWO

All through that weary night Josh, Miriam and Daniel clung together in the bottom of the boat as cold water slopped about them and the storm raged above. Daniel was sick. He was sick until the spasms completely exhausted him and then he lay motionless in his mother's arms. He was so still that Miriam frequently pressed her head to his chest to satisfy herself his heart was still beating.

More than once during that long darkness the feet of the two crewmen stumbled over the trio, and once one of them tried none too gently to kick them aside in the restricted space. Josh knew they were unwanted and resented, but he felt too ill to do more than accept the crewmen's curses and try to keep out of their way.

When dawn finally arrived wrapped in a cold grey shawl it found the small family group huddled together in the bow of the boat. The two seamen were bent over heavy creaking oars, pulling at them in ragged unison. Looking at the sea that heaved about them Josh thought their efforts were totally futile. Nevertheless, they were still afloat.

One of the seamen, as tall and thin as his companion was short and stocky, had been watching the small family group since it was light enough to see. When he spoke Josh recognised the voice of the man who had tried to make them leave the boat the night before.

'Can you pull an oar?'

Josh shook his head wearily and licked salt-caked lips before replying.

'I've never had to — but I'll try if it will be any help.'

'Trying won't help none in this sea. It'd most likely turn us over. You can either row or you can't.'

'You'd best do some bailing and get rid of the water in the boat,' said the other seaman. 'There's a bucket in the locker just by you.'

The locker was built into the bow of the boat, and Josh had

been leaning against the door. Unfastening it with difficulty against the movement of the sea he saw a metal-bodied bucket amongst a jumble of other things. Pulling it clear he began bailing. A great deal of water had been shipped during the night, and Josh scooped up bucketful after bucketful and flung it over the side.

The waves still heaved themselves high above the boat but they no longer fought with each other. They were now long swollen rollers, each following its precedessor, undefeated and hugely powerful, vast muscles of the sea. It was almost as though the sinking of *Pride of Liverpool* had been the sole objective of the fierce storm. Now it had been accomplished nature was relaxing. Only occasionally did the wind ruffle the creamy crests of the waves, and already the sky was lighter than it had been for days.

When Miriam raised her head to him Josh was shocked by her appearance. There was a great weariness in her eyes, and fatigue had etched deep lines on her face, but easing the sleeping Daniel to a more comfortable position in her arms she mustered a wan smile.

'We're safe now, Miriam. The storm is nearly over.'

'And the ship? Has it gone?'

It was the sailor who had suggested Josh begin bailing who answered her.

'The ship wouldn't have lasted more'n five minutes after we got away, missus.'

'What about all the others . . . ?'

Miriam did not complete her wide-eyed question.

The seaman shook his head. 'It's a miracle any of us is here. There were times during the night when I didn't expect to see the light of day again. Aye, it's a miracle right enough.'

He leaned on an oar that was thicker around than his own brawny arm.

'Seeing as how we're likely to be in each other's company for a while, we'd best introduce ourselves. Sam Speke from Kent, missus. A sailor all me life.'

He inclined his head towards the man on the seat behind him. 'And that's Isaiah Dacket.'

'I'm Josh Retallick. This is Miriam and my son Daniel.'

Sam Speke nodded acknowledgement, and the other man whose eyes had not left Miriam since she woke now shifted his gaze to Josh.

'You're the one who came aboard as a convict at Falmouth.'

For a moment Josh was genuinely startled by the words. The events of the night had cast away thoughts of everything else. Now he remembered and his spirits sank.

'Yes.'

'You was leading a riot in which some soldiers got killed, so I heard.'

'Then you heard wrong. I was trying to stop a riot, not lead one.'

Josh did not expect the seaman to believe him. Why should he? The jury at the Assize Court in Bodmin Town had not believed him. They had found him guilty. But it was no longer of any real significance. The fury of the storm, its power and destructive capability had shown the decisions of man to be trivial by comparison.

Yet Josh wished his past life might have sunk with *Pride of Liverpool* and allowed him to emerge from it a free man.

The son of a Cornish copper miner, Josh had received an exceptional education from the local Wesleyan preacher, William Thackeray. As a result he had been able to serve an apprenticeship and become an engineer in the mine where his father worked.

The same preacher had also schooled Miriam, who had been Josh's girl-friend since she was a barefooted girl running wild on the Cornish moor. When her father had been tragically killed at the hands of a group of vengeful miners led by Josh's father, Thackeray had married Miriam—even though she was carrying Josh's child.

But William Thackeray taught more than reading and writing, and it was a mutual interest in a union of miners that brought the three of them together again—for a brief while. It was not long before the preacher caused a violent confrontation between soldiers and miners—after ensuring that Josh would arrive on the scene in time to take the blame for the disturbance.

Josh's only share in the riot was an eighteen-inch sabre-slash across his back and a musket-ball through his arm. It was enough to earn him a sentence of transportation for life.

Only the determination and influence of Josh's former employer had secured for Josh the status of 'privileged prisoner' travelling on a passenger ship with a cargo of mine-engines to be installed in an Australian copper mine. It was this same man who had also arranged for Miriam and Daniel to travel on the same ship after she had left her husband. It was to be their chance to begin a new life together. Miriam had joined *Pride of Liverpool* as Miriam Retallick, and Josh had the satisfaction of knowing that this part of their secret at least would be safe.

'It doesn't matter, Josh. It doesn't matter.'

His mind came back to the present to find Miriam grasping his hand and whispering urgently to him.

'Whatever crime he was supposed to have committed couldn't have been so bad, I reckon,' put in Sam Speke. 'Otherwise they'd never have let him roam free on the ship.'

'Not unless he's got some friends in high places,' retorted the scowling Isaiah Dacket.

Josh had been looking at Miriam. Now he turned his head and raised his eyes to Isaiah Dacket's face. The sailor held his gaze defiantly for a few moments before his resolution wavered and he looked away. Angrily, he pushed the heavy oar an arm's length away from him as though it was to blame for his sudden discomfort.

Isaiah Dacket was deeply resentful of Josh's privileged treatment for a reason unknown to the others. The tall seaman had himself suffered the rigours of imprisonment – but with no one ready or able to help him. Isaiah Dacket had been taken prisoner when he was involved in the sale of other human beings, a willing crewman on a French slave-ship.

An orphan, Isaiah Dacket had been placed in the Royal Navy by the Parish when he was eleven years of age. Eight years later he was a deserter. It was then he discovered the money to be made by a seaman with no principles. He had no qualms about being part of such a trade. Indeed, he enjoyed it. For the first time in his life Isaiah discovered men whose lot in life was more wretched than his own – and they had with them women who were there for the taking.

But such a way of life could not last. More and more countries were outlawing slavery and making determined attempts to stamp it out. One morning, a day out from west Africa, the slave-ship was surprised by a French man-of-war. Isaiah spent two years in a stinking French prison where his suffering owed as much to his attitude towards the authorities as to his slaving activities.

Released under the terms of an obscure amnesty, Isaiah immediately returned to the sea on an English merchantman. He carried with him a hatred of Frenchmen and enough dark memories to bring him awake in a cold sweat in the middle of the night.

Isaiah Dacket could never forgive Josh for not having suffered as he had – or for having a woman of his own. One who had not been bought for a specified time, cash in advance. There had been no love in Isaiah's life, and, though he would have poured scorn on anyone who put it into words, he was fiercely envious of any man who had the love of a woman.

'If we stay out here talking and glaring at one another, we won't reach land until nightfall,' said Sam Speke.

'Land? Where?' Their tiredness suddenly forgotten, both Josh and Miriam scrambled to their knees in the bottom of the boat and peered out over the bow. The sudden movement woke Daniel. He sat upright in Miriam's arms, clinging tightly to her as his eyes sought something familiar in these extraordinary surroundings.

Josh and Miriam were eager for a first sight of land, but as each wave carried them upwards they looked into the sunrise in vain.

It was some minutes before Josh realised that what they could see on the horizon was not the gold of a tropical sunrise but a high bank of sand rising from the water's edge and extending for as far as could be seen.

Excitedly he pointed it out to Miriam and their son. Daniel was unimpressed.

'I'm hungry!' he exclaimed, with all the indignation of a three-year-old.

'If we got rid of some of this water in the bottom of the boat, we'd reach shore a lot sooner and find something to eat,' grumbled Isaiah Dacket.

Josh had already decided he did not like the surly Dacket. He would never be able to forget his attempt to prevent them from embarking in the boat during those last terrifying minutes on board *Pride of Liverpool*. He wondered how many others had been turned away from sanctuary in the boat.

Miriam could have been reading his thoughts.

'Do you think any other boats got away?'

Josh shrugged. 'Perhaps — but I doubt whether many passengers were in them.'

They might never know. In this sea a boat could be a mere hundred yards away and remain hidden.

Josh's glance went back to the tall swarthy sailor, and Miriam saw it.

'Don't let him rile you, Josh. We're alive. What was said last night is past. If it hadn't been for the sailors, we should have drowned.'

Josh remembered the tiny fingers slipping from his wrist. He fell silent and resumed bailing with excessive vigour.

It was early afternoon before they reached the shore. The fickle wind seemed reluctant to release them and veered round to westward, blowing from the shore. It was infuriating because the land was so tantalisingly close that grit blown from the sand dunes stung their faces and ground between their teeth.

Not until the ebbing tide turned did the boat begin to move in towards the beach again. By now the two seamen were near to exhaustion, their shirts soaked with the perspiration caused by pulling at the heavy oars in the heat of the fierce midday sun.

But the long delay in landing gave Josh ample opportunity to examine the strange and forbidding coastline in some detail. What he saw was not reassuring. The beach was a wide strip of sand heavily studded with rocks and long dark reefs. Behind it the sand dunes they had first sighted rose to great heights, their rounded slopes chiselled into concentric patterns by the wind.

The boat was only yards from the beach when Josh looked out over the side and suddenly saw a low barrier of glistening black rock protruding from the sea immediately ahead of them.

'Look out! Rocks!'

Sam Speke instantly dug his oar into the water in an attempt to slow the boat. His companion was less quick to react. Isaiah Dacket gave one more powerful stroke, causing the boat to slew sideways on to the beach. It was picked up by the next breaker, and seconds later the small party suffered their second shipwreck in the space of twenty-four hours.

The boat was dashed sideways against the reef, and with the sound of splintering wood ringing in their ears the occupants were flung into the water.

Held by the rocks the boat lay on its side for a moment or two until the next wave turned it upside down and carried it in towards the shore.

Josh floundered towards Daniel, who was choking and screaming a few feet from him. As he caught the boy and lifted his head clear of the water Josh's feet touched solid sand. He reached out a hand for Miriam and they waded ashore coughing and choking from the salt water they had swallowed.

Behind them the two seamen fought to drag the boat in through the surf that pounded heavily against the shore. Handing the badly frightened Daniel to Miriam, Josh went to their aid.

The three men righted the boat and, helped by the breakers, dragged it on to the beach. Waiting for the water to drain out through a foot-wide hole punched in the bottom, they heaved the boat up beyond the highest line of sun-dried seaweed.

As well as the hole, half a dozen of the planks had sprung apart. The longboat would never put to sea again.

'You should have seen those rocks,' exclaimed Isaiah Dacket angrily. 'Look at the bloody boat now – smashed.'

'It got us ashore safely,' retorted Josh. 'That's the main thing.'

'Is it? You don't know where we are. This is the place called the Skeleton Coast – and you'll soon see why. There's been many a fine ship wrecked here, and you'll find the bones of hundreds of good seamen picked clean by the crabs and bleached by the sun. Ashore we may be. Safe? I doubt it.'

Spitting scornfully on to the sand, Isaiah Dacket strode away to wade into the sea and recover an oar that was floating close inshore.

'Don't take no notice of Isaiah, Mr Retallick,' said the more affable Sam Speke. 'He's not the happiest of men but he's as fine a seaman as you'll find anywhere.'

'He's going to have to learn to be a good landsman,' commented Josh. 'Otherwise he'll be even more miserable.'

Turning away, he walked over to where Miriam was stripping the clothes from Daniel. After wringing the water from them she laid them out on the sand to dry. The sun beating down on them was so hot that steam began rising immediately.

'He's not worried, anyway.' Miriam smiled, nodding in Daniel's direction. His recent ducking and protested hunger already forgotten, the small boy sat enjoying his nakedness. Picking up handfuls of dry sand, he allowed it to escape between his fingers. All the drama of the shipwreck and the storm were already fading in his memory.

'You'd best put some clothes about the boy's shoulders, missus. This sun's fierce enough to peel the skin off an orange.'

As Miriam hurriedly put Daniel's wet shirt about his shoulders, Josh helped Sam Speke to pull the wet canvas sail from the holed boat's locker. It was stiff and heavy, but with it they could rig a shelter that would keep the sun off and allow the breeze to pass beneath it and help cool them.

When it was done Miriam put Daniel in its shade.

'What now, Josh?' she asked quietly.

Standing beside him, her hair hung damp and lank about her shoulders and her eyes appeared abnormally large in her tired face, but she was still able to stir feelings inside Josh that had no place here at this time.

'I want to go up to the top of those dunes and see what's on the other side.' Josh looked along the empty shoreline. 'We might even see some more survivors — or perhaps a boat.'

Miriam knew as well as Josh that no others had escaped from the ship with their lives, but it was not a thought to put into words just yet. The memory of their own skirmish with death was too cose.

'I'll come up there with you,' Sam Speke said to Josh. 'It'll be better if there are two of us; there's no telling what might be about. It looks empty enough from here, but this is a strange land.'

'I'd rather you stayed with Miriam and the boy,' Josh said pointedly.

'Isaiah'll do that,' replied the seaman. Then he caught Josh's expression.

'Oh, don't you worry about him. He'll have plenty to do.' Securing a loose rope on the canvas, he called to the tall seaman.

'Me and Mr Retallick's climbing up to the top of the dunes to see if there's anything about. While we're gone you can get a fire going and catch some fish for our supper. There's a good hook and line in the boat's locker.'

'You giving the orders now, Sam Speke? Fancy yourself as the bos'n of this party, perhaps?'

'All I fancy is fish for supper.'

'How can Isaiah get a fire going?' asked Josh as he paused to look back on the first gentle slope of the dunes.

'The same way as any sailor lights his pipe on a wet and stormy night,' replied the burly sailor, pulling a pigskin pouch from inside his shirt. 'A seaman learns on his first trip how to keep his baccy dry and the way to light it whatever the weather. By the time we get back there'll be a good fire going and fish to eat.'

After the first slope the going became harder. The soft coarse sand slid away beneath their feet and they sank ankle-deep with every step.

They struggled upwards but arrived at the ridge only to find a higher one beyond it. It was the same picture when they conquered that one. There was always one more that was higher. By now Josh's legs felt as though they had weights attached to them. Two months on board ship had done nothing to tone up his leg muscles. The two men climbed for an hour, yet when Josh turned around he was still close enough to the beach for Miriam and Daniel to return his wave.

The two men rested for a while on the next ridge. Sand dunes stretched on either side like a vast crumpled blanket, and they could see the narrowing ribbon of beach curve away until it was lost in the shimmering haze of distance. Beyond it was the sea. Calm now, it was coloured a deep dark blue with here and there a patch of light-green shallows, or a white-fringed black reef. In other circumstances Josh would have looked at it and thought it incredibly beautiful.

In the whole of the vast panorama the three people on the beach below them provided the only sign of life. In the burning heat of the tropical afternoon not even a bird stirred.

'Do you think anyone else got off the ship?' Josh asked the question, seeking confirmation of his own belief.

The seaman shook his head slowly. 'No. There wasn't a chance for any of 'em. We had but four boats on the whole ship, and I saw two of them smashed myself. I reckon the other one went the same way. Even if it had been lowered it would have gone straight down on to the rocks. No, Mr Retallick, there's only us left alive from the old *Pride of Liverpool*.'

'Then why didn't we try to get more people off with us in our boat? It would have held twenty or thirty others.'

Sam Speke looked everywhere but at Josh's face. 'It was the only way, Mr Retallick, believe me it was. In a shipwreck you've got to act quick. Them as is there gets away with their lives. Them as isn't don't. I've seen it all before and so has Isaiah. I was wrecked once on the Scillies and once on the coast of Jamaica. It was off the Scillies where I saw a brave captain make the crew of his boat stay close to the ship until they'd picked up so many survivors the boat became top heavy and capsized. All of 'em was drowned.'

He looked at Josh now. 'I don't expect you to understand, Mr Retallick, but you and your family are on land and alive. You remember that whenever you get to thinking we should have done something else.'

There was a note of aggressiveness in Sam Speke's voice that told Josh far more than the seaman's words. For all his reasoning the burly seaman knew he had behaved in a cowardly manner on *Pride of Liverpool* at the height of the storm. He had thought only of saving his own life. He would deny it and defend his motives vehemently, but the truth of it would stay with him for ever.

However, Josh found it easier to accept his explanation knowing Miriam and Daniel had been brought ashore safe and well.

Sam Speke sent dry sand trickling from one hand to the other. 'There's been more ships than enough wrecked along this coast. I can't recall hearing of anyone being taken off afterwards. It isn't called the Skeleton Coast for nothing. A wise captain keeps his ship well offshore from it. It's a place to know about from over the horizon. We can't hope that any vessel will pass close enough to see us.'

He dropped the sand to the ground and stood up. Dusting his hands against his trousers, he gave Josh a faint smile. 'Come to think of it, I've never heard tell of anyone going inland and living to boast about it, either. But I don't suppose that's going to stop us from climbing up that next ridge to look and see what's there.'

Miriam searched along the beach for small pieces of wood while Isaiah tore two of the thwarts from the boat and split them into long splinters with the aid of his seaman's knife. Miriam was surprised at the amount of wood to be found half-embedded in the sand, some of it well above the high-tide mark She thought it had doubtless been carried there by some great storm even worse than the one they had survived. One old plank was drilled with worm holes large enough to put her fingers inside, but it was dry and helped the fire get away to a good start.

As the first flames burst into life Isaiah fed it with wood shavings while Miriam knelt beside it and fanned it into life.

When the flames were biting into the larger pieces of wood Miriam brushed a long tress of hair back over her shoulder and looked up with eyes smarting from the smoke. Isaiah was standing close, looking down at her, and there was something in his eyes that made her body go suddenly tense. Slowly she rose from the sand to face him.

'You're a handsome woman to be married to a convict,' said the seaman.

Miriam did not correct him.

'What I am is of no concern to you.'

'I like spirit in a woman — just so long as her man has some control over it.'

'What you like is your own business. But I advise you to choose your words carefully in front of Josh.'

'You don't have to worry about me. Isaiah Dacket knows when to hold his tongue. I know a few other things too. You remember *that* when we get to where there's people. Your husband's a convict, sentenced to transportation. Any influential friends he might have are a long way from these parts.'

The seaman gave Miriam what might have been an attempt at a smile.

'You'll need someone to look after you when he's gone.'

'Taking good care of my son as well, of course?'

The sarcasm was lost on Isaiah Dacket.

'I'd treat him right. You wouldn't have to worry about that.'

Maintaining her self-control cost Miriam a great effort.

'Isaiah Dacket, I think you'd better save all that breath you're wasting for catching fish — and I hope you'll have a lot more success or we'll all starve to death.'

Isaiah Dacket turned away without a change of expression. Taking the line from the boat he made his way down to the water's edge.

Josh and Sam Speke returned just before the sun sank over the glittering horizon. A number of large fish were cooking on makeshift spits over the fire, and the two men sank to the ground within reaching distance of the sizzling food.

As they ate, Daniel leaned against Josh, worn out from the heat of the tropical day and the bewildering turn his young life had taken. He tried to stay awake to eat all the hot fish Miriam fed to him, but once the edge of his hunger had been dulled he found it hard going.

'Well? Is neither of you going to say more than "This fish tastes good"? What did you see from up there?'

Miriam put the question even though their very silence told her the climb to the top of the dunes had been a waste of time.

'There was nothing to see,' replied Josh.

'Only plenty of sand,' corrected Sam Speke.

'How far could you see?'

Miriam tried to glean some hope from their terseness.

'Twenty miles. Twenty-five, perhaps.'

'And there is nothing but sand for that distance inland?'

Josh nodded glumly.

'Well, we did think there could have been a mountain or something well to the south,' said Sam. 'At least, Josh saw it. I wasn't so sure. Not that it would make any difference,' he finished lamely. 'It would just be rock instead of sand, that's all.'

The news was depressing but it came as no surprise to anyone.

Night descended very rapidly in this part of the world, and as Isaiah Dacket lifted another spit of fish from the fire and threw on a piece of wood firefly sparks rose from it and chased each other into a star-sprinkled darkness.

'We'll have to move off first thing in the morning and find water,' said the tall seaman. 'The keg in the boat's dry. Without water we'll be lucky to last through the day.'

'That's true enough, Josh' – the burly Sam Speke had dropped the formal 'Mr Retallick' at Josh's insistence – 'it gets terrible hot in these parts. We've got to have water.'

'That needn't bother us. Not while we're by the sea,' Josh replied. 'We've got all the water we need.'

Isaiah snorted in disgust. 'You drink that and we'll have to tie you down. Sea water puts madness into a man's blood. But I doubt if a landsman would know about such things.'

'No,' agreed Josh quietly, 'but any man who's had anything to do with making engines knows how to purify water. Was the bucket saved when the boat capsized?'

'Yes,' Miriam answered. 'We've got two buckets from the boat's locker under the canvas – one metal, the other leather.'

'Good. What else is in there?' Isaiah Dacket was curious.

'There's some rope; a piece or two of canvas; a boat-hook; anchor; couple of tin mugs. . . .'

'Then we've got all the things we need to purify sea water and take plenty with us.'

Sam Speke looked at Josh as though he had pronounced he would turn the sand into gold.

'It's easy enough, Sam.' Josh smiled at the seaman's disbelief. 'It simply involves boiling the sea water and cooling the steam quickly. Then all we have to do is collect the water that forms.'

The seaman looked no less awed.

'Don't worry about it. You'll see for yourself tomorrow. However, it's going to take time to fill that fresh-water keg. We'll be here for a couple of days. The best thing we can do is get plenty of rest and eat as much fish as we can catch. We can salt some, too, with the salt we collect from the sea water. Then we'll be leaving here better prepared to face a journey.'

'So now everyone gets to be captain,' said Isaiah Dacket. 'No doubt it'll be the woman and the boy's turn tomorrow — while I'm left to catch all the fish.'

'If you do as well as you did today, you'll have done enough,' said Josh. 'Now I suggest we make up that fire and get some sleep. I feel as though I haven't closed my eyes for a week.'

Josh, Miriam and Daniel were to sleep beneath the canvas awning while the two sailors took the inside of the boat. Although they had been wrecked on a tropical shore, the night was surprisingly cool. After wrapping some of the loose canvas about Daniel, Josh and Miriam lay down together on the unyielding sand and held each other close.

Since the night when Daniel had been conceived, high on Cornwall's Bodmin Moor, much had happened to keep the two of them apart. It was not until Josh had taken passage as a privileged prisoner on the ill-fated *Pride of Liverpool* bound for Australia that they had come together as man and wife. They were still learning to know each other again. Even having their bodies touch was a wonderful renewed experience for them both.

'Josh?' Miriam's whisper was very close to Josh's ear. 'What will we find when we leave this place? What are we looking for?' It was the tremulous query of a young girl, suddenly uncertain of what the future held.

'Who knows what we'll find? Maybe a village. A farm. People like ourselves. Sam says the Cape Colony is somewhere to the south of us. There are lots of people there. English and Dutch mostly.'

'How far away is that?'

'Sam didn't know. He's not exactly sure just where we are. But if we head south and get clear of this desert I'm sure we'll find them. I believe there are probably people inland too, but we can't risk trying to cross that sand.'

'And what happens when we do find them, Josh? What happens to us?'

He pulled her even closer and kissed her forehead.

'Don't worry about that now. There'll be a place for us. I'll turn my hand to anything to give us a living.'

'But you are still a convict as far as the rest of the world is concerned. What will happen when people find out?'

'Why should they find out? I was convicted in England. We're thousands of miles away from all that now.'

'No, Josh. Isaiah knows all about it. He'll talk to whoever will listen. He doesn't like you.'

Josh fell silent. The grim memories of prison and the horrors of the prison hulk flooded back to him. This time it would be worse. He would be tortured by the thought of what was happening to Miriam and Daniel, unprotected in a strange land. He determined that whatever happened he would not become a convict again and no man would send him back to prison.

Miriam was aware of the tight knot of unhappiness inside her man. She began to wish she had said nothing. Then she remembered Isaiah's words and knew she had been right to speak.

'Josh?'

'H'm?'

'Don't ever trust Isaiah, Josh. Whatever happens never put any trust in Isaiah Dacket.'

Again there was silence.

'Josh?'

'Yes?'

'I love you — and Daniel needs you. I'll kill anyone who tried to part us now. Don't let it happen, Josh.'

Josh felt her tears warm against his cheek and he held her to him until the soft whispering of the surf lulled them both to sleep.

CHAPTER THREE

As Josh had predicted, the distilling of the sea water was a slow process. The water had to be boiled in the metal bucket, the steam cooled in one upturned tin mug and allowed to drip into the other. It meant someone had to stay by the fire the whole time to transfer fresh water to the keg and ensure that none of the delicately balanced apparatus fell into the fire.

But there were compensations. The wind had dropped to a breeze coming off the sea and, although the weather was hot, it was not unbearably so, making the three days they spent at the spot where they had landed a pleasant interlude after the horrors of the storm.

It was an opportunity for Josh and Miriam to get to know their two companions.

There was nothing complicated about Sam Speke. He was a slow-moving, slow-thinking reliable man of infinite patience. He had taken it upon himself to look after Daniel, and nothing the small boy wanted was too much trouble for him. The burly seaman spent the whole of one afternoon making a wide-brimmed canvas hat and matching sleeveless jacket for the boy, stitching both items with a sailmaker's needle, using fishing-line for thread.

'There, that'll keep the sun from burning you,' he said, putting the home-made garments on the boy. Daniel paraded in them proudly and from that moment refused to take them off.

Isaiah Dacket was a very different character. Even when he was in a good mood he was taciturn to the point of rudeness. Much of the time he spent immersed in his own thoughts, excluding those about him. In worse mood he muttered to himself and glared angrily at anyone who spoke to him. His uncertain temperament provided additional fuel for Miriam's uneasiness about him.

Miriam had much time to think as she worked hard in a largely unsuccessful attempt to preserve the fish that Isaiah Dacket caught in plenty. She tried to pack into two days a method of curing that required nine, using the salt produced from the distilling. It was not long enough. Although she rubbed salt well in, and finished off the process by smoking the partially cured fish, the end result was an evil-smelling product that she was glad to pack away into the pouches that Sam Speke made from the invaluable canvas.

On their third day ashore the castaways received a grim reminder of the fate they had so narrowly escaped.

The outgoing tide left two bodies behind on the beach only a hundred yards from their fire. One was identified by the two seamen as a fellow-crewman from *Pride of Liverpool*. The other body was that of an unknown boy aged about sixteen. He was committed, nameless, to a shallow sand grave alongside the man whose rough-hewn cross declared him to be the late 'Brendan O'Keefe. Seaman. *Pride of Liverpool*. Died 23rd February 1843'.

The following morning the shipwrecked party moved off along a coastline shrouded in early-morning mist with the keg and the leather bucket full of fresh water. Each of the travellers wore a canvas hat made by Sam Speke and carried a canvas pouch of fish which was already registering a strong protest against the hasty method used for curing.

The men took it in turn to carry the eight-gallon keg between them, and Josh also had Daniel riding on his back in a make-shift canvas sling. They had with them the tin bucket, mugs, and a boat-hook which closely resembled a pike-staff. This, together with the two knives carried by the seamen, comprised their total armoury.

Their plan was boldly simple. They would head southwards, following the coast, until they encountered people.

It was hotter now they were moving, fully laden. The dawn mist was soon burned away and the sun blazed down upon them from a clear blue sky. Even the beach underfoot was hot, and they walked as close to the sea as possible to take advantage of the firm damp water-cooled sand.

Miriam had an additional problem that she tried to keep from the others. She steadied the pouch she carried with fingers that were stiff and painful, the skin cracked and raw from two days of plunging them in brine water and working rough-grained salt into the fish.

All that day they trudged along the water's edge on weary legs unused to such exercise. They covered fifteen miles and sighted two wrecks. The first was a few hundred yards out from the shore, only the stern protruding from the teeth of the reef that had torn it to pieces not many years before.

The second wreck was much older, and they reached it at the end of the day. It was twenty yards inland, protruding from the sand dunes as though it had been carried ashore and half-buried by a giant hand. The castaways had yet to learn that the sands of the Skeleton Coast were never still. They advanced and retreated as the mood and the wind took them.

They had been speculating on the strange shape of the wreck for the last two miles, its plump dumpy lines provoking a keen professional interest from the two seamen.

When they finally reached it they examined it in great detail, pointed out the unusual method used to fit together the now crumbling timbers.

'I've never seen the likes of this,' muttered Isaiah Dacket, walking around the wide rounded bow, the timbers of which had been scoured to a fine smoothness by the sand.

'I have, many years ago,' said Sam Speke thoughtfully. 'But she wasn't still sailing. She was laid up in Lisbon, as unseaworthy a ship as you'd find anywhere, fit only for the breakers — but the Portuguese wouldn't hear of it. Belonged to one of their great admirals years and years ago, so I was told. That ship had the same pot-bellied look about it as this one.'

'I expect it'll burn as well as English wood,' said Isaiah Dacket practically, tugging at a piece of the timber. It broke away with a sound like a musket-shot.

He was right. It burned well and threw out a good heat.

As no one seemed anxious to sample the fish Miriam had preserved they set about catching fresh fish.

There were some low rocky outcrops just off the shore, and the ebbing tide had left one or two small pools. It was Sam Speke who found the first huge crab. Nearly a foot across its shell, it scuttled sideways from the rocks into a pool as Sam approached.

The sailor stalked it cautiously until he was able to pounce upon it and grasp it without endangering his fingers in the hard bony claws. Holding it in the air, he called triumphantly to the others, 'This will make a fine meal. Quick, now, look around for more while I put this one into the bucket.'

The crab struggled valiantly, its powerful claws grabbing helplessly as it attacked the air, but there was no escape.

Between them they found an incredible nine large crabs, and as darkness fell they all sat around a blazing fire enjoying a meal of delicious crab meat.

'All it needs to round this off is some bread and soft butter and a pint of good strong ale,' said Sam Speke wistfully as he threw away the last piece of broken shell.

'I'd settle for a warm woman to share my bed,' said Isaiah Dacket softly to Sam Speke. 'It was just our luck to get one who brought her own man along.'

'What's ale?' asked Daniel.

'Ale?' Sam Speke reached out and picked up the boy, swinging him kicking into the air above his head, hoping the others had not heard Isaiah's comments. 'Well, now, ale is something that makes good men feel better, bad men feel worse and young fellows like you feel ill.'

Daniel's chuckles brought a smile to Miriam's face. She had not heard Isaiah's remark — but Josh had. He frowned, remembering what Miriam had said to him about the sailor on their first night ashore. He guessed the surly seaman must have said something to her while he and Sam Speke were away. He determined Miriam would not be left alone with Isaiah Dacket again.

That night their sleep was disturbed by thunder rumbling in the north-east. Once when Josh woke he could see lightning flickering in the sky beyond the lofty sand dunes. But it was far away, and when Miriam murmured in his arms and pulled him to her he quickly forgot the distant weather.

The next morning the sky was dark and glowering above them and lightning tracked an angry course downwards to the sand of the dunes. Thunder grumbled all about them, but it was the wind that was to prove most troublesome. The wind direction had changed during the night and now it blew from the hot sand inland in ever-increasing fury. It culminated in a furious sandstorm that they heard minutes before it arrived bringing a choking cloud of sand in its wake.

They barely had time to gather their handful of possessions and scramble to shelter on the lee side of the wrecked ship before the battering wind was upon them. Josh held his hands over Daniel's ears so he would not be frightened as the wind buffeted the shell of the old ship and it creaked and groaned at the ferocity of the onslaught. Fortunately, the ancient wreck had weathered many such winds and would not yield to this one.

For an hour the five people huddled together while wind and sand howled about them. The sand trickled into their ears, stung their eyes and collected about their lips. At the height of the storm the sand became so dense that they began to breathe it in and choke upon the cloying particles. Any available piece of cloth was held up to nose and mouth as they coughed up the lung-clogging sand. Kerchiefs, the end of Miriam's dress and men's shirts all found a new use.

Then, as suddenly as it had arrived, the wind passed on. Opening red-rimmed eyes, the five castaways saw the dense cloud of sand racing away in a funnel-like spiral across the grey Atlantic waters.

But this strange land had not yet exhausted its supply of surprises. While they still crouched in the shelter of the wreck, so covered in sand as to appear part of the dunes, there was a sudden eruption of the sea a mere twenty yards along the beach. As they watched in astonishment a glistening sleek head broke the surface of the water and a fat bull seal rode the next breaker up on to the beach. Wheezing and groaning, he heaved himself clumsily across the sand until he was at least twelve feet from the sea.

Not until then did he remember he had broken the natural laws of caution. Pausing, he raised his nose in the air and looked about him. His big soft brown eyes passed over the castaways, moved on – then swung back.

With a startled snort the big seal began to make a clumsy and desperate turn in the sand.

It was too late. The bull seal would pay the full price for his error. The two seamen jumped to their feet and sprinted the short distance that separated them from the seal, pulling knives from their belts as they ran. Josh was on his feet scrambling after them a split second later.

Isaiah was the first to reach the panic-stricken creature, throwing himself at it as it humped down the beach to the sea. It was a close race, but even as the creature's front flippers raised a splash from the edge of the ocean Isaiah buried his knife-blade in its throat. The bull seal tried to throw itself forward into the safety of deeper water, but Isaiah's knife flashed again, the blade a dull red in the poor light before it struck again. Then Sam Speke was there, and his knife pierced the blubber protecting the creature's ribs. Josh plunged into the water to help, and between them the three men rolled the dying seal back up the beach. Miriam pulled Daniel's head in towards her and turned her own face away so she would not have to see the look in the creature's too-human brown eyes.

It was all over in a matter of minutes. In the distance the thunder still grumbled and lightning illuminated a black-shrouded sky, but bright sunshine was pursuing the shadows along the beach. By the time it reached the ancient wreck Isaiah had slit the seal from throat to rear flippers and the men were congratulating themselves on their good fortune, the discomfort of the sandstorm forgotten. Even Isaiah Dacket looked happy as his fellow-seaman praised the speed with which he had moved.

'I never knew you could move so fast, Isaiah,' chortled Sam Speke. 'And look at the size of the creature! It must weigh five hundred pounds. We shan't go hungry for a while now.'

Isaiah, his arms coated to the elbows with a grisly mixture of blood and sand, resumed his natural dolefulness before replying. 'There's meat enough,' he agreed, 'but how long will it keep in this heat?'

'Don't worry about that.' Miriam overcame her revulsion now the soft-eyed creature was dead, though she still avoided looking at it. 'I'll get a fire going. Josh, you fetch a bucket of sea water. We'll need as much salt as we can possibly get – and you must dig a hole down where the sand is wet. We'll bury the meat as it's cut up. That way it will be out of the sun and will absorb salt water until I'm ready to rub more salt into it.

We'll try smoking some of it too. I think both methods will work better on this meat than they did on the fish. We can't possibly take it all with us, but I'll make sure we waste as little as possible.'

'How long will it take?' asked Josh.

Miriam shrugged, trying not to think of the pain in her fingers. 'Far longer than we've got if I were to do the job properly. But I'll do what I can in three days.'

While the two seamen continued their messy task Miriam got a fire started and, with Daniel 'helping', set to work tearing pieces of wood from the old wreck. Josh was down at the water's edge digging a pit in the wet sand, using his hands and a plank from the old ship's decking.

Isaiah paused to wipe the back of a bloody hand across his forehead and slap angrily at the flies that the wind had brought from inland and that gathered in buzzing black clouds about the seal meat. Seeing that the others were out of hearing, he spoke to his companion in a low voice.

'Do you think we'll ever see England again, Sam?'

The burly seaman grunted. 'There's a chance.'

'But not much of one with the convict and his family to slow us down.'

'I can't say as I've noticed them lagging behind.'

Sam Speke paused in his work to give the other man a long searching glance.

'Sam! Be honest, now. I know you're soft on the boy — and I fancy the woman — but we're shipwrecked. We've got to look after ourselves. Just as we did on board ship before this lot jumped into the boat with us.'

Sam Speke winced. 'I'm not proud of what we did then, Isaiah.'

'But we're *alive*, Sam. That's better than being dead. *You* know that.'

Isaiah brushed a trickle of perspiration from his nose, attacked the flies again and did another rapid check on the whereabouts of Josh and Miriam. They were both fully occupied.

'Listen to me, Sam. There's food enough for everyone now. We can leave on our own during the night. We'll take the water and as much meat as we can carry. They'll still have enough meat left to last them for a couple of weeks.'

'Only if they stay here. They won't be able to carry much off with them. And what are they supposed to do for water if we take it with us? They've got no means of lighting a fire once it's gone out.'

Isaiah Dacket hesitated a shade too long to convince Sam Speke that he really believed what he said next.

'They'll manage. He'll think of something. He's an engineer and much cleverer than the likes of you and me. Are you with me, Sam? Tonight?'

'And if we get to safety—to where there's civilised folk? I suppose you'll send 'em back here to find Josh and Miriam and Daniel?'

Isaiah Dacket thought his argument had won his shipmate over. 'Of course we will. Why, we'll be helping them, won't we? Getting them rescued quicker than if we carry on the way we're going with them in tow. You'll come, then, Sam?' His voice was a hoarse excited whisper.

'I wouldn't come with you, Isaiah Dacket—not if you promised to make me Admiral of the Queen's navy, I wouldn't.'

The tall seaman's mouth dropped open, but Sam Speke had not finished.

'I'm not used to having to sleep with one eye open Bristol fashion. That's what it would come to if I travelled with you. If we ran short of water or food, I wouldn't dare to let you behind me for fear I'd feel your knife in my back.' Sam Speke shook his head sadly. 'We were good shipmates in *Pride of Liverpool*, Isaiah, but I don't like the man you are shoresides.'

Isaiah Dacket's mouth clamped shut and he hacked savagely at the fat carcase of the seal.

'You're a fool, Sam Speke. You'll regret not taking this chance. They'll hold us back until we die in this God-forsaken country. You'll see. All the way to hell you'll regret you didn't heed my words.'

At that moment a very hot Josh came up the beach for the first of the meat for the water's-edge cache and the two seamen fell silent.

For the remainder of that day and far into the night they worked on the seal meat, cutting and storing, salting and smoking. They also gorged themselves on the fatty meat. It smelled and tasted of fish, but Josh thought he had never tasted a finer steak.

They stayed at that camp for three more days. A Cornish country housewife would have thrown up her hands in horror at the methods used in an attempt to cure the seal meat as quickly as possible, but Miriam did her best with the resources she had. Her hands were much worse now, and there was no hiding their state from the others. Josh insisted that she keep them bound up with strips of her under-skirt while he and Sam Speke continued with the salting, but they did not appear to be healing.

They intended to carry with them as much smoked and salted meat as they could manage and, when they had sufficient, Miriam boiled down the inches-thick blubber and provided a bucket of seal oil to take with them.

The heat was great when they set off in the dawn of the fourth day. There was no cooling wind now. What wind there was still blew from the hot sand dunes inland. To make matters worse their fishy diet had brought Josh and Isaiah Dacket out in a crop of boils that did nothing to help either man's temper.

During the morning storm clouds blew up again and they could hear thunder grumbling away inland. They saw more of the dust spirals too. First one and then another snaked down the side of the dunes a mile ahead and spun out to sea, the spiralling plume of sand bending and changing shape with each unpredictable change of direction that was made.

'This is a terrible land.' Miriam eased her aching legs and tried to straighten her torn fingers as they made a midday halt. 'It's savage all through.'

'I don't think we've seen the half of it yet,' said Sam Speke. 'I've heard tales about this part of the world as would set your ears burning.'

'What sort of tales?' asked Josh.

'I'd rather not say, Josh.' Sam Speke threw a quick glance at Miriam. 'But sooner or later we'll meet up with the natives whose land this is and you'll likely see for yourself.'

'What he means is that if they say they fancy your woman it won't be for her looks. It'll be because they think she'll cook well.' Isaiah grinned maliciously.

Miriam looked to Sam Speke for confirmation and he shrugged uncomfortably. 'Take no notice of either of us, Missus Retallick. We're just repeating the old sailors' tales you hear on board ship. Neither of us has ever met anyone who's set foot here.'

'I'm quite sure Isaiah enjoyed telling us about it,' said Josh curtly. 'Now we've got something to look forward to. Let's get moving. Up you come, Daniel.'

The next day they were all in even worse shape. The sun shining on their faces had cracked their lips, and their legs and arms were chafed from the dried-in salt water in their clothes and the perspiration that ran from their bodies in the gruelling heat. Only Daniel was free from chafes and sores. But now there was a slight change in the featureless landscape. At first Josh thought he was mistaken, that perhaps the beach was wider here. But by midday they were all sure. The sand dunes were flattening out with clumps of thick coarse grass dotted here and there. Then, most exciting of all, they saw the peaks of a small range of mountains standing mauve against the blue sky far inland from them.

Another mile and the grass had become thicker and there was even an occasional bush. Finally, ahead of them the sand dunes disappeared altogether and they could see trees.

It gave the party a new lease of life. They stumbled forward excitedly, expecting at any moment to catch their first glimpse of people, convinced that their ordeal in the scorching sun was almost over.

But they did not know this part of south-west Africa, were unaware that for every promise made the land demanded a dozen disappointments in payment.

Their first was not long in coming.

What had appeared from a distance to be an expanse of flat featureless country turned out to be the estuary of a mile-wide sluggish river, oozing muddy brown water that stained the sea as far as the horizon.

Unslinging the heavy bundle from her shoulder, Miriam sank wearily to the ground, disappointment adding to the pain in her fingers and sore limbs. Josh eased Daniel from his back and, freed from restraint, perspiration ran down past the waistband of his trousers.

True to character, it was Isaiah who voiced the despair they all felt at encountering what was an unsurmountable barrier at the very place where they had been hoping their troubles would be at an end.

'We'll never cross that! We're finished. We might just as well give up and die now.'

'If you die here, you'll die alone,' said Josh firmly. 'As soon as we're rested we'll head up-river towards those mountains.'

'Walk inland? You're mad! How far away do you think those mountains are? They must be fifty or even sixty miles from here. It'll get hotter with every step you take away from the sea and, if the heat doesn't kill you, you'll die of starvation. Besides, what will you do when you get there? One place is much the same as another in this land, be it mountain or sand.'

'What's the alternative? To sit here chin in hands wishing we had a boat? No, we'll follow the river inland. At least we'll have water. If we can see nothing from the mountains, we'll discuss our next move then. You with us, Sam?'

'Of course I am – and so is Isaiah. He knows it's the only way for us to go. Isn't that so, Isaiah?'

The tall seaman glared at each of the two men in turn, then without a word took a tin mug from his bag and went to the water-keg.

'It's all right, Josh. He'll be with us, you'll see,' Sam Speke said in a low voice.

Josh shrugged. He was becoming impatient of Sam Speke continually making excuses for his companion. 'He can please himself. The hell with him. I've got my own family to look after.'

'If either of you has anything to say about me, then out with it. Don't whisper behind my back.' Isaiah threw the tin mug to the ground petulantly. 'I expect such goings-on from a convict, but not from you Sam. All right, I'll tell you what I think about going inland to those mountains. Look at us. We're covered in sores and boils. The woman can scarce pick anything up because of her torn fingers. If it was just Sam and me, I'd give it a try. Without the woman and the, boy we'd stand a chance. With them we might just as well stay here and wait for death. They've been a drag on us ever since we got off the ship.'

'Oh! Stop this stupid quarrelling.'

Miriam got to her feet as quickly as she could, willing her legs not to buckle beneath her.

'I'm as ready to move on as anyone else. So is Daniel.' She saw Josh's sudden grimace of pain as he moved. The boils on his legs and arms were worse than the others'. 'It's all right, Josh. Daniel can walk for a while. If anyone slows us down, it won't be a Retallick.'

'You don't have to force yourself to go on because of anything Isaiah says.' Josh was angry. 'We'll rest a while longer.'

'No, Josh. It's all right; really it is.' Miriam put a hand on his arm and squeezed it reassuringly. 'And it's time we moved on. We've got a couple of hours of daylight left. Let's make the most of it.'

They followed the course of the river until dusk, making perhaps four more miles. The mountains seemed no closer, but the nature of the country had changed yet again. The tall sand dunes were still dominant to the north, but down here by the river there was green grass backing off from the mud at the water's edge. Farther away from the water coarse spiky grass thrust upwards from the sandy soil, and there were many bushes and a few stunted trees.

There were also birds. They first saw them close to the estuary – tall long-legged birds standing higher than a heron in the water, curved dark beaks disturbing the water as they sifted it noisily, heads questing from side to side.

The birds took little notice of the small party of humans walking close by until Daniel ran towards them clapping his hands in excitement; then they took to the air with a clatter of noise, exposing the pink underside of their wide wings. They moved in a fluctuating pink cloud to the far side of the muddy river, leaving the newcomers to this land of surprises marvelling at their collective beauty.

That night the party camped on the river-bank alongside a dead tree whose trunk and branches were ravaged by the tunnelling of ants. Here they had their first encounter with mosquitoes. The insects descended in dense clouds, zooming and stinging and making life very uncomfortable. Not until the castaways had a good fire going with smoke billowing about them did the mosquitoes look elsewhere for a bloody meal.

But later that night the camp received a call from a much more dangerous visitor.

Everyone was asleep and the fire had burned low when Josh suddenly came awake. He was a light sleeper and knew an unusual sound had brought him awake. He lay listening for some minutes, the night seeming deep and still. Then he heard the sound again. It was a soft nerve-tingling cough — but it came from no human throat.

His heart pounding, Josh rose slowly and silently, standing clear of Daniel and Miriam. Across the dying fire someone else was awake and on his feet.

'Is that you, Josh?' Sam's hoarse whisper reached across to him.

'Yes. What's out there?'

'I don't know — but I saw its eyes. They were big and yellow like a cat's. Put some more wood on the fire. Maybe if we build it up whatever it is will go away.'

Josh picked up a length of the dead tree and, stirring up the ashes, provoked a flicker of life. Putting the piece of wood on the dull red ashes, he followed it with another.

From the darkness there was a sharp rattling cough. This time it came from a different place.

A piece of dry bark on the fire flared briefly and the light was reflected in two yellow eyes. At that moment the cough became a growl and the creature of the night bounded in to the attack.

At first Josh could see only the eyes, but then the heart of the fire shifted and he glimpsed the sand-coloured body of a leopard.

A sound, half-fear, half-bravado, left Josh's throat. At the same time there was a bellowed 'Haaa!' from Sam Speke as he lunged across the clearing with the outstretched boat-hook to intercept the leopard's charge, scattering the fire in a shower of sparks.

The makeshift naval spear took the animal in the ribs and it rounded on Sam with snarling spitting anger, but the noise of human voices accomplished more than the boat-hook. A concerted shout from Josh and Sam Speke caused the animal to lope off into the night.

In the last hectic few moments Josh had tripped over the water-keg and now he rose to his feet shakily, aware that a tawny death had passed very close to him.

'What's all the noise?'

'What's going on?'

Isaiah made his enquiry from one side of the fire as Miriam held Daniel to her and called from the other side.

'It's all right. It was only some animal come to see what we were doing here. That's all,' said Sam Speke.

'Thanks to your quick thinking "seeing" was all it did. I'm in your debt, Sam.'

'I'm sure we'll owe each other more than that before we're out of this, Josh. I didn't do nothing.'

Sam Speke was embarrassed by Josh's thanks.

'What was it, Josh. *What* nearly happened?'

'Everything's all right, Missus Retallick. You get the boy to sleep again. You'll be all right now. We scared the creature off. It won't come back again.'

'Then why's the water-keg turned over on its side spilling water everywhere?' asked Isaiah.

Josh seized hold of the keg and turned it right side up, but most of the contents had already spilled out on to the dusty ground. Anxiously shaking it, Josh estimated it now held no more than a gallon. This was a disaster.

Josh showed his dismay.

Sam said: 'We can get more water in the same way as we got this. We couldn't have fixed you up so easy. Don't you worry about it. Get back to sleep if you can. I'll sit here and keep watch for a while just to make sure that creature's gone.'

'We ought to take it in turns,' declared Josh.

'You two do what you like,' grumbled Isaiah. 'I've seen nothing. All that's woken me is you two shouting about something you imagine you saw. I'm going to sleep.'

'You too, Josh,' said Sam Speke. 'If it makes you feel any better, I'll give it a couple of hours then wake you. You can take the watch until dawn.'

Josh agreed and lay down beside Daniel and Miriam. But before he slept he had to tell Miriam what had happened to waken the camp.

Miriam reached across Daniel and her torn hands gripped Josh's very tightly when he had finished his story.

'I knew from the very beginning that I liked Sam Speke,' she said in a choked voice. 'Now I know why. He's a good man, Josh.'

In spite of his frightening experience Josh was soon asleep again and Sam Speke never woke him. He remained awake until the sky glowed red in the pre-dawn; then he, too, fell asleep.

Josh woke and saw him crouched against the tree-trunk, his arms hugging the boat-hook to him, and he managed a smile. He was making up the fire when Isaiah threw off his canvas blanket and climbed to his feet to make off in the direction of the river. He returned in such a hurry Josh thought he must have seen the leopard.

'What is it?'

'It's the river. . . . It's gone!'

'Gone? Don't be so—'

'Then have a look for yourself!'

Isaiah's shouting woke the others, and as Josh ran up the brief slope that separated them from the river Sam Speke lumbered after him.

Incredible though it was, Isaiah had been telling the truth. The water had gone. There was now nothing between them and the far bank but a wide trough of flat mud that was already hardening in the early-morning sun.

'I've never seen the likes of this before.' Sam Speke rubbed the sleep from his eyes as though he was still dreaming. 'One day there's a mile-wide river, the next morning it's gone! What do you make of it, Josh?'

'It must have something to do with those storms we've been seeing in the direction of the mountains. There's been a lot of rain up there and it must have run off down this river-bed. From the look of it now I'd say it stayed dry for most of the year.'

'And so will we if we don't get some water pretty quickly,' volunteered Isaiah. 'There's not much left in this keg. Now the river's gone we'd best get across and head back for the coast again.'

'I'd still like to get to those mountains and have a good look at this country from the top,' declared Josh.

'That's madness!' exclaimed Isaiah. 'Even you must see that, Sam. If we follow the coast, we've got a source of water and food — and we'll be heading towards the Cape settlements. Going inland doesn't make sense.'

Sam could not make up his mind. There was logic in his shipmate's argument, but he felt he owed Josh some loyalty.

Miriam provided him with a respite.

'Can I say something?' Without waiting for a reply she went on, 'I'm a bit worried about Daniel this morning. He's not very well. He's miserable and has a bit of fever. He's very sleepy, too. It isn't like him. I'd be much happier if we could stay here for today.'

'I thought the Retallicks wouldn't hold us up,' gloated Isaiah, throwing Miriam's words of the previous day back at her.

'Of course we'll rest up today. We could all do with it. We've been pushing ourselves pretty hard and the little chap's done very well,' said Sam Speke. 'It'll give us a chance to look for water in the river-bed and make up our minds what we're going to do. Personally I can't see why we shouldn't do as Josh suggests.'

Isaiah showed his displeasure by wandering off on his own.

Daniel slept for most of the morning and seemed a little brighter at midday when Sam Speke brought him a roughly carved boat he had made from a piece of wood found along the bank of the dried-up river.

Daniel was pleased with the small gift and immediately began pushing it through a sand sea at his feet.

'That was very thoughtful of you, Sam,' said Miriam. 'There's not much in this country for a small boy.'

'It was nothing. I enjoyed making it. I've whittled many of them on board ship. When I have the time I'll make a really good one for him.'

This was the first opportunity Miriam had found to have a private talk with the seaman. With the other two men out seeking water in the river-bed she determined to make the most of it.

'Do you have any sons of your own, Sam?'

'No, Missus Retallick. I've been at sea since I was eight and never found the time to take a wife, let alone settle down and raise a family.'

'Since you were eight? That was a very young age to be going to sea.'

'Well, it wasn't really being at sea at first – not on a merchantman, that is. My father was a fisherman. I used to go out with him. Then his boat was wrecked and my father lost, so I took on as a seaman in a deep-sea boat. I was twelve by then.'

Miriam looked at him sympathetically. 'You've had a hard life, Sam.'

The seaman looked surprised. 'Hard? No, it's been a good life mostly. Better than Isaiah's. You mustn't think too badly of him, Missus Retallick. He never knew either of his parents and was brought up by the Parish. They sent him off to sea as soon as he was big enough to hold a rope. He's had to fight for everything he wanted for as long as he can remember. It's not easy for him to understand that others aren't the same.'

'You're probably right, Sam. All the same I wish we had two like you here instead of Isaiah Dacket.'

Sam Speke coloured up and, mumbling that they would have no real trouble with Isaiah, he excused himself, saying that he wanted to look for the leopard's tracks.

It was another hour before everyone returned to the camp for a meal of near-rancid seal meat. While they were eating they discussed the events of the night and their future movements. To Josh's surprise he found that the others had accepted they would go on to the mountains. Even Isaiah raised no further objections and agreed they should move to a new camp before dark. Sam had found a site he was sure would afford them greater protection should the prowling leopard return to trouble them.

Daniel was now noticeably better, and the move of a mere half-mile was quickly accomplished. The new camp was in the shelter of a tall pile of huge balancing boulders. They were the first large stones Josh had seen since coming ashore. With dense thorn-bushes on two sides they had only to build a fire in the gap that was left and they had a stockade to protect them against any animal of the night.

There was shade here, too, most important in the airless heat of the afternoon. During the last two days the heat had become almost unbearable. It bounced back from the sandy soil and left a haze dancing above the ground like smoke from a skillet of boiling fat.

Josh had managed to locate a reluctant source of water in the middle of the river-bed by digging a hole two feet deep with his hands. The water seeped into it slowly and never rose to more than a depth of two inches, but with patience it could be scooped up and poured into the keg using a tin mug.

The men took turns at this tedious task and in the heat of the afternoon Sam Speke was lying beside the hole with the sun beating down upon his back when he was surprised to have Isaiah join him.

The tall seaman's words quickly told Sam that he had not accepted the trek to the mountains as readily as Josh had believed.

'We'll be here for days at the rate that water's coming through.'

'That's all right. We haven't got a ship to catch.'

'We'll be lucky if we ever see a ship again, Sam,' Isaiah prophesied gloomily. When Sam Speke made no reply he went on, 'We could still go back to the coast – just you and me.'

'I thought we'd already decided that.'

'You mean *he's* decided it.' Isaiah jerked a derisory thumb in the direction of the camp. 'I didn't notice him paying much heed to what anyone else wanted.'

Sam Speke had asked both Josh and Miriam to make allowances for the tall seaman. Now he tried to do the same. The sea had been father and mother to Isaiah Dacket, and Sam Speke knew he was uneasy away from it.

'We'd make out, Sam. You and me. It'd be like it always was. If we go on with the convict, we'll never see other folks again. He doesn't want to find people.'

'Now, what sort of foolish talk is that? He wants to find them just as much as we do.'

'He doesn't, Sam,' Isaiah persisted. 'You're not thinking

about it. He's a convict. As soon as he gets to where there's decent folk he'll be sent off to Australia to serve out his sentence. It stands to reason that the longer he stays away from others the longer he remains a free man.'

Isaiah saw that Sam Speke remained unmoved and he changed his approach. 'I'm not blaming him, Sam. A man has to look after his own. But there's no reason why *we* should suffer for it.'

His thoughts not on what he was doing, Sam Speke stirred up the dirt in the bottom of the hole and it muddied the water. He left the mug there to wait for it to settle and turned to his companion.

'Isaiah, I told you once before what my feelings are about leaving the others and going on with you. I think I've got more chance of coming through alive if I stay with Josh. You had your chance to put a point of view and chose to say nothing. Now you come to me and talk of sneaking off in the night and leaving the others in the lurch. I wonder how tough things would have to be before you did the same to me?'

Isaiah began to protest that he would never do such a thing, but Sam Speke cut him short.

'Go away, Isaiah, before I forget we were shipmates and treat you as I would anyone else who suggested we left three people to face certain death.'

'You weren't so particular when we were helping each other to get off *Pride of Liverpool*,' retorted the tall seaman.

'No. But I think of it with shame, not as something to be proud of. You'd be a better man if you felt the same.'

'I'm still thinking as a man who intends coming out of this alive, Sam. That woman and boy have addled your brain. When you've got your senses back we'll talk about it again.'

Sam Speke watched the angry seaman walk away from him and wondered whether he ought to speak to Josh about him. He decided against saying anything. Relations were already strained between the two men. He would only make it worse. He turned back to the water in the hole. The dirt had settled now. He hoped that the same might happen with Isaiah – that if he were left alone his resentment of Josh might go away.

Because of their stockade they were able to sleep in safety that night, but they maintained a guard. Armed with only a seaman's knife and the boat-hook, his main task was to keep the fire built as high as was possible.

Josh took the first shift. The temperature fell quickly when the sun went down, and it was pleasant to sit close to the fire and look out across a land shaded to a soft silver by the ripe moon. It became even more pleasant when Miriam slipped from the shadow of the rocks and nestled against him in the circle of his arm.

'Do you think everyone on Sharptor is looking at the same moon tonight, Josh?'

Sharptor was the small mining community on Bodmin Moor from which they both came.

'It's nice to think they might be,' Josh replied softly. 'They seem so far away now.' He took one of her hands. The skin was healing slowly, but Miriam would always carry the scars to remind her of these weeks in her life. 'These last few years haven't been easy for you and they don't seem to be getting any better.'

'Oh, they are, Josh.' She squirmed in his arms and her shadowy dark eyes looked up at him. 'We're together, and that's all I've ever wanted. Here, Sharptor or Australia. The place isn't important. I just want to be able to look up and see you near. Then I can forget everything else.'

'But there's Daniel to think of. What of his future?'

Miriam gathered her thoughts before answering.

'He'll be all right, Josh. He'll grow up to accept all manner of things we've never dreamed of. He'll see more, learn more and achieve far more than he would had he stayed in a Cornish mining village. All he could have looked forward to there would be having to support me when he became old enough to work.'

'I wish I could be as certain as you. I must admit I've had second thoughts about coming inland. Am I being selfish, Miriam? Am I more eager to find a place where I can keep my freedom than in trying to locate other people? Or did I just dig my heels in because Isaiah was against coming inland?'

Miriam smiled. 'You wouldn't be a Cornishman if you didn't resent someone else telling you what you ought to do. But I believe you made the right decision. It was far too hot on the beach with no shade at all. We wouldn't have survived another week there. It will be cooler in the mountains.'

'I hope we'll find water too. I'm worried—'

'Sh! We've found enough water in the river-bed to last for a day or two. There will be water in the mountains and we'll find it. Have faith, Josh. We weren't brought together after such a long time to have everything end here in this strange land.'

Josh held her close and said nothing more.

CHAPTER FOUR

The next morning something so extraordinary happened that it might have been conjured up by Miriam's confident faith in their future.

Sam Speke had the dawn watch. He afterwards swore he had not slept — and the well-made-up fire supported his statement. Yet someone managed to come to within six feet of the camp and leave two ostrich-egg shells filled with water in full view.

It was not until Daniel woke that they were even noticed. His loud 'What's that?' and pointing finger began the mystery. None of the castaways had ever seen such huge eggs before, and they approached them very cautiously.

Josh was the first to remove the dried grass stuffed into a hole at the top of each egg and discover they held water. Isaiah tried to dissuade him from tasting it, saying it might have been poisoned, but Josh tilted one of the great eggs and poured some water into his hand. Transferring it to his mouth he declared that, though brackish, the water was every bit as good as their own.

Who their benefactors were nobody would hazard a guess. Sam Speke insisted they must be invisible spirits, and Isaiah Dacket shook his head unhappily.

'They can't mean any good by it. Why else would they sneak in without showing themselves?'

Miriam accepted the water as a welcoming gesture from the unknown people whose land they now found themselves in.

'If they meant us harm, they could have killed us all during the night,' she declared. 'As for not showing themselves — we are strangers. For all they know, we might kill *them*.'

She emptied the water from the eggs into the keg, and when they broke camp she left the empty shells lying on the sand.

That day they travelled only until noon. By then the heat had become unbearable. As soon as a suitable camp site was found they all collapsed into its shade. It was so hot that breathing became an effort. Not until the shadows grew long and the heat became less oppressive did they stir again.

The mountains looked no nearer than they had the day before. This, together with the knowledge that there were unseen humans about — friendly though they might be — helped to make it a subdued and unhappy camp that night.

Isaiah Dacket had the morning watch and he was determined not to be taken by surprise by the visitors of the previous night. As the dawn light grew brighter he stood up alert for anything that might occur.

For a long time there was nothing to be heard but the morning insect noises and the song of a solitary bird in a tree by the dried-up river-bed. Then Isaiah heard a faint sound in the bushes to one side of the camp. It sounded to him as though someone was creeping stealthily towards them. Seizing the boat-hook, Isaiah went out of the camp and made straight for the place where he thought he had heard the noise.

'All right, you come out of there. I know where you are.'

There was not a sound.

Isaiah began prodding the boat-hook into the bushes. There were too many large and sharp thorns on the branches for him to go searching for the natives he felt sure were hiding there. It did not occur to him that the same consideration would have kept others out.

'D'you hear me? Come on out, now.'

Again there was complete silence, and Isaiah began prodding angrily into the bushes and cursing noisily.

The sound woke the others, and Josh called to ask what was happening.

'There's someone in here,' growled the angry seaman. 'I'll have 'em out in a minute.'

'How do you know they are there?' asked Miriam. 'Did you see them when they left the water?'

'What water?'

Isaiah swung around to look at her.

Miriam pointed. There, standing upright on the sandy soil not two yards beyond the perimeter of the camp, were two ostrich eggs. One of them was actually standing in one of the footprints Isaiah had made when he had gone out in pursuit of their elusive benefactors.

Isaiah took it as a personal affront. Charging across to the bushes on the opposite side of the camp, he thrashed about with the boat-hook in a vain attempt to flush out those who he imagined had humiliated him.

It was ten minutes before he returned scratched and hot and scarcely able to contain his rage.

'If I had a musket, they wouldn't be so keen to make a monkey out of me. A musket-ball would find them soon enough, that's for sure.'

'You'd shoot someone—for giving you water?' Miriam was aghast.

Isaiah stood looking at her for a long time, his mind groping for a reply. Finally he said, 'Damn you, woman! I wouldn't expect you to understand.'

Aware of the grinning faces of Josh and Sam Speke he stomped to the fire and lit his pipe with his back to them.

'I wonder who these people are?' mused Josh as he picked up one of the eggs and gazed about the parched scrubby country.

'They'll show themselves in good time,' said Miriam. 'For now let's just be grateful to them.'

When Isaiah had recovered sufficiently from his rage to talk again he was less philosophical about the unseen strangers.

'We should have left the water where they put it and not touched it. One day they'll show themselves and come to us expecting gifts. They'll want more than a drink of water, you can be sure of that.'

'If we have more than water, they'll be welcome to it,' replied Josh. 'I should think water is the most valuable gift it's possible to offer anyone in this place. I only wish they'd leave some food, too. My stomach heaves each time I look at seal meat.'

Isaiah spat into the sand at his feet. 'You're too soft—all of you. I know these people. I've met them farther up the coast. You can't make friends with them and you daren't trust them. If you do, they'll likely as not turn on you and cut your throat.'

'How many throats did you see cut?' Josh enquired.

'I don't have to jump off a yardarm to know it'll kill me,' the seaman retorted, his anger flaring anew. 'I can take the word of them as knows.'

Sam said: 'Don't take too much notice of him, Josh.'

Josh said nothing. It was apparent that he and the tall surly seaman could not agree on anything.

It was fortunate for everyone that Josh was keeping watch at dawn the next morning. The sun had shown only a thin orange rind in the eastern sky when he saw a movement about a hundred yards distant. He sprang to his feet, but it was a moment or two before he realised he was looking at three humans. There were two women, and a boy the size of Daniel.

From all the accounts he had heard Josh had expected the people of this land to be big, black and warlike. The three approaching the camp were all well below five feet in height with skins of soft golden brown reflecting the colour of the early-morning sunshine. The women were naked from the waist up, while the boy wore no clothing at all. They came this morning openly and with no attempt at concealment.

It was a very exciting moment and one to be shared. Josh went quietly to Miriam and shook her gently awake. Startled, she sat up and opened her mouth to speak, but Josh silenced her. He felt it would be better not to wake Isaiah for a while.

The three visitors were so small that, had it not been for the breasts of the two women, Josh would have said they were all children. The youngest was, in truth, newly matured, but what she lacked in years she made up for in natural dignity.

The two women each bore an ostrich egg. Without a glance at Josh and Miriam they stopped outside the camp and carefully placed their gifts on the ground. They knew they were being watched but chose to ignore the fact. This was a gesture of trust. They knew nothing about the strangers who watched them from only a few yards away and must have felt very vulnerable, but they did not allow it to show.

When the women had placed the eggs safely on the ground they turned and walked away. Josh became aware that Miriam had a tight hold on his arm, her fingernails digging painfully into his flesh in her excitement.

The visitors had almost reached a tumbled pile of rocks which would hide them from view when the younger of the women

51

found it impossible to maintain her dignity for a moment longer. Perhaps her action was prompted by the relief she felt that the tall white strangers had not harmed her. Whatever the reason she suddenly stopped and turned to stare at Josh and Miriam for about ten seconds. Then, with a quick smile that lit up her whole face, she raised a hand to them before turning and running after her companions.

Miriam and Josh had just seen a tragic fragment of a once numerous and gifted race. Their visitors were of the Bushman people.

'Oh Josh! They were just too lovely for words. And to think we've been worried about them! Did you see that beautiful smile?'

Her delighted cries woke the others, and with great excitement Miriam described their visitors to them. Sam Speke was relieved they had proved to be nothing more sinister than two women and a boy. Predictably, Isaiah did not agree.

'You should have woken us,' he muttered. 'It might well have been some sort of trick.'

'Isaiah! Don't you ever see anything nice in anything or anyone? It was a gesture of friendship on their part and nothing more. I'm quite certain of that.'

'All right, if that's what you want to believe, I'll keep my advice to myself in future.'

Isaiah shrugged his shoulders and turned to walk away, but Miriam moved quickly and blocked his path.

'Now, you listen to me, Isaiah Dacket. There are only four of us plus a child here. The rest of the passengers and crew of *Pride of Liverpool* were drowned—remember? We know there are people in this land and they might well have resented our presence. Instead they've chosen to bring us gifts of water. Isn't that something to be thankful for? A reason to be grateful and glad to be alive? It would make life so much easier if you sometimes agreed with the rest of us and didn't spoil the few good things that happen.'

Isaiah opened his mouth twice as though he was about to say something in reply, but then he clamped his mouth tight shut and walked stiffly past her.

'You might as well not have spoken,' said Josh.

'I had to try.' Miriam's dejection was showing. 'His resentment is such a destructive thing I'm afraid it will spill over and engulf us all.'

Before they moved on from that camp Miriam made up her own small gift to the Bushman women. She guessed they would collect the eggshells once the castaways moved on and she left behind three strips of smoked seal. As an afterthought she also poured some yellow seal oil into one of the eggshells. The oil was no great loss; already it was going rancid. In other circumstances Miriam would have discarded it, but she had grasped one of the elementary rules for staying alive in this hostile world of near-desert. Never throw away anything that might prove edible, however unpalatable it might seem.

This exchange of simple gifts might have been the sign for which the Bushmen had been waiting. An indication of mutual friendship.

The Bushmen were a shy and sensitive people, used to going their own way, with customs that had changed little since the Stone Age. Because of this they had become a misunderstood and tragically persecuted race, hunted and killed like animals by tribesman and white man alike wherever they were found. It was fortunate for Josh and his party that the Boers, pushed out of the Cape Colony farther south, had not yet trekked this far north. The Bushman family group who had found them had never before seen a European; had not yet been given good reason to fear them or to tip their arrows with the special poison so rarely used amongst themselves – the poison for which only one man among each group held the formula and who would offer up a special prayer to accompany its use. The poison for hunting man.

They showed themselves to the shipwrecked party when they had called a halt with the sun beating down upon them from directly overhead. When they actually arrived nobody knew. Had it not been for Daniel they might not even have shown themselves then.

The castaways were resting in the shade of the inevitable balancing rocks. Miriam closed her eyes for a few minutes and when she opened them again she could not see Daniel.

Hurriedly Miriam jumped to her feet, a shout on her lips. She as quickly bit it back.

Her movement had brought Josh to wakefulness and he climbed to his feet at Miriam's urgent whisper.

'Over there, Josh. Look!'

Twenty-five yards from the camp Daniel and the Bushman boy were squatting together examining the boat Sam Speke had carved.

Daniel's explanation of his toy was lost on his new companion, but when Daniel pointed out a feature of particular interest the Bushman boy nodded obligingly. He smiled happily, fascinated by the flow of strange words from the tongue of the white boy. When he himself broke in with a comment of his own, the language was a strange mixture of words and incredible rapid clicks which came from the throat of the Bushman boy yet seemed independent of the words he spoke. Daniel was fascinated by the sounds and tried to imitate them, much to the other boy's amusement.

Then three Bushmen stepped from the cover of some bushes only a few yards beyond the two children. They were the two women Josh and Miriam had seen previously and an old wrinkled man. He carried no weapons of any description, signifying that he came in peace and trust with no ill-intentions. Crossing to where Daniel and the Bushman boy held their mutually unintelligible conversation, they, too, examined the carved boat.

Josh had started forward anxiously as the newcomers approached his son, but Miriam stopped him with a quick gesture.

'No! Stay here. See that Isaiah does nothing foolish. I'll take care of Daniel.'

She walked slowly but deliberately from the camp towards Daniel and the Bushmen. The young girl who had smiled at her on the previous visit saw her coming. Her eyes widened fearfully like a nervous doe hearing a strange new sound. For a moment Miriam thought the girl would turn and flee but she maintained her slow walk towards them. She smiled, and to her relief the young girl relaxed and her mouth opened in a beautiful tooth-displaying grin that had not yet caught up with the maturity of her body.

'Hello!' Miriam said to the visitors. 'I would like to say you are very welcome but I'm quite sure you wouldn't understand a word of it.'

The two women and the old Bushman all clapped their hands together briefly and said something to Miriam in their inimitable language. A sharp burst of words from the older woman brought the Bushman boy to his feet to perform the same brief ritual.

For a few moments there was a hesitant silence. It was not an uncomfortable or embarrassed void; rather, a pause while all of them tried to think of a mutual means of communication, each side eager to express its evident goodwill to the other.

Then Miriam had an idea.

'Come!'

She beckoned for them to follow her, but the women hesitated. Miriam called to Daniel and, taking him by the hand, began to walk towards the camp, hoping the Bushmen would follow. Daniel held out his free hand to his new-found friend, and with none of the reticence of his elders the Bushman boy took Daniel's hand and walked into the camp with him.

The two children had bridged the gap, and with the old man taking the lead the women followed.

Josh had wakened the others, and for once Isaiah was not scowling. He was looking at the younger of the two Bushman women, his gaze on her golden breasts that stood out proud and firm from the young body.

Miriam's stomach knotted as she recognised the hunger in the seaman's expression, and she moved between him and the girl. Fortunately, the girl was totally inexperienced in the ways of white men and was unaware of his look; there was so much to be seen in this small camp.

Miriam took the Bushman group to their store of seal meat and gave each of them a fair-sized strip of the oily meat. They accepted the gift casually, with no sign of gratitude. To have shown gratitude would have been the height of bad manners. It would imply that they had thought the givers to be mean.

But the manners of the younger girl did not inhibit her excitement at the sight of some strips of hard-furred seal skin, rough-cured by Isaiah, that they had brought with them. Her delight was so great that Miriam turned to the seaman.

'Can I give them a couple of pieces of this seal fur? I'm sure it will help us in the future.'

'It's all right with me,' agreed Sam Speke. 'They're welcome to as much as they like.'

'No!' Isaiah Dacket jumped to his feet and advanced to the canvas pack. 'Don't give everything away on our first meeting. Save some to trade later. We'll cut one piece longways into two. Here, give it to me. I'll do it.'

He took the piece of seal hide from Miriam and laid it carefully on the ground. Drawing out his knife, he first cut a shallow mark down the centre of the strip and then cut it expertly into two. Standing up, he handed one piece to the older of the two women and then stepped to her young companion.

'Now, me young beauty. This'll make you a fine belt. There's enough here to go twice around that little waist. Here, I'll show you.'

Putting his arms about her near-naked body he wound the strip of skin about her tiny waist.

The young girl was wide-eyed with fear until she realised what Isaiah was doing, then she relaxed and took the ends of the strip from him. Crossing them over she tucked them between the new belt and her body. She was so engrossed in admiring her present that she was oblivious of Isaiah's hands lingering on her body, resting heavily on her hip bones.

'Yes, that's right, my beauty,' he murmured. 'You look at it often. It'll help you remember who has first call on you when the time comes.'

Miriam went white with anger, and Josh took a step towards the tall seaman. Sam Speke put a hand on his arm and restrained him long enough for common sense to prevail. If there was a scene now, the Bushman group might guess the reason and go away never to return. The friendly relations that had been forged already were too important to jeopardise. Nothing Isaiah said would have been understood by their visitors.

But the elder Bushman woman was not so naïve as her companion. She said something quietly to the young girl, who instantly slipped from the sailor's grasp and moved away from him.

The male Bushman looked at each of the men in turn and

then without hesitation walked to Josh. Standing in front of him, he made a brief speech in his own language. Josh could only shake his head apologetically.

The Bushman realised Josh was not understanding him and began using a simple but readily understood sign-language.

First he told Josh his name was Hwexa. The name contained one of the incredible 'click' sounds that were strange to the castaways' ears. Then he asked Josh if their journey were to the distant mountains. Josh nodded that it was. The Bushman then indicated that he wished Josh and his companions to accompany him and pointed in a direction a few degrees off their course to the mountains.

'Do you think it could be a trap, Josh?' asked Sam Speke when Josh put the Bushman's suggestion to the others.

'I don't see why he should come into our camp and risk his own neck for that,' Josh replied. 'If he'd wanted to kill us, he could have crept up on us during the night. No, I don't believe he means us harm.'

For once Isaiah was in full agreement.

Josh indicated to the Bushman that they were ready to follow him.

All the members of the Bushman group smiled their delight at the decision and with the two women still admiring their seal-skin belts they moved some distance away while the Europeans broke camp as quickly as they could.

Waiting only until the little Bushmen were out of immediate hearing, Josh rounded on Isaiah Dacket.

'You can put this down as one of your lucky days,' he said angrily. 'If it hadn't meant showing you up for the lecher you are, you'd have felt the weight of my fist just now.'

'I don't know what you're talking about.'

Isaiah began to turn away but Josh's hand shot out and, gripping the sailor's shirt-front, he swung him round to face him again.

'I'm talking of you molesting that young girl. You keep well away from her. She's just a child.'

'She's no child. You know nothing about these people. Their women aren't coddled and pampered like English women. They're taught that their purpose in life is to please a man.

What's more, they only accept a gift from a man if they're ready and willing to give him what he wants in return. That's their way.'

'I don't accept your word for that, and you'd better forget what you've heard from others. These women and children will be left alone. Is that clearly understood?'

'Since when have you been leading this party?'

'Since I decided you'd leave that young girl alone.'

Isaiah Dacket was not ready to accept Josh's assumed authority but neither would he go farther without some support.

'Sam! You're not going to stand by while a convict gives the orders, are you?'

'I'll do more than stand by, Isaiah. I stand with him — and not only over the girl, either. If I hear you speaking foul-mouthed in front of Missus Retallick one more time, I'll put you on your back. Remember it, Isaiah Dacket. I'll not waste words on you again.'

The tall seaman's face showed his frustrated fury.

'From a Cornish Wesleyan I expect no more than pious clap-trap, but I never thought to hear it from you, Sam Speke.'

Swinging his canvas pack on to his shoulder, the angry sea-man marched away to where Hwexa was watching the argument with great interest. Josh and the others wasted no time in following him.

Later Josh found the opportunity to talk to Sam Speke.

'I'm obliged to you for your support, Sam; but there's no need for you to fall out with Isaiah on my account.'

'I'm used to speaking my own mind,' replied the seaman. 'I doubt I'll change now.'

'We both appreciate that, Sam,' said Miriam, who was walk-ing just behind Josh. 'But I'm a miner's daughter, brought up among miners. Isaiah isn't likely to say anything I haven't heard before. My only concern is that he might offend one of the little women. I believe we'll need their help to get clear of this desert.'

'We'll have to do our best to make sure that he doesn't,' com-mented Josh and he determined to keep a very close watch on the tall seaman.

They walked for about a mile before they reached the Bush-man village. It was such a well-hidden inconspicuous group of temporary huts that they were in the midst of them before they realised it. Even the cooking-fires produced hardly any smoke.

Hwexa led them to a hut that appeared to have been made especially for them. It was certainly larger than any of the others, although it was constructed in exactly the same way: a half-circle of sticks stuck into the ground, bent over and tied with strips of soft bark. The whole was covered with coarse dry grass and branches of bushes to blend with its surroundings.

The fire in front of this hut was much larger than any of the others, giving additional proof that the shipwrecked party had been expected even though Josh could not imagine how the Bushmen had been able to anticipate their arrival.

There were twelve huts altogether in the little 'village'. Unaware of the nomadic ways of the Bushmen, Josh had been expecting a village on a grander scale than this one.

No sooner had they put down their belongings than a crowd of silent but intensely curious Bushmen gathered about them. They were mostly women and, although they were all light-skinned, the young girl to whom Isaiah had given the seal-skin belt stood out among them for her golden skin and shy beauty.

One thing immediately apparent to Miriam was the absence of children. Apart from the boy they had already met there was only one other child, a babe-in-arms, in the village. This, too, was a direct result of the harsh environment and the fragile barrier that divided life and death in this primitive country. If there was a particularly hard and prolonged drought or a shift of animal migration, nature stepped in and the Bushman women did not conceive. If this natural method of birth control failed during such a time of hardship, then the traditional and basic rules of survival were invoked. The old women of the village took the baby from its mother at birth and it was never seen again. There could be no exception to this rule. The desert provided just enough, and no more. If the baby were not killed, then the chances were that neither mother nor child would survive to see better years.

Once again it was the young Bushman boy who broke down the barrier of shyness between the newcomers and the villagers. He saw the bucket containing the rancid seal oil and, dipping a finger into it, immediately transferred it to his mouth. He had already tasted the gift Miriam had left for his mother and found it very much to his liking.

In an instant his mother was at his side, scolding him in a sharp rebuke liberally laced with angry 'clicks'.

Miriam laughed. This seemed a good opportunity to rid herself of the evil-smelling seal oil. She offered the bucket to the boy's mother.

The Bushman woman was reluctant to take it at first, but Miriam insisted and eventually the woman accepted it with obvious delight.

But such a present was one to be shared, as were most things in this tiny close family community. The woman put the bucket down and called for Hwexa to come forward and issue a fair share to a representative of each 'hut'.

The distribution drove away all shyness from the Bushmen. Within minutes the village was noisy with chatter, and more than one smile was flashed in the direction of their guests.

A generous supply of water had been left for the use of the newcomers, the eggshell containers being buried in the sand on the shady side of the hut. Now the Bushmen came and brought strange root-vegetables for the bewildered Miriam to cook, and a woman produced an evil-smelling paste, indicating it should be put on their boils.

Once the Bushmen had all had a good look at the strange newcomers the crowd quickly drifted away to their allotted tasks. Although life in this temporary village appeared disorganised and casual, this was a totally false impression. The castaways had joined a very efficient little community. The Bushman was master of his environment—but it was a mastery that had to be worked at and constantly asserted. Death was the only gift the desert handed out freely.

Shortly before dusk there was another break in the routine of the village. For a full hour there had been an air of excitement building up although no one had left and nobody had arrived. Josh felt it, and so did Miriam. They found themselves waiting expectantly for something to happen.

Then, as though there had been some silent signal, more wood was thrown on to fires, the women gathered at the edge of the village and the reason for their suppressed excitement came into view. It was the remainder of their menfolk, who had been out on a hunting expedition. Armed only with tiny bows and stone-tipped arrows they had been hunting for two days.

The reward for their perseverance was a large bushbuck. Cut into rough pieces, the hunters carried it into their village and deposited it upon the ground in the centre of the circle of huts.

The hunters received a vociferous welcome and, like the seal oil, the deer was distributed to each family group, Josh and his party receiving an over-generous share. A large hindquarter was carried to their fireside by the leader of this small band of Bushmen who had returned with the hunters. He was beaming with the sheer pleasure of bringing them such a gift, and there was something about his smile that made Miriam think of the young girl, Bele, who had visited their camp. In fact, Xhube, the chief, was Bele's father.

His brief speech of welcome, like his own name, was liberally sprinkled with the clicks that defied that Europeans' tongues and was totally unintelligible. But his smile needed no interpretation. They were welcome guests in his village.

He did not stay talking for long. He could tell by the way their glances wandered to the portion of deer meat that they were hungry for fresh food. It was a hunger he had known many times. He would not prolong their waiting.

Josh and the others had not tasted fresh meat since leaving England two months before. They did not count the seal meat which had been so fishy it was difficult to accept it as anything else but fish. So much had happened to them during those two months that England might have been a lifetime away. Already, in an uneasy way, they felt part of this strange and harsh new country.

Josh in particular, with only captivity awaiting him elsewhere, was looking at it with the eye of a prospective settler.

Every fire in the small village was cooking meat, and the smell hung tantalisingly on the still evening air. When their own meat was almost ready for eating one of the Bushman women came to their fire carrying a quantity of hot cooked root-vegetables wrapped in a broad fibrous leaf. They were of the same type as those previously brought to Miriam and which remained uncooked because she had been reluctant to try them.

Having already witnessed the Bushmen's idea of a delicacy in their enjoyment of the rancid seal oil, Miriam was apprehensive about tasting the vegetable; but the Bushman woman was waiting, and she had no choice. To Miriam's relief it was quite palatable – enjoyable even.

She served up a filling and tasty meal to the four male members of the party and they ate it squatting around a pleasant-smelling fire. Even the dour Isaiah looked almost mellow.

That night the camp fires of the Bushman village burned late as a dance was held to celebrate the end of a successful hunt and the presence of the tall white strangers.

The rhythm and dancing were like nothing Josh or Miriam had ever witnessed before. The musician sat in the shadows playing a primitive form of stringed instrument while all the other members of the tribe formed a small tight circle and shuffled around and around keeping time by clapping and chanting to the strange exciting rhythm. Only a couple of very old and incredibly wrinkled women did not join in.

Gradually the dancers worked themselves up into an ecstatic state that communicated itself to the European watchers.

The Bushman men and women were half-shuffling, half-hopping around the narrow circular depression they had worn into the soft ground. They kept this movement up for longer than an hour without any sign of weariness. Even the hunters who had that day trotted miles with the fruits of their hunt on their shoulders were enthusiastic participants.

At this point the small Bushman boy broke from the circle and extended a hand for Daniel to join him. Daniel went unhesitatingly, and the teeth of the Bushman dancers gleamed white in the firelight as they made room for him. Within minutes the small boy from the mining village on Bodmin Moor had become a part of the dance. He shuffled and hopped and swayed to a dance that was being performed when a Pharaoh sat on the throne of Egypt and denied the right of the people of Israel to leave his land and his service, and when the tribes of the British Isles were themselves as primitive as these little men of the African wastelands.

It was Isaiah Dacket who brought the celebrations to an early and embarrassing close.

Unnoticed by the others he had begun to edge towards the dancers when Daniel was taken into their circle. Miriam saw him when he was no more than a yard from them, half-hidden in the shadows farthest from the firelight. Clapping his hands in time to the music, he was leering at Bele, who wore her seal-skin belt as she danced.

Guessing his intention, Miriam spoke urgently to Josh.

'Look! Isaiah's over there beyond the dancers. He's watching Bele. Stop him before he does something, Josh.'

But she was too late. Even as she was speaking Isaiah Dacket lurched forward and clumsily forced his way into the circle behind the young slim Bushman girl. Immediately the rhythm faltered and the dancers stopped in some confusion.

An older woman spoke quickly to the young Bele, and the girl ran from the circle. The others followed in an embarrassed silence, and Isaiah Dacket was left standing alone in the disturbed circle of sand.

One of the women brought Daniel back to Miriam and with a broad smile on her face said something that Miriam knew was a compliment about his dancing ability. Miriam could only smile in return, wishing once again that there was some way she could communicate with these happy and generous people, to say 'thank you' – and to apologise for the actions of the tall seaman.

When she looked back at the circle Isaiah Dacket had gone.

Josh and Sam went out into the darkness looking for him.

'If you find him first, stay with him,' Josh said. 'And whatever you do don't let him start anything stupid.'

'He's a fool,' growled Sam Speke. They were well out of the hearing of Miriam now. 'But it's a foolishness that affects many sailors. He sees a girl he fancies and his brain moves down into his trousers!'

Isaiah was not successful in his amorous search for the young Bushman girl, and when Sam Speke found him he was already on his way back to their own fire. Curling up close to it, he shared his hard bed with nothing but his own angry thoughts.

*

Later that night when the moon stood high over the mountains, touching its peaks with a silver brush, the fires of the Bushman village burned low. But the men of the little tribe were gathered around the low fire of Xhube's hut.

'It is agreed, then,' he said. 'We will take the white men to the mountains of Gaua.'

'It is your will,' said Hwexa, uncle of Xhube. 'We will do as you say. It matters not that some do not agree.'

Xhube looked at the expressions on the faces of his men shadowed in the dull light of the fire and saw doubt among them. This was a family group. Every one of the men was related to him by birth or marriage. He had long ago learned to read their faces and know what they were thinking.

'It matters,' he said. 'Give me your thoughts and I will give you mine.'

Hwexa had expressed his opinion openly and it was to him Xhube looked.

'The holy painted cave of Gaua is in the mountains,' said Hwexa. 'It would give the God great offence if a white man were to enter. It would bring great troubles to our people.'

'Then we must lead them away from the painted cave,' countered Xhube. 'If we do not go with them they are more likely to find it. The path to the cave is not hard to see.'

'The white men are not children to be taken by the hand and led by us. They will go wherever they wish.'

'We will find a way, Hwexa – but not if we remain here.'

'Then use Bele to turn their steps from the painted cave. The tall white man would see no path if she walked before him.'

Xhube's face tightened momentarily. The girl was his first-born and the only one of five children to have survived the harsh years since.

'It would not please Gaua if such an important task was undertaken by a woman,' he said quietly. 'Bele will stay far from the eyes of the tall white man.'

'What of the other thing, Xhube? The bones of the white men who came in the time of our fathers' fathers?'

'I have thought about that. It is not right a man's body should stay in the sight of the sun. They must be buried by their own people. I will take these white men to them.'

'Is that wise? What if they think we killed them?'

'They will not think that. The bones have been lying on the mountain since before the time of my father and your father, Hwexa. The white men will see that. Is there anything else?'

Hwexa shook his head. 'No, it will be as you say.'

Xhube looked at the face of each of his men for confirmation of his decision. It was freely given. 'It will be as you say,' said each man.

'Good. When the sun warms us we leave for the mountains of the sacred cave of Gaua.'

'Xhube?' The young man who spoke was his half-brother. 'Why do the white men go to the mountains?'

The Bushman leader smiled. 'I, too, asked myself that question. Look about you, my brother. If you came to this land for the first time, knowing nothing of it, where would you first look?'

The young Bushman turned his head instinctively towards the silver peaks of the mountains.

'It is so. You did not need your tongue to give me an answer. Your eyes turned to the mountain of Gaua's cave. So, too, did the eyes of the white men. That is why they have to go there.'

'And when they have been there? What then, Xhube, son of my brother?' asked Hwexa softly.

'I think they will not return to the place of hot sand. They will go on beyond the mountains. To the land of the Herero.'

Xhube smiled sadly, his thoughts those of a leader whose people were not welcome in the lands of other tribes, whose very survival depended upon occupying land no others wanted, where others could not live.

'When they go perhaps our people will have a friend on the far side of the mountains for the first time.'

Xhube said it with hope, yet as a Bushman he was conditioned to expect nothing from anyone outside his own tribe.

CHAPTER FIVE

The Bushmen removed all traces of their village quickly and efficiently. By the time a thin wedge of sky separated sun from mountains there might never have been a Bushman encampment among the tall grass and bushes. This was the way the little tribe always left their stopping-places. It was not because of any love of tidiness; it was self-preservation. The places where a village could be sited to allow them to view the surrounding countryside without themselves being seen were few and had to be protected. By exercising care they would feel safe returning to this site time and time again.

The Bushmen did not follow the course of the river as Josh expected them to do but struck across country, and by the third day the ground was beginning to slope steadily upwards. Soon they were picking their way between weathered granite rocks and toiling up steep paths as the mountains rose dramatically from the parched plain.

Looking ahead, Josh estimated that the highest peak must be at least eight thousand feet high. It would not be necessary actually to scale the summit. He only needed a good vantage-point from which to see all sides of the mountain 'island'.

When they paused for a brief rest he pointed out a saddle-shaped pass some three thousand feet below the summit to the Bushman leader.

Xhube nodded that he understood, yet when Josh took what would appear to be the obvious route to it the Bushman leader touched his arm and shook his head, indicating another route — one that would take them diagonally away from the pass.

When Josh showed signs of uncertainty Xhube squatted into a crouching position by a flat expanse of sand and motioned for Josh to sit beside him. Miriam and the two sailors joined the group, and Xhube began to tell them a vivid tale in the now familiar and remarkable Bushman sign-language.

Using a stick to create line drawings in the sand and quick movements of his sensitive hands to mould shapes in the air, he told them a story as detailed as any Josh had heard related by one of his own countrymen.

Xhube described how two white men had come to this area from the sea. It had been many years before – two grandfathers ago. Xhube's forefathers had seen them soon after they landed and followed their progress. Once they had drawn close, intending to speak to them, but one of the white men had pointed a stick at them and caused it to make the sound of small thunder. Immediately, one of the Bushmen was stung in the side by a snake that could not be seen. It had drawn much blood, and the Bushman died in great pain. After this the Bushmen had kept a respectful distance between themselves and the white men.

Even when it became obvious the white men were weak from lack of food and water the Bushmen had been reluctant to draw near.

Xhube described how the two men weaved an erratic course towards these mountains, staggering along the way and occasionally falling to the ground. Still the ancestors of Xhube only looked on from a safe distance, but never allowing the white men to leave their sight.

They followed them up this very slope – and now the two men were falling down more frequently, sometimes crawling on their hands and knees. Then somewhere farther up the mountain they found a narrow sandy gully where there was shade but no water. Here the men lay down, too weak to go farther.

During that night one of the white men died, but his companion clung desperately to life during the next long scorching day.

Then – and here Xhube's magic fingers faltered for the first time – then, as the arms of the sun slipped from around the mountains, the second man died. Not silently as had his companion, but by putting his stick into his mouth and calling from it a thunderclap that had burst forth from the gully and flown from cliff-face to mountain sending the antelope that lived on the mountains leaping all ways in terror.

The Bushmen, too, had been frightened, but they had stayed long enough to climb part of the mountain and see from a distance that both the white men were now still. Then they had left the mountain.

Since that time no Bushman had entered the gully. The bodies were still there, and with macabre accuracy Xhube's fingers traced ribs, teeth and the hollow eye-sockets of a skeleton. His uncle Hwexa had looked down on the bodies from the height of a cliff-path many years before. Rain had never been known to fall on this slope of the mountains and it was dry and hot. Bones would be preserved for many, many years. Until one day a wind would blow between the rocks and gullies and touch the bones of the long-dead men. Then they would crumble to dust. But Xhube said that would not happen for many years. For now the skeletons remained.

When the sign-language story ended the little Bushman was surrounded by his own people as well as the survivors from *Pride of Liverpool*, and every one of his listeners was spellbound by his graphic tale.

'That was magic!' breathed Miriam, breaking the silence. 'I would never have believed one man could tell us so much without uttering a single word.'

'It was a sight more than that!' exclaimed Isaiah. 'Sam, you know what I'm talking about? What one of those men carried with him!'

'Yes, I'd say it was a musket,' said Sam Speke slowly.

'There can be no doubt of it!' Isaiah was more excited than Josh had ever seen him. 'And if it's as dry up here as Xhube says, then the musket and any powder that's left might be usable!'

'For what?' queried Josh.

'For what?' echoed the seaman. 'Why, for hunting — that's what. And for protecting us when we move on from here. There's not a native or any wild animal as would threaten us twice if we had a musket with us.'

Xhube saw the excitement of the white men and was well pleased. He would take them to the place where the skeletons lay. By so doing he would lead them away from the cave of Gaua and the risk of incurring the wrath of the Bushman God.

'Well, come on! What are we waiting for?' Isaiah was impatient to locate the skeletons and check on the musket he was sure was there.

68

Moving ahead of them along the path, Xhube beckoned them on.

The party toiled upwards for another thousand feet before the Bushman stopped and began unslinging his belongings. The other Bushmen followed his example. It became apparent that this was not merely another stop for rest. The Bushmen were making a camp.

Isaiah immediately protested that they should go on and reach the skeletons now. Xhube listened politely until the seaman stopped talking, then he raised his hand silently and pointed with a finger.

What had appeared to be just another shadow between the rocks above them could now be seen to be the entrance to a gully. They had reached the place Xhube had described.

'I'll keep Daniel here and stay with Xhube and his people,' declared Miriam. 'I don't want to see any skeletons.'

Josh hesitated. He had grown to like the little people they had fallen in with. He trusted them too. And yet. . . . He decided he would not leave Miriam and Daniel alone with them.

'I'll stay, too. I've seen enough bodies in my time.'

'You please yourselves. I don't care if no one else comes. I'm going in there.'

As Isaiah strode off Josh said, 'Go with him, Sam. Give whoever is in there a decent burial if you can. I doubt if Isaiah will think of it. He's interested only in that musket.'

Sam Speke hurried after his fellow-mariner, and Josh helped Miriam to set up camp in a sandy hollow between some towering rocks.

The entrance to the gully was in shadow but only twenty paces on it took a sharp turn to the left and widened out into a narrow sand-floored valley with a sheer cliff-face on one side and high tumbled rock on the other.

The seamen found the skeletons at the far end of the tiny valley at a place where it ended abruptly in a sheer rock-face.

They lay side by side, the bony fingers of one reaching out as though he had tried to touch the other in death. Except for sand-dust that lay thick upon them they might have been there for no more than a few months.

Yet the clothes that held the bleached bones together were of another age. In the Portuguese style, they had been tailored when America was still a British colony — almost eighty years before!

The two seamen could not immediately see a gun, but when Isaiah bent low over the skeletons he saw not one but two weapons.

One was a pistol dangling loosely from the slack belt of the skeleton with the outstretched hand, his disconnected skull resting wearily upon a dusty sleeve.

The other weapon confirmed Xhube's graphic story. A long-barrelled musket, it lay beneath the other man's skeleton, the end of the barrel gripped between loose-toothed jaws and a gaping hole in the top of the skull to mark the passing of a musket-ball. A finger-bone protruding from the trigger-guard of the musket provided a mute addendum to the story.

Isaiah unceremoniously pulled the musket from beneath the brittle skeleton, and at his touch the human form disappeared and became no more than a bundle of bones wrapped in old rags.

'Look, Sam! There's powder and shot here, too.' Impatiently Isaiah tugged a horn of powder and a pouch of musket-balls from the skeleton's belt.

Sam was more gentle as he removed the pistol and powder from the belt of the second skeleton. The pouch of lead shot was on the other side of the belt — and there was something else. The drawstring of a once fine large leather bag was looped about the belt.

Pulling it free with difficulty, Sam heard a dull jingling inside it. He loosened the drawstring, and the slanting rays of the sun found themselves in sudden competition with the contents of the bag.

It held a sizeable fortune in gold coins.

Sam Speke's gasp of incredulous surprise made Isaiah Dacket look up sharply. He had placed the flintlock musket on the ground and was busily searching the clothing of its late owner. He had chosen the wrong body. The only secret there was the secret of death.

Before Sam Speke could stop him Isaiah Dacket dipped his hand into the bag and pulled out a coin. He put it to his mouth and bit into it. His teeth left a faint mark in its surface.

'It's gold, Sam. Pure gold! There must be at least seven pounds' weight. We've found ourselves a fortune.'

Sam Speke could only nod his head, utterly bemused. In other circumstances, in more civilised surroundings, having so much money in his grasp would have terrified him. Here, on the side of a mountain with nothing but scrub and desert on all sides, the find lacked the same impact.

Not so for Isaiah Dacket. He could hardly control his eagerness to have his share of the valuable coins.

'We're rich, Sam. We're rich! When we get out of here we'll be able to pay our passage back to England. Travel in style. No need to go aloft in all weathers, or clean out stinking bilges. We won't be working all the hours God gave us. We'll be passengers, waited on by poor sailors. And when we get home we won't have to work again! Just think of it, Sam.'

'I am thinking of it.' Sam Speke tugged the drawstring of the bag closed deliberately, and the tall seaman looked at him quickly.

'Is that what you'd have said if you'd found the gold instead of me, Isaiah?'

'Why, of course I would, Sam.' Isaiah's voice oozed friendship. 'I'd share anything I found with you. Two ways, straight down the middle. I swear it.'

'This will be shared more than two ways. There's four of us — five, if we include the boy. And what about Xhube and his people? They brought us here.'

Isaiah's face showed utter disbelief.

'You can't share it with all of them. What would they do with it?'

'If I thought he'd use it, then Xhube would have his share. But I don't suppose he'd even know what gold was.' Sam Speke slipped the bag inside his shirt. 'I'll keep it until it can be shared out between the rest of us.'

'You're mad, Sam! We don't have to share it with anyone else. The Retallicks don't even know we've found it. Getting a musket and pistol will be enough to keep them happy. Let the gold be just between you and me. Anyway, Josh Retallick won't be able to do much with his share. He'll be back in prison when he gets to where he could spend it.'

'All the more reason for Missus Retallick and the boy to have money. They'll likely have need of it.'

'Sam. . . .' Isaiah pleaded with his companion to reconsider, but Sam Speke cut his protests short.

'There's no more to be said about the matter. Now, give me a hand to dig a couple of graves in this sand. They won't be deep, but it will show we cared enough to bury them.'

'What difference is that going to make now? There's little enough left of 'em as it is. They'll rot as well above ground as beneath it.'

'Happen you're right, but I'm not walking away from an un-buried man with his gold in my shirt. It's little enough to do. Come on, down on your knees and dig.'

Isaiah had no alternative but to help Sam bury the remains of the two unknown men who had perished so tragically many years before.

When their task was finished the twin mounds were scarcely discernible. Sam felt they should be marked in some way and he found enough stones to pile upon each other to make a small monument at the head of each grave. He knew even the promise of their gold would not persuade Isaiah to raise a prayer for the souls of the long-dead men, so he stood in silence by himself for a few moments, thinking a small prayer, too self-conscious to utter the words aloud.

While he was doing this Isaiah was examining the musket, peering down the long barrel, blowing sand from it and gingerly cocking the weapon. Then he twisted the top from the elaborately engraved powder-horn and, shaking some of its contents into palm of his hand, examined the black powder carefully. He sniffed it, rubbed it gently between his hands and blew on it gently. The examination over he said, 'I can't see anything wrong with either the gun or the powder. It's dry – drier than some I've used in cannons. I don't see any reason why it shouldn't fire, although some of the musket parts are just as dry. If I can cadge a spoonful of that seal oil back, we'll have our-selves a musket every bit as good as a modern one. Now, show me that pistol.'

Isaiah took the pistol and after a keen inspection handed it back to Sam Speke, declaring it to be in an even better condition than the musket.

By the time the two seamen emerged from the gully Josh had begun to worry about them. He was relieved to see them and pleased they had found the weapons. He examined the guns with great interest; it was the first time he had held one in his hands.

He was excited about the gold, too, but he had some gold coins sewn into the belt he wore beneath his shirt and so he had less need of it than the others. His money had been brought on to *Pride of Liverpool* by Miriam, royalties earned from the man-engines invented when he was a mine engineer.

But he was delighted for Sam Speke's sake. Although the seaman showed few outward signs of excitement, Josh knew the gold could provide him with a future far more comfortable than the crew's quarters on some merchantman. He also thought Sam should keep the gold for himself. 'You found it. There can be no other claim upon it, so it's yours by right.'

'It's for all of us,' said Sam Speke doggedly. 'When the time is right it'll be shared five ways.'

'If it's all the same to you, I'll take my share now,' declared Isaiah Dacket.

'No, you won't.' The stocky seaman gave his shipmate a long hard look. 'I'm keeping the gold until we are out of this mess and all go our separate ways. Then I'll share it out – but I'll hold on to yours until Josh has left with Missus Retallick and the boy.'

'He'll be going to prison on his own,' asserted Isaiah Dacket.

Sam Speke shook his head. 'No. Not unless *he* says something to put himself there – and I doubt he's fool enough for that.'

Isaiah Dacket's face grew redder and redder as he struggled to control his temper. 'There's only one fool here,' he blurted out. 'That's you, Sam Speke.' With that he threw the musket into the crook of his arm and walked towards the Bushman fires to obtain some seal oil.

'Poor Isaiah!' said Sam Speke, looking after his fellow-seaman. 'He's never seen so much gold before. He can't wait to hold his share of it in his hands.'

'And what about you, Sam?' Miriam asked gently. 'Doesn't

it mean just as much to you?'

Sam Speke frowned as he thought about it.

'No,' he said finally, 'I don't think it does. I mean, when I found it up there in the gully all I could think about was the man I'd taken it from. I wondered what he meant to do with it. I felt sorry for him because he'd died without being able to use it. I felt he'd been cheated.' The burly seaman gave Miriam a sheepish smile. 'You'll think that's foolish talk.'

'Oh no!' Miriam rested her hand on his arm for a moment. 'I think you're a good man, Sam Speke, and I've said so before.'

The seaman's neck and face darkened to the colour of a roach's fin, and Josh rescued him by changing the subject.

'Do you think these guns will work, Sam?'

'Isaiah says they will. He knows about such things. He was a gunner's mate in King William's navy and looked after the two cannon we had on board *Pride of Liverpool*.'

The tall seaman certainly appeared to be knowledgeable about firearms. He used the seal oil to grease all the moving parts on his musket, then wiped them clean again. He ran a ramrod with a lightly greased strip of cloth down inside the barrel of the musket and as carefully dried that, too. Finally he had the musket ready for firing. Pouring a small measure of powder into the long barrel, he followed it with a small wad from the pouch. Then he took a musket-ball and wrapped it in a tiny strip of cloth torn from his own shirt. Thumbing the wrapped musket-ball into the barrel of the musket, he rammed it home carefully with the ramrod. Then he shook a little of the black powder into the firing-pan and, selecting a flint from the pouch, screwed it into the cock.

'Now comes the real test,' said Sam Speke in a low whisper. 'Xhube reckons it never rains on this slope of the mountains. We'll know for sure in a moment. If there's ever been any damp hereabouts, the powder will have picked it up and there'll be nothing more than a fizzle when Isaiah pulls the trigger.'

Just then a remarkable freak of timing occurred that would have placed Isaiah Dacket securely in Bushmen legend had the outcome been different.

A large antelope not expecting to encounter anything representing danger on this usually deserted mountain slope leaped into sight against the skyline a mere seventy yards away. For several seconds it froze in astonishment at the unprecedented scene before it.

Isaiah Dacket threw the musket up to his shoulder and squeezed the trigger. The 'little thunder' reverberated from cliff-face to rock-pile. Isaiah had not fired a musket for some years. He had no knowledge of whether this one threw a musket-ball true, and the measure of gunpowder used had been a guess. But the musket-ball sang only inches wide of its target, and the startled antelope threw up its head and bounded from view.

'Hard luck, Isaiah!'

'But the gun works, shipmate.' Isaiah accepted the commiserations of his companions with surprisingly good grace, but the effect of the shot upon the Bushmen bordered on complete panic. As the sound of the shot reverberated around the mountainside they scattered in terror, some of the women screaming as they ran to get away from the 'stick-that-made-thunder'. Only Xhube, who had recounted the story of the musket, was not totally unnerved. It was his voice calling to his people that brought them all back, although some of the younger women were actually trembling with fear.

They kept their eyes averted from Isaiah and the musket and, although Xhube tried to explain what had happened, they were totally unable to grasp the principles involved and Xhube himself had only the very vaguest idea.

They spent a hot night on the mountainside with the stars so clear overhead they hardly needed any other light; but the flickering yellow flames of a fire provided a comfortable glow, and as they sat around it Isaiah checked Sam Speke's pistol. Satisfied that it was in perfect working order he handed it back to his shipmate.

'That's a fine pistol, Sam. It's French and the inlay is silver. I wonder what a man with a silver-inlaid pistol and a bag of gold was doing in this place?'

Sam shrugged. 'Whatever it was never got done.' He balanced the pistol thoughtfully in his hand and then held it out to Josh.

'Here, you take this. You'll likely find some use for it. There's plenty of powder and shot to go with it.'

'But I've never touched one of these in my life!' protested

Josh. 'I wouldn't know how to use it.'

'Then it's time you learned,' replied Sam. 'I'll show you how, and maybe you'll have a chance to practise later on. You'd best not try while we're here or Xhube's people won't stop running until dawn.'

Sam Speke showed Josh how to load and prime the pistol. It had two barrels and two triggers. Sam made Josh load and unload it, then practise priming and aiming, and also showed him how to squeeze the trigger without jerking it off aim. All the while this was going on Isaiah sat nursing his musket and scowling at his own thoughts. Josh thought it unlikely the seaman would have checked the pistol so thoroughly had he known that he and not Sam Speke would use it.

Although they were not desperately short of food, their stocks were running low, and when a keen-eyed Bushman sighted an eland near the bottom of the slope the next morning there was great excitement among the little men. The largest of the deer family, this was a particularly fine animal. Almost six feet high at the shoulder, it must have weighed more than all the men of the small tribe put together.

Eland were not often found on this side of the mountains, and Xhube made an immediate decision. The top of the mountain would be there tomorrow. Such a vast supply of meat as this large creature promised was all too seldom encountered. It could not be passed up, and such an important hunt needed to have the tribal head leading it. Only Hwexa and three of the older men of the tribe were left behind with the women and the white castaways.

It was no hardship to remain upon the mountain slope in the shade of the rocks for a day. A couple of hours after dawn the sun was already heating the rocks and it promised to be even hotter than on the previous days.

With the aid of Sam's knife, a piece of canvas and a length of fishing-line, Miriam was making a shapeless wide-brimmed hat for Daniel. The boy himself and his little Bushman friend were playing a game with a number of small stones. Josh had found an interesting quartz fault in a border and was explaining it to Sam Speke while Isaiah Dacket wandered off with his musket, hoping to make amends for his wasted shot of the previous day.

The Bushman women had their own work to do. While their men hunted the spiral-horned eland they combed the mountain slopes for whatever food might be found. Mostly they sought the tuberous-rooted plants that sometimes grew in this shallow sandy soil, watered by springs that occasionally flowed from the mountain fed by the storms high on the far side. But the Bushman women scorned nothing that might provide food. There were many insects that were considered to be particular delicacies.

Bele followed the slope for some distance, working her way along the ridge above the camp. She searched a shallow depression that had once held water, knowing that the incredible plants of this country could lie dormant for years waiting for the next trickle of water to come and promote near-miraculous growth. Bele was not disappointed. In a sandy bed between two rocks and sheltered from the full blast of the sun she found some veldt tubers, roots resembling mild onions.

Digging one up, she laid it to one side, and had begun to uproot another when a long silent shadow reached out and stopped a foot from her hand. Bele started up to see Isaiah standing watching her, his musket resting easily in the crook of his arm. She was startled more than frightened. Among the Bushman people it was unknown for a man to hurt a woman. Isaiah did his best to put her at ease. He smiled, an unaccustomed expression for his face.

'Don't mind me,' he said. 'Go on digging your roots.'

Bele understood his actions, if not his words, and she crouched down and began digging with the short sharp stick all the women carried for the purpose. She was uneasy at having Isaiah watch her, but it was merely a feeling born of her shyness.

The seaman moved closer to stand by her shoulder and look down at what she was doing. The gun was supported solely by his left hand now, leaving his right hand free. As he leaned over to watch, his fingers brushed against her bare shoulder as though by accident. Bele had just unearthed a large juicy tuber and she held it up to show him, smiling happily at her success.

Isaiah leaned lower to look at her find and let his hand rest fully on her shoulder for a moment before it moved on, his fingers tracing the line of her collar-bone.

The smile left Bele's face as Isaiah's hand dropped suddenly lower and he grasped one of her breasts. She tried to stand; but the seaman pushed his knee into her back, knocking her off balance. Bele screamed as he dropped the musket and pushed her flat to the ground. She screamed again as Isaiah tugged at the cord holding the narrow strip of animal skin she wore as an apron below the seal-skin belt the seaman had given to her.

The thongs of the apron dug into the skin of her hips before they broke and Isaiah cast the apron away to one side. By now Bele was struggling violently, and as the seaman tried to stifle her cries with his hand she bit deep into the flesh at the base of his thumb.

Cursing, Isaiah pulled his hand back and struck her heavily across the mouth. Her generous lower lip caught on her teeth, and she tasted blood. He struck her again but with clenched fist this time, and Bele felt as though her head had exploded into a thousand shooting stars. The sensation lasted only seconds, but it was long enough for her to have his weight upon her and his legs kneeing hers apart.

Bele screamed yet again and redoubled her struggles, but there was no stopping the thoroughly aroused seaman now. Still raining punches upon her face, he took her while she moaned and writhed in semi-conscious pain and blood bubbled from her battered lips.

But Bele's screams had been heard, and one of the Bushman women reached her just as Isaiah pushed himself up from her with chest heaving as he gasped in warm air.

Hardly pausing in her rush forward the Bushman woman picked up a piece of stone and swung it against Isaiah's head.

The seaman heard her coming and was moving away from the blow as it struck. It did no more than glance from his forehead, grazing the skin.

Another woman came up the slope and leaped at Isaiah with her hands extended before her like claws. He brushed her aside as easily as a doorway curtain; but now other women were converging on the spot and, snatching up his musket, Isaiah backed away from them.

Bele began to regain consciousness, and two of the women picked her up and, half-carrying and half-dragging the semi-conscious girl, took her down the slope. The remainder of the women began picking up stones and hurling them at the sea-man. Some of the stones were as large as a man's fist, and one of them took Isaiah in the mouth and he felt a tooth go.

Throwing the musket to his shoulder, he aimed at the woman who had thrown it and pulled the trigger.

The sound in the confines of the rocks was deafening, but the shot went wide of its intended target. However, unlike Isaiah's previous shot at the antelope, the musket-ball did not disappear harmlessly into the wastes of the mountainside. It snicked a bloody furrow across the skin on the upper arm of one of the older women before tearing into the back of young Bele.

The two women supporting her felt her body jerk in their hands as the thunder of the shot assaulted their ears. Fear and thoughts of self-preservation took the place of concern for their young relative and, dropping her to the ground, they fled from the scene in terror.

Isaiah Dacket was also in a hurry to get away but he had to reload his musket first. He knew there were still the men of the tribe to face and was thankful that the hunters had gone after the eland. He worked his way down the slope, loading the musket along the way, his eyes only on powder and shot. That was how he almost stumbled over Bele at the moment he was ramming the musket-ball down the long barrel with the ram-rod.

The little Bushman girl was dying. Blood stained the seal-skin belt that was still twisted about her waist, and it spilled on to the ground from her open mouth. But her eyes held his. There was no fear in them now she had crossed the threshold of pain. Her expression was one of sorrow. Deep unfathomable sorrow.

It unnerved Isaiah Dacket. He stepped to one side of her and sidled past her body but he could not avert his gaze from her face. The beautiful doe-like eyes followed him until he backed out of sight behind the next pile of rocks.

Josh and the others heard the shot and were still wondering

what had happened when the first of the women stumbled half-hysterical into the camp. She tumbled out breathless words to Hwexa, and he and one of the old men snatched up all the weapons to hand and ran away up the mountain slope carrying little Bushman bows and bone-bladed spears.

Josh was even more concerned when Miriam hurried to the distressed Bushman woman only to have her run away from her in terror, pausing just to snatch the hand of the small Bushman boy and take him with her.

Before this happened Josh had thought perhaps the tall seaman had shot a deer and the Bushmen had gone to help him with it. Now he knew something far more serious had occurred.

'Get Daniel and hide in those rocks over there,' he said to Miriam. 'Sam, you stay with them. I'm going to find out what's happening.'

Miriam did not argue. She picked up Daniel, who was still protesting at being parted from his young companion, and had started for the rocks when there was another shot. Seconds later Isaiah Dacket ran into the clearing.

'Quick! Get out!' he shouted. 'The Bushmen are after us.'

'What for . . . ?' Josh asked as the seaman reloaded the musket with frantic haste.

'There's no time for talking. We've got to move. They'll be after us all now.'

Josh was about to argue that they had done nothing to cause the little Bushmen to attack them when an angry arrow fired from the extreme range of one of the small bows looped through the air and landed with a soft hiss in the ground at his feet.

Then Hwexa showed himself and, reaching back with his arm, hurled a bone-bladed spear with all the strength of an angry and determined man. Josh jumped out of its way just in time, and the bone blade shattered into splinters on the rock behind him.

Isaiah brought the musket up to his shoulder to fire, but as he had Hwexa lined up with the long barrel and squeezed the trigger Josh knocked the gun up and the musket-ball sped harmlessly through the air.

'What did you do that for? I'd have got him. He wouldn't have thrown no more spears!' cried the angry seaman.

'You'll "get" no one until you've told me what happened out there to turn them against us like this.'

'There was an accident. One of them got shot—but I'm not staying here to talk about it, and neither will you if you value your life.'

Isaiah was lying. Josh was certain of it, but now was not the best time to try to extract the truth from him. The little Bushmen were closing in quickly, moving forward from rock to rock.

Josh fell back to where Sam Speke was keeping Miriam and Daniel sheltered behind him. On the way Josh managed to snatch up one of their canvas bags with preserved seal meat in it. To attempt to collect the water-keg was out of the question.

They retreated from the camp along the way they had come, but had not gone more than a few hundred yards when they saw the hunting party returning far below them and Hwexa making his way down to intercept them.

There was a fairly level strip of ground running northwards at the foot of a tall cliff, and to Josh it seemed there might have been a faint path along it.

'We'll go that way,' he pointed northwards. 'If Xhube and his men decide to come after us, they'll try to circle around us. We need to stay fairly high if we are to see them coming.'

The wisdom of his words was soon apparent. Hwexa reached the returning hunters, and minutes later the group of Bushmen split into two parties—half the men coming straight up the mountain towards them, the remainder doubling back on a curving course that would put them ahead of Josh and the others.

Isaiah Dacket was leading the way and he set a gruelling pace. As the only one aware of what had happened he knew how determined the Bushmen would be to catch them. Whatever might be the fate of the others he would certainly die—and it would not be a pleasant death.

But no matter how fast they travelled the Bushmen who were trying to cut them off went faster. By the time Josh and the others had covered a mile the Bushmen were well ahead. But then the little men turned towards them and had to scramble up the steep and rocky slope, and this slowed them down.

There was no doubt in Josh's mind now that he and the

others were following a path. It was as wide here as a wagon track and smoothed by centuries of Bushman feet.

'We've got to go faster to beat those Bushmen.' Josh took a firm grip of Daniel and broke into a trot. The boy protested breathlessly, but the little men were scrambling towards them in a last desperate attempt to cut them off. However, the Bushmen had lost their race.

The path swung around a tall single boulder and then suddenly ended at the mouth of a tall cavern set in the cliff-face.

Nobody needed Josh's urgent call to seek refuge in its shadows. They flung themselves through the entrance gratefully. Josh handed Daniel to Miriam then, turning back to the mouth of the cave, loaded his pistol and prepared to meet the expected rush of the Bushmen.

Xhube kneeled by the body of his daughter. His eyes burned and the muscles of his throat knotted as though they would choke him. Yet none of his people must be allowed to see his grief lest it be interpreted as weakness.

His hands longed to reach out and touch her young face in a vain attempt to give her back the gift of life he had first passed to her through the body of his wife. His heart cried out to tell of the twofold love he had borne for his daughter since the death of her mother.

But Bele, too, was now dead, and his eyes told him of many things he would rather not have known. Her young body had been abused by the man who had killed her. One of the lost white men he himself had ordered his people to help. It was now his duty as her father and the leader of his people to avenge her death. The white men must die.

His grief was disturbed by news from the hunters he had sent to intercept the murderers.

'The white strangers have gone into the sacred cave of Gaua. We were too late to stop them.'

The Bushman messenger had been part of the hunt, had raced to cut off the retreat of Josh and the others, then run back to his chief, yet his breathing was no heavier than that of the others standing about him.

But his news could not have been worse.

Xhube stood up and looked at the faces of his people. Now it was not only the murder of Bele that had to be avenged. The strangers had offended the god Gaua by entering his great painted cave. This was undoubtedly the worst day in the history of Xhube's people.

He looked down again at the body of his daughter. Ripping off the seal-skin belt she wore, he threw it far from him. Speaking to Hwexa, he said, 'Bring my daughter. She shall sit before the cave of Gaua and her spirit will witness the death of the strangers so it may rest when she is laid in the ground. Gaua can look from his cave and see that we, too, have been wronged.'

CHAPTER SIX

'I think you're lying!'

Josh's words were the answer to Isaiah's explanation that his musket had gone off accidentally and the ball had struck and killed one of the Bushman women.

'You think what you like. I don't expect you to believe anything I tell you – but that's what happened.'

At that moment a remarkable natural phenomenon occurred inside the great cave. The midday sunlight slanted through a cleft in the top of the cave and touched a previously unseen lake of deep-blue water. The reflected light illuminated the whole cave as though a million candles had been lit. It was this incredible and beautiful daily happening that had first made the cave a holy place for the Bushmen and their deity Gaua. This, and the truly remarkable graffiti that covered the walls of the cave to a height of more than twelve feet.

Josh had been having his heated argument with Isaiah Dacket at the entrance of the cave with the eyes of Miriam and Sam Speke upon him, and it was Daniel who first saw the sun's magic transformation of the inside of the cave. His delighted cry of 'Pretty!' brought all heads around.

It was much more than pretty. The scene was awe-inspiring in its beauty. The height of the great cave and the colours conjured up by the reflected light reminded Josh of the sun shining through the stained-glass windows of the village church at St Cleer in faraway Cornwall. But the parish church had possessed nothing to compare with the painted walls of this cave. Here, in reds, blacks, browns and whites, were a hundred stories and centuries of history. There were vivid action-packed hunting scenes, battles, births and deaths, and celebrations.

There were many animals depicted, too, most of them unlike any that Josh and Miriam had ever seen. But it was the figures of the men that really lived in the pictures. Painted with a minimum of brush-strokes the history of the Bushman came alive. Here was the little man of the wastelands at the moment of painful birth, his mother far removed from the village lest death come to her or her child and force the superstitious Bushmen to abandon that place. Farther along the wall the pictures traced the Bushman's life through the dangers and privations of a nomadic existence culminating in his death and his reunion with long-gone ancestors in a Bushman's heaven on the moon.

One could study these pictures and obtain a deep understanding of the little man they depicted—his ways, his thoughts and his religion. Here was the soul of the man.

But this was not the time for such a study. Of far more importance at the moment was the presence of water. Now Josh knew they had some chance of survival—if the Bushmen did not manage to kill them.

He was the first to recover from the wonder of the painted cave and see the little men moving in to the attack. They advanced from rock to rock, wriggling on their bellies like lizards.

Josh shouted to the others and, taking out his loaded pistol, aimed it at a low rock which was sheltering a Bushman. The report of the pistol was deafening in the confines of the cave but it achieved the desired effect. The lead ball glanced off the rock with a sound like a finger plucking a high note on a harp-string. The Bushman promptly bolted from his hiding-place, two others leaving theirs to flee with him.

It was the first time Josh had ever fired a gun, and he had not been prepared for the way it had bucked in his hand, or the choking cloud of gunpowder smoke that drifted back into his face from it, but he had hit the target he had aimed for and he was well pleased. He reloaded the barrel he had fired, content in the knowledge that this was a tool he could master if ever he put his mind to it.

The watchers in the cave had to wait for an hour before the Bushmen made their next move. It was a macabre and unexpected one.

The Bushmen arrived in a tight group, fifty yards from the cave, and Isaiah Dacket put up his musket to fire at them. Once again Josh stopped him.

'Wait! They aren't attacking this time. Let's see what they intend doing.'

But Isaiah Dacket had seen they were carrying something

between them and he had a shrewd idea what it was. Side-stepping Josh, he aimed the musket and fired. It was a snap shot, made in desperation without a proper sighting, and the musket-ball went harmlessly above the heads of the clustered Bushmen.

The sound of the shot caused great consternation among the little men, but Xhube's stern voice prevented them from dropping the body of Bele on the spot and running away.

Hwexa backed his nephew's words. 'Only a fool runs from thunder,' he declared. 'To hear it is to know that the lightning has already struck.'

Although the Bushmen heeded the words, they made great haste to the spot Xhube pointed out to them and, laying down their tragic burden, quickly scurried away to seek shelter amongst the scattered rocks.

This thing was against all their customs. When a Bushman died the body was buried in a shallow grave as quickly as possible and the whole tribe immediately moved far away so that the spirit would not follow and seek to remain with them. It was only out of respect for Xhube's leadership that they broke with tradition on this occasion. Even so, it was left to Xhube to prop the slight figure of his daughter's body up against a rock, seated so that the sightless eyes would gaze unblinkingly towards the holy cave of Gaua and witness the vengeance of her father.

Inside the cave Isaiah's desperate shot went without comment as the beleaguered party watched what was happening outside. Not until Xhube turned to face them and raised his arms in a promise to Gaua that he would avenge the death of his daughter and the desecration of the holy cave were they able to recognise the victim.

'Oh no!' The cry of deep anguish was forced from Miriam.

Josh was momentarily stunned. Then fierce anger welled up inside him. He turned on Isaiah Dacket at the moment the tall seaman aimed his musket with the intention of downing the little Bushman chief by the side of his dead daughter.

This time Josh did not try to persuade the sailor not to shoot. His clubbed fist struck Isaiah on the temple and knocked him sideways. Staggering across the cave on rubber legs, the sailor tripped and measured his length on the hard stone floor of the cave.

86

The long barrel of the musket began to swing towards Josh, but stopped suddenly when Isaiah looked into the two barrels of the shaking pistol, Josh's knuckles gleaming white as he gripped the weapon fiercely.

'Do it, Isaiah! Point that musket at me and give me an excuse to kill you.'

Isaiah Dacket dropped the musket to the ground quickly.

'Pick it up, Sam, and watch what's going on outside.'

Without looking at his shipmate Sam Speke did as he was told, careful not to step between the two men. He could see the anger in Josh and was afraid the pistol would go off accidentally.

When Sam Speke moved out of the way Josh gained control of himself, although he found it difficult to speak to Isaiah in his normal voice.

'So your gun went off "accidentally" and just happened to kill the girl you've been after since she first came to our camp? I think I could tell you a story that would come much closer to the truth!'

Some of Josh's anger returned again at the thought of what Bele had probably suffered at the seaman's hands.

'I ought to throw you out of this cave and let Xhube and his men have you.'

'You can't do that, Josh.' Sam Speke was thoroughly alarmed. 'You haven't seen what these people do to a man. Whatever Isaiah's done you can't let that happen to another human being.'

'And why not? He's put all our lives at risk as well as killing a young girl who did nothing but give us her friendship.'

'Josh, Sam's right. I feel just as upset as you about this, but you can't give Isaiah to them.' It was an emotionally choked Miriam who spoke.

Josh looked at Miriam and knew what she was thinking. Her father, crazed with drink, had also raped a girl, years before in Cornwall. He had been hounded to his death at the bottom of a deep mineshaft because of it. She would not allow any man to be handed over to certain death.

'No, you're right. But he'll answer for it when we reach civilisation.'

Isaiah Dacket showed no sign of the relief he felt. The first people they were likely to encounter would be Boers. If Josh made a complaint to them about the murder of a Bushman, he would make himself a laughing-stock. No Boer would penalise a white man for killing any native — but especially a Bushman. To a Boer, or indeed any native, a Bushman was something to be exterminated. A Bushman neither planted crops nor kept herds. He would not accept the rights of others to do so. It was beyond his comprehension that the land over which his people had roamed at will for thousands of years could be owned or taken possession of by others. As for cattle, they were merely slow-moving game — an easy meal.

There was another, economic, reason for hunting Bushmen. Taken young enough a Bushman woman would make a passable unpaid servant. Not so the men. A love of freedom was too deep-rooted in a Bushman to be beaten out of him, whatever his age. Killing him was the only solution.

All this was known to Isaiah Dacket, but he had no intention of being around to witness Josh's discomfort when he learned of the Boer way of thinking. He had plans.

On the way to the mountains with the Bushmen, Isaiah had observed that whenever they left camp the little men always buried a few ostrich eggshells full of water beneath the sand in a shady spot. Isaiah was satisfied he could find the camps again — and he would not be sharing the water with anyone. Josh's reaction to the death of Bele had made escape a little more difficult but he had little doubt that the dawn would find him many miles from Josh and the Bushmen.

Xhube's men made two forays before nightfall. They were not determined attacks, and a single shot on each occasion had been sufficient to drive the little men back to the shelter of the rocks. Josh's guess was that the attacks had been Xhube's way of holding the interest of his men. This would be a long siege. Time was entirely on the side of the little Bushman. He knew how much food they had in the cave.

Now that Isaiah had been deprived of his musket and his knife it meant that the watches would have to be shared between Josh and Sam, although in the grey dark of the pre-dawn they would both need to be on guard at the cave entrance.

The cave was wide enough for Josh to feel safe having Isaiah sleeping on the side farthest away from all the others while he or Sam kept watch.

Sam Speke kept the first look-out while Josh and Miriam, with Daniel, lay on the hard floor of the cave, well back in the deep black shadows. While Daniel slept Miriam wept for the young Bele, and Josh did his best to comfort her. Then the events of the day caught up with him and he dozed off.

He was brought awake by the sound of a shot, but it had come from so far away that Josh could not immediately identify it. Then from much closer he herd a groan of pain. Josh pulled the pistol from his belt before waking Miriam.

'There's something wrong. Take this pistol and stay with Daniel. Be ready to move quickly if I call.'

On hands and knees Josh crawled towards the cave entrance. There was something lying across it, and as he moved closer the shape moved and groaned. It was Sam Speke.

Josh rose to his feet and half a dozen paces took him to Sam's side. He took a quick look out from the cave. The moon was directly overhead, lighting the whole clear space before the cave. There was not a single shadow in which a Bushman could have been hiding, and the space was empty.

Sam Speke groaned again and stirred painfully.

In the moonlight Josh saw a dark patch staining the side of the seaman's forehead, and when he put his hand down to it his fingers came away sticky with blood. Then Josh knew this had not been the work of a Bushman. He made a rapid search of the area around the unconscious seaman, and when he could not find the musket he knew for certain this was Isaiah Dacket's doing.

'Miriam. Sam's been hit on the head and he's bleeding. Get some water and something to use as a cloth. Hurry! I want to bring him round and talk to him.'

By the time Miriam arrived with her underskirt soaked in water Sam was already regaining consciousness. A few minutes later he was sitting up, holding his head between his hands and cursing himself for a stupid fool.

'I never even heard him, Josh. And now he's taken the gold with him—and he's got the musket.'

'We've still got the pistol—and your life. It's my fault. I should have known he would try something like this. We should have bound him. But—'

A terrifying sound cleaved the night air and took his words away. It was a man's scream. Rising to a horrifying crescendo, it jerked along on the highest note for a full half-minute before dying away in bubbling breathlessness. It was another half-minute before Miriam's fingernails freed themselves from Josh's arm. Nobody said a word as they waited for the agonised sound to repeat itself.

There was nothing but the moonlight and a million silent stars.

'It is done,' said Hwexa.

'It is done,' agreed a weary-hearted Xhube.

The other Bushmen murmured their approval.

'This one has the stick that makes thunder,' said Hwexa. 'Now we can go to Gaua's cave for the others without losing more of our people.'

There was a moment's hesitation before Xhube declared, 'No! It is over. This is the white man who killed Bele. Now he is dead. There will be no more killing on the mountain.'

'You are forgetting the anger of Gaua. The white men and the woman and child are in his sacerd cave. They must die for that.'

'That is not Gaua's will.'

Xhube spoke as though from a great distance, and the others recognised the signs. Xhube was hearing the voices that sometimes came to him at moments like this.

'Gaua himself took the white men into his sacred cave and gave them his protection. This one was not a good man. Gaua turned him out and led him to us to pay for Bele's life. Now it is done and we will go.'

'We will go,' echoed Hwexa, and the three words were repeated by every one of the little golden-skinned warriors.

CHAPTER SEVEN

For the remainder of that night Daniel was the only occupant of the great painted cave of Gaua who slept. Sam's head throbbed painfully, but he sat keeping watch in the shadows of the cave entrance as the night gave way to the dark-grey dawn.

Still the expected attack did not come. Then, as it became lighter, Miriam said, 'Bele's body, Josh – it's gone!'

It was a few more minutes before they could be sure, and then Josh knew that Xhube and his small family tribe had gone away. He was sure of it even before the sun reached over the mountain and shone on the sandy plain below them, revealing the tiny Bushmen moving away from the mountain, travelling in single file.

Josh felt no animosity towards them, only a great sorrow. The little people had helped strangers to their land, asking nothing in return. Their reward had been murder and anguish. Josh doubted whether future travellers would find them as ready to make friends.

He lost some of his compassion when he and Sam Speke found Isaiah Dacket. The tall seaman was lying spread-eagled on the ground and the Bushmen had meted out a crude justice before spearing the life from him. Had he lived, Isaiah Dacket would have raped no other young girl.

Josh felt sick and was glad Miriam and Daniel had been left in the cave, but Sam Speke suffered no such queasiness. He searched the mutilated seaman and was jubilant to find the bag of gold slung on its cord about Isaiah's neck. His happiness was complete when he found the musket where Isaiah had dropped it after firing the shot that had wakened Josh. Only then did Sam Speke think of burying his late shipmate.

It was a very shallow grave and neither man bothered to pile stones upon it.

'Josh,' the seaman spoke as they scraped the last of the earth over the body, 'I'd like you to know that with Isaiah gone no one need ever know you've seen the inside of a prison hulk.'

The full impact of Sam Speke's statement took a few moments to sink in. He was right. Josh trusted the burly seaman and, with Isaiah Dacket dead, he realised he could hope for a future once more.

'I'm obliged to you, Sam. Not only for my sake, but for Miriam and Daniel, too.'

'Daniel's a fine boy, Josh. He'll grow up a boy to be proud of, and with this gold you'll be able to give him a good start in life.'

With their thoughts on the future the two men walked to the cave without a backward glance at the shallow grave that marked the violent passing of an English seaman.

There was no longer any choice about the direction they should take. They could not return to the coast for fear of meeting up with Xhube and his small tribe. It would be stretching his forgiveness too far.

The only way lay inland, across the mountains. But, as always in this parched land, they had to be sure of a supply of water. Isaiah had not been the only one to observe the Bushman habit of leaving a supply of water at camp sites, and so Josh and his party trekked to the site of their last unhappy camp to see if they could find some of the ostrich-egg containers.

They found something far more useful – the water-keg. It was probably too heavy and clumsy for the Bushmen to carry with them and of so stout a construction that to destroy it would have required unwonted effort. Josh chose to think that the leader of the little people had left it as a final generous gesture of friendship towards them.

They took the keg back to the great cave to fill with water for their journey and had a last look at the remarkable paintings. Then they set their faces to the east and headed for the low ridge Xhube had turned them from on their way up the mountain.

The ridge must have been four thousand feet above the surrounding country, but the view they had hoped to see was not there. Instead there was a wide broken valley with another ridge two miles in front of them.

It was the story of the sand dunes over again. For four days they slithered and scrambled down crumbling banks and toiled up steep slopes. Always there was another mountain ahead of them.

On the third day they found a valley where it was apparent that a river occasionally flowed. Here there was lush vegetation and plenty of animal life. Sam shot and killed a bustard, a bird as big and fat as a large turkey. It required no special skill. The big bird showed no inclination to move away and allowed Sam to approach to within easy shooting range.

They ate well that night, and it proved to be a turning-point in their gruelling trek across the mountains.

The next morning they topped a rise and instead of gazing out across more peaks and valleys they found themselves five thousand feet above a transformed land. Before them were miles of rolling bush veldt. It was not brown and parched like the land on the far side of the mountains, but green and fertile. The recent rains had brought plenty of water here – and it was still running. Water gushed from a spring below them, sparkling in the sunlight as it tumbled into a sheer hundred-foot drop from a smooth rock-shelf.

'We've done it, Josh. I told you we were right to come this way.'

Miriam hugged Josh in delight, and he squeezed her to him happily.

'There's life out there, too,' said Sam Speke more soberly.

'You mean all those animals?'

There was a great herd of zebra far in the distance, though from up here it was impossible to identify the species.

'No. I mean the fire over there.'

Sam pointed farther out towards the horizon, to one side of the grazing animals. A barely discernible wisp of smoke threaded the still, hot air.

'There's our civilisation. I hope it turns out to be all we are hoping for.'

Josh looked thoughtfully towards the distant fire. It *had* to be all right. They needed to make contact with people again and were totally committed to travelling in this direction. There could be no return across the mountains.

'We'll head towards the fire tomorrow. But we'll be cautious. I'd like to know what sort of people they are before we call on them.'

The ground was much steeper on this side of the mountains, and they descended slowly and cautiously, reaching the plains below by mid-afternoon. After filling the keg at the stream they followed the foot of the mountains for a while, keeping an almost vertical cliff-face on their right.

They had only travelled half a mile when they discovered a fissure in the cliff-face. It was no more than a six-foot-wide notch and would be ideal for a camp. A fire built at the entrance would provide an efficient barrier against any prowling creatures of the night, but as a double protection they cut down some of the thorn-bushes that seemed to grow everywhere in these lands and built a low barrier across the entrance beyond the fire.

Trees were more numerous here, and with the fire piled high with slower-burning wood they felt secure enough to bed down without a guard when darkness fell with typical tropical abruptness.

Sam Speke was the first to wake the following morning and seconds later he shook Josh with vigorous urgency. Josh sat up, and his hand went immediately to the loaded pistol.

Sitting cross-legged on the ground beyond the thorn-hedge were a dozen natives. Each was naked except for a short animal-skin 'apron' secured about his waist.

Sam also picked up his gun, and there was a nervous movement among the men beyond the fire. One of them stood up slowly and deliberately, leaving his spear lying on the ground beside him.

Unlike the golden-skinned Bushmen, this man was very dark-skinned and tall — taller than either Josh or Sam Speke — and his body was well formed and muscled. The castaways had met up with a hunting party of the Herero tribe.

'We come in peace. We have no guns.'

The Herero warrior spoke English slowly, his voice deep and melodic. Josh and Sam looked at each other in delight. Being able to communicate with these people meant there was far less chance of a misunderstanding occurring between them. It also meant they must be close to English-speaking people. Things were looking brighter already.

'We, too, come in peace,' replied Josh. As proof of his words he tucked the pistol back into his belt.

Behind him Miriam had awakened, and sight of her caused much interest among the Herero beyond the thorn-barrier which this morning looked frail and ineffectual.

'You have journeyed far?'

The Herero's manner was polite, his command of English good, but Josh found it necessary to concentrate on what was being said as the other man's pronunciation was unusual.

'We come from beyond the mountains. From the sea. Our ship was wrecked.'

A frown crossed the Herero's face, and he said something in his own language to those sitting beside him. One of them replied at some length.

'Do you think they mean us any harm?' Miriam whispered to Josh.

'I don't think so.' Josh's reply was as low as Miriam's query had been as he included Sam Speke, 'But keep your musket primed, Sam. Just in case.'

The Herero turned back to them.

'It is far from the other side of the mountains. Did you meet with any of the gatherers on the way?'

The question was casual—too casual. Josh sensed a sudden dangerous air of expectancy among the tall black men beyond the flimsy hedge. He knew that for some reason his answer would be important—but he did not know what he was expected to say.

'I don't know who "the gatherers" are. We met some small people on the other side of the mountains.'

Immediately the tension mounted.

'The small people are the gatherers. They helped you? They are your friends?'

Josh looked from the face of the man who had spoken to his companions and he knew what his answer had to be, though he choked on the words.

'We fought with them. One of my people was killed.'

'Ah!' The sound went up from many throats, indicating that a number of the Herero understood what had been said. Sud-

95

denly the tension was gone.

'It is always so with the gatherers,' said the Herero spokesman. 'They are not to be trusted. How many days since did this happen? We have killed three of the gatherers but know there must be more.'

He seemed disappointed when Josh told him the Bushmen were more than four days away.

'It does not matter. You are with friends now. The Little Father will be pleased to see you.'

'The Little Father?'

The Herero smiled and made the sign of the cross with his forefingers. 'The one who comes to us from the Great Father.'

'A missionary!' Josh and Miriam spoke as one, and Sam grinned at them.

'I knew I was right to follow you, Josh. You was born lucky. Shipwrecked a thousand miles from anywhere, a hundred different ways we can go — and you guide us right to some missionary's doorstep!'

They were not exactly on the missionary's doorstep. The Herero — his name was Mutjise — was leading a hunting party a hundred miles from the village where the mission station was situated and it took them another four days of hard travelling to reach it.

Along the way Josh learned to like and respect the tall muscular Hereros. They were cheerful and good-tempered and carried Daniel for much of the way on their shoulders. The only thing Josh found difficult to understand was their unreasonable hatred of the Bushmen. It was an attitude he was to find among men far more sophisticated than the Herero — and with the same apparent lack of cause.

On the way to the Herero village they met up with a great deal of game, including many animals Josh had never seen before. Elephant, giraffe and the tall ungainly bird, the ostrich, among them. Sam Speke shot two zebra and a giraffe, and the hunters were overjoyed. They would return with more meat than they had expected.

Unlike the Bushmen, the Herero were quite familiar with firearms, although none of them possessed one. Instead, they hunted with long-handled, broad-bladed assegais which they could hurl incredible distances; but they were quite content to allow the sailor to hunt for them.

They arrived at the Herero village an hour before dusk. At this time the bare-breasted women surrounded by wide-eyed naked children, were busy preparing a meal of maize porridge washed down with slightly curdled milk for their men. The men themselves were returning from the grazing-lands about the village, driving their numerous cattle into dusty wooden pens on the edge of the village.

There had been no attempt to conceal this place. It had all the bustle and dust of a small town. Round mud huts with thatched roofs were bunched together in orderly family groups while cattle, goats, children and dogs cluttered the packed earth 'streets'.

The arrival of the hunting party was greeted with acclamation, but this meat would not be distributed amongst all the people as a matter of course. It would go only to the families of the hunters. As had been the case with the Bushmen, the white strangers came in for much attention, Miriam most of all. She was the first white woman most of the villagers had ever seen. Certainly there had not been one here before.

Mutjise led them straight to the centre of the village, to where the mission church stood, its symbolic wooden cross standing high above the surrounding huts. When they arrived at a small hut standing in the shadow of the cross, Mutjise signalled them to wait. Pushing aside the blanket that served as a door, he went inside.

While they waited Josh and the others took in the details of their surroundings. The beehive-shaped huts were deceptive. At first sight they appeared tiny, but there was room in each of them for a whole family. As Josh estimated there were at least five hundred huts in the village it added up to a sizeable population.

There were many shady trees left standing, too, and the hard-packed earth beneath them was evidence that full use was made of their shade during the hot days. There seemed no shortage of water. On the far edge of the village Josh could see orderly green patches of vegetation. These people were cultivators as well as herdsmen. They were altogether a more prosperous and settled people than the little Bushmen of the desert, who lived out their precarious lives on a day-to-day basis.

'Good evening. I have been awaiting your arrival with great excitement. You are the first visitors from the outside world I have received here in Otjimkandje.'

Josh had been looking towards the pens where hundreds of cattle were raising great palls of dust as they milled about restlessly prior to settling down for the night. At the sound of the voice he swung around, startled. He had heard the accent before. It brought back memories of a German mine-captain who had once terrified the small mine where Josh's father had worked—the man who by his callous disregard for Cornish miners had caused much hardship among them. His contempt for human life had been such that he had once tried to leave injured miners entombed in a tunnel after a roof-fall.

Miriam, too, had known the German mine-captain and like Josh her initial reaction to the voice was one of dismay.

But missionary Hugo Walder was as strong a man as any to have come out of Germany and he had none of the faults of his mining fellow-countryman. Hugo Walder's capacity for loving his fellow-men was as large as the frame that held his great heart. In his early fifties, the missionary stood well over six feet tall with a large-boned frame and huge hands that would tackle any task, no matter how menial. With an eagle nose dominating a full-bearded face he was a formidable figure.

He took in the state of the ragged travel-weary party as he grasped first Sam Speke's hand and then Josh's hand, learning their names before turning to Miriam.

'My child! What a terrible time you must have had. This is no country for a woman to travel through on foot. But who is this little gentleman?'

Hugo Walder swung Daniel easily off his feet and held him out at arm's length to look at him.

'You are so young to have travelled so far!' Daniel grinned at him. 'And so brave and cheerful.' With a gentle friendly shake he lowered Daniel to the ground. 'Come, you must be hungry. I have food ready. Please come into my little house.

Holding the blanket aside, Hugo Walder ushered them inside

the hut. It was as though they had stepped over the threshold into another world. A civilised world of tables and trestle stools; of shelves with books and piles of newspapers; crockery and cutlery; oil-lamps and grass mats. In a corner of the room was a discreetly curtained-off bed, in another a small writing-desk with brass-handled drawers. Around the walls portraits of severe-faced men and women looked down. There was another picture, larger than the others, of a blood-stained Christ hanging on the cross of Calvary with tearful men and women kneeling about him.

'Welcome to my home,' said the missionary. 'While we are eating, your own huts will be made ready. I knew how many of you there were but very little else.'

'How did you know we were coming?' Josh put the question that was in all their minds.

Hugo Walder smiled. 'A runner was on his way here with the news of your presence before you knew you had been seen. Since Jonker and his tribe of Afrikaners moved into this country it is as well to know everything that happens. You were brought to Otjimkandje by Mutjise, son of Tjamuene who is the chief of this tribe of Herero. Tomorrow you will meet Tjamuene, but while you are in the village you will be my guests. That is less likely to offend Jonker.'

It was apparent that Jonker the Afrikaner had considerable authority here, but Josh's questions about him would have to wait. The big German missionary was ushering them to places at the rough-planked table which, together with the two long wooden stools, had been brought from the church for the occasion.

The missionary offered a prayer before the meal and they all sat with bowed heads as he said, 'Lord, bless all who eat at this table. And for deliverance from the trials I am sure they have suffered we thank you. Amen.'

'Amen,' they repeated.

The meal was of hot meat and gravy poured liberally on top of a generous base of thick cornmeal porridge and was served by two Herero women. It did little to cool them, but it was a happy gathering and there could be no doubt of the missionary's very real pleasure at having guests.

'It came as a great surprise to me when I heard you were found in the north, in the mountains. Where had you come from — and where are you going?'

Josh told Hugo Walder of the storm and the shipwreck as the missionary's expression changed from one of concern to incredulity.

'You were shipwrecked on the coast and crossed the desert to the mountains? You crossed that desert on your own and are here to tell of it? It's a miracle! There is not a Herero who would even attempt it, and I fear you will meet many people who will not believe you. Before today I would not have believed it possible.'

'We had some help. . . .' Rather hesitantly Josh told the missionary about the little men who had helped them. He told him the whole story — of the Portuguese skeletons, of the great cave and of Isaiah's way of repaying their kindness. He ended with an outline of the seaman's death and their subsequent trek over the mountains.

'So you met the Bushmen and they showed you kindness,' mused the missionary, emotionally moved. 'You have been more successful than I — and I have been in Africa for nine years.'

He signalled to one of the Herero women, who brought in large slices of a juicy melon while the other woman cleared the plates from the table.

'The Bushmen are a tragic people — so very tragic. It is most unusual for them to show themselves to strangers. You must have met a remote group who have little contact with other tribes. You have been lucky.'

In spite of the guttural accent Hugo Walder had a scholar's command of the English language.

'Why are the Bushmen such a tragic people?'

The missionary wiped melon juice from the thick beard about his lips before he answered. Conversation in this remote African village was a luxury in which he was rarely able to indulge himself, and there was not a man of his acquaintance, white or black, to whom he could have expressed a sympathetic opinion about the little Bushmen. In consequence he had to think about his words.

'Why is the Bushman a tragic figure? It is because he is an anomaly in this age. He should rightly be extinct. He does not own cattle, neither does he till the land. He will not live in a village such as this one, and so he cannot be overrun and made to pay homage to an overlord. He will not understand that the land from which he and his people have fought a living for longer than history belongs to anyone. To him it is not something that can be picked up and taken, and so the land belongs to no one but itself. Unfortunately he has the same nonconformist ideas about cattle. When a Bushman is hungry he looks for food. An elephant or a cow is all the same to him. Lastly, of course, he has no powerful tribe to back his actions. Africa is no different from any other part of the world in one respect: the weak are bullied by the strong. The only difference is that in a civilised country bullying is carried on within certain accepted limits. Here there are none. Death is the only boundary. The Bushman will not conform to the will of those about him, so he is hunted and killed. The Bushman is an elusive prey with only limited power to fight back, and so the whole thing has become something of a sport. The party that found you was supposed to be a hunting party – it *was* a hunting party – but I think their quarry was the little men who helped you to cross the desert.'

Josh remembered Xhube as he had told the sign-story of the Portuguese wanderers whose bones lay in the mountain gully, and recalled the pride and sensitivity within the little golden-skinned man.

Miriam's thoughts were of the shy and beautiful smile that had belonged to the gentle Bele.

'But you are a missionary. Surely your teachings are against such things? Can't you put a stop to the killing?'

'My child, every Sunday I preach to an empty church. The Herero watched me build it with my own hands. They did not help. I treat their illnesses and their injuries. I fall to my knees and pray to a god they cannot comprehend. Things have improved since I learned their language, but they have first to accept me as a man before they will listen to what I have to say. I must teach them by example and by proving to them that their life and their hardships are mine also – that I will not desert them when things become even harder.

'I was with Tjamuene when Jonker and his Afrikaners came from the south and took the valley of the hot springs for his own, forcing the Herero to move here to Otjimkandje. That helped, but I have far to go.'

Hugo Walder stroked down his heavy black beard.

'It may seem a strange and sad thing to say, but your dead companion may have done a great service to that little tribal group. They will never again trust strangers. Because of that they may stay alive for a few more years. Who knows?

'I came here to bring the word of the Lord to a people who have walked their own path for centuries. I doubt if my mission will succeed during my lifetime. It requires much patience, and the things that are bad can only be changed slowly. Sometimes because of my years they seek my advice. Perhaps that is to be the sum of my life's work. Who can say?'

During the missionary's sincere and quiet-voiced talk Daniel's head had leaned sideways against Miriam and his eyes drooped closed. Hugo Walder saw it and immediately rose from the table.

'What am I thinking of? You must be so tired, and all I can do is talk. I am being a selfish old man because I enjoy your company so much. Come, I will show you to your huts. I think you will find them quite comfortable. Tomorrow we will discuss your plans and see what I might be able to do to help them.'

Sam Speke was given a hut adjoining the mission. Josh carried the sleeping Daniel to a larger hut on the far side of the church. After showing them in through the blanket-covered door and lighting a single yellow-flamed oil-lamp for them the gruff but kindly German missionary wished them 'Good night' and left them alone.

When he returned to his hut Hugo Walder sat down to think. After a while he crossed to the piles of ageing and tattered newspapers and, selecting one bundle, untied the string that held it together and began slowly thumbing through the pages.

The mud walls of Josh and Miriam's hut were unadorned, and above them a latticework of bowed saplings supported the thick dried-grass thatch of the roof. An upside-down lizard, red-eyed in the lamplight, was spreadeagled motionless against the thatch, waiting for an exploring fly to walk into the range of its whiplash tongue.

Two beds made up from cured animal-hides covered with colourful woven blankets were ready for them, one for Daniel and the larger one for Josh and Miriam. The lamp stood on a rough square table in the centre of the one-roomed hut, and three stools were placed around it. Hugo Walder had even managed to gather together an assortment of cooking-pots, and two large earthenware jars of water stood near the door.

After undressing Daniel and tucking him into his bed Miriam said to Josh, 'Do you realise that this is our very first home?'

Josh smiled wryly. 'That doesn't exactly make me the greatest of providers.'

'Don't say that.'

Miriam came to him quickly. 'Do you remember where I spent my childhood? In that rock cave on Bodmin Moor? This is far, far better than that. We are all three of us here because of you, Josh. Four people from *Pride of Liverpool* are alive because you insisted we should head inland instead of following the coast.'

She kissed him and he held her close, surrendering to his need for her. Miriam responded immediately, and the fears and uncertainties of the previous weeks fell away. They were alone, and for the moment there was only an all-consuming love for each other. It was a force as primitive and powerful as any that might be found in the untamed lands surrounding the mud walls of the hut in Otjimkandje.

Later that night Miriam lay awake in the crook of Josh's bare arm. Above them in the roof the lizard scratched a zig-zag path across the tight-knit thatch. The drums of the village had long since fallen silent and with them the loud voices of the Herero men returning to their huts. From the cattle-pens there was only the occasional complaint from a cow crowded by her fellows. Miriam had lain awake for a long time before she felt a slight movement from the arm about her.

'Are you awake, Josh?' she whispered.

'Yes.' His whisper was hoarser than her own as his arm

tightened about her.

'What will we do now? I mean, now that we've reached safety?'

'I don't know. Probably move on to a place where there are more Europeans. Where they might have need of an engineer. But first I must learn more of the country – who it belongs to, and how the law is administered. Whatever happens, I am not going back to prison, Miriam. I would rather die here.'

'You won't have to go prison again, Josh. Sam is the only one who knows anything about your past and he won't say anything.'

'Oh, I trust Sam. But if we made our way to a place where there was a British administrator he would ask questions. Then he would have to inform the owners of *Pride of Liverpool* of our survival, and before long news would come back that I am a convicted man.'

'Then why move on? Perhaps there are some mines in this area where you can can work.'

'I haven't heard of any – certainly none that might need a mine engineer. Not that it would be necessary for them to have engines. I had a thorough apprenticeship, and there are many other jobs I could do. Blacksmith, founder, smelter – I'll do anything.'

'It would be a completely new start, Josh. We could stay here and forget there was ever anyone or anything before. You and I and Daniel could build a whole new life together.'

'All right. I'll find out all I can about the country from Hugo Walder first thing in the morning.'

Miriam slid her arm across his chest and snuggled closer to him.

'Then I'll not worry about the future anymore. Everything is going to be all right – and we'll always be together.'

CHAPTER EIGHT

Sam Speke was as contented with his little hut as Josh and Miriam were with theirs, and by morning the strain of the arduous trek from the sea had begun to fall away from all of them. Hugo Walder visited them early, assuring himself that they had slept well and were provided with all they required.

'I had a visit from one of the chief's messengers last night,' he said. 'Tjamuene wishes to meet you this morning. You have aroused his curiosity. White men coming here from the south are rare enough. White men, a woman and a child coming from the north are unheard of!'

Tjamuene had his own tiny kraal within the village. It consisted of some thirty thatched round huts sited within a six-foot-high wall of sticks and dried grass.

The missionary had sent word ahead of him that he was bringing the newcomers, and they found the chief waiting, seated beneath a tree on a pile of cow hides, a lion skin draped about his shoulders. The chief was flanked by the warriors of his personal bodyguard – tall, powerfully built men each armed with a broad-bladed battle-assegai.

If Tjamuene's idea had been to impress his visitors, then he was successful. Josh thought it would be a brave or foolish man who would dare to attack a chief surrounded by such warriors.

'Welcome!' Tjamuene spoke English with difficulty. 'You have come far.'

'From beyond the desert and across the sea,' agreed Josh.

Mutjise spoke to his father in their own tongue, and the chief nodded, carefully appraising the newcomers.

'From the lands of the Little Father. It is far.' His face took on a calculated expression. 'You have guns, Mutjise tells me.'

'We have guns.'

'It is good. Chief Jonker of the Afrikaners would be angry if the Herero had guns. It would mean war. But you are of the Little Father's people. You will hunt for us.'

'We will need more powder,' said Sam Speke.

Again there was a conversation between father and son.

'Mutjise will fetch you whatever you need.'

'Then I am sure they will be happy to hunt for Tjamuene's people for as long as they stay in Otjimkandje,' said Hugo Walder before Josh could speak. 'But their travels are not yet over. They have far to go to reach the towns of their own people.'

This time the talk between Tjamuene and Mutjise was carried out in lengthy whispers, and the missionary took the opportunity to explain his intervention.

'Unless it is made clear to Tjamuene that you are only passing through he would regard you as being a permanent hunter for the Herero. That would not please Jonker. It might provide him with an excuse to fall upon Otjimkandje and order me from the country.'

Tjamuene spoke again, looking at Josh. 'There will always be milk in my house for you and yours.' He pointed to Daniel. 'This is your son?'

'Yes, he is my son.'

Tjamuene called over his shoulder, and a tall boy of about ten years of age came forward proudly. Tjamuene put a hand on the youngster's shoulder briefly, then motioned him forward towards Josh.

'This is my son, Kasupi. He will be as a brother and a shadow to your son. You may go now.'

It had been a good meeting. Mutjise was smiling, and there was satisfaction on the faces of the tribal elders standing behind the chief. Only Tjamuene felt an emptiness in his heart. He was chief of the Herero, but because of Chief Jonker and the Afrikaners he was unable to guarantee the safety of his visitors, or offer a guide to take them on their way. He could only give away his younger son to them.

'Tjamuene was well pleased,' said Hugo Walder as they left the chief's kraal. His relief was apparent. 'He has paid you two of the highest honours it is possible for him to bestow. Telling you there will always be milk for you in his house means you are as close to being part of his household as is possible for a stranger. And poor Kasupi has taken on an awesome responsibility. To him has been given the task of protecting Daniel –

absolutely. If danger threatens, he will be expected to give up his own life to save him. If Daniel has an accident and hurts himself, Kasupi will be whipped for not preventing it from happening.'

'You can't put responsibility like that upon a young boy!' Miriam was shocked.

'For Kasupi it is a great honour. It shows his father's trust in him.' Hugo smiled. 'It also means that you must get used to having that young man sleeping in your doorway at night and staying with you every minute of the day while you are here. He is part of your family now.'

Miriam was not at all sure it was an arrangement of which she wholeheartedly approved, but her opinion would have made little difference to Tjamuene. His gesture had been one that contained more than friendship. As Hugo Walder knew and Josh had guessed, there was a secondary motive. They had arrived as strangers from an unknown land, with unexplained intentions. Kasupi would certainly be a guide and companion for Daniel. He would also report to his father any suspicious moves the newcomers made.

'Well, now you have met Tjamuene. What would you like to do today? Are you still tired? Perhaps you would like to rest?'

'How soon can we move on?' asked Sam Speke. 'And how many days' travelling-time is it to the Cape Colony?'

The thought of what he might do with the gold he had hanging inside his shirt was beginning to weigh almost as heavily on him as the bag itself.

'Well, now.' The missionary became more serious. 'First it will be necessary to let Jonker know you are here. Then you will need his approval to pass through his territory. Once you have that no one will dare to attack you. Without it you would not get far. Then you will need an ox-wagon. When the time comes I will supply that for you, together with drivers. As for the journey itself, it will take you longer than three months.'

Josh was astounded. Until now he had believed that they were at the borders of civilisation, that towns and villages occupied by Europeans were only a few days' travelling away.

Hugo Walder interpreted his expression correctly and smiled. 'This is not like any of the places you have ever known before, my friends. This land where we stand is not wanted by any of those countries who are fighting elsewhere for colonies. The Cape was once a Dutch colony. Now it lives uneasily under the British flag and, as more and more of your countrymen arrive there, the Boers – the Dutch – move farther away to escape their jurisdiction. Even so, you will travel five hundred miles from here before you reach the first Boer farm. On the way you will pass through three mission stations. If you are lucky, you may avoid the tribal wars that are going on. If not. . . .' Hugo Walder shrugged. 'No place on this great earth is God-forsaken, but I sometimes think the Lord has yet to look upon this corner of Africa.'

The missionary saw that his words had cast a pall of deep gloom over his guests and he put a friendly great hand on Josh's shoulder.

'I am sorry – but as a missionary it is my task to light a candle to guide Him to us. Come and see the candle I have built for His glory. The church of Otjimkandje.'

Upon their arrival the previous evening the mission church had seemed large and imposing to the travel-weary party. Today they saw it was both small and incomplete. Inside there were only four long benches, and wood and crude building materials were strewn about. But at one end of the building beneath a high glassless window a silver and mother-of-pearl crucifix stood on a spotless white cloth that covered most of a wooden table, and the area around it was swept clean.

'As you can see, there is much to be done. It is very slow work, and I feel it is more important for me to learn the Herero language. That takes much of my time, but is necessary if I am to translate the hymns and prayers into Herero. Then I also have my garden to attend to. My allowance is small, and I must feed myself as much as I can.'

Hugo Walder looked about the little incomplete church with pride.

'Here I am selfishly happy, watching it grow slowly with time. However, it will have to wait a while longer. My tools are worn out, and it will be many months before more arrive from the Cape – Chief Jonker of the Afrikaners permitting.'

Josh picked up a poor-quality hand-axe from the floor. The

head of it had cracked down one side of the handle-holder.

'A blacksmith could do something with this.'

'My friend, there are so many things a blacksmith could do in Otjimkandje. Unfortunately there is not a blacksmith north of the Rehoboth Mission Station. The last one we had was an Ovambo tribesman who was put to death by Jonker. He realised the error of his ways too late and now Jonker, too, is without a blacksmith.'

Josh became thoughtful. 'Did the last blacksmith only carry out repairs, or did he also make things?'

'He did everything! To the west of here, not many miles distant, is much of the ore that makes iron and the Ovambo used it a great deal. We have other tribesmen living here who can make iron, but they lack the skill to make useful tools.'

'Well, if there is still some of the last blacksmith's equipment to hand, I think I can do something about these worn-out tools.'

After the conversation with Miriam the previous night it seemed to Josh that this was a great opportunity to exercise his skills as a blacksmith and at the same time help this man who had so little and yet was prepared to give so much to others.

'You get some of your men to produce some iron and I'll see about setting up a smithy.'

'You are a blacksmith?'

The joy on the missionary's face was touching.

'I'm an engineer. Learning to work as a smith was part of the training. I can do that while Sam does the hunting.'

'And when I'm not hunting I'll help with some of this.' Sam pointed to the unfinished church furniture. 'I'm pretty useful at carving and carpentry and the like. It will keep me out of mischief before we move on.'

Hugo Walder took a deep breath and spoke with a voice choked with emotion.

'I think the Lord must have sent you as a reproach to me for my lack of faith. My friends, your stay here is going to be a happy time for me.'

When Josh first began working on the smithy and stripped off his shirt the Herero tribsmen flocked from all over the village to look upon the vivid red scar that bisected Josh's back from shoulder to waist. When Hugo Walder asked about it Josh said only that the wound had been caused by a soldier's sabre, and the missionary asked no more questions.

By the end of two weeks Josh, assisted by Herero workmen, had almost completed the setting up of the smithy. Although no man had raised a hand to assist Hugo Walder in the building of his church, Tjamuene had taken a great interest in Josh's project. He had even handed over the crude anvil which had belonged to the murdered Ovambo blacksmith and which the Herero chief had appropriated as a piece of furniture.

It was then that Jonker's Afrikaners paid their long-awaited call.

The Afrikaners, known to the Herero as 'Aich-ai' — 'the war-like people' — rode into the village at midday, a party of about forty of them. They were shouting arrogantly, half their number brandishing muskets and most wearing at least one item of European-style clothing. The speed and recklessness of their riding kicked up a cloud of dust and scattered Herero cooking-fires.

There were no streets in Otjimkandje, only wide open spaces between the rows of huts. Jonker's men ignored these natural thoroughfares and rode direct to the mission, forcing their way between the closely packed huts and trampling over everything that lay in their path.

The manner of their arrival led Josh to think the worst and, putting aside the bellows he was shaping, he hastily loaded and primed his pistol. Tucking it into his belt, told Miriam to stay inside their hut. There was no sign of Daniel, who was off somewhere with Kasupi, and Sam Speke had gone on a hunting trip with Mutjise.

Josh returned to his embryo smithy close to the church walls and awaited the arrival of the Afrikaners. They rode straight at him, waiting until the very last minute before tugging hard on the short reins, causing their horses to rear and mill about, foam flying from abused mouths.

One of the horsemen said something to Josh in a harsh and unfamiliar language. Josh shook his head without taking his eyes from the Afrikaner's pock-marked face, and Chief Jonker's man repeated his brief statement.

'If you say it in English, I'll try to answer you,' said Josh, and this time it was the Afrikaner's turn to look blank.

At that moment the bearded German missionary came from his church, his demeanour unruffled. Armed horsemen riding up to his church could have been an everyday occurrence.

'You would appear to have a language problem,' he said, smiling at Josh. Turning to the leader of the Afrikaner horsemen, he spoke to him in the same harsh language Josh had just heard.

The conversation moved back and forth between the two men, and from the frequent nods in his direction Josh knew he was the subject of their talk.

Eventually Hugo Walder turned to Josh. 'Jonker has heard of your presence here. He would like to meet all of you.'

'The way he was putting it didn't sound much like a request to me,' commented Josh, jerking his head at the Afrikaner horseman.

'Coming from Chief Jonker even the vaguest suggestion should be interpreted as a command,' said the missionary.

'When does Chief Jonker want to see us?'

Hugo Walder put the question to Jonker's emissary.

Josh did not need a translation of the single-word answer to know that he was expected to set forth immediately.

'How long a journey is it?'

'Two days by ox-cart, a matter of hours only if we had horses.'

Josh looked at the smithy taking shape about him. 'I've another week's work to do here. Tell them we'll set off to visit their Chief Jonker then.'

Hugo Walder gave an amused smile. 'Yes, Jonker's orders bring out the worst in me also. All the same, I think we should make immediate arrangements for the journey.'

Josh pushed his way between the Afrikaner horses, slapping the rump of one of them to make it move out of his way and almost unseating its rider. Between the little church and Hugo Walder's hut was a small garden on which the missionary had put in a great many hours' work. The effort of carrying water to it was a daunting task in itself. The healthy green of the plot's well-ordered crops had been evidence of the missionary's perseverance. The arrogant Afrikaners had charged their horses through the fertile little plot and churned up mature plants and frail seedlings alike.

Josh pointed to the chaos. 'Tell Jonker's men I would have been happy to set off immediately. Unfortunately my departure will be delayed until this has been set right.'

Without another look at the horsemen Josh walked back to the smithy and resumed work on the bellows.

Hugo Walder translated Josh's words exactly as they had been spoken.

From his horse the Afrikaner looked down at Josh, his nostrils flaring angrily. Jerking his restless horse to a halt he said, in Afrikaans, 'I have carried Chief Jonker's words to you. You would do well to obey them.'

Pulling the horse's head around, he led the other horsemen away, carefully avoiding the missionary garden.

'What happens now?' Josh said to the missionary as they walked together back to his hut to deposit his pistol and tell Miriam what had been said.

The missionary smoothed his beard and smiled. 'Who knows? Perhaps the great Jonker will call personally with his invitation.'

Josh looked to see if he was serious, and the big German missionary shook his head. 'If that happened, Jonker would not come alone and we would be left in a deserted village. Tjamuene and his people would flee before him. But that must not happen, my young friend. We must prepare ourselves to pay Chief Jonker a visit.'

'What is it about him that makes him so terrifying?' asked Miriam. 'What has he done?'

'If you are asking me for a list of his misdeeds, it would save much time if I listed the few things he has *not* done.'

The missionary began pacing the confined area of the hut.

'Jonker is the younger son of a thief and murderer who fled from the Cape Colony with a band of like-minded followers. They were not really a tribe, and so for want of a name they became known as the Afrikaners – the people of Jager Afrikaner, as Jonker's father called himself. They were a strange mixed band with some white blood flowing in their veins. When the father died Jonker, as a younger son, inherited nothing. So, gathering all the worst elements of his father's people about him, he fought his way northwards, conquering the people and taking whatever he wanted. He forced Tjamuene to leave Ai-gams, in the valley of the hot springs, and now Jonker lives there and has opened up some form of trading post, exchanging stolen cattle for brandy, guns – and now horses. He calls his new capital "Winterhoek".'

'And all the other tribes pay homage to him in the hope that he will leave them alone?'

'That is so.'

While they were talking they became aware of a growing commotion outside the hut. At first Josh thought it was nothing more than excitement caused by the visit of the horsemen; but the noise was swelling and coming nearer, and now a desperate wailing accompanied the general hubbub.

The missionary was the first to the door of the hut, and as Josh and Miriam emerged into the bright sunlight the noisy crowd swarmed about them.

The missionary snapped a few questions at the noisy Herero. When he turned back to Josh he was almost as agitated as Tjamuene's people.

'What is it? What's happening?' Josh asked.

'It is Jonker's men.' Hugo Walder's face had paled beneath his beard. 'They saw Daniel over by the cattle-pens with Kasupi. They have carried both boys away with them.'

CHAPTER NINE

'How many miles is it to Jonker's village?' Josh intended going there on foot; he had already dismissed an ox-cart as being too slow.

'Thirty — thirty-five miles,' replied the missionary. 'But you cannot go alone!'

'He won't be alone. I'm going too.'

Miriam was busy stowing food into one of the haversacks that had stood them in such good stead on their travels from the coast.

Josh did not even start to argue with her. One look at her determined expression was sufficient to tell him it would have been a waste of time.

'What is Tjamuene doing about his own son?' he asked the missionary.

Hugo Walder spread his hands wide. 'He dare do nothing. To march on Jonker's village would mean annihilation for his tribe. Tjamuene is father to his people first — to Kasupi second.'

'Will he at least provide us with guides to show us the way to Jonker?'

'There will be no need for any Herero to come. I will take you.'

Josh paused in the act of slinging the powder-horn over his shoulder.

'There's no reason why you should involve yourself in this. You are here to preach the gospel to the Herero. If you offend Jonker, all your years of work will be undone. Just give us a guide.'

'My work will be finished here unless I am seen to do something to return Daniel. If it is seen that Chief Jonker holds me in such little regard that he can come here and interfere with those afforded my protection, then I might as well return to Germany. No, my friends, this outrage affects the lives of us all. Give me a moment or two to change my footwear and I will be ready.'

It seemed that the whole village assembled to watch their departure, the Herero warriors standing in humiliated silence. Only Tjamuene, their chief, was absent.

By taking advantage of the bright moon and sleeping for only two hours they reached Jonker's village early in the morning of the next day, taking the despotic chief completely by surprise.

The village was sited in a beautiful fertile valley, and from the wide pass in the hills above it looked very large and well laid out. There was even a train of ox-wagons trundling westwards from the village on a well-defined road.

The long forced march had brought Miriam close to the point of exhaustion, but now they had come to within a mile of the place to which her son had been taken she was stubbornly determined not to allow her tiredness to show.

'Is that Jonker's hut?' Josh pointed to a large square-built building closely surrounded on three sides by many of the now familiar round huts and with a large empty space on the fourth.

'I don't know.' Hugo Walder ran a cloth kerchief around his neckband. He had grown unused to walking long distances since moving to Otjimkandje. 'But it is the largest hut in the village, and Chief Jonker would not settle for anything less.'

Josh checked the priming in his pistol. 'It might be as well if you waited up here, Miriam.'

'I could have stayed in Otjimkandje if I'd wanted to avoid danger,' retorted Miriam. 'We'll go down there together.'

'Do you have any plan in mind?' asked the missionary as they set off down the hill to Chief Jonker's village.

'None – beyond getting Daniel and Kasupi back and returning to Otjimkandje.'

Hugo Walder could think of a great many reasons why Josh's simple and naïvely direct plan should fail – not least of them being the thousand or so armed warriors who occupied the huts they were rapidly approaching.

But luck has always reserved a special place for the brave and the foolhardy. They had arrived at a time when most of the men were beating the valley a couple of miles away to flush out a lioness who had killed a herd boy and one of his charges, and so the determined trio were actually in the open space in front of the large hut before their presence caused a stir.

Nevertheless, by the time they stood before the entrance to the hut it seemed that everyone who remained in the village was noisily rushing to surround them.

The sound brought a man from inside the hut. He was not a particularly impressive figure, being slightly built in comparison with the Herero of Tjamuene's tribe. The only distinctive thing about him was the leopard-skin cloak he wore slung over one shoulder.

'I'm looking for Chief Jonker of the Afrikaners,' Josh blurted out before the other man could speak.

'I see you have brought the Little Father with you. Does he have so short a memory that he has forgotten the chief of the Afrikaners so soon?'

The leader of the warlike Afrikaners smiled mockingly at Hugo Walder. His English was more strongly accented than the missionary's, although a recent influx of traders from the Cape Colony had given him some practice.

Slowly and deliberately Josh began to draw the heavy pistol from his belt, but the strong hand of the powerful missionary reached out quickly and took his wrist in a bone-crushing grip. Behind them the noise from the Afrikaners swelled ominously.

Chief Jonker looked deliberately at the hand gripping Josh's wrist, then raised his eyes to Josh's face.

'It is only to be expected that a man will sometimes act foolishly for love of his son.'

His quiet dignity was solidly backed up by half a dozen warriors standing a few yards away, their muskets aimed at the hearts of the three Europeans.

When Hugo Walder was sure Josh had seen the armed men he released his grip, a movement that was acknowledged by a nod from Chief Jonker.

'The child should not have been brought here. I gave no orders for it. The man responsible has been punished, and I have sent for your son.'

'We are grateful to Chief Jonker.' Hugo Walder inclined his head to the leader of the wild tribe of Afrikaners.

A tribeswoman dressed in the silks that were reserved for Jonker's favourite wives came around the corner of the hut holding Daniel by the hand. When he saw Miriam he released his hand and with a shout of 'Mamma!' ran to her, and she gathered him in her arms.

'I rode on a horse.'

That was all the whole frightening incident had been for him —an adventure, a ride on a horse.

'He is well,' said Chief Jonker and, looking at his affable smile, Josh found it difficult to believe that this was the man who was feared so much by Tjamuene and his Herero.

'But where are my manners?' Chief Jonker stood to one side of the doorway to his hut. 'You have travelled far. You must come inside to eat and rest.'

'No.' Josh spoke before the missionary could answer for him. 'We came for my son and the boy Kasupi. When we have them both we will return to Otjimkandje.'

'Is Chief Tjamuene of the Herero so afraid of the Afrikaners that he cowers in his village and sends strangers to beg for his son's return?'

'I know nothing of Tjamuene's feelings. I know only that he gave me Kasupi to serve my son. Because of that I have a responsibility for him.'

'That is so,' agreed Chief Jonker. 'He shall be returned to you now. It is fitting that Tjamuene should produce sons to be servants. Now that matter is settled you will stay. See! Your woman is tired.'

Now that Daniel had been safely returned to her, Miriam was indeed feeling the effects of the journey. Clasping Daniel tightly to her, she leaned heavily against one of the posts that supported the overhanging thatched roof of Chief Jonker's hut. But Josh had no wish to be a guest of this man he still believed to have ordered the abduction of Daniel.

'I intend to be clear of this place and back in Otjimkandje by nightfall. We'll all sleep safer there.'

For a brief moment the chief of the Afrikaners looked angry. He realised that Josh did not accept that he had not been responsible for carrying off Daniel. He turned and snapped an order in his own language at one of the musket-carrying warriors. As the man turned and hurried away Hugo Walder looked thoroughly alarmed and made a plea to the chief, also in the Afrikaner language.

Chief Jonker smiled thinly, his eyes still showing anger, but he said nothing.

The missionary turned to Miriam in a state of agitation. 'Turn away and cover the boy's eyes. Whatever you do, don't look until I tell you.'

He was too late. Miriam was able to push Daniel's face into her breast but she did not miss the gruesome trophy that the member of Chief Jonker's guard bore into their presence. She just managed to stifle the scream that rose to her lips.

His fingers locked in the short black crinkly hair, Jonker's man carried the severed head of the warrior who had ridden into Tjamuene's village and demanded that Josh leave to see his chief immediately.

The Afrikaner thrust the head at Josh, and he recoiled in horror, trying not to gag at this example of Jonker's savagery.

'Take it with you,' said the chief, satisfied with Josh's reaction. 'It will help you to remember that Chief Jonker does not lie. Neither does he deal lightly with those who do not obey his orders. You have your son. The man who took him has been punished. There is nothing between us now.'

'We will stay in your village and rest,' said Hugo Walder quickly.

'Good!' The Afrikaner chief waved the guard with the gruesome trophy away.

Had the face of the dead horseman not haunted Josh throughout the day it would have been difficult to fault Chief Jonker as a host. That he had full and absolute sovereignty over his tribe was beyond dispute. His every command, every gesture was obeyed immediately. He also possessed a natural dignity and charm that would certainly have impressed Josh and Miriam greatly had they not had tangible proof of his primitive cruelty.

The feast he put on for them after they had rested and the dancing he ordered in the space outside his hut went on until well into the night. Jonker asked many questions of his guests and seemed very impressed when he heard Josh had a knowledge of smithying and ironwork. There were many guns in his village that needed repair, and wagons, too. Would Josh not consider moving to Winterhoek where Jonker could find much more work for him? Many traders were arriving in the town with wagons damaged from the long overland haul.

Josh replied that he had no intention of operating the smithy at Otjimkandje permanently. He planned to move south to the Cape Colony as soon as possible.

'That will not be for a very long time,' said Jonker. 'There is much trouble in the land. I cannot allow you to go on until I can be sure of your safety. An attack upon you would be an attack against me. It might even bring trouble from the government at the Cape. No, you must stay. I have trouble enough.'

Josh knew from the way the Afrikaner chief spoke that his words constituted an order, not a suggestion. His talk of trouble was exaggerated. If trading wagons could get through, then so could Josh.

But Chief Jonker accepted that Josh should remain at Otjimkandje and help Hugo Walder with his mission church. He also extracted a promise from Josh that he would carry out any work that Jonker might send him from time to time and also train an Afrikaner tribesman in the art of smithying.

That night Chief Jonker and his guests parted, if not as friends, then certainly with more warmth than had been present upon their arrival in the Afrikaner village at Winterhoek.

The next morning Chief Jonker rose early to see his visitors on their way and demonstrated that there was both generosity and a bizarre sense of humour in his nature.

He loaned his visitors an ox-wagon and an escort to take them back to Otjimkandje, and gave Josh two gifts. The first was a new musket together with a quantity of lead and powder. The second gift was the horse that had belonged to the man Jonker had beheaded.

'The gun will kill from afar,' said Chief Jonker, touching the musket. 'With this you need never be short of meat.'

Reaching out, he pulled the pistol from Josh's belt. 'With a gun like this you may only shoot a chief when you stand before him. It is better to send him a message from afar with a long gun.'

On their way back to Otjimkandje the party met up with Sam Speke, Mutjise and a much enlarged hunting party of Hereros heading for Jonker's village. Not all of Tjamuene's warriors were as ready as their chief to accept an insult to the tribe.

The Hereros approached in battle formation, and Jonker's men prepared to meet an attack. Only the swift intervention of Hugo Walder prevented an incident.

Even when Mutjise and his warriors saw Daniel and Kasupi and heard of the fate of Jonker's lieutenant, they looked at the tribesmen from Winterhoek with hot-eyed suspicion. The missionary deemed it wiser to send Jonker's men back to their village with the ox-cart and walk the remainder of the way to Otjimkandje with the Hereros.

Along the way Josh jokingly asked Sam Speke whether he had intended taking on the whole of the well-armed Afrikaner tribe with his small hunting party and one musket.

'No,' replied the seaman seriously. 'But Mutjise wouldn't have thought twice about it. I don't think he's afraid of anything. Me, I'd have appealed to Chief Jonker's better nature.'

He pulled the bag of gold from inside his shirt. 'Mutjise tells me Jonker has developed an expensive taste for brandy as well as guns and is in debt to the traders. I'm sure we'd have been able to come to some arrangement.'

'You'd have parted with your gold for Daniel?' Miriam asked.

Sam Speke shrugged. 'Well . . . I'd have given him your share first, of course. But likely as not I'll waste most of mine, anyway.'

'You take care of it, Sam. One day some sensible woman will come along and snap you up. When she does you'll be able to put that money to good use.'

Sam Speke said nothing, but Miriam had touched upon a subject to which he had been giving a great deal of thought since their arrival at Otjimkandje. Among the Herero a man was not expected to run his own household, and the girl sent by Tjamuene to help with Sam's chores looked upon it as a living-in situation. She was an attractive pleasant girl, but Sam did not know how his companions would react if he told them that he seriously contemplated marrying a Herero girl.

The incident with Chief Jonker marked a turning-point in Hugo Walder's mission among the Herero. Warriors of the all-powerful Afrikaner chief had carried off a son of their own leader.

The Little Father had gone after him and returned the boy to his people. In order to achieve this he must have had the protection of a very powerful god. Such a god should not be offended.

The Herero tribe, led by their chief, flocked to the little church to learn about the missionary's god and his ways.

While Hugo Walder scattered the seeds of his religious teachings among the people, Josh brought his smithy into full operation and Sam Speke proved that not only was he a competent carpenter but was also capable of producing wood-carvings of considerable skill and imagination to decorate walls and pulpit.

While all this was happening, Miriam transformed her hut into a comfortable home, and Daniel pried into the childish mysteries of village life in company with his faithful guardian Kasupi. Miriam spent much of her day surrounded by inquisitive women. It was very difficult to order them from the hut as they pretended not to understand what she was saying. Eventually she gave up and made the best of their presence by making them teach her the Herero names for all her household items. Soon she had gained a fair command of their language.

The shipwrecked party had found their way to the village of Otjimkandje in early March of the year 1846, when the minor change in the weather introducing winter had just begun. By November, when the hot airless days of summer were upon the land, the essential work on the interior of the church was complete.

It had been a pleasant season, and somehow the urgency of moving on to seek other communities had faded. Josh's temporary smithy was kept busy from dawn to dusk with work for the Herero and the Afrikaner chief.

The small valley where the Herero village was situated was also a pleasant and healthy place. It had a permanent supply of water and ample grazing on the surrounding plains for all the cattle the tribe possessed. When cattle sickness decimated Jonker's herds during July it was far enough away to prevent the Afrikaner chief from casting envious eyes upon its prosperity.

One evening Hugo Walder invited the others to his hut for the main meal of the day. An easy relationship had developed between them, each aware of the strengths and weaknesses of the others and appreciating their worth.

The meal was over before the missionary broached a subject that had been increasingly on his mind since the completion of the church became an accomplished fact.

'This has been a most enjoyable evening,' he began. 'In fact this has been a splendid year. Because of your arrival I have seen so many of my hopes achieved. Your presence has been a great help and a constant pleasure. I realise it is a selfish pleasure. My life is here, serving God. My happiness is in His service. For you life has other things to offer. You are young.' The missionary paused uncertainly, toying with the spoon on the table in front of him. 'What I am trying to say is that I realise you have made a great sacrifice by remaining here to help me. I have always known you must go your way one day. I don't think Chief Jonker will put any obstacle in your way now. You can take my own ox-wagon and a Herero driver and I will help you in any way I can. That, coupled with my constant prayers, is the only way I know of expressing my deepest gratitude to you all.'

Now it had been said, the big bearded missionary felt relieved but very sad. He had believed for a long time that it was only a form of loyalty to him that had kept Josh and the others in Otjimkandje.

Josh and Miriam, too, were relieved that the missionary had broached the subject. It had kept them talking until very late into the night during recent weeks – but not because they wished to hasten their departure.

Josh cleared his throat noisily.

'Yes, it's something we have been thinking a lot about – at least, Miriam and I have.'

Hugo Walder nodded. 'Then I was right to speak of it. Have you decided when you would like to leave? It is becoming hotter every day. Soon travelling will be most uncomfortable – although some traders are beginning to arrive by sea at Whalefish Bay. It might be possible to arrange a sea passage to the Cape Colony for you.'

Miriam shuddered at the thought of ever again travelling by sea, but it was Josh who spoke.

'That isn't quite what we had in mind. As I said, Miriam and I have given it much thought. We've been very happy here – and are still happy, thanks to your great kindness. I'm pleased you feel we have helped you, and I believe there is much more we could do. I could extend the smithy to undertake simple foundry tasks, and when I was riding west of here some weeks ago I saw signs of a large copper-ore deposit. That could be exploited and a profitable trade built up, using Chief Jonker's sea route via Whalefish Bay. I know he would expect to be paid tribute, but that could be negotiated.'

Josh's words generated an air of excitement in the smoky lantern-lit interior of the hut, and Miriam took it up.

'I've picked up a fair knowledge of the Herero language. If I work hard, I feel sure I could master it, at least well enough to open a school.'

'I know we're taking a great many things for granted,' put in Josh. 'We came here uninvited and now we're proposing we should stay. But that's the way Miriam and I feel. I can't speak for Sam.'

'There's no need for anyone to speak for me.'

Josh's declaration had come as a great relief to Sam Speke. His relationship with the Herero girl who looked after him had grown into something very special for the lonely seaman. His love for the girl he had named Mary had grown slowly but very surely; and there were nights when he suffered torment as he lay awake holding her sleeping body close to his, dreading the day when Josh would decide to move on and he would have to make his own decision – whether to cut his ties with everyone and everything he had ever known, or leave this girl and the loyalty and love he had never before experienced.

'You've both said things I couldn't have put into words. If I was to leave here, I'd end up back at sea sooner or later – no matter how much money I had. That's no life for a free man. I can't offer you the talents Josh and Miriam have, Hugo, but I can promise you one thing. Give me a few years here and I'll make you some beautiful carvings for your church.'

Hugo Walder looked from one to the other, and even in the dim light from the smoky lamp it was possible to see the tears in his eyes.

'You *want* to stay but are not sure of the way I feel about it? My very, very good friends, if you say you will stay with me and help me in my work, I will go out to my little church tonight, fall on my knees and give heartfelt thanks because the Lord will have answered my prayers.'

Now this momentous decision had been reached Josh felt the need to tell the missionary something of the events that had brought him to Africa.

He began his story hesitantly, but Hugo Walder cut him short.

'I wish to hear nothing! God works in His own ways, and I neither question nor doubt Him. He guided you here and allowed me to judge the man you are. I am happy to have you as my helper and friend. What is more important is that together we can all do so much for the Herero – both in this life and in the greater one to come. My friends, life will begin anew for us in this great year.'

Looking at the honest old missionary, Josh thought he was right. Here in this remote African village Josh had found a freedom he would have in no other place.

Two hundred miles north-west of Otjimkandje another decision was being made. It had been a disastrous season here between the sea and the mountains of Gaua. No rain had fallen, and the few animals that normally lived here had died or moved on. Now the underground water-holes that had kept the Bushmen supplied for centuries were drying up one by one.

Xhube looked around at his people and thought their bodies were like the old wreck lying among the sand dunes, with little more than a gaunt frame remaining.

They sat about a single fire, picking listlessly at the flavourless pulp of a stringy giant desert aloe, the only food the women had found in two days.

It pained Xhube to see his people like this, the joy and laughter gone from their lives. There had not been a dance for many months. Life had become a daily fight for existence – and his people were not winning.

The little Bushman said what was in his mind.

'Tomorrow we will leave this place. We will go to meet the

rising sun and seek a home in the land beyond Gaua's mountains.'

His words meant little to the women. The land to the east promised little more than the land in any other direction. The only thing that would bring hope to them was water. But the men looked wide-eyed at their chief.

'Those are the lands of the Herero. To go there is to invite death for us and slavery for our women.'

'Death shares our fire now,' declared Xhube. 'And he will enslave our women more surely than the Herero.'

There was not the heart in the other men to argue. Only Hwexa expressed his disquiet.

'We do not know the lands beyond the mountains. We will be strangers in the land of others.'

'Are you any more familiar with the land beyond the grave, Hwexa? No, we must go to where there is food. Rain has fallen beyond the mountains. We must go there. We will travel fast and unseen to the desert beyond the Herero. Perhaps there we will find the freedom for which we are both concerned. The freedom to live as we will – and freedom from hunger.'

BOOK TWO

In the Herero village of Chief Tjamuene, Josh and Miriam enjoyed a good life for more than a decade. They had the friendship of the tribesmen and of the missionary. They built a wooden hut for themselves and made it a home, and with a well-contented pride they watched their son grow to near-manhood.

Daniel grew up learning the ways of the Herero alongside the things taught to him by Josh and Miriam. His friend Kasupi was always present to explain the customs of his people, and Daniel learned well. By the time he was sixteen he could hunt the lion with a spear and bring down a buck with a single musket-shot at a hundred paces. The child from Cornwall became a young man for whom the Herero warriors had respect. To the young Herero girls and their mothers he was the subject of much speculation. Such a hunter as Daniel would be a great asset to any family.

Meanwhile, in his little church Hugo Walder sowed the seeds of his religion with hope and honest belief, and was content to see God reaping a sparse but growing harvest.

These were the good years, and it was difficult to say when they first began to change.

The changes came as gradually as did the traders who pushed their way northwards from beyond the Orange River to Jonker's village in the valley of Winterhoek. The Afrikaner chief also established a trade route from his village to the small but safe anchorage at Whalefish Bay, one hundred and fifty miles to the west.

From the traders Jonker developed a taste for brandy, and his wives pestered him for the colourful silk dresses in which it pleased him to see them clothed.

But the traders demanded payment for the goods they lavished upon Jonker's people, and when the Afrikaner chief was not left with sufficient cattle of his own with which to pay his debts he turned upon those who had – and the Herero were his closest neighbours. Gradually, the small villages had their cattle wrested from them and, if they were foolish enough to raise their voices in complaint, the Herero lost their lives too. Soon there were but half a dozen Herero villages within a radius of one hundred miles of Winterhoek, and the only one of any size was Otjimkandje.

This was the way of things by the time Daniel was in his seventeenth year and Christmas Day in the year eighteen hundred and fifty-eight drew near.

CHAPTER ONE

Christmas in Africa did not possess the magic of the same day in Europe. Even Hugo Walder had to admit to that. The Holy Day needed snow, holly and the wide-eyed anticipation of children to give it the proper atmosphere. Somehow the pagan trimmings made it easier to imagine the birth in the manger and the Three Wise Men travelling on their journey to destiny.

In his own simple way the German missionary was a far greater man than any of the celebrated ancient trio. They had been given a star to follow – something visible to guide them on. There was no such guiding light sent to Hugo Walder. For years he laboured in total spiritual darkness – years when the tide of his faith sometimes ebbed so low that there was nothing but the ugly jetsam of doubt all about him.

Yet still he had gone on.

It was his belief that when the tribesmen saw for themselves the good that stemmed from His teachings they would turn to him for spiritual guidance. This was the basis of Hugo Walder's mission among the Herero.

He had not come to Otjimkandje to decry their customs, to demand that they conform to the strict rules he imposed upon himself. He tried hard not to interfere in their tribal way of life, although he was totally convinced the Church offered a better path for them to follow. He was equally certain he could show them that path by example. Because of these beliefs he determined not to take sides in the complicated and bloody tribal strife that sprung up in the lands around the village of Otjimkandje.

The tide had turned for Hugo Walder with the arrival of the survivors from *Pride of Liverpool*. Suddenly there was help with his physical problems: his church and his garden – and his schemes to make the material life of the Herero of Otjimkandje easier. He already had the attention of the villagers when Sam Speke provided him with an unexpected bridge between them.

The missionary had known that Mary was sharing Sam's bed;

but the fact was not blatantly thrust upon others, and Hugo Walder chose not to bring the matter into the open. Nevertheless, it came as a great joy to him when Sam Speke and Mary stood before him one day early in 1847 and said they wished Mary to be baptised and then have Hugo Walder marry them in his little mission church.

At first Hugo Walder tried to deter them.

'I am happy you wish to behave as an honourable man,' he said to the ex-sailor, 'and I know that here in this little village such a marriage would be accepted by all of us. But there is a whole world beyond Otjimkandje. Your marriage would be as binding out there as here. If you decided to move on, Mary, as your wife, would go with you. There are places not so very far from here where such a union would make you both outcasts. Mary is a good girl but all her life has been lived in Otjimkandje. She would be unhappy away from her own people.'

'I've thought of all that,' said the burly Sam Speke, fidgeting like a child before the missionary's honest searching eyes. 'I don't want to move any farther than here. I've knocked about the world a bit in my time and seen many places. There's none where I've been happier. Here I'm looked up to by Mary's people. I've never had that sort of respect before. I've been used to the lower deck, where you expect everyone to kick you. Even ashore it's only a sailor's money folks are after. When it's gone they'll kick you as hard as any ship's officer. No, I like it here. There's no reason why I should want to go anywhere else. If I have to — well, Mary has looked after me well here where I came as a stranger. I reckon I could do the same for her elsewhere.'

'In that case, Samuel Speke, I will be proud to marry you and Mary. You'll be getting a good wife, and she'll have as fine a man as any in Otjimkandje for her husband.'

There were a few formalities to be completed. Tribal custom decreed a bride must be bought, whether there was to be a Christian wedding or not. After suitable negotiation the bridal price was set at six cows and a small bench of the type Sam had made for the mission church. He also had to provide two goats for the wedding feast.

Sam Speke produced the Portuguese gold coins, Hugo Walder

carried out the trading for the livestock and the wedding went ahead.

It was the first marriage in the little mission church, which was packed to stifling overflowing for the occasion. Hugo Walder made it a very moving occasion and conducted the marriage in both English and Herero. The wedding set a precedent that other Herero couples were quick to follow.

Less than eighteen months later, in June 1848, the christening took place in the same little church of Victoria Mary Speke, newly born daughter of the mission's first marriage.

Then followed the good years for Hugo Walder — years when he saw the growth of Christianity in this remote village. The baptisms and marriages began to spread across the pages of the mission register. Soon Miriam's teachings, too, bore fruit. Some of her brighter pupils were sent to the Cape Colony and would one day return to their own tribe as teachers.

But Africa is a restless continent, ever changing and shifting its moods — a vast rumbling pot-pourri where fortunes swirl this way and that, like the sand shifting before the four winds.

So it was with Hugo Walder, his companions, Otjimkandje and the Herero. The good years did not disappear overnight, but by Christmas in the year of 1858 it seemed doubtful whether the life they had known and the community they had built about them would last for very much longer.

The cause of their uncertainty was Chief Jonker of the Afrikaners.

The years had not made the Afrikaner chief any more tolerant. He had always welcomed traders and accepted their presents. He was flattered by the deference they showed him as factual overlord of the whole territory.

The traders supplied Jonker with guns and powder and introduced him to brandy. Soon he was buying many barrels of spirits, but as Jonker's love of brandy grew and his debts to the traders mounted he no longer tried to find excuses for plundering Herero cattle. He helped himself to whatever he wanted. If the owners objected, they were killed. Jonker's warlike followers took their cue from their leader. Herero in remote villages were slaughtered and their possessions stolen by the well-armed Afrikaner warriors.

Soon it became a genocidal war, and only the strong personality of Tjamuene's missionary kept Jonker from treating Otjimkandje in the same manner as all the other Herero villages. It helped that Jonker received dues from the copper mined by Josh in the hills beyond the village. It was not a large working but it was profitable.

At the moment, however, Hugo Walder was very concerned with the situation. He voiced his thoughts at the Christmas meal he shared with Sam and Josh and their two families.

'I don't think Jonker will dare to raid us here,' said Josh. 'He's frightened that any interference with a mission station will bring trouble for him from Cape Town. Besides, Sam and I are building some ox-wagons for him. He needs them to bring his own goods up from Whalefish Bay if he's ever to break clear of the traders.'

'I wish I shared your confidence,' replied the missionary. 'Too many of Tjamuene's people are leaving and heading north with their cattle, while the ones arriving here to seek refuge have none. Very soon we will find ourselves with a feeding problem.'

'There'll be no helping them by hunting,' put in Daniel. 'Jonker's men and their guns have killed everything within two days' riding. Kasupi and I have been out twice in the last week and didn't find a single track around the usual water-holes.'

Almost as broad-shouldered as his father, Daniel possessed an air of confidence that was due to the responsibility he had assumed as hunter for the two families and Hugo Walder. It was nothing for him and Kasupi to be away from the village for a month at a time.

'We won't starve,' said Sam Speke. The ex-sailor had put on a great deal of weight since he had settled down ashore and he had the manner of a solid contented man. 'Our credit's good with the traders. If Jonker would allow them to come up as far as Otjimkandje, it would be even better.'

'It's the Herero I feel sorry for.' When Miriam had arrived at Otjimkandje she had still been a young girl, for all that she was a mother. She had matured into a beautiful woman. The bond of love and understanding between her and Josh had kept at bay the strain that aged many young women in Africa. 'They are terrified of Jonker and his men. It's a pity his last missionary gave up and left Winterhoek. He needs some sort of restraining influence.'

'For today let us try to forget Jonker,' said Hugo Walder. 'There was a full church for my service this morning. Perhaps prayers will do what the Herero cannot – keep Jonker from our village.'

But the Afrikaner chief chose that very day to pay a visit to Otjimkandje. He came with fifty mounted warriors, and their arrival threw confusion and terror into the Herero. Many of them were refugees from previous 'visits' made by Jonker and his men and they had witnessed the slaughter that followed. The screams of the women and the excited babble of the men brought the small party of Christmas celebrants out of the missionary's hut.

Chief Jonker of the Afrikaners showed his contempt for the chief of the Herero by riding past Tjamuene's small kraal without so much as a sideways glance. He did not stop until he and his party reached Hugo Walder's hut.

His first words made it clear that his business should have been with Tjamuene.

'Someone has been stealing my cattle. I have come here to look for them.'

The Afrikaner chief swayed in the saddle, and Josh realised he was dangerously drunk. He hoped the missionary also recognised the signs.

'Since when have the Herero of Otjimkandje been stealers of cattle?'

'The Herero have always been cattle thieves. Now I have come to claim back what is mine.'

All his listeners knew that Jonker had come to Otjimkandje because he needed cattle – Herero cattle – to pay his debts.

'This should be a matter between chiefs. Have you spoken to Tjamuene about this matter?'

'The chief of the Afrikaners does not talk to old women who tremble when the wind blows.'

Some of Jonker's followers laughed uproariously. Their chief had not been drinking alone.

Daniel wished his gun was closer to hand. He sensed serious trouble here. But the missionary had known Jonker for many years. He would not lose any battle of words. He looked pointedly up at the sky that was beginning to darken as the sun sank low over the skyline.

'It is unfortunate that the light is failing or I would help you seek your cattle amongst those in the cattle-pens. It would not do to make mistakes. Many of the cattle belong to the mission while others are owned by those who are friends of Chief Jonker. Besides, this is Christmas Day. We are celebrating the birth of the Son of God. But of course you will know of these celebrations. I remember your father died a Christian. Step down from your horse and join us in our celebrations – or return tomorrow and we will seek your cattle together. The great chief of the Afrikaners is always welcome in my mission.'

The missionary had turned the tables neatly. He had hinted that, if Jonker went off with any of the cattle, he might well be stealing missionary property – a matter that could have far-reaching consequences. Hugo Walder had also reminded Jonker that his father, who had himself once terrorised Namaland to the south, had turned to Christianity before his death and celebrated this day. Any trouble Jonker now caused would signify disrespect for his father's memory. It was something that not even a drunken Afrikaner chief would contemplate.

But Jonker had no intention of leaving without giving the missionary and his party some very disturbing news. It was even possible that the whole story of his 'missing' cattle had been invented and this was the real reason for his visit.

'The copper mine at Meneheke can be worked no more. There is too much water in the mine.'

Josh nodded. Meneheke was a copper mine on the other side of Winterhoek worked by a syndicate of Europeans with Jonker's blessing. Water had begun to seep into the workings years before, and they had ordered an engine from England – only to discover when it arrived that they had no one with the skill to put it together and set it to work. Josh had offered his services and done the job for them. He had told Andrews, the mine-owner, that the engine would never cope with any deep mining. The mine's closure came as no surprise to him. The Afrikaner chief's next words did.

'I have told Andrews he can work the copper at Sesebe.'

136

This was the small copper mine Josh had successfully developed with the help of the Herero. It was only a few miles from Otjimkandje, and Josh had used his knowledge of mining to make it an efficient and profitable undertaking. The mine had provided additional meaning to his life here. It was worthwhile and satisfying work. He was happy — and now Chief Jonker was saying he was taking it away.

'The mine is on Tjamuene's land. We've been working it for years. We made an agreement with you to work it — and you receive tribute.'

'The tribute is not enough. The Herero are lazy; they do not work hard enough. As Tjamuene's land is my land I have given it to Andrews.'

With that, Jonker jerked his horse's head around and he and his men rode away into the lowering dusk, leaving a stunned group of people behind them.

For all Hugo Walder's bluff about missionary cattle, in truth the mission and its occupants owned very few. Their livelihood depended heavily upon the modest income from the copper mine at Sesebe.

'Perhaps Jonker's bluffing.' Sam's words contained more hope than belief.

'Why should he bluff? He claims the land. He doesn't have to ask us what he can do with it — and he'll have no opposition from Tjamuene.'

Josh spoke bitterly, unaware of the figure that slipped noiselessly from the shadow of the nearby huts.

'My father is beyond the years when a man should have to fight to prove he is the chief. But he has sons. Would you have me lead my father's people to their deaths against the guns of Jonker's warriors?'

Mutjise was a man with much pride and, though he was more aware than anyone of Tjamuene's weak leadership, he would have no criticism of his father. He was wise enough to know that the day when the Herero could successfully rise against the Afrikaners was not now. They should have risen *en masse* when Jonker had led his men on their first foray into Hereroland. Now there was nowhere that could rightly be called 'Hereroland'. It was Afrikanerland.

'I'm sorry, Mutjise.' Josh liked the chief's eldest son and respected his position. It was not easy for him to lead and guide the tribe when another man was its head. 'But Jonker has given our mine at Sesebe to Andrews.'

'That is very bad.'

The Herero shared the profits with the mission and their men were paid for digging the ore.

'Perhaps Jonker would listen if I went to Winterhoek to speak to him.'

'No.'

Hugo Walder's rejection of the idea was decisive. On the last occasion Mutjise had gone to the Afrikaner chief to plead the cause of his people he had spent three days and nights tied to a wagon-wheel for his pains.

'It would serve no purpose,' Josh agreed. 'Jonker has already made the agreement with Andrews. I suspect the brandy he's been drinking today was part of the settlement. All I can do is speak to Andrews and ask him to employ Herero labour to work the mine for him. I expect he'll agree, especially as any sort of work is beneath the dignity of Jonker's men.'

Harold Andrews was only too happy to accept Josh's proposal. He was a merchant, not a mining man. He might even have been embarrassed at taking the mine away from Josh and the Herero but, as he explained to Josh, had he not agreed to mine the copper ore from Sesebe someone else would have been brought in. As a merchant Andrews had to remain on good terms with Chief Jonker. To fall out with him would be committing trading suicide.

Josh did not believe the trader. He had a shrewd suspicion that it had been Andrews who had pointed out to Jonker the money he was losing by not taking the lion's share of the profits from the Sesebe mine. But Josh kept his own counsel.

Then Harold Andrews made Josh a generous proposition. He wanted to expand the trading side of his business and explore the trading potential of the interior with his partner, a Boer trader named Jacobus Albrecht who had recently trekked overland with three wagons from the Boer territory beyond the Orange River, four hundred miles to the south. Andrews asked

Josh to manage the mine for him.

Josh accepted. The prospect of working with professional miners excited him. He told Miriam about it that evening.

'We're going to have a whole new community out here,' he said, gulping down great mouthfuls of food so he could talk more quickly. 'Andrews is going to build cabins and mess-halls and a smithy, and there'll be a wagon-shop run by Sam. We can go and live there in a new house. It will be just like a village at home.'

Miriam did not share Josh's enthusiasm.

'I thought we had found what we wanted here in Otjimkandje.'

Josh nodded vigorously, still carried along on the high tide of his enthusiasm. 'We have, but this will bring civilisation closer. There'll be new people to talk to.'

Miriam was aware that European civilisation could bring more than neighbours.

'Will there be other European women there?'

'Yes. Well . . . not at first, maybe. They will come later as the mine goes deeper and more men move in with their families.'

'Then I've a pretty shrewd idea of how the men will keep themselves entertained until then. No, thanks, Josh. We'll keep our home here. You know what miners are like when they've been paid. These men will be no different. I expect Andrews has made provision for selling liquor to his men?'

'Yes, he's going to build a place where they can buy drink.'

'Of course he is. That way he'll get a week's pay back from his men in one night.' Miriam shook her head sadly. 'We've seen it all before with Cornish miners. They'll arrive full of good intentions – to save their money and send for any kin they might have. Then the loneliness will get to them in the evenings, and they'll gather together to drink and talk about what they'll do when their families arrive – or when they return home. Before long their families will fade farther into the background and the girls in Otjimkandje begin to look more and more attractive to them.'

Miriam stood across the table from Josh, hands on hips in a stance that reminded him of his mother.

'I don't think you need me to spell out what happens then!'

Daniel had been listening in fascination. He had never before seen Miriam lecturing to his father in this way. He paused with a food-laden knife halfway up to his mouth.

'Spell it out for me, then, Ma. I don't know what happens then.'

Miriam transferred her glare to him and snapped, 'I'm pleased to hear it. That means the rumours I've been hearing about you and Kasupi and the young girls working the maize fields can't be true.'

Daniel choked on the maize-meal porridge. It was fortunate for him that Josh was too concerned with what Miriam had said about the miners to pay heed to his son.

'Yes, I'm aware of what miners are like when they have money in their pockets. I'll do what I can, but it will be little enough. I'll be paid by Andrews to run his mine, not to stop miners spending money on his liquor.'

Miriam shrugged. 'There's really nothing you can do, Josh, except to bring one or two of them here for a meal sometimes and try to encourage them to attend Hugo's church. They're grown men and will lead their own lives.'

'Of course they will – and there will be good and bad among them as there was at home, you'll see.'

'Will they need someone to hunt for them?' Daniel asked.

'Not on a regular basis. They'll buy cattle. Besides, there's little game to be found about here now. You told me so yourself.'

'There hasn't been,' agreed Daniel. 'But a tribesman from the north came in yesterday and said he'd seen signs along the Omuramba Omatako flats. I'd like to take Kasupi and check for myself.'

'How long do you expect to be away?'

'Two – maybe three weeks.'

'Are you and Kasupi taking a large party with you?'

'No, just the two of us. I'll take a horse for Kasupi and borrow Sam's old gun for him.'

'All right, but there have been reports of Bushmen up there. Keep out of their way and don't interfere with them.'

'I have no quarrel with our little brothers.'

Daniel gave his reply in the Bushmen's own click language. He had learned it from a Bushman slave kept by Tjamuene. Daniel was one of those fortunate beings to whom the learning of languages came easily. In addition to the strange Bushman language he was fluent in Herero and most of the local tribal dialects as well as German, taught to him by Hugo Walder. He also had a working knowledge of the Dutch used by the Boer traders and voyageurs and favoured by Jonker's Afrikaners.

'Keep out of the way of Jonker's warriors,' warned Miriam. 'By all accounts they're spoiling for trouble.'

'Jonker and his men will be too busy seeing what they can take from the men coming to the Sesebe mine to go that far away.'

Josh had taken Daniel hunting on many occasions since he had first been able to ride a horse and he had no qualms about his ability to take care of himself. He was sixteen years of age, and in this country a boy was not allowed to remain a child for long. Daniel had been brought up in a Herero village where a boy was expected to do a man's share of the work at thirteen. At sixteen a Herero would be a warrior and most likely married. Although Kasupi had forgone his right to marriage when his father appointed him to be Daniel's personal bodyguard, being a favourite son of the tribal chief made him very attractive in the eyes of the young village girls. He took full advantage of the situation, and as Daniel was his constant companion it was inevitable that his tuition had covered more than native languages and customs. Daniel had become a man in everything but years.

CHAPTER TWO

The tribesman from the north had been correct. The game had returned to the Herero's traditional grazing-lands. With few Herero cattle remaining, they had no competition for the grasslands. The two hunters came across a black rhinoceros only thirty miles from Otjimkandje. They gave the animal a wide berth. A rhinoceros could be killed with the gun that Daniel had, but it would need to be a perfect shot. Anything less would leave two tons of angry and possibly wounded rhinoceros running wild. The animal's horn would have fetched a high price from the Herero tribal doctors, but it was not a worthwhile risk.

For Daniel, checking on game was merely an excuse to get out of the village and away from people. He loved the wide-open emptiness of the bushveldt. He especially enjoyed the country inland from the village, where the rolling landscape of coarse grass gave way to the desert, broken here and there by high rocky outcrops protruding hundreds of feet towards the sky. They were volcanic islands in a dried-up sea.

Everything about the desert fascinated Daniel. Here it was not the sand dunes of the coastal strip but a vast area, barren but for the stunted thorn-bushes and the occasional clump of sword-sharp grass defying sun and wind. This was the desert of the dry season which lasted for most of the year. But when the rains did come it changed, literally overnight. When that happened a man could be excused for thinking he had been transported in his dreams and had woken in a new land. The coarse dry grass had become green, and unseen tubers lying dormant beneath the ground pushed up stems topped with bright flowers to capture the magic of the rains.

There had been rain here in the last week and, although it had been no more than a brief rehearsal for the rainy season soon to come, it was enough to transform the whole desert.

'It is good to leave the smells of the village behind,' said Kasupi.

'And the weeping of the unmarried girls because we are away

will be good for the maize,' commented Daniel.

Kasupi's grin threatened to split his face.

'Their gratitude will be all the greater when you return me safely to them.'

Daniel snorted. 'One day Tjamuene will lose all his cattle to fathers demanding payment for the gratitude of daughters.'

Kasupi's smile disappeared. 'Better to lose his cattle that way than to the robber Jonker.'

Kasupi was as much the son of a chief as his older brother Mutjise. The domination of the Herero people by the Afrikaners was a constant source of shame to him. Kasupi was proud of being a Herero. He believed that had his people been allowed to buy guns they would have defeated the Afrikaners before they had established their dominance, but successive missionaries had frowned upon Herero trading for arms. Once Jonker arrived it was too late. No one was more aware of the importance of firearms than the Afrikaner chief. He promptly issued an order to every trader entering the country forbidding them to sell arms to the Herero. It was an order that was confirmed by the Cape government. Although their jurisdiction did not extend to this part of Africa, they warned traders against selling guns to any of the tribes in the region. It was a directive that rankled with Kasupi and the young men of his tribe because it seemed to be aimed directly at the Herero. The Afrikaners already had guns.

'We've left those troubles behind us for the moment, Kasupi. I can see something moving up ahead. Let's go and shoot our supper.'

But what Daniel had seen was not an animal. It was a tiny Bushman trotting along doggedly, eyes on the ground following a spoor that only he could see. When they were close enough to recognise him Kasupi kneed his horse forward excitedly. Animals he would kill only for food. A Bushman would provide sport.

Daniel galloped his horse alongside his friend and shouted at him.

'No, Kasupi! Don't hurt him. I want to find out what a Bushman is doing in this country.'

The keen-eared Bushman had heard them behind him and

was running for the shelter of a clump of thorn-bushes. When Daniel slid his galloping horse to a halt between the Bushman and his refuge the little hunter slung an arrow in his bow and pointed it mechanically in Daniel's direction.

'We come in peace,' Daniel said in the musical click language.

The hunter did not lower his bow, but neither did he let the arrow fly. As the two men looked at each other Daniel noticed the protruding ribs and emaciated body of the Bushman.

'Had we wished you harm you would already be dead.'

Daniel nodded to where Kasupi stood his horse twenty yards behind the Bushman, his musket aimed at the little man's back.

'We meet as friends.'

The Bushman stole a quick glance over his shoulder. Realising the hopelessness of his position, he lowered his bow, and his shoulders slumped helplessly.

'My people have no friends in this land.'

'It is long since your people were last here.'

'We live in the great emptiness where the sun rises.' He waved his arm to the east and the vastness of the northern Kalahari. 'There has been no water there for far too long. My people are dying.'

'How many of your people are with you?'

The Bushman held up nine fingers; but Kasupi had circled around to rein in alongside Daniel and, seeing the look on the Herero's face, the Bushman began instinctively to draw back the arrow in his bow.

'He's too old to make a good slave. Kill him!' the Herero said in English.

'Shut up!' Daniel glared at his companion. 'And stop behaving as though you were one of Jonker's warriors.'

The insult silenced Kasupi, and Daniel turned back to the Bushman.

'How long since you've eaten?'

'Many days. Some of my people are too weak to walk.'

'Then you'd better take me to them. Kasupi! Go and find something for our supper. When you've got it come back to here and follow our tracks. Here, you'd better take my gun and give me yours.'

He threw his modern gun to Kasupi and took Sam Speke's

old musket from him. Kasupi's pleasure at having the new weapon superseded all other feelings, and he rode away eager to test his skill with it.

The Bushman relaxed the taut string of his bow and slipped the small arrow into the tight curls of his hair, taking care not to scratch his skin with the sharp tip. When he caught sight of the musket Daniel was holding the Bushman moved to look at it more closely.

'This is yours?'

Daniel shook his head. 'No. It belongs to my father's friend.'

The Bushman looked at Daniel for some moments, his eyes showing nothing of his thoughts. Suddenly he turned away. 'Come, my people wait for me.'

He set off at a trot, and Daniel followed. The Bushman was weak and occasionally staggered, but he refused an invitation to ride on the horse with Daniel.

They travelled for about three miles before the Bushman led Daniel to a thick low clump of coarse grass. Here were the remainder of the little man's tribe. They were in desperate straits and had reached that apathetic state which comes to a Bushman when he has decided it is time to die.

The arrival of Daniel and their hunter roused them from this morbid surrender, and Daniel bullied them into getting a fire going. They had been afraid to light one before for fear they would be seen by local tribesmen. Daniel was able to assure them there were no tribes in the area at this time.

It was dark before Kasupi arrived, guided by the fire. Blood dripped from the soft nostrils of a reedbuck slung across the saddle in front of him.

The Bushmen's hunger was such that the meat of the reedbuck was barely scorched on the outside before they were cutting pieces from it and tearing the meat apart with their teeth, swallowing painfully.

Kasupi watched them with unconcealed contempt, Daniel with a strange mixture of pity and fascination. All he knew of these people were the stories he had heard from Sam Speke and his parents and the scant information gained from the slave of the Herero chief.

When the buck had been devoured and the fires were burning

low Daniel talked to the little hunters while Kasupi went some way from their camp and slept. Daniel asked them of their way of life, of their traditions and of their more recent troubles. The Bushmen in their turn questioned Daniel about the local tribes, their disposition and the hunting prospects in the land to the west. Not until the moon was on its downward journey did Daniel curl up in a scooped-out hollow in the sand and sleep.

When he awoke in the morning Kasupi was already up and scouring the ground about them. The Bushmen had gone without a track to show their direction. The Herero was angry, saying the Bushmen had made fools of them. Daniel was amused. He could well understand why the Bushmen trusted no one to know which way they had gone. But they had not left without expressing gratitude. Alongside his blanket Daniel found a miniature Bushman bow. It was a simple symbol of friendship.

From their hiding-place on a rocky outcrop the Bushmen watched Daniel and Kasupi ride away.

'You saw the stick-that-thunders?' asked the hunter who had brought Daniel to his people.

'I saw,' said the wrinkled man by his side.

'Then was I right?'

'You were right, Xhube. It was the one taken by those who came from the bitter water.'

'And this was the child. It was truly Gaua's will that we did not kill them to revenge the death of Bele.'

'It was truly Gaua's will,' agreed the aged Hwexa as he looked at their people, who would now live until they found the better hunting country Daniel had told them lay only a few miles distant.

Harold Andrews' men trekked in from the south with twenty ox-wagons and as much equipment as they had been able to carry from the played-out mine. Few of them were family men seeking to make money for their dependants. They were tough adventurers, living only for the day and taking as much from it as they were able. Josh recognised their type immediately. Theirs was the mentality adopted by generations of itinerant Cornish miners – the attitude of men with no purpose in life, no ambition but to drink their lives away in the shortest and most boisterous manner possible. Managing them was going to be tough.

The miners had been liberally supplied with Cape brandy for their journey, and because of this they arrived accompanied by a large party of Jonker's men. The chief himself was not with them. He had heard that a ship had been wrecked on the dangerous coast to the south of Whalefish Bay and had gone there to see what could be plundered.

In spite of all the drinking they had done, the miners wasted no time in setting up camp when they reached Sesebe. For the time being, the wagons would serve as bedroom and cookhouse, storeroom and mine office; but the men had brought with them the tools with which to begin the task of putting up buildings, and no sooner had they outspanned the trek oxen than they began digging out the foundations of their new mining camp.

Once work started the Afrikaners drifted away, and with their departure Herero from Otjimkandje moved in. They were immediately signed on and set to work.

By the end of a week the rough-timbered buildings were taking shape and the smithy, transferred from Otjimkandje, was in full operation. Sam Speke was working hard on wagons battered by a journey across the trackless country between the new mine and the old. In a month there were communal living-quarters, a cookhouse, office and bar surrounding the copper-rich dust of Sesebe mine.

By the time Harold Andrews arrived with his first wagon of trade goods the mine was in full operation.

'You've done well, Josh,' said the mine-owner, 'I knew I could rely on you to get things moving quickly.'

'The mine might be working well – but what about storehouses for the goods we trade, eh? And pens for cattle? Where are they? The speaker was a big blond sun-tanned man of about thirty. He spoke with a very strong Dutch accent.

'I'm sorry. You two haven't met. Josh, this is Jacobus Albrecht, my partner.'

The blond man nodded curtly at Josh.

'I repeat. Where are the cattle-pens?'

'What do we need cattle-pens for? The cattle coming in to

feed the mine will be slaughtered as they arrive.'

'Agh! I'm not interested in the mine. That's Harold's baby. I'm talking about profit — real profit. *That's* going to come from trading, and Jonker will pay for his goods with cattle. So we'll need a place to put them. Does that make sense to you, man?'

It made too much sense to Josh. He realised there was much more than copper behind Andrews' transfer of operations to Sesebe. It was closer to Jonker's Afrikaners, it was true. It was also much too close to Otjimkandje.

'Where is Jonker supposed to get his cattle from? His herds are already so small that he wouldn't dare deplete them any more by trading. The only herds of any size in these parts belong to Tjamuene's Herero.'

Jacobus Albrecht shrugged nonchalantly. 'Where he gets them is his own business. Kaffir cows are Kaffir cows. As long as they arrive in prime condition I don't ask any questions.'

'I'm sure you don't. But so far Jonker has left Otjimkandje and the mission alone. If he starts raiding their cattle to pay for your cheap brandy, you'll have no mine working here and then you'll learn where your steady profits are coming from.'

'You've lived among the Kaffirs too long. You're beginning to sound like a missionary. You just look after the mine, Retallick. Leave Harold and me to do the trading.'

'Start a war between Jonker and Tjamuene and you'll have no mine and no trading. You'd better be sure your partner understands that, Mr Andrews. At the first sign of trouble for Tjamuene I walk out of this mine and the Hereros go with me; and I guarantee that within months it will be making a bigger loss than you're able to cover by trading — that's if you are still able to trade.'

After looking contemptuously at Josh, Jacobus Albrecht gave him a tight-lipped smile and turned away. Striding off to his wagons, he shouted at the Africans working on them, using the bastard language the Boers expected all tribesmen who worked with them to understand.

'Come on. Get that load off. You — lazy Kaffir! Pakanisa lo bokisi. Pakanisa! Lift the box. Lift!'

'I shouldn't worry about Tjamuene's cattle, Josh. Most of our trading will be with the tribes farther inland. It's ivory and skins we're really after, not cattle.'

Harold Andrews spoke placatingly, but Josh knew that talk came easily to the trader.

'Have you explained the rules to Jonker? Or your partner? It seems to me Jacobus Albrecht has other ideas.'

'We've very little to trade that would interest Jonker. He's after guns and powder and, as you know, the Cape government has forbidden any trade in arms.'

'I didn't see any shortage of guns among Jonker's men when they came to Otjimkandje on Christmas Day.'

'You can't blame Albrecht or me for that, Josh. I've heard there's a Jew named Aaron who's supplying them. He's got a place down the coast from Whalefish Bay. His ships put whatever he wants ashore there. Albrecht's a hard trader but he won't go against the Cape government.'

'He must be the only Boer in Africa who won't,' retorted Josh.

The pleas of missionaries like Hugo Walder had resulted in the Cape administration banning arms shipments to the tribesmen who roamed and fought in the vast spaces of this unwanted corner of Africa, but it was a ban that was near-impossible to enforce. Even more so since numbers of resentful Boers had pushed farther northwards, refusing to accept any British-made laws. Their frontiers were still many miles away, but men like Jacobus Albrecht were their vanguard. If they thought selling arms to tribesmen would harm the Cape government more than themselves, then they would provide the guns.

Jacobus Albrecht and his people took their own laws with them wherever they went — and they would rewrite them to suit the occasion.

It was not long before the Sesebe mine was producing as much ore as they had the capacity to carry to Whalefish Bay to await the bi-monthly ship that came there. There were rumours that an ore-ship would soon arrive every month, and in the wagon-shop at the mine Sam Speke and his men worked away to provide more wagons to carry the extra ore, while other men were brought in from the Cape.

Mining the copper presented no problems for Josh. The ore was quarried rather than mined, a method that kept costs down.

But Josh was of the opinion that Sesebe, like the mine Andrews had owned, would one day simply run out of ore. He kept these thoughts to himself. While Andrews thought he needed him he would keep Jonker away from Tjamuene's cattle and Otjimkandje would survive.

But survival had to be paid for.

Hugo Walder rode over to the mine one evening to visit Josh and he was appalled by what he saw there. Although it was not yet dark, the wooden building that had been named 'The Miners' Inn' was well patronised, and ill-sung and bawdy songs rang out. Outside, a few Hereros sat on the slatted wooden steps, passing a jug of brandy around between them. Alongside the hut a number of Tjamuene's people lay in drunken sleep. Among them were two women. Shrill laughter indicated that more of the village women were inside.

'What sort of people have we allowed into this land, Josh?' asked the missionary as Josh came to the door of the mine office to meet him. 'How can I justify keeping my mission running on the proceeds of such evil living?'

'It's part of the price we must pay to keep Tjamuene's people alive,' Josh reminded the missionary. 'Having women here is a way of stopping the men from going looking for them at Otjimkandje.'

'I cannot bring myself to accept such a thing, Josh. To pay a toll to the Devil in order that I may carry out the Lord's work is totally wrong.'

'You've come on a bad day, Hugo. The men were paid today. I'm working closely with Mutjise on the effect this is having on his people and I believe we're keeping it under control. I'm sure both the Devil and Chief Jonker would be happy if they thought that together they might drive missionaries away from this land.'

'Then I have surprising news for you, my friend. Jonker has applied to have an English-speaking missionary sent up to Winterhoek for the Afrikaner people.'

Josh was genuinely startled. 'A missionary? But why? He's had three missionaries before and driven every one of them out —but I've no need to tell you. You know more about it than anyone.'

'Ah! That is where Jonker is being very clever. I and the others were German- or Dutch-speaking. Now there is a strong British administration at the Cape – strong enough to prevent Jonker from getting as much powder and guns as he would like. He thinks if he can get a British missionary he will be in a stronger position than the Herero or any other tribe. He might even be allowed to bring in new guns and powder and shot.'

'The British will never accept that! They must know what's happening here – what Jonker is trying to do. They won't send him another missionary.'

'It isn't up to them, Josh. Besides, what church will refuse the opportunity to save a soul – especially where other churches have failed? Jonker's request has already been granted. The London Missionary Society is sending him a man from England. He may already be on his way.'

'I suppose we really ought to be pleased. He could turn out to be a restraining influence on Jonker.'

'Never! The most we can hope for is that the new missionary has the strength of purpose to stay at Winterhoek – and the ability to remain alive.'

'Jacobus Albrecht wants me to act as a guide and take him inland. He's going to try to reach Lake Ngami.' Daniel broke the news to his family at the Sunday-evening meal.

Miriam paused in the act of serving him his plate. 'Wouldn't that mean crossing the Kalahari Desert?'

'Only the northern part. Pa and I went halfway there two years ago. It's not bad country.'

'How do you feel about taking him?'

'I don't care for Albrecht one way or the other, but I'd like to see Lake Ngami. Is it all right if I go?'

Miriam had grave reservations. Daniel was an only child, and it was difficult for her to accept that a sixteen-year-old was capable of looking after himself out in the uncompromising desert of the Kalahari.

Josh had more confidence in his son's ability and he recognised the eager look in Daniel's eyes. Setting aside his dislike of the Boer, he agreed.

'It's all right with me – but don't do Albrecht any favours.

Agree on a share of his profits before you tell him you'll accept. What men will you be taking with you – Hereros?'

'No. Albrecht says he'll feel safer with Jonker's armed Afrikaners around him.'

'H'm! I'm not so sure that's a good idea. The Bechuana chief at Lake Ngami might not be pleased at having such a well-armed party riding into his territory. You'd better be sure Albrecht saves the best of his trade goods for him. Whatever you do, don't underestimate the Bechuana, Daniel. For all their apparent timidity they're fierce enough to have beaten the Zulu in battle.'

'Do you really believe Daniel will be safe travelling with Jacobus Albrecht?' The question came from the darkness beside him as Josh lay half-asleep. Miriam had asked the same question half a dozen times since he had given Daniel permission to go on the journey. Josh turned over with an exaggerated sigh and slid an arm beneath Miriam, pulling her to him.

'Should I have said he mustn't go? Made him stay here with us?'

'No, of course not.' She snuggled into Josh. 'I'm just a worrier, that's all – and you and Daniel are all I have. I know he's such a very capable boy but I sometimes think we expect him to be able to do anything a man can do. He's not a man yet.'

'Oh! And how old was I when you decided I was man enough for you?'

'Have you forgotten the mess I made of both our lives when I was a lot older than Daniel?'

Josh squeezed her comfortingly. 'I haven't forgotten one thing about you, but all that's in the past. People do some funny things when they're in love.'

'That's another thing that worries me, Josh. How is Daniel ever going to meet any nice girls when we're living way out here?'

Josh grinned in the darkness. 'One minute you're telling me our son is still a child; the next you're trying to marry him off! Perhaps you'll decide whether he's a man or a boy so I can get some sleep.'

'It's not a laughing matter, Josh Retallick. Some things are more important than sleep!'

'All right, you've convinced me. Come here.'

'That wasn't what I meant. . . .'

Although she protested, her resistance was merely a token one and she came to him readily enough. Afterwards she lay still beside Josh, listening to his heavy breathing as he slept. She thought of Daniel and of his future. Of what the future held for Josh and herself. They had found their freedom here in this ungoverned land. It was an unquestioned freedom that would not have been possible anywhere else in the world. Even if it ever became known that Josh was a convicted felon, nothing could be done about it while they remained within these undefined borders.

But Josh's freedom depended so much on others: Tjamuene and Jonker. Otjimkandje was the last remaining Herero village. The rest of the large tribe had fled hundreds of miles away to escape Jonker. How long would the unpredictable Afrikaner allow this village to remain? At the moment he needed the Herero to work the copper mine at Sesebe. He was also reluctant to offend Hugo Walder. The German missionary had powerful friends at the Cape. But Jonker was getting deeper and deeper in debt to the traders who supplied him with brandy and with silk for his wives. He was probably receiving guns and powder, too, and the Cape government's ban on their sale would have increased the price he had to pay for them. One day his need for the Herero cattle would outweigh all other considerations.

If the mission closed down, what then? Where could Josh go? The only place was the Cape Colony — and there was British justice there. Even after all these years Miriam knew that someone would remember that Josh Retallick had been sentenced to transportation for life for conspiracy to treason.

The thoughts of the past caused her to remember the families she and Josh had left behind in Cornwall. Soon after they had settled in Otjimkandje Josh had sent one letter to inform his parents they were alive and well. He had not said where he was and he knew that by the time the letter reached them it would have passed through so many hands no one would know from whence it had originated. The news would have been passed on to her mother and to their friends. But that had been twelve years ago. She wondered what they were all doing now, whether

Josh's parents and her mother were still alive.

Her memories strayed to others they had known all those years before. She wondered about Preacher Thackeray, the man she had married while she was carrying Daniel, Josh's son, inside her; the man to whom the law still bound her. It was the first time for many years that the past had returned to her thoughts in this manner. It was not a good feeling. Lying awake in the darkness, Miriam felt suddenly afraid and turned for comfort to the sleeping bulk of Josh lying beside her. For a long time she clung to him as though the darkness might spirit him away.

CHAPTER THREE

'Come on, damn you. Throw those guns inside and hitch your horses to this wagon. If we don't get out of this vlei, we won't need guns and you might as well have left them behind.'

Jacobus Albrecht tongue-lashed the reluctance of the Afrikaners to help pull the ox-wagons through a bed of wet glutinous mud.

The expedition to Lake Ngami had degenerated into near-disaster. Jacobus Albrecht had delayed it until the end of the accepted rainy season, even though these inland areas had suffered a severe drought for four years. At first this year had seemed no different. The rains had threatened, but only from a tantalising distance. Then, when the trek to the Lake was a week north-west of Winterhoek, the skies darkened and a morning wind brought the clouds scudding in across the Kalahari. With them came the rain. It came down so hard that men and horses were blinded by a near-impenetrable curtain of water. It lashed into their faces and poured inside the canvas of the wagons. The oxen, plodding forward in dogged resignation, became confused when the flickering tongue of the lightning brought deafening thunder in its wake. River-beds that had been dry and dusty for decades filled to overflowing and were impassable. The small expedition swung off course first to the east and then to the north in an effort to ford rivers and find higher ground. For two days they lost their sense of direction altogether. It seemed to them that no matter which way they turned the rain still beat into their faces. Then they floundered into the vlei, and the oxen sank to their knees in mud and the axles of the wagons were under inches of water.

Jacobus Albrecht's expedition had ten grim days of this weather. It was impossible to hunt, and tempers flared at the slightest imagined provocation. The party did not go hungry. Two of the oxen broke legs in the treacherous terrain and had to be slaughtered.

'I should have my head examined!' said Jacobus Albrecht.

'Trusting wagonloads of trade goods to a wet-nosed kid who wouldn't know a vlei from a kopje!'

Daniel had grown tired of explaining that the timing of the expedition had been the trader's choice and marshland or hill was equally indistinguishable when rain prevented a wagon-driver from seeing as far as his lead ox.

'Half my goods are ruined already from this damn rain. If we ever get as far as Lake Ngami, I'll be lucky to break even.'

'We'd stand more chance of shifting this wagon if you wasted less of your breath on the Afrikaners and put that whip away. It's not helping oxen or men to pull any harder.'

'I'll do what the hell I want,' said the big Boer, and as if to emphasise his words he cracked the tip of the long bull-hide whip viciously across the flanks of his leading pair of oxen. The sudden pain caused them to throw up their heads and their horns clashed together in panic.

Daniel did not like Jacobus Albrecht's way of handling either the animals or the Afrikaners. He used the bull-hide whip far too frequently on the oxen and had twice curled its heavy leather thong about the shoulders of an Afrikaner, accusing him of riding too close to the oxen and scaring them.

Then on the eleventh day after the start of the rains they woke to see a blue sky above them, and as the sun rose higher it spread a steamy layer of haze above the sodden ground. For the first time in days they were able to get a good fire going and have hot coffee and a filling meal.

While it was cooking, Jacobus Albrecht examined the loads on his wagons while Daniel and Kasupi rode to the top of a small rise, hoping to see a recognisable landmark. For as far as they could see the land rose and fell in gently rolling folds and with its unfamiliar cloak of green plant life and shallow low-lying lakes it presented an unfamiliar landscape.

When they returned to the camp-fire the Boer had completed his inspection. The loads had been well packed and protected, and the rain-damage was negligible. But he was still no more kindly disposed towards Daniel.

'Well, where are we?'

'I don't know,' Daniel replied honestly. 'We might have been going around in circles for days. But we won't go far wrong if we continue to head north-east.'

'What you really mean is that we're lost and you *hope* that's the right way to go?'

Daniel looked at the big man in surprise. Lake Ngami was to the north-east. Sooner or later, if they kept heading that way, they would reach a landmark that either he or Kasupi would recognise. It might not be for a couple of days, but with no shortage of water two days' travelling in this country meant nothing.

'Can you think of an alternative?'

Jacobus Albrecht made no reply, and Daniel went on, 'Get the Afrikaners to help the wagons up that far slope. The ridge is wide and flat and runs in the right direction. I'll take Kasupi with me and scout ahead.'

'Don't get lost!' was the Boer's sarcastic parting remark.

'He is not a good man,' said Kasupi when they paused on the ridge and looked back. They could hear the Boer's shouted orders and the crack of his whip. 'No Herero would treat oxen like that. They, too, have been through a bad time. He should stay and rest them for a day.'

'I'm glad you didn't suggest it,' said Daniel. 'I don't think he's too pleased with us at this moment.'

'I say nothing to him,' replied the Herero. 'He has no ears for my people.'

The two friends rode until midday when in the distance they sighted a low jagged outcrop against the skyline that neither recognised. They were probably more off course than Daniel thought, but they had plenty of time and game was plentiful.

Daniel shot a small buck and with it slung across the saddle of Kasupi's horse they set off to return to the wagons.

Daniel had never seen so many varieties of wild animal as there were all about them. They saw zebra, gnu and buck of many kinds and once saw a pride of lions running almost leisurely away from them across the wet desert.

Then they heard two shots ring out from some way ahead. They were followed by a ragged volley and then another single shot.

The two men looked at each other in alarm and without a word passing between them they kicked their heels into the horses' flanks. They heard two more shots before they gained the ridge and saw the wagons stopped in a straggling line a mile and a half away.

Jonker's Afrikaner horsemen were some distance from the wagons, milling around a number of objects lying about on the ground. Others lay singly farther away from the Afrikaners. Daniel and Kasupi slowed their horses to a canter as they headed towards the main body of riders.

When they were still to far away to establish what had been happening one of the horsemen detached himself from the group and galloped towards them. It was Jacobus Albrecht. He carried a gun and looked happy for the first time in days. Daniel and Kasupi pulled their horses to a halt as he reached them.

'I see you've been hunting too,' he said, pointing to the buck.

'But, man, we've done better than that!'

He waved his gun to where the Afrikaners were still gathered, some of them whooping loudly with glee.

'We surprised some Bushmen and killed thirteen of them. I got three for myself. Two I shot and the other one I clubbed down. I was only just in time. He damned near had an arrow fitted in his bow. It was great stuff.'

There was a shot from the scene of the slaughter, and mounting their horses the Afrikaners made their way noisily and happily back to the wagons.

The big Boer grinned. 'They've had their fun, too. There was a young Bushman girl they only wounded. She wasn't my type, but Jonker's boys enjoyed her.'

It was a quieter older Daniel who sat eating the evening meal in Otjimkandje four days later. To Miriam's repeated questioning as to why he had left the big Boer and his party to fend for themselves he would only say that he did not like the way Jacobus Albrecht ran his trading expedition.

Josh asked few questions during the meal but afterwards he announced that the elderly Tjamuene wished to speak to him about the mining camp and suggested Daniel went along with him to the chief's kraal.

They took the long way, going past the cattle-pens. Josh had recently adopted Sam Speke's habit of smoking a pipe and he stopped to light it by one of the pens.

The sudden flame caused the cattle to mill about in momentary panic, and Josh tasted dust as he drew heavily upon the pipe. He watched the cattle for some minutes until the aroma of tobacco smoke hung heavy on the night air.

'What really happened out there with Albrecht, son?'

Daniel had been expecting the question but that did not make the telling any easier. Hesitantly at first but with growing emotion Daniel told the story of the disastrous trip. Of Jacobus Albrecht's arrogance, his attitude towards Kasupi and Jonker's Afrikaners, and his uncontrolled rages when the bad weather hit them. It was a story he needed to tell someone. He was still a young man and in spite of his proven capability was dogged with a young man's uncertainty. He felt that he had somehow failed; that had he possessed a stronger personality he might have prevented Albrecht's expedition from becoming a complete débâcle – might have prevented the massacre of the Bushmen.

It was when he was talking about this last incident that his voice choked on the words and Josh understood what was really troubling his son.

'You couldn't be held accountable for the rain,' he said at length. 'And a good trek-master would have been prepared for anything that might come his way. You'll never change his attitude towards Kasupi and the others – he's a Boer. We think they're too hard with the people of this land. They think we're too soft.'

'He said I'd been living on a mission station for too long. I'd become a kaffir-boetje.'

'Would you consider it an insult if Kasupi called you "brother"?'

'No, of course I wouldn't.'

'It is something Hugo has preached for years. Don't let a man like Jacobus Albrecht change the value of the word. As for the Bushman . . . well, you know the Herero are just as bad. They'll hunt them down and kill them wherever they find them. How did you explain your feelings to Kasupi?'

'I didn't have to. Kasupi knows how I feel about them. We've met with them before. Anyway, I told Jacobus Albrecht that the Bushmen could have guided us to Lake Ngami and that killing them was not only unnecessary but stupid. Kasupi agreed with that.'

Josh nodded in the moon-filled darkness. They walked on for a while in silence until Daniel's feelings erupted once more.

'Why do they slaughter the Bushmen wherever they find them? They don't do that to animals. The Bushmen don't go looking for trouble.'

Josh knew the outburst came straight from his son's heart and he responded, gripping his shoulder sympathetically.

'I've spent many years wondering about that myself. If you ask, you'll be told it's because the Bushman is a thief, a predator. That he neither understands nor respects ownership – particularly with regard to cattle. To him any animal is something to be killed and eaten when a man is hungry. He sees little difference between a buck and a cow. Neither does he recognise tribal boundaries. He was in this country long before any other tribe arrived and he won't accept their right to exclusive use of any part of it.'

Josh paused. They were at the entrance to Tjamuene's kraal, but his thoughts were back in the past – to twelve years before and the little family group of Bushmen who had found them when they were wandering in the hot sands of the Skeleton Coast.

'Perhaps it's even more than any of the reasons I've given to you, Daniel. For the Bushman life is a continuous battle for survival. He has no wish to war with others. He doesn't covet another man's lands or possessions. He won't fight to win power over other men. He has his own rules but he does his best to live at peace with his fellow-men. Such a philosophy makes others feel uncomfortable – inferior, even. And no man can be happy if he believes himself to be inferior to a Bushman. So he goes out to prove himself against them.'

Josh tapped out his pipe on the heel of his boot and carefully ground the wad of glowing tobacco into the hard earth.

'Don't let any man change your attitude towards the Bushmen, son. You'll be unpopular for it but you can always be sure of having Sam Speke and me behind you. Without them I doubt if any of us would be alive today.'

*

Tjamuene reclined on a pile of cow hides and blankets. The years had not gone well with him. He was an old and tired man. It showed plainly in his slow movements and dull resigned eyes. The Herero of Otjimkandje still had their village and their cattle, but Tjamuene had paid for it with his pride – the pride of a hereditary Herero chief. It had been a great price to pay.

He had watched the scorn of his young men grow with the changing of the seasons. They openly declared that death was preferable to life as a vassal of Chief Jonker.

Chief Tjamuene could have told them that the Herero people could not fight their way back from the grave; that life always held a spark of hope for the future.

He could have told them but chose to keep silent. Time would tell it for him. Jonker, like Tjamuene, was growing older. He would not live for ever. The day of the Herero would dawn once again.

Room was made for Josh and Daniel and tea was served to them by one of Tjamuene's younger wives.

'My son serves you well?' Tjamuene asked of Daniel.

'He is my friend and guide,' Daniel replied in Herero, in the formal manner one was expected to use when addressing a chief. His good manners did not pass unnoticed and there were nods of approval from the elders.

'It is good. He has told me of your troubles with the trader. The man behaves like one who has no mind to think with. You must take care. Trouble sits like a vulture on the shoulder of a fool. He can cause you much sorrow.'

Daniel nodded in acknowledgement of the chief's words, and the old man turned his attention to Josh Retallick.

'How goes the work at the mine?'

'Enough copper ore is being brought out to keep Andrews happy.'

'Is it enough to keep Jonker happy?'

Josh shrugged. 'Who knows what makes the chief of the Afrikaners happy?'

Tjamuene grunted. 'Who knows, indeed? I have heard it said you do not believe the copper will always be there for the digging?'

'There is less than a year's supply of ore. I've started tunnelling to see how deep it goes. We may find more, but once we're down to a certain depth we'll need more equipment and that will push the cost up. We'd have to increase the price of the ore and become less attractive to the buyers. If other countries can produce the ore more cheaply, we'll go out of business.'

Tjamuene nodded. 'And when that happens Chief Jonker will no longer have a need for the Herero of Otjimkandje – only for our cattle.'

'He would not dare to raid Hugo Walder's mission station.'

Mutjise's laugh was devoid of mirth. 'Even the Little Father cannot tell Chief Jonker what he dare not do.'

'Then perhaps his own missionary will be able to influence him,' said Josh. 'One has been sent for and is on his way.'

'There have been missionaries at Winterhoek before,' replied the old chief. 'Now the mission church there is strewn about the ground. There was also a time when a man could ride a hundred miles in any direction from here without losing sight of Herero cattle. Now the cattle and the Herero have gone. Only we at Otjimkandje remain – but Chief Jonker is also still with us. I fear greatly for the lives of my people, but when I ask for guns to protect them I am told, "No. The White Father far away to the south says guns must not come into this land. They would be used for killing people." At first I told myself this was good. The White Father is right. There must be no guns for killing. But then Chief Jonker and his men ride through my village and each of them has a gun and a horse. Only the Herero do not have guns. Is it the wish of the White Father that only the Afrikaners should kill and only the Herero be killed?'

'Chief Tjamuene, if you wished to talk of this, you should have asked the Little Father to come here tonight. He is the one who can talk to the White Father in the Cape Colony. I only run the mine at Sesebe.'

'I know, my friend. I should not burden you with the troubles of the Herero. They are not of your doing. Forgive me. I am an old man and the things that fill my heart pour too easily from my mouth. Forgive me.'

'There is nothing to forgive. I too, feel these things. I have spoken to Andrews about Jonker's guns. He says they are not being brought in by his ships. I believe him.'

'Thank you. But let us speak of the matter for which I asked you to call on me. It concerns the women from Otjimkandje who come to Sesebe.'

Josh had realised this was behind Tjamuene's summons. The men at the mine were well paid, with little on which to spend their money but drink and Herero women. The women had taken to hanging about the mining camp. There they could earn more money and trinkets in one night than most of their fellow-tribeswomen acquired during a lifetime of more moral activities — and with none of the hard work that accompanied tribal life. Recently their numbers had increased, and Josh had noticed that some of the more regular visitors had more than bangles and beads as mementoes of their way of life. Sesebe would soon have its population increased by children who would belong to neither the European community of their fathers nor the tribe of their mothers.

'It is not natural that a man should be without a woman,' said the chief. 'We knew when Andrews and his men came to Sesebe that some of our women would go there. That had to be accepted. There are many of our women who have known men before. Women who have lost their men and have no families to take care of them. For these women it does not matter that they give themselves to the men at the mine. They can do as they will. But when our young girls see the gifts given to these women they say, "Come, we will go and get gifts for ourselves." This is not good. It is bad for the foolish young girls and it makes my young men angry.'

Josh nodded seriously, 'It is wrong, Tjamuene. But it is difficult for me to tell a Herero woman who has known a man from one who has not.'

'That is so,' Tjamuene accepted. 'Mutjise will go to Sesebe to send the young girls home.'

Josh saw serious trouble ahead of him if the proud Mutjise went to Sesebe and arbitrarily ordered the young Herero girls back to Otjimkandje in front of the tough miners.

'It's not fitting that the first son of a chief should carry out such a task,' he said diplomatically. 'Let Kasupi come and point out the young girls to me. I'll see that they return to Otjim-kandje.'

Kasupi was often at Sesebe with Daniel. His presence would pass unnoticed and he would be more discreet than the man who would one day be the chief of the Otjimkandje Herero.

'Good!' The old chief nodded his agreement. 'If only all the troubles of the Herero could be settled as easily.'

'They could if they didn't have a Chief Jonker behind them,' commented Josh.

As they made their way back to their own hut Josh said, 'We've got to handle this pretty carefully. If the miners realise what we're doing, it will cause a resentment that might build up to serious trouble for Tjamuene. Come to Sesebe with Kasupi tomorrow and make sure he understands the need to carry this out quietly. See how many of these girls there are, get their names and give them to me. I'll have them rounded up and sent packing. That way the miners will only be angry with me, and that's nothing too unusual.'

Jacobus Albrecht returned to Sesebe five weeks after Daniel's return. The remainder of his trading trip had been no more successful than the first few weeks. There had been an argument between the trader and the Afrikaners about the direction they should take. The trader had won and led the party straight out into the featureless wastes of the Kalahari Desert, too stubborn to acknowledge that he was wrong. Half the Afrikaners deserted him; and then the strain of pulling the laden wagons became too much for the heat-stricken oxen. They began to die.

Albrecht abandoned two of his wagons in the sands of the Kalahari before he would admit his mistake and change his direction northwards. Soon afterwards his weakened party met up with a sub-chief of the Bechuana who made exaggerated demands for gifts before allowing the trader into his territory.

Jacobus Albrecht grudgingly parted with some of his trade goods in exchange for a promise of ivory. The ivory never came, but the demands of the Bechuana grew daily more menacing. Eventually the Boar decided to cut his losses and head back to Sesebe.

The Bechuana said they could not go until they had given

him more gifts. After two days of argument Jacobus Albrecht and his small party of Afrikaners quietly packed their wagons and made a run for it.

All pretence of friendship gone, Bechuanas pursued them and in the ensuing fight three of the Afrikaners were killed. But the guns of the trader's party inflicted heavy casualties on the Bechuanas and they withdrew leaving Jacobus Albrecht to find his way back to Sesebe as best he could.

He blamed Daniel for the unsuccessful outcome of his expedition, but the Boer received little sympathy from the miners when his exhausted party eventually returned. They were of the same opinion as Josh. Jacobus Albrecht was an experienced trader and should have prepared his expedition more carefully. In the strangely perverse way of men who have to perform manual work for a living the miners were pleased that the venture of Andrews' partner had not succeeded. Far from deriding Daniel for his part in the affair they fêted him as a man who had 'put one over' on the trader!

Josh was not happy that part of their lauding Daniel took the form of treating him to drinks in the Miners' Inn. But he said nothing, and soon there were many other things to keep him busy.

CHAPTER FOUR

The Jew, Aaron, rode into Sesebe at midday on a hot January day in 1860. He was driving a large covered wagon pulled by a team of raw-boned oxen. Seated beside him on the high seat and dressed like a slim youth in cotton twill trousers and a soft flannel shirt was his daughter Hannah.

It was the hour when the day shift of miners stopped work to eat, and many of them sat drinking with the off-duty miners in the inn. They spilled out on to the wide veranda in front of the inn, feet up on the hand-rail, taking advantage of the light breeze that blew through the mining town.

The arrival of strangers in Sesebe was unusual enough. When one of them was a girl – even one aged only fifteen and wearing boy's clothing – it became a major event. The whistling and cat-calling brought miners pouring from the inn and living-quarters to add their voices of crude approval to the ribald din.

Ignoring the many invitations for Hannah to sample the doubtful pleasures of the inn, Aaron kept the scrawny oxen plodding on to where Josh stood in the doorway of the mines office, drawn outside by the noise.

Heaving on the long reins, the black-bearded Jew brought his wagon to a halt. He climbed stiffly to the ground, the movement disturbing the dust that clung to his clothes.

'You must be Joshua Retallick?'

'That's me.'

'My name is Aaron and this is my daughter Hannah.'

The dark-eyed girl on the wagon nodded unsmilingly.

Josh shook the hand the Jew proffered but did not return the other man's smile of greeting. This was the man who was rumoured to be illegally smuggling guns in for Chief Jonker's warriors. His presence here could bring nothing but trouble.

'I thought you traded only along the coast. What brings you here?'

The Jew shrugged and held his two hands out, palms upward. 'Business. What else? Things were too quiet for us there.

We tried Whalefish Bay but found folk too unfriendly. A bit too high and mighty for the likes of us. So "Hannah," I said, "I'll take you to see a copper town. Somewhere for a young girl to see a bit of life." And so here we are.'

There was a roar of approval from the miners who had deserted the inn to crowd around the wagon. They listened to the Jew and looked slyly up at the impassive girl on the high seat of the wagon.

'You let the girl come down here, Aaron,' one of them called. 'We'll show her a bit of life.'

'Come and have a drink, girl,' shouted another. 'There's no need to be shy with us.'

Josh rounded on the miners.

'If you don't get back to work, you'll be shy of a job. Your break-time is over. The rest of you return to the inn if you've nothing better to do.'

The men grumbled and were slow to move, but Josh stood firm and gradually the crowd began to break up and the miners move away. Josh's recent purge on the young Herero girls at Sesebe had convinced them that, although they might refer to him as a narrow-minded Methodist, Josh was not a man to argue with. Some of them had tried, with the result that two miners had received cracked heads and four others were on their way back to the Cape Colony to seek fresh work.

When the miners had drifted away Josh turned back to Aaron.

'Well, now you've seen your copper town and you'd be well advised to be clear of it before dark. Apart from my wife your daughter is the first white girl to set foot in Sesebe, and I won't guarantee her safety when the serious drinking starts.'

'I'm quite capable of looking after myself.' The girl on the high wagon-seat spoke for the first time. Her voice was soft but firm and she emphasised her words with the gun she pulled from beneath the seat. Josh observed that it was a gun of far more modern design than any he had seen in this part of the world. It served to confirm the rumours he had heard about the Jew's involvement in gun-smuggling.

'I'm sure you are — but so are my miners, and there are more of them.'

He turned to the girl's father. 'What's your real reason for coming to this part of the country?'

Aaron shrugged again. 'I'm a trader. I want to make money. I met Jacobus Albrecht a few weeks ago and heard of his unhappy trek inland. . . .'

'He had bad weather and his own foolishness to blame for that,' said Josh quickly.

'I never doubted it for a minute. That's why I am so sure I can do better.'

A thought came to Josh. 'Does Chief Jonker of the Afrikaners know you're here?'

The Jewish trader made a vague movement of his hands. 'I have spoken to him about such a trek. He knows how interested I am in the interior. Mind you, I haven't seen him for some months. However, that need not bother you. I've done business with Jonker many times in the past. I know how to smooth over any objections he may have.'

'Both you and your daughter seem supremely confident of your own capabilities,' said Josh. 'If you don't mind, I'd rather not have them put to the test here in Sesebe. You'd best come to Otjimkandje and stay with us there until we've sorted out your future plans.'

'Your kind offer I'm pleased to accept,' said Aaron. 'My future plans I know already. I want to trade between Whalefish Bay and the interior. To do that I'll need to establish a store and build a house here in Sesebe.'

Aaron saw Josh's astonishment. 'I won't be trading until I've built a stout wooden building with bolts and locks. You needn't worry that it will affect you. It won't be a place to sell goods to your miners, merely a staging post between the coast and the interior. There's plenty of scope for good healthy competition there, and Jacobus Albrecht says it will be all right.'

Josh wondered whether he imagined the fleeting moment of uneasiness in the young girl's eyes when Aaron mentioned the name of the Boer trader, but her father had not finished speaking.

'You'll have no need to concern yourself with Hannah or me, Mr Retallick. I promise not to upset your miners. I've looked after my little girl since she was two years old and always steered her well clear of trouble.'

'In case you haven't noticed, your "little girl" is now a very attractive young lady,' said Josh drily. 'But we can talk about that later. You get your wagon moving along that track.' He pointed the way to Otjimkandje. 'I'll send someone on ahead to warn my wife to expect company and I'll catch up with you before you reach the village.'

Miriam had put on her 'best' home-made dress to greet the new-comers. Visitors had become increasingly rare these troubled days. The occasional trader or hunter preferred the less-inhibited pleasures of the mining town to the mission station.

The Herero messenger had told Miriam one of the visitors was a white woman. 'She's young, missus, like Daniel, and dressed like a white man – but she's a woman.' His open hands rocked on his breast to emphasise the fact.

Hugo Walder stood with Miriam as the wagon rolled up to the mission. Daniel was off somewhere with Kasupi.

The young girl showed none of her earlier bravado in the presence of Miriam. She became quiet to the point of extreme shyness. Hannah had not come into contact with many other women during her lifetime.

Her father was less inhibited.

'Miriam, eh? A lovely name. Miriam the prophetess. Sister of my great forefather and namesake, Aaron. Delighted to meet you, my dear.'

Miriam smiled. The Jew was over-effusive, but there was nothing offensive in his manner. He was a man whose zest for life was continually bubbling over.

'I'm happy to have you here, Aaron – and Hannah, too. Do you have a surname?'

'My dear Miriam, if plain Aaron was good enough in Israel, why should I try to improve upon it?'

Miriam laughed. It was a lovely sound, and Josh realised that it had been a long time since he had last heard it. Life in Otjimkandje had become all too serious in recent times.

'My father's name was Moses,' she said, 'but he didn't let his pride prevent him from claiming the name of Trago also.'

The Jew spread his arms in a gesture of defeat. 'Then who is Aaron to think himself better than Moses? Copping, my dear.

Aaron Copping. It's not the name my father was given at birth, but I like it. It's easier to say.'

Hugo Walder's welcome was far cooler than Miriam's. Like Josh he had heard the rumours of Aaron's illegal traffic in guns. He had also inherited his countrymen's vague mistrust of these children of Israel who maintained their own faith and their own language even though they were a people without a country. He would allow father and daughter to remain under the protection of the Otjimkandje mission, and in time his own warm nature would encompass them, but for the moment he reserved judgement on them.

They all went into the sizeable wooden home that many years before had replaced the Retallicks' mud hut.

'You'll be staying here with us, of course,' said Miriam.

'Please! You must not put yourselves out in any way for Hannah and me,' protested Aaron. 'The wagon has been our home for a long time. We find it quite comfortable.'

'Nonsense! All the more reason why you should enjoy the advantages of a comfortable house for a while. You come with me, Hannah. I'll show you the room that will be yours while you're here. It will give you a chance to wash some of that trail dust away before we eat.'

Hannah emerged from her room wearing the same shirt and trousers as before; but the dust had been shaken from them, and her long black hair was swept back and caught behind her head, leaving it to hang in a single thick tress halfway down her back. The style brought her high cheekbones into prominence and highlighted her expressive brown eyes. She was a tall girl, standing eye to eye with Daniel when he came in fresh from another escapade with Kasupi and the girls working the fields.

Apart from an initial polite nod of greeting the young Jewish girl ignored Daniel. He did not share her indifference and was unable to take his eyes from her throughout the meal. When Miriam quietly reminded him that it was rude to stare he coloured up alarmingly.

It was with a sense of shock that Miriam realised this was the first white girl her seventeen-year-old son had seen. She had so completely accepted their isolated way of life here at Otjimkandje that it was easy to forget there were whole communities of their own people elsewhere. Whole countries of men and women, boys and girls with settled ways, different values and a code of conduct alien to all that was accepted here.

For a few seconds Miriam missed all she had once known in Cornwall.

The feeling was quickly forgotten when the Herero girl carrying in a dish of maize-meal porridge dropped it and the dish smashed into a hundred fragments on the hard dirt floor.

Hugo Walder's unease at having someone of an alien faith living in his community fought a losing battle with his generous nature. He suggested to Aaron it might be safer for Hannah if they remained in Otjimkandje instead of setting up house in Sesebe.

'Quite true,' agreed Aaron. 'Just as it would no doubt have been safer for you to remain in Germany rather than come here. No, Father Hugo. We all take our chances – you for your church, and me for my business. It's kind of you to suggest it, and I will remember that. But there's another reason why I shouldn't stay here – Chief Jonker. I have traded with him for many years. If he thought I was transferring that trade to your Herero, we would both have serious trouble on our hands. Hannah and I will move to Sesebe when our store is finished.'

The work on Aaron's combined store and home began within a few days but it was going to be a long time in the building. Its construction was more reminiscent of a fort than a trading store. Aaron justified it by saying he wanted to be sure that whenever he had to go away neither Hannah nor his goods would be in any danger inside.

While the store was being built by Herero workmen supervised by Sam Speke, Aaron decided to put the time to good use. He knew Hannah would be safe with Miriam and suggested that Josh accompany him on a trading mission to the same mysterious lake that Jacobus Albrecht had attempted to reach on his ill-fated expedition months before.

After a token show of resistance Josh agreed. Harold Andrews was in Sesebe and could look after the mine while Josh was away. Daniel wanted to go with them and was more than a little surprised and hurt when Josh refused.

'It's not that I don't want you with us,' Josh explained, seeing his son's disappointment, 'but with Sam working in Sesebe and Hugo Walder taking ship to the Cape for some meeting I want someone here I can trust to look after your mother and Hannah.'

Daniel was only partly mollified. He was never happier than when he was away from the village on a hunting or exploration trip. However, he knew his father's reasons were sound. There was no threat from the Herero, but the unpredictable Jonker was an ever-present menace.

The proposed expedition created great excitement in Otjim-kandje. Josh intended taking about forty Herero warriors with him, and there was much competition to be among those chosen. It was so unusual for the subjugated tribe to venture such a distance from their village that Mutjise himself decided to go. The Herero had neither horses nor guns, but to trek long miles with spears in their hands and a hunting song on their lips would make them feel like men again – warriors, breathing the air of the hills and plains and desert.

The send-off was all a Herero warrior could have wished. The old chief Tjamuene sat surrounded by his household to witness their departure, and the women of the village sent them on their way with the exciting ululating cry that had sent generations of warriors and hunters on their journeys with hearts filled with pride.

It was quiet in Otjimkandje with so many men away. Daniel's awareness of his responsibility quickly wore off. Hannah did not help. She behaved as though he did not exist.

Daniel found her indifference both irritating and puzzling. It was totally removed from the behaviour of the Herero girls. They would giggle and nudge each other when he and Kasupi approached them. If one of them were alone, she would walk past with eyes demurely fixed upon the ground until she was alongside. Then she would raise her eyes to look slyly sideways from between long black lashes.

Hannah did none of these things. She went about whatever she happened to be doing as though he was not there, ignoring him completely. It was as though he did not exist for her. It annoyed him even more to know that she spoke freely to his mother and to the Herero women who frequented the house, and he had heard her laughter ring out when one of the young Herero men brought some produce from the mission garden to the kitchen.

After some weeks Daniel could take her diffidence no longer. Choosing a time when he knew his mother was away at Hugo Walder's house, he went into the kitchen and found Hannah alone, kneading the coarse bread the women made.

It would have been impossible for the Jewish girl not to know of his presence, but she said nothing as she pummelled the brown dough with her fists. In her own time she finished and carried the wooden board with the mixture to a corner cupboard and placed it inside. Rinsing her hands in a small bowl of water she dried them on the apron she wore, then made to walk from the room past Daniel.

He put an arm across the open doorway in front of her and she stopped abruptly. For the first time since she and her father had arrived in Otjimkandje she looked directly at him and he became acutely aware of the depth of her dark eyes.

Daniel wanted her to say something, to be the first to speak; but he found her eyes so disturbing, her look so intense, that he was thrown off balance.

'Why are you in such a hurry to leave the kitchen?'

The weakness in his own voice was apparent to him.

Hannah looked faintly surprised. 'Hurry? I'm in no hurry to leave, but I've finished what I was doing and have other things to do elsewhere. So if you will kindly remove your arm. . . .'

His arm stayed where it was. He had won. She had spoken to him.

'So you *can* speak!'

'I can speak.' Her self-assurance was so complete as to be unnerving. 'But I've been brought up to believe that speech is a gift from God. To waste it is to belittle its value and insult Him.'

Daniel was bewildered by such a deep philosophy.

'It's not wasting words to say "Good day" to me, is it?'

'Yes. You are quite capable of seeing what sort of day it is for yourself. You don't need me to tell you.'

'It isn't supposed to be a way of telling what sort of day it is.' Daniel was floundering; his confrontation with Hannah had rebounded on him and he could see no way of extricating himself.

'It's ordinary courtesy, that's all.'

'You mean it's just like the courtesy shown by yourself and that friend of yours when you talk about me in Herero when I'm standing within hearing?'

Daniel's jaw dropped. 'But you can't speak Herero. You've never been in this land before.'

The blood rushed to his face at the thought of the first conversation he and Kasupi had held about Hannah when she ventured forth from the Retallick house the day after her arrival in Otjimkandje with her father.

Secure in the knowledge that she could not know the language they had discussed her virtues and defects, and Kasupi had stated after due deliberation and discussion that Hannah would one day develop into a woman who could bring much pleasure into the life of a man like Daniel.

Daniel had scornfully replied that she had as much bosom as a hearth snake and he would as soon try to lie along the thin branch of a tree as make love to her.

There had been other remarks made in her presence since then, and his face burned at the thought of some of them.

'I have been trading north of the Orange River with my father since I could first talk,' said Hannah bitingly. 'I doubt if you could teach me any new languages. As I said earlier, words are not meant to be wasted. None of yours has been.'

To complete his utter rout at her hands Hannah's next words were in the Herero tongue.

'Words are like arrows. A man should not let them fly unless he knows where they will land.'

At that moment Miriam arrived back at the house carrying a large basket of vegetables.

'Hello, you two. It's nice to see you getting together at last. I was beginning to think you didn't like one another.'

Daniel fled from the house, and Miriam looked after him startled.

'Oh dear! Have I interrupted something?'

Hannah laughed. 'No, there's nothing to worry about. Daniel and I have just discovered that we speak the same language. We'll get along fine now.'

*

Aaron's trip towards Lake Ngami was as successful as Jacobus Albrecht's had been disastrous. He and Josh made their way steadily north-westwards without a hitch. It was a great help having Hereros with them. In former days, before Jonker had come upon the scene, some of the Hereros had led a semi-nomadic life, taking their cattle to wherever the grass grew, following the rains and searching for new grazing- and hunting-grounds. A few of their escort had been with these people. They knew the country and were able to follow the elephant tracks from water-hole to water-hole, always heading towards their goal, 'the great water'.

Only six weeks from the time they left Otjimkandje, Aaron and Josh rode off to a nearby ridge to shoot down a big bull elephant with enormous tusks. It would provide much-needed meat as well as a handsome profit. Good ivory was much sought after by the captains of trading ships.

The huge grey animal turned with flapping ears and slowly lashing trunk to meet their advance. As they moved closer it began to sway, shifting its four-ton bulk from side to side, lifting its front feet alternately, choosing its moment to charge.

Before it had arrived at a decision Josh brought it down with a single shot. The huge creature buckled at the knees and collapsed sideways, raising a huge cloud of dust as it crashed to the ground.

Not until the dust had settled did the two men see the shimmering blue line on the flat horizon.

They had reached Lake Ngami!

Recklessly galloping their horses, they confirmed their discovery and tasted the bitter waters of the lake before riding back to the wagons. They had seen enough for a decision to be reached to make a camp some miles away from the reed-beds and mud-flats of the huge inland lake. It abounded with mosquitoes and the deadly tsetse fly which could kill off all their oxen.

The lake reflected the blue of the sky as they squatted in the shade of their wagons watching the Herero warriors bringing in the meat of the bull elephant.

Josh felt a great sense of contentment and achievement inside him.

'This is the life, Aaron. It's better than being shut away in a mine office with dust and noise all around. I sometimes wonder how I put up with it.'

'This is a great country,' agreed the bearded Jew, beaming as two huge bloody-ended tusks were stowed away inside one of his wagons. 'Have you seen the tracks about here? Some of them are better than Cape roads – and they are all made by elephants. There must be hundreds of them. A man could get rich on ivory alone in this place.'

'It might well prove less troublesome than many other items of trade,' said Josh pointedly. He had seen the Jewish trader and Mutjise in earnest conversation on a number of occasions. Their talk always broke off abruptly whenever he approached. Josh had not forgotten his earlier reservations. Aaron was a shrewd trader with a reputation for dealing in forbidden goods. Mutjise wanted the Herero to become a great nation once again. There was one commodity which might well satisfy the ambitions of both men – guns!

'With so much ivory here for the hunting what more could any man wish for?' asked the trader with exaggerated wide-eyed honesty. 'Unless it be copper, perhaps?'

'You can forget copper this far inland,' said Josh. 'It's here all right. We've passed some first-class ore in a number of places along the way. But most of it's too far from the sea. Transport problems would make it uneconomical to mine.'

'Isn't that just like the good Lord!' said Aaron, rolling his eyes towards the sky. 'He shows us the door to the promised land and then goes off with the key still in His pocket.'

Josh smiled. It was impossible not to like this black-bearded man. A keen trader he most certainly was, but he was always cheerful and even-tempered. They had been lucky and the trip had gone well this far, but Josh thought Aaron would have been the same had they met with adversity all along the way.

'It's a pity Daniel couldn't have come with us,' said Josh. 'A trip like this would have made up for the last one.'

'Ah yes! The trek with Jacobus Albrecht.'

Something about the way Aaron spoke the Boer trader's name reminded Josh of Hannah's expression when Jacobus Albrecht had been mentioned on the day of her arrival in Sesebe.

'Of course, I was forgetting you know him. I must admit it

surprised me that he agreed to your opening a trading post at Sesebe. Jacobus Albrecht doesn't impress me as a man who would invite competition into his territory.'

'No, he's used to getting his own way,' agreed Aaron, his manner more serious than usual. 'Perhaps that's way he's let me open my store.'

Josh looked at him uncomprehendingly.

'Jacobus Albrecht wants to take Hannah for his wife.'

'But she's a mere child!' Josh was shocked.

'Oh no.' Aaron Copping stroked his beard and looked directly into Josh's eyes. 'Hannah is enough of a woman to refuse to have anything to do with him.'

'What about you?' Josh sensed the Jew was being devious. 'Don't tell me you would agree?'

Aaron shrugged. 'With Hannah what I think would make little difference. She will marry whoever she decides to take for a husband.' He smiled. 'If Jacobus Albrecht believes it could be him, then who am I to bring disillusionment into his life?'

The calculating look returned to his face again. 'No, I don't think Jacobus is the man for her. For a man of my religion it would be nice to think she might choose to marry someone with a more appropriate name. A good strong Hebrew name like — Daniel?'

The dark-bearded Jew began nodding his head thoughtfully 'Yes, there's a good name. Daniel. The good book says he was a man of strong beliefs. Prepared to enter a lion's den rather than back down.' Aaron looked up at Josh and smiled again. 'But perhaps such a dramatic sign of his faith will not be necessary.'

As it happened, Daniel had found his own special lion's den in which to set foot. After his humiliating conversation with Hannah he located Kasupi and together they made a desultory foray into the maize fields. The young girls working among the tall wind-rattled plants were as giggling and willing as ever, but Daniel found he had lost his taste for women.

Leaving his companion to make uncomfortable love to the enthusiastic and overdeveloped younger daughter of a tribal elder, Daniel rode into Sesebe. His ego was immediately boosted by the welcome given to him by the miners in the Miners' Inn. Two new men had recently come up from the Cape and Daniel was introduced to them as 'the one who put it across Jacobus Albrecht'.

The story of the previous year's trek was told and retold. Incidents, real and imagined, grew as darkness covered the mining camp and brandy blurred the young man's memory and loosened his tongue.

As loud laughter and the singing of bawdy songs drowned conversation in the smoke-filled room Daniel leaned back in his chair and beamed about him. This was where a man belonged: among friends who understood him and respected his maturity; friends who looked up to him as a man who got out and did things, a man capable of making a fool of a hard-living Boer trader. They did not look down their noses at him or ignore him, did not try to humiliate him as Hannah had.

He frowned, and one of the miners leaned across the table and blinked drunkenly at him.

'Hey! What's the matter with you, man? Ain't you enjoying yourself? Come on, drink up. Your old man's away. Let's all make the most of it.'

He splashed Daniel another drink from the bottle and more brandy spilled over the edge of the glass on to the stained table-top.

It was sheer bad luck for Daniel that Chief Jonker chose this night to pay another of his unheralded visits to Otjimkandje. He, too, had been drinking cheap brandy with his men, but his drinking lacked the bonhomie of the miners.

Hugo Walder's mission and the Herero village were thorns in the flesh of the Afrikaner chief. He knew that one day he would have to do something about them. For as long as Otjimkandje remained, Jonker's authority would not be seen to be absolute in the country he had claimed for his own. It had been the land of the Herero before his coming and, while they clung to Otjimkandje, Tjamuene and his followers still had a claim to it. They had to go.

All the same, Jonker knew he could not risk an outright attack on the village lest a European be killed and bring the wrath of the Cape government down upon him. Jonker had once

178

travelled to Cape Town in his younger days and he retained considerable respect for the organisation and might he had seen there. His control of his Afrikaner warriors was not sufficient to ensure the safety of Hugo Walder and the others. So Jonker was forced to resort to less direct tactics.

It was the night of a late-rising full moon and the shadows of Jonker and twenty or so mounted warriors cast long shadows before them as they rode from the bushveldt across the cleared space to the eastern fringe of Otjimkandje village.

As usual, they rode scornfully past Tjamuene's kraal and through the village, squeezing knee to knee between the closely spaced huts, the hoofs of their mounts scattering the dying embers of the deserted cooking-fires as they went.

Although it seemed no one had witnessed their arrival, the news that Jonker and his warriors were in Otjimkandje had reached every hut within minutes. As women and children trembled in the darkness of their homes men nervously fondled spears and wished the warriors who had gone off with Aaron were at hand. They had feared the Afrikaners for so long that no man ventured outside to see what Jonker wanted.

The Afrikaner chief rode directly to the mission area and he and his men reined to a halt outside Hugo Walder's hut.

'Little Father, I wish to speak to you.'

The Afrikaner was fully aware that the missionary was absent at the Cape, but he called loudly for the ears of those who listened and would report on the night's events to Hugo Walder when he returned.

'Little Father, I have heard bad reports that the Herero trade for guns with strangers from the sea. I wish to discuss this with you.' In a quieter aside to one of his men he said, 'Take five men and search the mission church. Turn over the benches and other things – but cause no damage. Do you understand?'

The Afrikaner nodded and, dismounting from his horse, beckoned for some of the other warriors to accompany him.

When they were gone Jonker swung down from his own horse and, flanked by two warriors, entered Hugo Walder's hut.

Not far away a figure hidden in the shadows retreated silently from the scene and hurried away to the Retallick house.

Kasupi had only to knock once. Miriam had been woken by

the Herero girl who helped in the house.

'Who is it?' she called from behind a bolted door.

'It's Kasupi. Is Daniel there?'

There was a brief pause. 'I thought he was with you.' The bolt was drawn back and the door opened to allow the Herero to slip inside.

'Where's Daniel? Why aren't you with him?'

'He will be all right.' Kaspui's heart pumped blood to his head madly. Daniel *had* to be all right. If anything had happened to him, the Herero would forfeit his own life. 'He went to Sesebe earlier. I thought he would have returned by now. Jonker is in the village.'

'I know. What's he doing?'

In the moonlight that filtered through the curtains Kasupi saw that Miriam held a pistol in her hand.

'He and his men are searching the church and the house of the Little Father. He will come here soon. Do you have a gun for me to use? If we keep the door locked, we can kill some of the Afrikaners and perhaps frighten the others away.'

'No! Do that and we give them an excuse to destroy the whole village and us with it. Go into the back room and don't show yourself. I'll deal with Jonker.'

Kasupi shook his head. He was the son of a Herero chief. He would not hide behind a woman when danger threatened. Besides, there was the question of Daniel's whereabouts. . . .

'You must stay inside here and keep the door bolted. Perhaps Jonker will not trouble you. I will go to find Daniel.'

'Wait!' Miriam clutched his arm. 'Find him and make sure he's safe — but don't bring him back here until the Afrikaners have gone.'

It was a promise Kasupi had no intention of keeping, but he nodded. Slipping from her grasp, he opened the door quietly and vanished into the night, heading for the pen where the few horses were kept.

Jonker and his men searched Hugo Walder's hut, but apart from deliberately moving some of his belongings to let him know they had been inside they disturbed very little. Hugo Walder would be furious at the invasion of his home, but he would have little of substance to complain about to the Cape authorities.

Jonker waited until his warriors rejoined him from the church before he moved off to the house of Josh Retallick.

'Mr Retallick?'

Once again Jonker made a great show of announcing his presence, although he was fully aware that Josh, too, was away from Otjimkandje.

'Yes, what do you want?' The door opened and Miriam stood in the doorway. She had decided to play the Afrikaner at his own game. If he wanted every move to be made in the open, witnessed by others, then she was quite prepared to have it that way.

'Tell Mr Retallick that Chief Jonker of the Afrikaner wishes to speak to him.'

'You know very well that Mr Retallick is away—just as I'm quite sure you know Father Walder is not in the village. If you want to speak to them, you must return some other time—in daylight, if you please.'

Chief Jonker was not used to having a woman speak to him in this manner in front of his men, not even a white woman.

'I come in peace but I am unhappy at the talk of guns being brought into the country for the Herero. I come to speak to the Little Father and see for myself that this is not so. The Little Father is not here and I am happy there are no guns in his house. I wish to be sure there are no guns for the Herero in your house.'

'The only gun in this house is the one I have here in my hand. You will take my word for that.'

The Afrikaner chief frowned. He did not want trouble at this house. On the other hand, he could not lose face in front of his men. He wished he had brought more brandy with him; the effects of his earlier drinking were beginning to wear off.

'I must be sure. We will look.'

Miriam used both thumbs to pull back one of the cocks on the double-barrelled pistol. The noise it made as it clicked into position was very loud in the night air.

The sound genuinely alarmed Jonker. He had not been prepared for events to go this far. He had merely wanted to remind the residents of Otjimkandje that he was the sovereign ruler of

Hereroland.

One of Jonker's men was not so sensitive to the diplomacy of the situation – or perhaps the effect of the brandy he had drunk was slower in wearing off. Contemptuously he kneed his horse forward to where Miriam stood outside the door and reached down to take the gun from her.

He had made the same mistake as his chief in underestimating Miriam's determination. Pointing the gun in the Afrikaner's direction, she closed her eyes and jerked the trigger.

There was a loud bang as the pistol jumped in her hand.

The ball sped harmlessly over the head of the Afrikaner warrior, but his horse was not used to having a gun fired at a distance of only six inches from its nostrils. The noise and flash terrified the animal and it reared back from the gun.

The warrior had been leaning forward and was caught off balance. The violent reaction of the horse threw him high into the air, and he landed with his arm twisted beneath him. His scream of pain was lost in the snorting of prancing horses as the frightened mount of the unseated warrior jumped among them.

Opening her eyes to the confused moonlit scene, Miriam waited for the holocaust she believed must now come down upon her.

To her amazement Jonker began to laugh. Following the example of their chief, the Afrikaner warriors joined in. A wound inflicted by a man from another tribe would have started a war. An injury caused by falling from a horse frightened by a woman was a joke. It was also Jonker's way of extricating himself from a situation he did not care for.

'Come!' he said to his men as the injured warrior was unsympathetically assisted to his feet. 'Before she fires again and dismounts us all.'

Still laughing, the Afrikaners rode away and Miriam slumped back against the doorpost. Her arm brushed against cold steel, and she looked down at the barrel of Hannah's musket which protruded through the door opening.

'Thank goodness you didn't fire that thing, too,' Miriam said weakly. 'That would have finished me off. The sound of my pistol frightened the life out of me. When that man fell to the ground and I thought I'd killed him I could have died myself.'

'Then you had both Jonker and me fooled,' replied Hannah. 'You were so cool I felt sure you must have known I was behind you with this.'

'Had I known I would have been even more frightened,' said Miriam. 'One bang like that was enough. I don't think I'll ever stop shaking!'

'I only hope Chief Jonker appreciated his luck, too,' said the Jewish girl. 'My gun was pointing at his heart – and I'm a very good shot. I wouldn't have missed. Had he not called off his men when he did the Afrikaners would be electing a new chief tomorrow and I would have been happy to die for it.'

There was such intense emotion in her voice that Miriam said, 'Hush, child! What a thing to say. Nobody's going to die tonight. And why should you hate Jonker so much? He's not a good man, but I doubt if he's any worse than many others in this world.'

'Yes, he is. Jonker is the worst man I've ever met. He can't be trusted.'

Hannah's hatred of Chief Jonker had to come out, and Miriam waited in silence in the doorway. It was dark just here and she knew from her own experiences that difficult words slipped out easier in the darkness.

'When we first came to Whalefish Bay I wasn't very old and we didn't have much money. But Father worked hard day and night doing anything to earn a living. After a couple of years he began trading and for a while things started to improve. Then he met Chief Jonker. He came to Father full of talk about how he would make him rich. He said he was the greatest chief in the country and he insisted that Father should trade with him alone and break with all the other tribes. Father agreed and from that time on everything that came in went to Jonker. It wasn't long before it became obvious that all we were getting in return were promises – and abuse. But we carried on trading with him because Father said that one day Jonker would allow us to trade farther inland and then everything would be worthwhile.'

Hannah paused and the only sound was her own heavy breathing.

'Eventually he did agree to allow traders to come inland – but he gave the concession to Jacobus Albrecht and Harold Andrews. We got nothing.'

Miriam resisted the urge to put out a hand and touch the girl. There had been nobody before to listen to her story and but for the emotive events of the night it would still have been bottled up inside her. But there was more to come.

'Jonker was still willing to trade with Father for "special" goods. But it meant moving away from Whalefish Bay and going a long way to the south — away from people to where there was nothing but sand and sea mists, where most of the trading was done at night so no one could see.'

'This trade was in guns?'

Hannah shrugged into the darkness. 'It must have been. When I asked Father he said the less I knew the better it would be for me.'

The emotion had drained away now, and Miriam did reach out and squeeze the girl's arm reassuringly.

'You've had a very hard life, Hannah, with no mother to turn to. That's over now. You're here among friends. Everything else is in the past.'

'Is it?' The bitterness returned to Hannah's voice. 'I don't suppose Jacobus Albrecht thinks so.'

'Albrecht? What's he got to do with anything?'

'He persuaded Jonker to allow us to come inland to trade.'

'He did that? Such generosity doesn't sound like the Jacobus Albrecht I've met.'

'Oh, he didn't do it out of kindness!' Her laugh was an ugly sound. 'He wants to marry me.'

'Good God! You're much too young to marry Jacobus Albrecht.'

'I was only fourteen when he first mentioned it.'

'The man must have been drunk!' Miriam's indignation crackled in the darkness.

'No. I could have excused him had he been drinking. He was quite sober. He told Father he wanted to take me for his wife. I was there when he said it. What made it even worse was that he didn't look at me during the whole time he was talking. I felt like some dog he wanted to buy.'

'Your father refused him, of course?'

'Had he done so we would still be down there among the sand dunes. Father didn't say no and he didn't say yes. He told Jacobus he would think about it if he helped us to get a trading concession from Jonker.'

'Well, we'll see about marriage to Jacobus Albrecht if it ever crops up again. If there's even the breath of a whisper about it, you come and see me, young lady. I've seen enough misery caused by wrong marriages. I'll not let it happen to you.'

She sensed the immense relief in the young girl at having someone to share the burden she had been carrying alone for so long. Miriam moved before the relief overflowed into tears.

'Now let's go inside and settle the house down for the night once more.'

The Afrikaners had gone, but there was to be little sleep for Miriam and Hannah that night. The sound of the shot she had fired had been heard in every hut in Otjimkandje; but it was not until the hoofbeats of the Akrikaners' horses had faded into the far distance that the Herero dared to leave their huts.

Cautiously at first, but in ever-increasing numbers, they made their way to the Retallick house. Soon the hut was surrounded by anxious villagers. When no one appeared from inside, the rumours began to circulate. 'The white mother Retallick has been killed.' 'No, it is the tall daughter of the Trader.' 'Both women have been taken by the Afrikaners.'

Finally Tjamuene himself arrived at the house surrounded by men of his personal bodyguard bearing bright flaming torches. 'Having first made sure Jonker has left,' commented Hannah disdainfully.

'Hush! At least he's come himself and hasn't sent one of his men,' said Miriam. 'He's an old man who would stand no chance against Jonker. Put some more tea in that pot, Hannah. We'll have to ask Tjamuene in.'

The old chief was full of genuine concern for the two women and relieved to see them both safe.

'Jonker has gone too far this time,' he said. 'I will post some of my own guards outside your house. The Afrikaner will not bother you again. You have Tjamuene's word for that.'

'Thank you, Tjamuene. That won't be necessary,' said Miriam firmly. 'He won't come again. If he did, and your men were here, there would be a fight and many men would be killed. It is better such a thing does not happen. Come, sit down and have some tea with us. It's very kind of you to be so concerned.'

While they drank the tea Tjamuene heard the full story of all that had happened. By the end of it he, too, was chuckling. The laughs came from deep in his ample belly and erupted in short uncontrollable bursts, spilling from his lips into his tea-cup.

'You are right,' he said, using a fat finger to wipe away the tears that overflowed from his bloodshot eyes. 'Jonker will not return. A chief who allows his warriors to be sent running by one woman would not dare to risk it happening for a second time. If it did, he would be their leader no longer.'

The Herero chief suddenly stopped laughing. 'But where is your son? Was he not here when Jonker came?'

'No.' Tjamuene had awakened the worry that was nagging at Miriam. 'He is in Sesebe tonight.'

The chief gave no hint of his thoughts. 'Kasupi is with him'

'Yes.'

It was not a lie, Miriam told herself. Kasupi would be with him by now.

'It is good. They are as brothers and both are sons to me.'

The old chief stood up to go. 'My eyes are pleased to see you well but my heart is heavy that as chief of the Herero I am not able to protect you while you are in my village. If we, too, had guns, perhaps Jonker's people would tremble in their huts at night. . . .' Tjamuene gave a resigned gesture. 'I will not live to see such a thing come to pass. All I can do is try to bring my people safely through each long day and night and leave my hopes for their future to those who will follow me.'

'You are the chief of the Otjimkandje Herero,' said Miriam. 'You have the love and respect of your people and your friends.'

'I am the chief of the Otjimkandje Herero,' agreed Tjamuene. 'And I have the love of my family and friends. A man can ask for little more.'

Nodding to Hannah, Tjamuene shook Miriam's hand and left the house with a quiet dignity that brought a ridiculous lump to Miriam's throat.

'We'd better get these tea things cleared away,' she said briskly to Hannah, 'otherwise we'll get no sleep at all tonight.'

186

But there were more visitors yet to come on this strange eventful night.

Miriam had extinguished one of the two lamps when she heard the pounding of hoofs on the hard dirt road leading into the village. For one fear-filled moment she thought it must be Jonker returning to take revenge for the humiliation she had caused him. Then she realised that the horses were coming along the road from Sesebe.

Lighting the second lamp again quickly, she unbolted the door and threw it open as the first of the foaming horses was reined to a halt outside the house.

'Daniel? Is that you? Where . . . ?'

'It's not Daniel, ma'am. It's me. Harold Andrews. Your boy's friend – the Herero – came galloping into Sesebe saying Jonker was attacking the village. I gathered up half a dozen of my men and we've come here as fast we could, thinking you was in trouble. There'll be more men following.'

'Oh dear! Yes, Jonker and his men have been here and there was some trouble, but it's over now. But Kasupi went to fetch Daniel. Where is he? Why isn't he with you? I thought he was at Sesebe?'

'He is, ma'am. He's spending the night at Sam Speke's place. If I send one of my men back along the road to stop the others, perhaps I might step inside and have you tell me what's been going on here tonight?'

'Of course. Please come in.'

Hannah had not gone to bed and she came into the kitchen when Miriam went indoors.

'You'd better make some more tea, Hannah. We'll give up any idea of sleep tonight.'

As the girl hurried away Miriam said to the trader, 'Is Daniel all right? Why didn't he come here with you?'

Harold Andrews looked sheepish. 'To tell you the truth, ma'am, he was drinking with some of my men last night. He's a big lad for his age and sometimes it's easy to forget he can't take a man's share of hard drink. He wasn't feeling too good. When I heard about it I thought it best he be taken to Sam Speke's place for the night. I didn't think it would be a good idea to bring him with us. He might easily have had an accident

187

in the dark — especially if he was worried about you.'

'Mr Andrews.' Miriam was tight-lipped as she faced the trader. 'What you're trying to tell me is that my son got so drunk last night that he was incapable of getting himself home.'

It might have appeared to an onlooker that the hat Harold Andrews held in his hand had a red-hot brim.

'That's about the rights of it, ma'am.'

'Then don't beat about the bush. Say so. Now, you'd better get your men inside, and I'll tell you what's been going on to-night. But if I catch any of them leering at Hannah they can wait for you outside. Is that understood?'

'Yes, ma'am.'

Miriam glared at the other men through the open doorway, and when they had all nodded that they understood she led the way into the house and told her story yet again.

It was a very pale and shaken prodigal son who returned to the Retallick house the next morning. He had awakened feeling very sorry for himself, but received no sympathy from Sam Speke. The one-time seaman had hurled the news of the night's events at Otjimkandje in his face before his feet had swung to the heaving floor.

Sam described what might so easily have happened in the Herero village in such vivid detail that the thought of it had immediately combined with the stale brandy in his system to make Daniel violently sick.

Kasupi had been able to put his mind at ease when Daniel made his way to the stable to collect his horse. The Herero had spent a great part of the night riding back and forth between Otjimkandje and Sesebe. He, too, had a guilty conscience.

When he arrived at Otjimkandje, Daniel tried to apologise for his absence, but Miriam cut his words short.

'What happened here could not have been prevented by you. What does upset me is that you should undermine your father's authority by getting helplessly drunk with his men. You know very well he's concerned about the drinking in Sesebe getting out of hand. How can he do anything about it when his own son is as bad as the worst of them?' Daniel mumbled something about it not happening again. 'I'll believe that when you've proved it. But I tell you one thing. No son of mine is going to become a drunkard. If you make this a habit, I'll come to Sesebe and bring you back here myself if I have to go into that place and walk you out by the ear to do it. Just you remember that.'

Daniel's shame was heightened by the presence of Hannah. She stood in the kitchen making pastry, her back to them during the whole of Miriam's tirade.

'And don't think you're going to moon about here all day because your head feels like a bucket filled with thunder. We're out of meat. You can take that gun of yours and go and shoot something. You'll find the game in the east — in the opposite direction to Sesebe.'

'But I could be gone for days! What if Jonker comes back?'

'He won't; but, if you're so worried, you'd best be on your way, then you'll be back here quicker.'

'What sort of gun do you have?'

The question came from Hannah.

'A Spanish one — with rifling.'

'Show me.'

Only too pleased for an opportunity to escape from his mother's wrath Daniel went to his room and returned with his gun. It was a long-barrelled flintlock of excellent quality but a long-outdated model.

'That's a Kaffir gun. If you want to get back here in a hurry, you'd better take mine. Here!'

She handed him the gun she had placed in a corner of the kitchen the previous night. It was a new percussion rifle, far more reliable and accurate than a flintlock.

'Take the pouch, too. You'll find all the percussion caps, paper cartridges and moulded shot you're likely to need.'

Ignoring his stuttered thanks, Hannah turned her back on him and resumed her own task.

Daniel's dejection showed in the way he sat his horse as he rode away from Otjimkandje with Kasupi.

'You were very hard on him,' said Hannah quietly as she and Miriam stood together by the window watching him go.

'It was no more than he deserved.' Miriam's tone of voice belied her words.

'It was a good thing Daniel was in Sesebe last night,' commented Hannah. 'Had he been here it would have been him standing out there facing Jonker. His shot wouldn't have missed, either, and the Afrikaners would have killed him.'

'Don't you think I know that?' Miriam's voice broke as she added, 'I was giving my thanks to God for that as Daniel left to ride away just now.'

Turning away, she hurried into her bedroom before she could make a fool of herself in front of Hannah.

CHAPTER FIVE

Josh and Aaron were away for almost four months and returned well pleased with the results of their long trek. Although Lake Ngami had been discovered some years before, very few Europeans had yet been there.

The two men from Otjimkandje had not only reached the lake, but had also made friends with the unpredictable Bechuana chief who claimed the lake as his territory. More, they had established trading links with him. Their wagons were laden with ostrich feathers and elephant tusks. Some had been taken from animals shot by Josh, but the majority had been received from the Bechuana. Trade with Lake Ngami would take the form of a lengthy trek, but the profit at the end of it would make the journey well worthwhile.

Josh had also brought a few samples of copper ore back with him. Most of the deposits he had found had been too far inland to make working them a practical consideration, but there was one spot only two days' journey from Otjimkandje that looked promising. Josh thought that, if a road were made from it direct to Whalefish Bay, the distance would be little more than from Sesebe.

One of the Herero warriors with him said this copper deposit had been known to some of his people who had once had a village near the spot. They had fled before Jonker and no one had shown the ore to the Afrikaner. Josh said it would be as well to keep the secret with the Herero people.

Hugo Walder was still in the Cape Colony, and Miriam had suggested that nothing be said to Josh of Jonker's visit until the missionary returned. Daniel would not agree. Such an incident could not be kept secret in this land. If Josh were not told about it by the Herero, he would hear the details from the miners at Sesebe.

Daniel told his father about it himself that night when the family was having its evening meal. Aaron and Hannah were also there. Daniel made no attempt to hide the reason for his absence, and Hannah watched Josh very closely for his reaction.

Josh was angry — very angry. But whether it was directed at Jonker or at Daniel she did not know.

'Jonker knew we were all away,' Josh said finally. 'Otherwise he would never have dared to come here like that. But it was an insult directed against Hugo and Tjamuene rather than against us. I think we'll discuss it with Hugo on his return before we decide what action is necessary.'

He looked at Daniel and frowned. 'I thought I could rely on you to take care of things while I was away. It seems I was wrong.'

'Had he been here it would have been a different story,' Hannah blurted out. She repeated what she had said to Miriam the morning after the raid, adding, 'If Daniel had been here, you'd have come back to find none of us left alive.'

She stared so defiantly around the table when she had finished that Josh raised an eyebrow questioningly at Miriam and Aaron stopped his fork halfway to his mouth, looking from his daughter to Daniel with great interest. Her outburst took Daniel by surprise. Since the incident with Jonker she had been more civil to him and they had held a number of brief conversations, but no more. Aware of the interested expressions of the others his own face reddened and matched Hannah's.

'H'm! That may be so,' said Josh. 'But Daniel's had his seventeenth birthday. When I'm away he's the man in this house. I expect him to accept that responsibility.'

'It won't happen again,' mumbled Daniel.

'Of course it won't!' said Miriam, putting an end to the subject. 'Now, let's talk about Aaron's new house and store. I've been down there to help Hannah get things ready. It's far and away the finest building in these parts, and there's already been a delivery of trade goods from the Cape. Sam had them stored away for you.'

'I'll have to settle my debt with Sam,' said the Jew. 'He's a useful man to have around. Do you think he'd come to work for me, Josh?'

'He might. He's his own boss. There's more than enough work for his wagon-building in Sesebe; but, as you say, he's a good man to have around. Make him an offer he can't refuse.

He'd be especially useful if you intended trading with the Herero. He's married into the tribe, and they trust him.'

'I don't think I'll have any difficulty trading with the Herero,' said Aaron, 'but I'll ask Sam anyway.'

He pushed his plate from him and leaned back in his chair. 'That was a delightful meal, Miriam. Now, as a "thank you" for looking after my Hannah I've brought you back some specially treated sable antelope skins that the Bechuana traded from the Matabele Zulus. They are so dark and soft that if you cover your chairs with them you'll swear they are finest velvet.'

The remainder of that evening was spent talking about the things the two men had seen during their long return trip to Lake Ngami.

Aaron and Hannah left Otjimkandje for Sesebe the following day. Miriam was going to miss the tall Jewish girl. She had grown very fond of her and learned to appreciate her intelligence and quiet self-assurance. Miriam also felt sorry for Hannah. As the only white woman in Sesebe her every action would be observed and commented upon by the miners. She would need all her sound common sense to remain level-headed. Miriam's only consolation was that Hannah had promised to come and stay with her in Otjimkandje whenever Aaron went away for any lengthy period.

A week after their departure Hugo Walder returned from his long stay in Cape Town. He looked healthy and fit in spite of his advancing years. The meetings he had attended in the administrative capital of the Cape Colony had gone well for him. Owing to their patient diligence over the years, the German missionaries had gradually consolidated their precarious foothold in the country to the north of the Orange River. English missions, encouraged by the success of Robert Moffat at Kuruman, were concentrating their evangelical efforts on the southern Bechuana tribes and were poised to take advantage of Moffat's incredible but strong friendship with the bloody Matabele Zulu chief, Mzilikazi. They hoped he would help them to extend their sphere of influence to the more central regions of southern Africa. Because of this they were content to allow the German missionaries to work in the near-forgotten south-west corner of Africa.

Yet there were exceptions to these loosely defined missionary 'sees'. Jonker's request for an English missionary made one inroad into the influence of the German missions.

Hugo Walder had news of this religious incursion, and his words were to bring the whole life Miriam and Josh had built for themselves crashing down about their ears.

The two of them sat in the missionary's hut on the night of his return, listening to his news and looking at the many new things he had brought back with him.

'My society wishes me to establish new mission stations among the tribes to the north,' said Hugo. 'They are sending me two young missionaries from Germany to help. Their youth and enthusiasm will give my work new impetus. They will provide a newly sharpened edge to the time-tempered blade that is old Hugo Walder. No doubt they will also prove a great trial to me until they learn to accept the ways of the Herero.'

'It's time you had some help, Hugo.' Josh drew contentedly on his pipe. 'You've pushed yourself far too hard for too many years.'

'You need a woman to look after you,' commented Miriam, who was unpacking the missionary's clothes and inspecting them for tears or missing buttons before packing them away into the drawers and cupboards Sam Speke had made more than twelve years before.

'I still have much work to do for God if he will grant me the years,' said Hugo Walder. 'And now that Jonker has his own missionary perhaps I will be allowed to continue my work among the Herero untroubled by Afrikaner warriors.'

'His missionary is in Winterhoek? We've heard nothing about it. When did he arrive?'

'We came up from Cape Town to Whalefish Bay on the same ship,' said Hugo Walder. 'He arrived there from England only a few months ago.'

Miriam failed to notice Hugo Walder's reluctance to talk about Jonker's missionary. 'We'll have to invite him to Otjimkandje for a visit. It will be nice to hear the latest news from England. I don't suppose you know from which part of England he comes?'

'He told me he had been working in London for some years,'

replied the German missionary heavily. 'But before that he was working in the part of England from which you come – Cornwall.'

Miriam saw Hugo Walder's expression for the first time and she put a hand to her mouth. Josh froze as he lowered the pipe to the table in front of him.

'Yes, my very loved friends, I see you fear the worst – and I wish I could allay those fears.'

Hugo Walder's concern caused his German accent to thicken, but there could be no mistaking the name he was to give to them. 'Jonker's new missionary is a Wesleyan preacher named William Thackeray.'

'Oh no!' The room suddenly spun about Miriam as the words were torn from her. She reeled, and Hugo Walder caught her and sat her in a chair.

Josh's hands clenched so tightly that his nails drew blood from his palms.

Hugo Walder had just uttered a name that bridged fourteen happy years. A grim and unhappy past had caught up with them.

The foundering of *Pride of Liverpool* had set Josh free and the mission at Otjimkandje given him a new and worthwhile life. Now all that would change. The preacher's presence here had to be more than coincidence. What was more, according to the law Miriam was still William Thackeray's wife – and Daniel his lawful son.

Josh and Miriam looked at each other in utter despair.

'He asked about you,' said Hugo Walder, his misery almost as great as their own. 'I told him as little as was possible in the circumstances, but I fear he will seek you out.'

'He obviously told you about Miriam and me,' said Josh. 'I'd like to tell you our version of what happened—'

'He told me nothing,' interrupted Hugo Walder. 'And I have no need to know anything more about either of you. You have lived and worked here as my very good friends for fourteen years. What more does a man need to know?'

'But he must have told you what happened before we left England,' insisted Josh. 'How else could you know we have something to hide from Thackeray? Nobody here knows of his connection with us – not even Sam.'

'Ah. But you are wrong. You are wrong.'

The missionary sat down heavily on a tall-backed chair. 'It has always been one of my worldly weaknesses that I enjoy knowing what is going on in my beloved homeland. Every month my brother goes to the docks at Hamburg to put a package of newspapers on board a ship bound for the Cape Colony. From there they are sent here to me. But you already know this; you have seen me reading them many times, and I have given some of them to Daniel to improve his German.'

Josh and Miriam both winced at the mention of Daniel. The Wesleyan preacher's arrival would have a profound effect on his life.

Hugo Walder was speaking again. 'Not long before you were first brought to Otjimkandje I received newspapers which gave great prominence to the trial of a number of men on a charge of riot and treason in some little port in Cornwall, in England. The report said these men had fought with soldiers. There were rumours that it marked the beginning of an uprising such as the one France had experienced fifty years before. The leader of the rioting, so the newspapers said, was a young engineer named Joshua Retallick. They also reported that he was badly wounded during the battle.' The missionary spread his hands. 'Even had the name been a coincidence all doubts would have gone when I first saw you working in the smithy with your shirt off. That huge scar across your back is as distinctive as the spots on a leopard.'

'But that doesn't explain how you know about Miriam – or Preacher Thackeray. They weren't involved.'

'Oh, but they were,' corrected the missionary. 'One of the newspapers reported a disturbance at the end of the trial and observed that a woman evicted from the court was one Miriam Thackeray, wife of a local Wesleyan preacher, well known for his union activities. The reporter was surprised that he had not put in an appearance at the trial as a witness in your defence. For me the newspaper reports left many questions unanswered. For the reporter, too, I think.'

'You mean you have known about this all these years and yet said nothing?' Josh could hardly believe it was possible.

'What was there for me to say?' Hugo Walder tried to shrug

his silence away. 'Men and women leave their own countries for many reasons. I had mine; you have yours. Those who find their way to this part of the world usually have stronger reasons than most. There was a time when I was concerned for the child, but as Daniel grew it became ever more apparent that he was Josh's true son. It is not what you were before but what you have become now that matters. For me you have become my very dear friends.'

'Even though the Church says I am another man's wife?' Miriam's eyes were brimming with tears she was fighting hard to hold back.

'I have forgiven the Herero far worse sins,' said Hugo Walder. 'The final judgement must be the Lord's. Even so, I do not think he will be any less compassionate than a humble man like myself.'

'Hugo, you are a truly wonderful man. . . .'

Miriam burst into tears and turned to Josh for comfort. He held her until the shuddering sobs grew still.

'We'll go home now, Hugo,' said Josh. 'We have much to discuss.'

'Of course.' The missionary put out his hand and rested it on Miriam's head. 'All seems black now, but it is not so. We cannot shut off our past as though it never happened. It always catches up with us. Much better, my friends, that we face it here rather than in the Kingdom of Heaven. If there is anything I can do, I will be here.'

As Josh led Miriam from the hut Hugo Walder called, 'And remember, the decision of an English court means nothing in Otjimkandje. Here you are a free man, and so you will remain.'

Josh was relieved that Daniel was not in the house when they arrived there. He did not feel like making his explanations tonight. Miriam was so upset that Josh insisted she went directly to bed.

When she had gone he stood in the doorway of their home for a very long time, smoking his pipe. He watched as the huge three-quarter moon rose, plump as a golden pumpkin, above the horizon, dominating the star-strewn sky. All about him lively fires danced in front of the Herero huts, and he listened to the village sounds as though hearing them for the first time:

loud voices, laughter, restless cattle sounds from the animal-pens —and the drums. They throbbed out across the warm and comfortable African evening. Later the singers would join in and a dance would begin.

It was during this time that Josh arrived at a decision. William Thackeray would not drive him away from Hereroland as he had from England. He and Miriam had made a good life here for themselves and Daniel. It was a life worth fighting for.

Josh went to Miriam and they talked until the sun took over the duties of the moon on the eastern horizon.

CHAPTER SIX

Josh rode into Winterhoek when the sun stood tall in the sky. It was hot, but he was not sure whether the perspiration that followed the course of his spine was caused by the heat or the thought of meeting William Thackeray again.

His name conjured up so many memories and images: of green moors and yellow gorse; miners and the heartbeat throb of mine-engines; family and friends. It brought back less pleasant memories, too: of heavy chafing wrist- and leg-irons, and the foul-smelling inhuman darkness of a prison hulk. Josh shivered in the heat. He would not forget that it was the man he was about to meet who had given him these last memories of England.

Winterhoek was three times the size of Otjimkandje and shut in by mountains. It was a straggling untidy village, the Afrikaner huts surrounded by the hovels of their Bergdama servants and hangers-on from other tribes. Away to one side were the more substantial huts of the traders.

Josh threaded his way through the village, his horse trampling the scattered rubbish of a lax and badly organised community. But there was plenty of activity at the church. William Thackeray had only been in Winterhoek for twenty-four hours but he had wasted no time. A whole gang of Bergdama men were busy rebuilding the walls of the mission. Beyond them were women working on the thatch of the previous missionary's hut. Bustling between the two was William Thackeray.

It came as a shock to Josh to see once again how small the missionary was. Josh had always been tall, and time and work had filled him out. It had done the opposite for William Thackeray. Always a slight man, he now looked fragile, with a frail man's slight stoop.

As Josh cleared the native huts and rode into the space before the church the missionary's face wrinkled as he shielded his eyes against the sunlight with one hand and looked up at the horseman.

'Why, Josh! What a pleasant surprise. How good to see you after all these years. My word, but you're looking well. Come into my house — or "hut" I believe I must call it. There's a terrible mess inside, but I'm sure we'll find somewhere to sit. At least we'll be out of this dreadful sun. I don't think I'll ever learn to accept the heat!'

He took out a large handkerchief and wiped his face, then ran the damp cloth around his stiff neckband to emphasise his words.

Josh ignored the preacher's elaborately friendly greeting and made no move to dismount.

'Let's not play games with one another, William. I have no fond memories of you, and you proved your regard for me many years ago by having me falsely convicted of involvement in your scheming. Why are you here?'

'I am here to serve God, Josh — as I have served Him elsewhere. This place was once a Wesleyan church and will be again. That's why I am here. As for the other things you speak of, they happened a great many years ago and bitterness has undoubtedly clouded memory. It would be futile for me to protest my innocence now. No doubt your own conscience rests easier for believing the worst of me.'

'If that remark refers to Miriam, I have no feelings of guilt about taking her from you. She was never your wife in anything but name, and you know it well. But for your interference she would have been my wife in Cornwall — as she *is* my wife here.'

'And Daniel . . . how is he?'

'My son is almost a man, as tall as his father and nearly as broad across the shoulders.'

The Bergdama workmen had stopped their labours. Few of them spoke or understood much English, but it needed no command of language to recognise the antagonism between their new missionary and the white man from the Herero village.

William Thackeray brought out his damp handkerchief again, and it pursued its limp course as before.

'Josh, I have been sent here at the request of the chief of the Afrikaners. I come to preach the gospel, not to follow a vendetta.'

'Are you saying your coming here is mere coincidence? That you didn't know Miriam and I were here? I don't believe that.'

'I won't lie to you. I thought to find you here. Some years ago I returned to Cornwall, seeking Miriam.' William Thackeray saw Josh's expression harden. 'My motives are irrelevant now. It is sufficient to say she was not there. Neither would anyone tell me anything, but I heard rumours. It was said that Miriam and Daniel were with you; that you were living as a family somewhere in Africa. If you were a free man, I knew you would be in no land that was under British rule. It greatly reduced the number of places where I needed to look. I was working in London, helping in a mission in the docks area. I spoke to seamen for years and heard nothing. Then I was told about two men, a woman and a child rumoured to have survived a shipwreck and living in a village inland from the Skeleton Coast. The sailor had heard the story when he was working on a ship trading between the Cape Colony and Whalefish Bay. I checked with the headquarters of all the missionaries in this area, and from Germany I was informed that an English family named Retallick had survived a shipwreck together with a sailor. They told me you were living at Otjimkandje with missionary Hugo Walder.'

'You went to all this trouble, yet expect me to believe you came here only to preach God's word? I may have been ready to believe you once, William, but not anymore. That was a lesson I learned well from you.'

William Thackeray shrugged his thin shoulders. 'I would most probably have done nothing with my information had a request not been received in London for a Wesleyan preacher to come here to this place, only a few miles distant from Otjimkandje. I felt it was an omen; that I was being given an opportunity. For what I did not know – but I came.'

'So here you are. What happens next?'

The narrow shoulders shrugged again. 'I carry out the work for which I was sent here. No doubt that will involve occasional visits to my fellow-missionaries. I hope to see you again, Josh. And I look forward to meeting Miriam and Daniel.'

Josh's horse danced as the shadow of a low gliding bird crossed the clearing in front of him. Josh fought the animal around in a tight circle to confront the preacher again.

'Many years ago I came to your house to see Miriam in an attempt to prevent your wedding. You refused to let me talk to her. You said it would serve no purpose. This time it's my turn to give you that same message — and I'll add a warning for your safety. Chief Jonker is hated by the Herero. Any of his men entering Otjimkandje unarmed would be hacked to pieces. You're Jonker's missionary, brought here by him in an attempt to gain some degree of respectability in the eyes of the Cape government. You'll be neither welcome nor safe in Otjimkandje — so stay away.'

He swung his horse's head to face towards Otjimkandje.

'Josh?'

Josh turned to look back at William Thackeray.

'I was in Cornwall for a few weeks last year. I saw your mother and father. They were well. Miriam's mother died several years ago. I thought you would both wish to know that.'

Josh inclined his head in acknowledgement of the news, then kneed his horse into a canter away from the mission at Winterhoek. He was more sure than ever that the arrival of Preacher William Thackeray meant serious trouble, if not actual disaster, to the happy little family in Otjimkandje. The newly recruited missionary was thinner than he had ever been before, but the light in his eyes showed his physical form was being fed to the furnaces of some inner force. William Thackeray remained what he had always been — a zealot. Once it had been for the cause of unionism, the unity of Cornish miners. Josh wondered what direction his crusading would take in this hot and explosive country. Jonker needed very little incentive to massacre Tjamuene's Herero. At the same time tribes of opposing interest were being driven from the south into ever-closer proximity by the northward trek of land-hungry Boers. One spark of ill-directed fervour could cause the country to erupt in bloody war.

When Josh arrived back at Otjimkandje he was not able to tell Miriam of his talk with William Thackeray because Aaron and Hannah were at the house and the Jewish trader was very distressed and extremely angry.

'When is someone going to do something about that man? He

is no more than a common thief, a scourge to honest traders. We can do nothing, and even the Cape government seems to be frightened of him.'

'Who are you talking about? What's happened?'

'Who else but that son of a renegade, Chief Jonker!'

'Well, stop prancing about the room; you're making me dizzy. Hannah, will you close that door, please. Your father's voice is loud, and there are too many ears about outside.'

Otjimkandje was no different from any other village. Not every man was loyal to Tjamuene. There were some who would be happy to repeat Aaron's words to Jonker in the hope of currying favour with the Afrikaner chief.

'So who cares who hears me? A thief is a thief, be he an Afrikaner chief or a Bushman slave.'

Hannah hurriedly closed the door of the hut, and Josh steered the Jewish trader to a chair and sat him firmly in it. 'For God's sake be sensible, Aaron. We can do without another of Jonker's visits!'

'*You* can do without another of Jonker's visits?' shouted Aaron. 'Me and my wagons, we've had one already.'

'Miriam, get some tea for all of us, then perhaps we'll get some sense from Aaron in place of this disjointed rambling.'

Aaron threw up his hands in a gesture of exaggerated resignation. 'Agh! What does it matter? What does anything matter anymore? It's no use trying to trade honestly in this country — not while Jonker is allowed to do whatever he wishes, with no man with the courage to stand against him.' He caught Josh's eye. 'All right! All right! I still talk in a riddle for you, so I tell you. I am on my way to Whalefish Bay with two wagonloads of the goods we traded from the Bechuana when I meet this — this — Afrikaner!'

Aaron made the word sound like an oath, and spluttering with indignation he went on, 'He and his men are waiting for me on the road. I cannot ride through them and so I have to stop. Without so much as a "Good day to you, Aaron", they jump on to my wagons and start to throw out all my elephant tusks and ostrich feathers. "What is all this about?" I ask Jonker. 'Is the chief of the Afrikaners so poor that he has to rob traders now in order to live?"'

Josh winced. 'You said that to Jonker?'

'I said much more. When a man sees all he's worked for being taken from him should he remain silent?'

Josh shook his head. 'No. Go on.'

'Jonker accused me of taking the trade away from his people and of bartering with the Bechuana without his permission. He said he was not taking everything, only that which was his due as paramount chief of all these lands.'

'A pity some of the other chiefs weren't around to hear him say that,' murmured Josh. 'He may have control of Hereroland, but there are bigger men moving in to crowd him. How much "tribute" did he take?'

'About three-quarters of the total,' replied Aaron bitterly. 'There wasn't enough left to cover the cost of the trip to Lake Ngami.'

'You said you had two wagonloads,' put in Miriam. 'But you returned from the lake with three. What happened to the other wagonload?'

'Ah!' Aaron managed a thin smile. 'Trusting I may be. Stupid I am not. The third wagonload is in my store in Sesebe.'

'Then you'll still make some profit,' said Josh, 'if you can get the wagon to Whalefish Bay without Jonker knowing.'

'A *little* profit I may make,' corrected the Jew, 'though it will be small enough when I've paid my debts. But with three wagons of goods I would have been clear of all my money worries. However, I don't intend to let that Afrikaner thief steal this load. I'd like to talk to Mutjise. If I take the wagon to my old trading post farther down the coast, I'll need him and some of his men to come along with me and wipe out my tracks as we go. If we set out at nightfall, we'll be out of sight of the Whalefish Bay road by sun-up.'

'What happens if Jonker discovers you've tricked him?' asked Josh.

Aaron spread his hands wide. 'Why should he ever find out? Mutjise will only bring trusted men, and no one from this house will tell him. But in case anything should go wrong I'd like to leave Hannah here with you. Is that all right?'

'Of course it is,' said Miriam, and she saw the pleasure that lit up Daniel's face. He had been silently watching the trader's daughter as the others talked. Hannah was aware of his interest but chose to pretend she had not even noticed his presence.

'I'll come with you if you feel an extra gun would help.' It was an unselfish offer from Daniel in the circumstances.

'Thank you. If I intended having an armed escort, I could ask for none better.' Aaron was not averse to praising Daniel in front of his daughter. 'But I travel in peace and trust I will avoid the paths of the Afrikaners. Now, perhaps you would send your friend to find his eldest brother. Tell him I would like to speak to him at the cattle-pens. It will not be thought unusual for a trader to talk to Mutjise about buying cattle.'

With all the bustle in the house that evening it was not until Josh and Miriam were alone in their bedroom that he was able to tell her about his meeting with William Thackeray. Miriam was upset at the news of her mother's death, although it came as no surprise to her. Her mother had been in indifferent health for some years before they had left England, and Miriam had accepted she would never see her again. Even so, there were memories of the hard years of poverty they had shared when Miriam's mother had done much to make her daughter's lot an easier one than her own.

Of more immediate concern was William Thackeray's next move. They were both quite certain there would be one. The missionary was a very devious and determined man. They would never be able to relax while he remained at Winterhoek.

Daniel was Josh's main worry.

'He will have to be told the whole truth,' he said to Miriam.

'But how can you tell him, Josh? What will you say? That his name is not really Retallick? That he was conceived out of wedlock and his mother married another man while carrying him? You can't tell him that, Josh. You can't!'

'Would you rather he heard it from William? I must tell him, Miriam, no matter how difficult it is for me.'

'But how? What will he do when he knows?'

'I'll take him on a hunting trip tomorrow. We'll stay away for a couple of days to give him time to think about it. It's not going to be easy for either of us but it must be done. You can see that?'

'Yes,' Miriam agreed finally. 'But what sort of man is it who will travel thousands of miles to find us after all these years? Why is he here, Josh? What does he want?'

'If I knew that, I might be able to do something about it without Daniel ever knowing. William Thackeray is not a man to shout his intentions, but I've no doubt we will know soon enough.'

Chief Jonker had greeted his new missionary civilly enough upon his arrival a Winterhoek. He gave him women to repair his hut and men to help in the rebuilding of the mission church. He would, he said, be pleased to give William Thackeray all the help he needed to establish a church in the mountain-bordered valley.

But on the third morning no women arrived to tidy the now-completed hut and there was not a Bergdama workman to be seen.

William Thackeray waited patiently until noon before he strode off to speak to the Afrikaner chief. He found the way to the chief's door barred by an Afrikaner warrior bearing a gun.

'Chief Jonker rests,' said the guard. 'He says he will see no one.'

'Unless he also told you to shoot his missionary you'll let me through,' said William Thackeray. Scornfully brushing aside the weapon, he walked past the astonished tribesman.

He did not knock at the door. To do so would have given the guard time to recover his wits and upset the odds against the chance the missionary was taking.

The hut was in semi-darkness and smelled abominably of human perspiration, smoke and stale brandy fumes. Jonker was reclining on an untidy heap of bedding, the level of the brandy in the bottle he held already well down the bottle.

'What are you doing here? I am resting.'

The startled Jonker was belligerent but his eyes avoided meeting William Thackeray's.

'You said you would have men work on the mission church until it was completed. There are no men working today.'

'Even Bergdamas must have a day of rest.'

'Sunday is the usual day of rest. It gives the Bergdamas and your Afrikaners the opportunity to attend their church — when it's completed.'

This missionary was showing none of the deference Jonker had come to expect from those with whom he dealt. True, he had found white men to be far more casual when dealing with tribal authority, but with the exception of Hugo Walder he had always found missionaries eager to please. He changed his tactics.

'One of the white men from Otjimkandje came to see you. Why did you not tell me of this?'

'He came to see me because I knew him in England. It was nothing to do with you.'

'The Herero of the Little Father do not look kindly upon Chief Jonker of the Afrikaners. My people are greater than the Herero. They do not like this. Anyone from Otjimkandje is not my friend.'

'This man is not a friend. He came to tell me I must not visit Otjimkandje. Your Bergdamas must have told you we did not touch hands as do friends.'

'They told me. I wanted to hear it from you.'

William Thackeray took note that, although alcohol might have become an essential ingredient of life for the chief of the Afrikaners, it was not yet his master. He was still the man who had made his small tribe the most powerful in this corner of Africa. He had achieved this position by out-thinking his rivals, resorting to open warfare only when he was quite sure his small tribe could decisively beat the enemy. The Bergdama workmen had told him of the loud words between Josh Retallick and William Thackeray. He had known that by withdrawing the mission workmen Thackeray would come to him.

Chief Jonker had yet to learn that his new missionary was also a past master at the art of manipulating other men.

'Why is the white man from Otjimkandje not your friend?'

'That is between him and me. What about the men who should be working on my church?'

'They will be there when you return.'

'Good.'

William Thackeray hesitated before continuing. He had found out a great deal about Jonker while he was at the Cape. He had spoken to one of his previous missionaries and to officials of the

Cape government. There were traders there, too, who had left Winterhoek because of the Afrikaner chief. He thought he knew enough of the chief's own ambitions to be able to speak freely, but William Thackeray was unused to expressing his own ambitions to others.

'The British administration at the Cape has become very strong.'

Jonker took a noisy gurgling swig from his bottle.

'So I have heard.'

'You were wise to ask for a British missionary.'

'It is a chief's duty to be wiser than others, even though it is seen that the German missionaries have much power with other tribes.'

'I doubt if that will last for much longer.' Jonker's reticence returned once more, and William Thackeray said, 'The missionary at Otjimkandje is not a friend of the Afrikaners?'

'Without the Little Father the Herero of Otjimkandje would have gone north with their brothers long ago and their cattle would not be taking good grass from the mouths of Afrikaner cattle.'

That Afrikaner cattle had never grazed on Tjamuene's land meant nothing to Jonker. The Afrikaner tribe was stronger than the Herero, therefore it was their land.

'If the "Little Father", as you call him, were removed from Otijimkandje and the Herero left, what would happen to their village?'

Jonker tried to understand in which direction the conversation was travelling.

'I might bring in more Bergdamas to work the mine at Sesebe, or send for my brother to bring his tribe up from the south. But I cannot do this. The Little Father will not leave Otjimkandje.'

'But if he did', William Thackeray persisted, 'would you ask for another missionary from my church to take his place there?'

'Why? If every tribe has an English missionary, they, too, can speak to the Great Father in Cape Town.'

'If you can persuade other chiefs to ask for English missionaries, I will pass their requests on to the correct authority in the Cape. I will tell them they have been asked for because of your great influence over all other chiefs. I will make it clear that because of this great influence there must be no risk of offending Chief Jonker of the Afrikaners. His missionary must be chief of all other missionaries just as he is chief of all chiefs.'

Jonker put his bottle down on the floor carefully and looked at William Thackeray with new respect. He had never before met a missionary with ambitions that went much farther than persuading the village women to cover up breasts that only the missionary himself gazed at with undue interest. This man was different. He was a double-ended assegai, to be handled with care.

'The Little Father has been many years with Tjamuene's people. He would not leave them.'

'But what if I could persuade the Cape government to recall him?'

Jonker was puzzled. 'Why would they do that? Even I know the Little Father has done no wrong.'

'Leave that to me, Chief Jonker. It can be arranged, I assure you.'

The Afrikaner tried to discover more.

'All the white men would leave, too?'

'Yes, they, too, would go.'

'And the white woman? She would leave, too?'

'No. She would stay.'

The answer came too quickly, and Chief Jonker reached for his bottle again. This missionary had the weaknesses of all the white men the Afrikaner chief had ever known. He would not prove invincible. Jonker knew how to control such men.

'It will not be easy to persuade the other chiefs.'

'I did not say it would be easy. Neither should it be hurried. Until it's done you can help me by proving to your own people that you are happy to have a missionary with you again. I will expect you to be at my church every Sunday. We will speak again, Chief Jonker.'

William Thackeray smiled at the slightly bemused chief. 'I'm quite sure our association is going to be both happy and fruitful.'

Jonker nodded and as the door closed behind his missionary he leaned back on his bed thoughtfully. He had got his missionary – one who had brought with him the possibility of more influence with the Cape government than Jonker had dreamed of. Yet the Afrikaner chief was not happy. This man was seeing beyond a hill that had not yet been climbed and planning his own schemes for his own reasons. Jonker was used to having ambitious men about him, but they had always been men whose aims fell short of his own. If they went beyond a certain limit, he would have them killed. This missionary might prove more troublesome. He would have to be watched to ensure he did not gain too much authority.

If he did . . . ? Jonker sighed and poured more brandy down his throat. The missionary was still a man. He needed air to breathe and blood to keep him alive. Men of the Church had a great way with words. They wielded them as a warrior might wield a spear. But Jonker had always found the spear and the gun to be weapons of greater finality.

The Afrikaner chief smiled. He was no longer a young man but he would still be chief of the tribe when William Thackeray was no more than a vague memory for them. Yet he liked some of the things the missionary had said. If the Herero could be removed from Otjimkandje, Jonker would make quite sure their cattle did not leave with them. They would buy him much needed trade credit. Jacobus Albrecht was particularly well disposed towards trade in cattle and he was not fussy from whence they had come. It was a pity he had fallen out with the trader Aaron. The Afrikaners were hard on their weapons and at least half of their guns were no longer serviceable. But Jonker believed their differences would quickly be smoothed over. It had been necessary to show Aaron that being so friendly with the Herero did not meet with his approval. Such friendship could carry with it no profit for the Jew.

By morning Aaron's wagon and its escort of Hereros were far enough from the main trail to be safe from prying eyes. The Hereros had carried out their task well. Using blankets, they had carefully erased the tracks of men and wagon. There was nothing left for a curious Afrikaner to follow, and no one was likely to stumble across the tracks now. Aaron was taking the wagon across empty land where few men cared to go. It would take longer, and for many miles the strong shoulders of the Herero would be as necessary as oxen to heave the wagon wheels through the miles of soft sand, but it would be safe.

'How will the boat know when to expect us?' asked Mutjise as they rested among endless hot sand dunes.

'I sent word for them to meet me,' replied the bearded trader. 'I know that was before I set out for Whalefish Bay and we'll be a day or two late unless we can make it up by coming straight across country, but Captain Klopper will probably wait. He's done good business with me in the past.'

'What happens if he doesn't wait?'

Aaron's shrug successfully hid his inner feelings. 'Then we'll all have had a wasted journey and I will have to go north to Whalefish Bay and hope Chief Jonker isn't there to steal this load.'

It took fifteen gruelling days to reach their destination — fifteen days of toiling beneath a scorching sun, heaving the wagon up sand slopes so soft that the wagon wheels sank in to axle depth, then sliding down the far side, the wagons going down backwards so that men and oxen could hold them back. More than once they ended in a tangled heap at the bottom of the slope and had to right the wagon and repack the load.

But their perseverance paid off. When they topped the last rise and looked down upon the blue sea of a sheltered cove there was a small sailing vessel riding at anchor with sails furled not a hundred yards from the shore. The small crew were enjoying their unaccustomed leisure by swimming between the ship and the sandy beach.

'You and your men stay here,' Aaron said to Mutjise. 'When guns are being traded the fewer men who know where they're going the better it is for everyone. Tongues can't wag about things they don't know.'

Aaron took the wagon carefully down the slope, and some of the sailors came up to meet him and helped him get the wagon the last few yards on to the firm sand of the beach. There the captain of the small vessel was waiting.

'You've taken your time getting here, Aaron. Another day and I would have had to sail. It doesn't do to stay in a place like this for too long. There's been a naval frigate nosing along the coast, heading north. If we'd still been here when it came back, I'd as likely as not have had a longboat in to see what I was doing. There's a cargo on board that I don't want the likes of them knowing about.'

'Then you've got guns with you, Cap'n Klopper? Good guns I'm looking for, mind. None of your old useless flintlocks.'

'I've got some of each – but where's the rest of your wagons? I was told you'd been up to Lake Ngami and brought back some prime trade goods.'

A look of pain crossed Aaron's face.

'And so I did,' he growled. 'I was on my way to you, coming along the Whalefish Bay road, when Chief Jonker stopped me and stole most of it. Two wagonloads of good tusks and ostrich feathers.'

'Leaving you to bring me the rubbish he didn't want, I suppose?'

'Now, how many years have we done business, Cap'n Klopper? Have I ever tried to trade you rubbish? No, in this wagon I've got good ivory with a few pair topping two hundred and fifty pounds – and there are enough ostrich feathers to make your fortune in England. I kept this load back in my store and brought it out in the dead of night. I've travelled with it across country where no ox-wagon should have to go. That's why it's taken me so long to get here.'

'Hm!' Captain Klopper had known Aaron for enough years to recognise the truth. 'It seems to me high time someone singed the beard of this Afrikaner chief.'

'One day that might well happen, Captain. Sooner than Jonker realises. Now, get your men to help me with this canvas and we'll get down to business. How much are your guns this trip? You've brought plenty of power and shot?'

'More than one wagonload of trade goods will buy, Aaron. Guns are hard to come by. Prices are high.'

'But my credit? That's good, surely?' The wily old Jew knew better than to let Captain Klopper know just how desperately he needed credit at this time.

Captain Klopper shook his head. 'No credit this trip, Aaron. The Navy's getting too nosy – and your Afrikaner chief could meet up with you on your way back. We're neither of us a good enough risk for credit to be given on either side.'

Aaron said no more about it, and the two men got down to the ritual of hard bargaining. The Jew threw up his hands in mock disgust at the type of guns he was being offered, and Captain Klopper found imaginary cracks and splinters in the first-class ivory Aaron was trading.

Finally both men reached agreement and the deal was sealed with a clasp of hands and a bottle of good brandy.

It was almost dark when the last boatload of ivory was rowed out to the ship. Not until then did Aaron signal for Mutjise and his men to come down to the beach and help him to load the guns and powder on to the wagon. Even as the Hereros reached the beach the sails of the small ship were unfurling, and the clatter of its anchor chain tumbling into the chain locker rang out loud across the still water.

'You have many guns for us?' Mutjise and his men could not hide their excitement at the sight of the weapons.

'Enough.' Aaron was pleased with the results of his bartering.

'And you will teach us how to use them on the way back to Otjimkandje?'

'I'll teach you how to use them, but there won't be enough powder to make anyone an expert shot—not if you want to save any of it.'

'It must be saved. One day soon we will need to use it against Chief Jonker and his Afrikaners.'

'That's your business, and I don't want to know about it. Let's get the wagon loaded and over that ridge before we camp for the night. There's a British Navy ship around, and if they see our fires they might send men ashore to check on us. We can do without that kind of trouble. Let's have everyone with his shoulder to the wagons. Come on, heave! Up we go!'

Aaron cracked his long whip over the backs of the oxen, and the wagon creaked away from the sea's edge.

Later that night, the wagon safely away from the shore, Aaron sat eating with the Hereros.

'Why are you doing this for my people—getting guns for us and risking trouble with Jonker?'

Mutjise asked the question that had been with him for some days.

'Because I'm a trader. I get people what they want and take the goods I want in exchange. From you I will be getting cattle.'

'But we can only give you a few cattle at a time, so Jonker will not be suspicious. You could trade with him and he would pay you more with other things. He could even take all our cattle and give them to you now. I know he will try to do it one day.'

Aaron thought before answering. Mutjise was an intelligent man. He would know if Aaron tried to lie to him. But the trader was not certain of his own reasons for trading with the Herero. He urgently needed money or goods to pay off an outstanding debt to Jacobus Albrecht. Had he traded with Jonker it would have brought him greater — and quicker — profit. But so would the goods Jonker had stolen from him. Had Aaron been able to bring three wagons to Captain Klopper instead of only one he would have received guns for Mutjise and enough gold to pay Albrecht what he owed him.

'I have always tried to be an honest trader,' said the Jew eventually. 'I drive a hard bargain, yes. I deal in goods that are sometimes forbidden for political reasons. Yet I have never made a promise I have not kept and no man can claim he has been cheated by Aaron. Because of this I have no liking for a man who cheats and robs because he believes himself too strong to be stopped. Jonker has driven the Herero from their homes and scattered them over the land until only your father's people remain. The Herero are a persecuted tribe. The Jews, too, are a people without a land. We have much in common, you and I, Mutjise. The difference between us is that you have a chance to fight back and regain your lands. If I can help you to do that and defeat that thief Jonker, I will be happy.'

Mutjise had watched the heavily bearded Jew's face throughout the whole of his quiet speech. When it ended he nodded, satisfied.

'We will beat Jonker, and there will always be trade for you with my people. You will not lose because of your help to the Herero.'

'Good!' Aaron became the efficient trader once more. 'When I have some more trade goods sent up from Whalefish Bay your warriors must take me to Lake Ngami again. On the way back we'll take the wagons overland direct to the coast without returning to Sesebe. We'll all beat Chief Jonker in our own ways.'

CHAPTER SEVEN

Although he had been hoping to enjoy Hannah's company, Daniel was delighted when Josh suggested they went off together on a hunt.

'I'd like to leave Kasupi behind just this once,' said Josh. 'It's doubtful if Jonker will make a move while Hugo is in Otjimkandje but, if he does, Kasupi can come and find us.'

Daniel accepted this, and father and son set off early in the morning with Miriam and Hannah waving them on their way.

'I hope Josh is right and Jonker doesn't pay us another visit,' said Miriam, trying to take her mind off the real reason for the hunting trip as Daniel and Josh disappeared from view.

'I've go my rifle already in my room just in case,' said Hannah, smiling. 'How long do you think they'll be away?'

'I don't know.'

For an instant Miriam sounded so unhappy that Hannah looked at her quickly.

'Is something wrong?'

When Miriam seemed not to hear Hannah said, 'Please tell me. Is there something I can do to help?'

Miriam escaped from her thoughts. 'No, child. A fifteen-year-old in this country has enough troubles of her own without taking on others.'

Hannah's smile had a trace of sadness of her own this time. 'I'm not fifteen anymore, Mrs Retallick. I was sixteen yesterday.'

Miriam was instantly full of remorse, her own cares temporarily forgotten. 'Oh, Hannah! I'm so sorry. Why didn't you say something? I could at least have baked a special cake for you. To think your birthday passed without so much as a "happy birthday" wish from a single person.'

'I didn't mind,' Hannah lied. In fact the thought of it had lain inside her like a lead weight throughout the whole day. 'I nearly forgot it myself. Nobody here knows, and father began to forget it years ago when mother died and we came from the Cape. He had a lot of worries then.'

In a sudden unthinking statement that bared her soul Hannah

added, 'It's no fun remembering a birthday if no one else does.'

'Then we'll make certain this one doesn't pass entirely un-remembered. When Daniel and Josh return we'll have a special birthday tea. That's a promise, now.'

The mention of her two men brought back thoughts of William Thackeray, and Miriam lapsed once more into a deep silence.

'I wish you would share your unhappiness with me. Something is troubling you very much. What is it?'

Hannah had spent most of her life with only her father for company. She had never learned the subtleties needed to wheedle secrets from other women. Miriam found her directness disconcerting. It was impossible to sidestep the girl's blunt questions.

'It's nothing you can help with, Hannah. Something from the past has caught up with me — something that should have remained forgotten for all time.'

'Is it a very bad thing?'

'Yes.'

'Does it affect Daniel?'

'Very much, and it's him I'm particularly worried about. It's a secret his father and I have had to live with for many years; but Daniel knows very little about our lives before we came to Otjimkandje.'

'It doesn't mean Daniel will go away from here, does it?'

Hannah accepted that Miriam was not going to tell her the nature of the trouble that had caught up with the Retallick family. The most she could hope for was to learn about its probable effect.

'I doubt it. Where is there for him to go?'

Miriam looked at the tall and attractive Jewish girl. 'You seem very concerned for Daniel. Don't tell me you've grown fond of him?'

'I don't know.' Hannah looked honestly at Miriam. 'I've never met anyone else of my own age before. I'm not sure how I feel about him.'

'H'm! Well, I'm glad you're here, Hannah. Daniel will need someone he can talk to when he and his father return.'

*

After a day of hard riding Josh saw a small herd of gemsbok in the distance, recognisable by their grey bodies and long straight horns. They were moving away slowly, but the two men followed for more than thirty minutes without gaining on them. Then Daniel called to Josh and, jumping from his horse, examined a couple of distinctive paw-marks in the soft ground.

'Lion,' he said. 'I don't think we're the only ones after the gemsbok.'

'The lion is probably hungrier than we are,' said Josh. 'We'd better find a good place to camp before it gets dark and get a good fire going.'

Daniel nodded his agreement. 'And we'll tether the horses tonight.'

There were no rocks near them but plenty of thorn-bushes, and they used them to build a loose stockade about themselves and the horses, hoping it was high and wide enough to deter a hungry lion.

'This reminds me of our early days in Africa,' said Josh as they ate beside a crackling fire. 'We were never quite sure just how frightened of fire the wild animals were, but a good fire always made life seem more cheerful. You won't remember those times, Daniel; you were much too young. I'm talking about the weeks before we reached Otjimkandje. We were marooned in a strange country – exactly where we didn't know. We weren't even sure where we were hoping to get to. It was sheer luck that took us to Otjimkandje, and good luck too. We've all been happy there.'

'You've never said much about those early days, Pa. I know about the shipwreck – *Pride of Liverpool*, wasn't she? – and a little about our trek across the mountains to where Mutjise found us. But everything I know I've learned from Sam. You've never told me anything.'

Josh could not have wished for a more opportune moment to tell Daniel what needed to be said, but it was not going to come easily. His throat felt dry, and his heart was making noisy work of pumping blood around his body.

'There is a reason for that, Daniel. There are some things I hoped never to have to tell you, things I dismissed from my mind for many years and would dearly love to forget for ever.'

Daniel was puzzled; but Josh had his full attention, and now he had started the story the words came a little easier.

'One of them was that I joined *Pride of Liverpool* as a convict.' Josh looked into the fire and not at his son. 'I wasn't in chains — I wasn't even locked up — but that was only because I had a good friend in Cornwall. He got me sent out on a special ship bound for Australia because it carried some engines I was meant to assemble and work there. It was he who put you and your mother on the same boat with me.'

Josh glanced up and saw the disbelief on his son's face.

'It's true, Daniel. I was sentenced by an English court to be transported for life for being a party to treason and sedition.'

'Why?' It came out as little more than a hoarse whisper. 'What did you do?'

'I did nothing more than try to stop a crowd of foolish miners from fighting with soldiers for something they believed to be a just cause.'

'But, if you did nothing wrong, why were you sentenced to transportation?'

It was the cry of a young man who desperately wanted to believe his father.

'I was trapped by another man's ambitions, Daniel — a man who planned that I should be present when the miners started fighting with the military, not only present but in their midst. It didn't matter that I was calling on them not to be fools, to return to their houses. I was there for everyone to see. The Court of Assize said I was their leader and had organised the whole thing. There were some who believed in my innocence and a few — your mother was one — who knew I had done nothing wrong, but they could not convince the court.'

There was relief in Daniel's face. 'Well, nobody knows about it here, do they? So it doesn't matter anymore. Why have you told me after all this time?'

'Because there is more to the story, Daniel. Someone has arrived here who *does* know about it and was very much involved in what happened then.'

This was going to be the most difficult part of all and, try as he would, Josh could not keep emotion from affecting his voice.

'Your mother and I were sweethearts from the time we were

twelve years of age. During all the years I spent away from home learning to be a engineer she waited for me, knowing we would be married when I returned and was earning enough money to keep a wife. I came back to her, but then something terrible happened. Her father had too much to drink and attacked a girl. . . .'

Josh deliberately over-simplified this part of his story. Miriam's father had been a drunken bully who viciously raped a young widow in Josh's own home.

'A party of miners led by my father went after him, and he was killed. It was an accident, but the truth of that doesn't matter anymore. Your mother never believed it to be an accident — and she saw it happen. She was so upset she hardly knew what she was doing. She turned away from me to the one good friend she had, the man who had given us both our schooling — a preacher.'

Josh had to make a big effort not to mumble what had to be said next. The result was that it tumbled out louder than he had intended.

'Your mother was so upset that she married that preacher, Daniel. Even though she was carrying you — my child—at the time. It didn't take either of us long to realise what a terrible mistake we had both made. Even then we tried to behave honourably. For three years you were brought up as the preacher's own son. Then he plotted to have me falsely accused of treason, and stood back and said nothing when he could have proved my innocence.'

Josh was perspiring as though he had been working hard in the heat of the midday sun, the palms of his hands wet as he clasped and unclasped them.

'Not until then did we flout the laws of the Church and come together again on *Pride of Liverpool*, bound for Australia. A convict and his family.'

Josh drew in a deep breath. 'The shipwreck, terrible though it was, meant a new start for us, Daniel; a new life in a country where no one would know of my past — or so I thought; a chance to live as a free man and for us to become a family. It worked, Daniel. We've had fourteen good years. I've got a wife I love very much and a son I am proud of.'

The fire had burned low while Josh was talking, and he could not see Daniel's face.

'Now you know my secret, the reason why I've avoided talking about the past.'

'This man who had you sent to prison, the man' – Daniel could not bring himself to say the words – 'the preacher you have been talking about. He's come here as Jonker's missionary, hasn't he? He's the man you went to see?'

'Yes.'

'What's his name?'

'Thackeray. William Thackeray.'

'So my name is really Daniel Thackeray.'

It came out as a flat statement that hit Josh and hurt more than any physical blow could have done.

'No! You're Daniel Retallick. My son.'

'Why haven't you told me about this before? Why?'

There was a fierce anguish in Daniel's voice.

'There was no need. I thought there would never be any reason why you should know.'

'But I had a right to know. Something like this shouldn't have been kept from me for ever.'

'Your mother and I believed otherwise, Daniel. I wouldn't have told you now had it not been for William Thackeray's arrival at Winterhoek. As it is I'd rather you heard it from me than from a stranger.'

Daniel made no reply, and they sat in silence for some minutes. Then Josh began to pile wood on to the low fire.

'Don't allow William Thackeray to ruin our lives again, Daniel. This will have come as a great shock to you and I'm sorry it was necessary for you to learn about it, but it doesn't alter the way I and your mother feel about the life the three of us have had together. It's been a good life. We're a happy loving family and we'd do the same again if we had to. I hope you'll be able to agree with us when you've had time to think about things.'

Daniel did not say another word that night. When Josh woke in the dark hours before daybreak the fire had been made up and he knew Daniel had lain awake all night. He wanted to say something to him but held back. It was up to Daniel to make the next move.

The silence continued into the morning, and Daniel avoided meeting Josh's eyes as they ate their breakfast. When it was finished Daniel saddled up his horse before kicking out the remains of the fire.

When he did speak it was the thick slurred speech of a man who has not slept and is tired.

'This hunting trip was just an excuse to get me out of Otjim-kandje so you could tell me about William Thackeray, wasn't it?'

'I wanted us to be alone when I told you. I knew it wasn't going to be easy for either of us.'

'Does that mean you don't want to shoot any fresh meat?' Daniel's interruption was devoid of emotion.

'We could use it. Why?'

Daniel pointed to westward of the camp. 'There's a small herd of eland over there. They'll have the sun in their eyes, and we could get one before they wake up to the fact that we're about.'

'Then what are we waiting for? Get after them.'

Josh was relieved to have something else to think about. He hurriedly stowed away the remainder of the breakfast things and saddled his horse while Daniel rode off to stalk the great humped antelope.

Even when he had cleared everything away and swung on to his horse Josh hung back to watch his son hunting, proud of his calm efficiency. Daniel loaded and primed his gun during his first cautious advance. Then he and his horse disappeared into a wide depression and came out of it at a gallop not fifty yards from the eland.

The startled antelope barely had time to kick up their heels before Daniel brought his horse to a slithering halt, the gun already to his shoulder.

He fired, and one of the six-feet-tall animals somersaulted in its tracks, sending up a cloud of pale orange dust as it thudded down in the earth.

The animal had stopped twitching by the time Josh reached it.

'That was a first-class shot,' he said. 'I can't remember ever seeing a better.'

222

Daniel nodded his head in acknowledgement of the well-earned praise, and Josh said no more.

The eland must have weighed a thousand pounds and cutting it up proved to be a major task. When it was completed and the horses fully laden the two riders turned their faces towards Otjimkandje.

Apart from a casual necessary remark they did not speak on the return journey. They arrived in the Herero village soon after dark, and an envious Kasupi helped them to carry the meat into the house.

'You've never seen a shot like the one that Daniel brought down this eland with,' said Josh when they were inside the house. 'I don't think there's another man in Hereroland who could have equalled it.'

Daniel's lack of reaction to the praise was not lost on Miriam. She looked to Josh quickly, and he nodded his head.

Miriam understood and pretended not to notice her son's silence.

'Well! With all that fresh meat we've got double cause for celebration. You'll never guess the secret Hannah kept from us. The day before yesterday was her birthday, and she never said a word about it. I've spent all day baking cakes and tarts. I'll invite Hugo Walder and we'll have a special birthday meal to-night for Hannah. It's not every day a girl is sixteen.'

'Fancy not telling us a thing like that! Happy birthday, Hannah.' Josh kissed the young Jewish girl on the cheek.

But Hannah was waiting for some response from Daniel. It never came.

'Here, I'll give you a hand with that.'

Josh went to the assistance of Kasupi, who was struggling into the house with the hindquarters of the eland.

Daniel turned away and walked out of the house, and Hannah followed him.

'Is something the matter, Daniel? Can I help?'

'No.'

He had not intended it to sound so harsh and abrupt, but that was the way it came out. He stood by his horse making un-necessary adjustments to a stirrup.

'Why are you and your mother so unhappy, Daniel? Please

223

let me do something to help.'

'It's nothing. Nothing at all.'

Gripping the pommel of his saddle, Daniel swung himself up on to the horse.

'Daniel! You're not going? My birthday treat—'

'I'm not hungry.'

He knew she was hurt and at that moment he hated himself for causing it, but he could not stay in the house for any celebration. Not tonight. Savagely he jerked the horse's head around and kicked his heels into its flanks.

'Daniel . . . where are you going?'

Ignoring the plaintive call from the darkness, Daniel shook out the reins and urged his already tired horse to a gallop.

He had nothing planned, but when the hoofs of his horse struck the hard-packed earth of the road he turned on it and headed for Sesebe.

'Josh, you'd better go after him before he does something silly,' said Miriam.

Josh listened to the sound of the horse's hoofs fading away into the night and shook his head. 'I'd like to go after him, but this is something he's got to work out for himself.'

He felt weary and heavy-hearted. The trip and the talk with his son had taken a lot out of him. He felt it had all been in vain. Aware of a silent figure standing in the darkness beyond Miriam he said, 'Didn't you say it was someone's birthday? Come along. Hannah. Let's enjoy your birthday meal. Perhaps Daniel will come back later.'

Daniel did not come back and the meal was a dismal affair. The three adults managed to find small presents for the girl and Hugo Walder told amusing stories of his recent trip to Cape Town, putting on his most jocular manner, but the shadow of Daniel's absence hung over the table like a pall.

A mile from Otjimkandje, Daniel slowed his horse to a walk. It had been a hard day for the animal, returning from the hunt with a double load before this final gallop. Daniel patted its neck reassuringly, and the horse dropped its head and blew through its nostrils. At Sesebe Daniel would put it into the stables and bed it down for the night.

The thought of Hannah and the manner in which he had left her standing outside the house came back to him. He had ruined her 'party' and he was not proud of his actions.

Then he thought of what his father had told him. . . .

His father? Even that was no longer a straightforward fact. The whole foundation on which his life had been built had crumbled away.

Then Daniel thought of the tension in his father's voice when he was telling him of those years back in Cornwall, and a feeling of deep remorse swept over him. It could not have been an easy thing to talk about. They must have been difficult years. And his mother? What torment must she have suffered?

For a moment Daniel thought of turning around and going back to Otjimkandje. It was then, although he did not realise it, that Daniel took an important step towards accepting the things he had been told and understanding the very difficult situation. He had managed to break through the barrier of his own self-pity.

His thoughts were disturbed by the sound of pounding hoofs coming from Otjimkandje. He pulled his horse off to one side of the road, and the rider was almost upon him before the starlight gave both horses away.

'Daniel, is that you?'

It was Kasupi.

'Yes, it's me.'

The presence of his friend brought back much of Daniel's earlier mood. It was a simple defensive reaction. He had wanted to sort out the confusion that was in his mind before having to converse with others.

'You left in a great hurry. Where are you going?'

'To Sesebe.'

'At this time of night and after a hunting trip? Why?'

'Because I feel like a drink.'

Daniel kneed his horse forward, urging it to a trot, thus making conversation difficult.

Kasupi brought his horse alongside Daniel's to avoid the dust it was kicking up. He did not attempt to speak again but he believed Daniel would probably have need of him later tonight. It would take a great deal of brandy to drown the unhappiness that fought within him.

The Miners' Inn was well patronised. Smoke from the miners' pipes rose above a dozen plank tables and swirled lazily around the ceiling like a heavy rain-cloud.

A number of men called to Daniel as he went into the inn, and he accepted an invitation to join a young miner named Simon van der Byl who sat at one of the tables farthest from the door. Van der Byl was only a year older than Daniel and had been one of the latest miners to reach Sesebe, coming overland with his father, who was also a miner.

The talk here was chiefly of mines and mining, but they all showed interest in Daniel's latest hunting trip.

'Only a day's ride away, you say,' said one of the men. 'What wouldn't I give for the taste of fresh eland meat.'

His words were echoed by a number of other miners, and Simon van der Byl said, 'There's a great opportunity for you, Daniel. Bring back fresh game meat to Sesebe and you'll be able to name your own price for it.'

The idea appealed to Daniel. 'All right. I'll bring you fresh meat. You'll have all you want the next time I come in here.'

'Ha! They'll have to send someone out to find you first.'

There was a sudden hush at the table, and Daniel swung around in his chair to face Jacobus Albrecht. The big Boer trader stood with a bottle in his hand.

'I found my way home, Mr Albrecht. As I remember it you were the one who got lost.'

Someone laughed, but the sound was hurriedly broken off and nobody else joined in.

Jacobus Albrecht flushed angrily. 'When I hire a guide I expect him to know where he's going and not leave me when the going gets tough.'

Now it was Daniel's turn to look angry.

'If you and your Afrikaners hadn't been so eager to kill Bushmen and rape their women, we wouldn't have been lost – and we would have got to Lake Ngami.'

There was a murmur of interest from the miners. Not all of them were from Boer stock and a few of the newer arrivals had some sympathy for the little men. A human life was not something to be taken lightly, in their opinion — and neither was a woman.

'Agh! Kaffir-boetje.'

With this Boer expression Jacobus dismissed Daniel from his thoughts and sat down with two other men at the next table.

Their presence sent Daniel back into his earlier mood and he drank in brooding silence.

To Kasupi, who waited outside, things did not look good. Had Daniel merely become hopelessly drunk Kasupi would have carried him to Sam Speke at Aaron's store, but with Jacobus Albrecht at the next table he feared trouble. There was nothing he could do about it. The inn was for white men only. Neither Herero nor Afrikaners were allowed inside. All Kaspui could do was make himself comfortable outside the window and prepare for a long wait.

The Boer trader was not allowing the presence of Daniel Retallick to spoil his enjoyment. He was as noisy as Daniel was silent.

The trader had been drinking for about an hour when someone at his table brought the talk around to Aaron and his store.

'It's a beautiful building, Jacobus. A man could fight off an army from in there. Why don't you build one like it?'

'What for? The Afrikaners are the only fighting kaffirs around here, and Jonker wouldn't turn on me. If he did, he'd get no brandy and starve to death.'

When the laughter died down the Boer said, 'Anyway, I'll have Aaron's store before too long. You wait and see.'

'How will you manage that, Jacobus? Buy him out, eh?'

'I won't have to pay anything. He'll give it to me. Just as he's going to give me that daughter of his, in spite of her high and mighty ways.'

Daniel's half-filled glass stopped in mid-air.

'Give you his daughter? Away with you, man! What would you do with his daughter, Jacobus? You're too bloody old, man!'

The speaker nudged the men on either side of him, and their ribald laughter made Daniel grit his teeth angrily.

'What do you think I'll do with his daughter? The same as I do with any other woman. I'll take her to bed and knock the backside off her. I'll show you whether I'm too old or not. She'll never wear those denim trousers for riding again. One night with me and she'll find it too painful to sit it on a horse. I tell you, man—'

Daniel's pent-up temper exploded from him. Standing up, he turned and hurled the contents of his glass into Jacobus Albrecht's face.

'You've got a filthy tongue, Albrecht. Keep it for talking about your Afrikaner women—if they'll have you.'

Kasupi disappeared from the window. He had seen enough.

Jacobus went pale for a few seconds. As the blood rushed back to his face he took a dirty handkerchief from his pocket and carefully wiped the drink from around his eyes. Not until they were dry did he look up at Daniel.

'You've got a bit above yourself, young man. You've been around your Herero for so long you've come to think of yourself as a man. I'll have to teach you otherwise.'

Slowly and deliberately the Boer stood up and tucked the handkerchief inside his pocket.

Simon van der Byl jumped up and tried to push his way between Albrecht and Daniel. 'He didn' mean anything by his talk, Mr Albrecht. He's had too much drink like the rest of us. He'll apologise in the morning.'

'Of course he will,' called another voice. 'He's only a boy, Jacobus.'

'Boys are like Kaffirs,' said the Boer trader. 'They have to be taught to hold their tongues in the presence of their betters.'

He pushed Simon van der Byl to one side without taking his eyes from Daniel. 'You might be having second thoughts now, eh, boy? Thinking perhaps you heard wrong? Well, you didn't. I was talking about Aaron's daughter Hannah. I said I'll have her and that by the time I've finished with her she'll be as slack as a calving Afrikaner cow.'

Daniel's right fist swung in a great arc towards Jacobus Albrecht's face. It missed. So did the left that followed, and the next right swing.

The Boer trader smiled mockingly. 'Wish you'd kept your mouth shut now, boy? Is this what you're trying to do?'

His fist smashed on to Daniel's nose, and blood spattered in a wide circle on the floor about him.

'Or was it this?'

Albrecht's next punch took Daniel hard on the side of his face, knocking him to the ground, the room gyrating about him. He rose to one knee and spat out a tooth. Albrecht's face was somewhere in the haze above him and he lunged to his feet, arms flailing. He felt his fists strike home. Once, twice. Then a fist crashed into his face again, and Daniel went backwards over a table, lost in a world filled with brilliant coloured stars.

Again he rose to one knee, and this time it was one of Jacobus Albrecht's boots that sent him back to the floor again. Another kick as he lay on the ground broke two ribs – but by now Daniel was not aware of anything that was happening to him.

Sam Speke was woken by a mighty hammering on the door of the store.

'Who is it? What do you want at this time of night?'

'Come quickly. Daniel and Jacobus Albrecht are fighting. Hurry!'

Throwing the blankets from himself and his startled wife Mary, Sam Speke paused only to put on a pair of trousers. Pulling back the heavy bolts on the door, he flung it open and sprinted barefooted after Kasupi.

He arrived at the Miners' Inn just in time to see Jacobus Albrecht's second kick land in Daniel's ribs. Men went sprawling to either side as the burly ex-seaman pushed his way through them to where the Boer trader stood over the prostrate Daniel. He reached Albrecht in time to knock him off balance as he drew back his foot for another vicious kick.

The trader staggered among the watching miners, and they stopped him from falling. Recovering his balance, he saw who it was who had pushed him.

'Keep out of this, Sam. You and I have no quarrel.'

Sam Speke looked down at Daniel and saw the blood pouring from his shattered nose and trickling from the corner of his mouth. Anger rose like bile in his throat.

'What's the matter, Jacobus? Do you only fight children?'

'He started it – ask anyone. He struck out at me first.'

'There was no need to beat him the way you have. You

goaded him on to hit you first.' Simon van der Byl spoke the words, and there was a murmur of agreement from others.

For the first time Jacobus Albrecht realised he was in the midst of a hostile crowd. 'He started it,' he repeated.

Daniel groaned, and Sam Speke said to the men about him, 'Get him over to the store. I've a mind to finish what he started.'

'I've no quarrel with you, Sam,' Jacobus Albrecht repeated.

Stepping across Daniel's unconscious body, the angry Sam Speke brought a short powerful punch up on to the Boer trader's mouth. 'Now say we have no quarrel,' he said.

Jacobus Albrecht took two backward steps on his heels and wiped the back of a hand across his lips. It came away smeared with blood.

'You'll regret that,' he roared and lurched forward angrily. He walked straight into another powerful punch to the head. But his momentum carried him forward and he found himself wrapped in Sam Speke's powerful arms. It was a rib-crushing hold, and when the trader tried to shout it came out as no more than a faint breathless gasp. The more he struggled the tighter Sam Speke held him, constricting Albrecht's ribs, crushing all the strength from him.

Sam Speke had been involved in many seamen's brawls during his sea service and his name was known in the ports of the world for this one hold. He had more than once hugged a man to him until he lost consciousness.

But he had no intention of letting Jacobus Albrecht off so lightly. Daniel would always have an irregularity in his nose to remind him of his beating. Sam Speke had decided that Jacobus Albrecht would carry a similiar reminder.

At the moment the trader began to go limp in his arms Sam Speke released one arm and swung Albrecht around. He propelled him through the onlookers like a battering ram. Had the rough wooden wall been of a less stout construction Jacobus Albrecht's head would have gone straight through that too. As it was the trader's face suffered far more damage than the wall. Three times Sam Speke crashed it against the timber, then he released his hold on Albrecht.

The Boer trader dropped to the floor and rolled on to his back, his nose broken in half a dozen places.

Sam Speke looked at the men who crowded around, jostling for view of the trader's face.

'Anyone here got anything to say about what I've just done?'

'Nothing at all, Sam.'

'You did what needed doing, Sam.'

'He had no call to beat the boy the way he did.'

Sam had difficulty in hiding his contempt for them. They were unanimous in their approval of his actions and condemnation of Jacobus Albrecht but not one of them had done anything to prevent the Boer from beating Daniel.

He inclined his head towards the unconscious trader. 'When he comes round tell him if he thinks this isn't finished he knows where to find me.'

Daniel had already been taken to the store, and the crowd of miners parted respectfully as Sam Speke walked to the door and out into the clean air and soft moonlight of the African night.

CHAPTER EIGHT

The following day Sam Speke took Daniel back to Otjimkandje in one of the mine's wagons. He was having trouble breathing owing to the damage to his ribs, and the bruising on his face showed the severity of the beating he had taken.

Sam Speke's twelve-year-old daughter Victoria sat in the back of the wagon with Daniel, constantly bathing his brow with water, breaking off only to turn her head when a paroxysm of coughing took her. When this happened her shoulders hunched forward with pain, and she had to fight to draw in breath. The cough had been with her for a long time, and she was used to it now, but Sam frequently turned around to look at her with great concern.

When the wagon arrived at Otjimkandje, Josh's first reaction was to reach for his gun and go after Jacobus Albrecht. Sam Speke stopped him.

'You'd be doing yourself and Daniel no good, Josh. The thing began and ended last night. I've left Jacobus Albrecht with a face that will remind him of the fight every time he looks into a mirror. Daniel's nose will set. I doubt if Jacobus's will. Anyway, he's already gone from Sesebe – some say to Winterhoek, others to Whalefish Bay.'

'He'd better stay away a long time,' breathed Josh. 'I'm in your debt, Sam.'

'In my debt nothing! When we first got ashore from *Pride of Liverpool* we all shared each other's battles. It's been some years since then, and maybe we haven't seen so much of each other just lately, but I've got a long memory.'

'So have I, Sam, and good friends are all too rare. Come into the house for a while.'

'Later, Josh. As you can see, I brought young Victoria with me. I thought it might be better if she left Sesebe for a while. Jacobus Albrecht might do something to make life difficult there, and I'd like Hugo to have a look at her. She's not a strong girl, and I'm worried about her cough. She's had it a long time, and it's showing no sign of clearing up.'

'I'll tell Hugo,' said Josh. 'And don't worry about her while you're in Sesebe. I know she has plenty of relatives here but I'll keep an eye on her.'

Inside the house Hugo Walder finished examining Daniel. Although never qualifying as a doctor, the missionary had received medical training and had long ago accepted that he was as much of a doctor as they were likely to see for very many years in this part of the world.

He discovered Daniel's broken ribs and bound them up tightly. Gingerly he felt the bone in Daniel's nose between thumb and forefinger.

'He'll always have a bump to show for this little adventure,' he said. 'But it could have been worse. It is his ribs I am more worried about. I can't tell whether one of them might have punctured his lung. You'd better keep him in bed for a week or two, and he'll need careful looking after.'

'Hannah and I will take care of him,' said Miriam. 'But God help Jacobus Albrecht if he ever shows his face around Otjimkandje. I'll shoot him myself.'

'That was the way I felt,' said Josh. 'But it seems Sam has already settled the score for us. From his account I doubt if you'd recognise Albrecht if he did come here.'

'What started the fight?' asked the missionary.

'I don't know.' Josh was evasive.

'Yes, you do.' The assertion came from Hannah. 'It was what Jacobus Albrecht said about me. I overheard Sam Speke telling you. Daniel told Jacobus he had a foul mouth and then hit him when he repeated it.'

Josh cleared his throat noisily. Sam Speke had used seaman's language and been very explicit about what the Boer trader had said about Hannah. 'Er . . . yes, it was something like that.'

'Then the least I can do is to look after him while he's confined to his bed. Will that be all right, Mrs Retallick?'

'Why, yes, Hannah. We'll both look after him, but if you care to take charge of things it will be a great relief to me.'

Miriam would spend just as much time as Hannah fussing about her only son, but the Jewish girl's aggressive determination defied argument – and Aaron was not the only one with ideas about the future of his daughter Hannah and Daniel.

When Josh told Hugo Walder about Sam's young daughter the old missionary had her brought into the house in order that he could examine her. It was here that Hugo Walder came face to face with the inadequacy of his medical knowledge. One did not need to be a doctor to hear her breathing and know there was something seriously wrong with her chest, but the missionary could not give a diagnosis. He did not know what was wrong with her. But her condition was not one that would be as easily resolved as Daniel's.

Hannah turned out to be a devoted and efficient nurse. At night she would leave the door of her room open and, if Daniel did more than turn over in bed, she was up and in his room, satisfying herself he was all right. The fight had created a closer bond between them than Miriam would have dared hope for a few weeks earlier.

It had done something else. Although Daniel would never be able to forget the things he had learned on the hunting trip with his father, they no longer assumed such gigantic proportions in his mind. He now had a long time to think about them and accept much more than he might otherwise have done, much to the relief of Josh and Miriam.

There was another matter on Daniel's mind. Kasupi was a frequent visitor to his room and they had many whispered conversations together. After each of them Hannah was always rather less enthusiastic in her role of nurse, and after the latest meeting she tidied his bed with such scowling abandon that Daniel swore she must have broken at least another two ribs.

'You're lucky I haven't pitched you out on your head,' said Hannah. 'If you and that ne'er-do-well friend of yours want to make arrangements with village girls, then at least have the decency to wait until you're well out of my hearing.'

Daniel only grinned by way of reply. The 'arrangements' with the village girls were not of the kind Hannah imagined.

After a briefer than usual visit by Kasupi, Daniel called Hannah into his room.

'Yes, what do you want?' Hannah's hands were white with flour. 'I'm helping your mother with the cooking.'

'Come here a minute.'

'Daniel, what is it? I really am busy—'

'Come here.'

Hannah advanced into the room cautiously.

'Over here by the bed and close your eyes.'

'Why? Daniel, I've already said—'

Daniel let out an exasperated sigh. 'Will you do as you're told without arguing—just this once?'

Hannah did as she was told.

'Now, mind you keep your eyes tightly closed.'

She felt Daniel's hands go about her neck. It was so unexpected that she almost opened her eyes and only just managed to resist the urge.

Daniel was fastening something beneath her long hair at the back of her neck.

'All right, you can open your eyes now.'

Hannah opened her eyes and gave a gasp of delight. About her neck was a long necklace made up of pieces of delicately carved ivory and mother-of-pearl culminating in a beautiful polished mauve gemstone.

'Daniel, it's beautiful! But why? And where did you get it?'

'It's a late birthday present—to make up for the party I spoiled for you. I had it made specially by some of the women in the village. The stone I found in a river when I was out hunting about a year ago. Now you know all about the arrangements Kasupi and I have been making.'

Unwanted tears sprang to Hannah's eyes. 'Oh, Daniel, it's a lovely present. I've never owned anything so beautiful.'

Sitting down heavily on the bed beside him, she threw her arms about him and kissed him on the mouth.

She felt him wince and was immediately full of concern. 'I'm sorry, Daniel. Did I hurt you?'

Her eyes were very dark, the eyelashes about them very long. For perhaps the first time Daniel realised that Hannah was a very beautiful woman.

Hannah, too, realised that their relationship was undergoing a sudden dramatic change. She saw it in Daniel's eyes and responded to the emotions that rose within her. When Daniel reached out for her she came to him eagerly.

Holding her to him hurt Daniel's ribs, but the real pain went much deeper than that for both of them.

When Hannah returned to the kitchen to show the necklace to Miriam the older woman found the look on Hannah's face of far more interest to her. She recognised it immediately and felt a strange mixture of youth and age stir within her. She had once worn the same look for Josh, when she was even younger than Hannah. She knew the joy and the pain that were part of being in love, the fire and the water that tempered the steel of true love.

Her affectionate hug took Hannah by surprise. 'I'm very happy for you, Hannah.'

'Yes.' The tall dark Jewish girl coloured up. 'It's a birthday present.'

'I know.'

Miriam's fond smile said much more than her words. It said that she knew, as Hannah knew, that the gift was so much more than a birthday present. It explained why Daniel had tackled the Boer trader in the one-sided fight in Sesebe.

Aaron was less far-sighted about their relationship when he returned to Otjimkandje and heard about the fight. To him it spelled instant and total disaster for his business. Unknown to the others he owed Jacobus Albrecht money that was already overdue for payment. He could not tell the Boer trader of the long-term arrangement he had made with Mutjise to receive cattle as payment for the Herero's guns. It was quite certain now that the Boer would not agree to any deferment of a full settlement.

Aaron arrived just before dawn, having travelled as fast and as quietly as possible during the night hours in order to elude Jonker and reach the Herero village before Tjamuene's people awoke.

The guns and kegs of black powder were hurriedly carried into the grass-walled kraal of the chief and hidden away. Aaron did not want to know their exact hiding-place. It was safer for everyone this way.

Josh was puzzled by the unusual time of the party's arrival. In this country men did not travel at night. He said as much to

Aaron, but the Jew passed it off by saying they had hoped to arrive before dusk the previous evening but had run into trouble with the wagon. He said it had not been worthwhile to make camp when they were so close to home.

Although Aaron was tired, he slept for only a couple of hours before rising and going to Sesebe to his store. All was in order there, and Sam Speke was busy building an extension to house his wagon-building workshop.

Harold Andrews had been to speak to Sam, saying he hoped the fight with Jacobus Albrecht would not affect the business relationship between the mining company and Sam. He promised to try to smooth things over with the Boer trader.

Sam Speke promised to carry out any repairs to the wagons owned by Andrews and Albrecht, though he intended trying to build up other business. He would not trust his future to a man whom he had disfigured in such a violent manner.

To Aaron's great relief Jacobus Albrecht was not at Sesebe. But his relief was short-lived. He had hardly put the wagon into the yard behind the store and sent the Herero driver off with the oxen when a messenger arrived from Harold Andrews' office. Jacobus Albrecht was at Winterhoek and had said he wanted to see the Jewish trader as soon as he returned to Sesebe.

Aaron would have liked to put off the evil moment, but it was not his way of dealing with problems. Neither would it have helped. The Boer would know the moment he returned. Deferring the meeting would only make things worse — if such a thing were possible!

The Jewish trader rode to Winterhoek that same afternoon, and a feeling of apprehension overtook him as he topped the pass into the valley and saw Jonker's untidy village sprawled out before him. He was not sure whom he dreaded meeting more, the Afrikaner chief or the Boer trader.

Jacobus Albrecht was not in his store. The European who managed it for him said he was with the new missionary, and the news gave Aaron heart. If he could broach the subject of the money he owed the Boer in the missionary's presence, the Boer trader might be inclined to be more understanding towards Aaron's problems.

His hopes fell when he saw the state of the Boer's face. Even the presence of a missionary could not make a man forget such an injury. Jacobus Albrecht would be out for revenge on everyone even remotely connected with his humiliation – and Aaron knew that Hannah had been at the root of the fight.

Another surprise to Aaron was seeing brandy standing on the table between the two men. It was true William Thackeray did not appear to be drinking very much, but most missionaries were opposed to alcohol on all but the most important occasions.

Jonker's missionary greeted Aaron warmly and motioned him to a chair, pouring him a drink and saying how pleasant it was to meet another trader.

'It's you traders we missionaries depend upon so much to bring the trappings of civilisation to our peoples. It makes a missionary's work much easier when a native can see tangible proof of our words; when he can see that by following our spiritual teachings his whole life can gain materially as well as spiritually.'

Aaron doubted the wisdom of such a sweeping statement. Standing on the table was one of the more doubtful material 'blessings' that traders had brought into the lives of the English missionary's new flock.

'I know I will need to lean heavily on Jacobus's knowledge of Jonker's people,' went on William Thackeray. 'He has traded with the chief for a great many years and knows a great deal about his ways.'

'I know a few of them myself,' said Aaron, thinking unhappily of the two wagonloads of trade good pilfered by the Afrikaner chief.

'Of course,' said William Thackeray. 'I was forgetting that you had traded with him. But most of your business is now with the Herero, is it not?'

'Trade is with whoever has something to sell or something to buy,' said Aaron. 'At the moment Jacobus is in favour with Chief Jonker. Next week it might change again.'

'Next week a lot of things might change,' said Jacobus Albrecht, scowling. He spoke as though he had a heavy cold. 'You owe me some money, Aaron. Where is it?'

The hopes Aaron had entertained of the Boer trader being more reasonable in the presence of the new missionary were dashed by his uncompromising tone of voice.

William Thackeray stood up.

'If you gentlemen are going to talk business, I'll find something else to do. . . .'

'No . . . please. . . .' Aaron still entertained a faint hope that the presence of the missionary might help him. 'It's business, yes – but honest business. Nothing that should not be heard by others.'

'He's right. Sit down, William.' The fact that the two men were on first-name terms was not lost on Aaron. 'This isn't going to take long. Either he has the money or he hasn't. If he can't pay, I've got a little proposition that might involve you professionally.'

'Jacobus, business hasn't been too good lately,' Aaron began his excuses. 'It's picking up now. Picking up well. The Herero are a good people. I'm sure they'll let me have a few cattle in advance for you. I'll pay the remainder of what I owe within three months – maybe two. How will that suit you?'

'It doesn't suit me at all,' growled Jacobus Albrecht nasally. 'The settlement is well overdue now, and I've been a very patient man. Profitable trading doesn't run on promises, Aaron. You should know that. As for business being bad – you've had a good trading trip to Lake Ngami. If you couldn't turn that into a profit, what hopes are there of my ever getting my money from you?'

'It was a good trip,' agreed Aaron. 'The profit would have been there but for Jonker. He took almost everything I had, claiming it as the tribute due to him for allowing me to trade in his lands.'

Jacobus Albrecht shrugged. 'Jonker makes the rules in his own land. Who's to say he won't do the same thing again? No, Aaron. I can't let the debt drag on any longer. You're a bad risk, man.'

'You said you had a proposition,' urged William Thackeray. 'One that might involve me.'

'I did,' agreed the Boer trader. He downed his drink and poured himself another. Then he leaned back in his chair and looked across the table at his Jewish counterpart, giving him an ugly smile. 'You can't pay your debt, Aaron, and as I see it you have two alternatives. One, I take over your store, your wagons, oxen and all your property. It may sound hard to you, but if we were down south that's what would happen. You know it well.'

This was even worse than Aaron had anticipated but nothing showed on his face.

'If your second alternative is as attractive as your first, I can't wait to hear it.'

Jacobus Albrecht stopped smiling and leaned forward across the table, pushing his face closer to the bearded Jewish trader.

'It's much better, Aaron. It's one that no good businessman could possibly refuse. You know how I feel about Hannah. I've mentioned marriage before. Now I'll put it on a businesslike basis. You give her to me and I'll have William marry us right away. Then your debt to me will be wiped out. More, I'll have an agreement drawn up to say that should anything happen to me all my trading assets will come to you. Of course, I'll expect you to have a similar agreement drawn up in my favour.'

He leaned back in his chair again and, carrying his brandy to his mouth, watched Aaron.

'That sounds very generous to me,' murmured William Thackeray. 'Very generous indeed.'

Aaron looked from the Wesleyan missionary to the Boer trader, wondering what these two men could possibly have in common. Had they already discussed this 'business' proposition? Wiliam Thackeray might consider it a generous offer, but it left the most important detail out of the reckoning.

Hannah and her feelings.

'It's an interesting offer,' Aaron said cautiously. 'But I will have to discuss it with Hannah and see what she has to say about it.'

'What for?' Now the traditional Boer attitude to women came out. 'Agh! She's your daughter, man. You tell her what to do. Tell her she's got to marry me. That's all there is to it.'

'I don't do things that way,' said Aaron quietly. 'As you've just said, Hannah is my daughter, not some object in my store. I'll put your proposition to her. If she agrees to marry you, then so be it. If not. . . .' He spread his hand in a habitual gesture.

'You'd better do more than to *ask* her,' said Jacobus Albrecht angrily. 'You go home and *tell* her what to do. I'm not a patient man, Aaron. I've waited long enough for both Hannah and my money. You've got until sunset the day after tomorrow to give me my answer. If you can't persuade her by then, you'd better be out of that store of yours by the following morning. And don't take anything more than you are wearing away with you. Everything else is mine: building, stock, wagons, oxen and horses – the lot.'

Pale-faced, Aaron stood up. 'Thank you for your hospitality, Preacher Thackeray. I'll go now.'

William Thackeray shook the other man's hand and smiled enigmatically. 'It's been a pleasure meeting you, Aaron. I hope you can find a satisfactory solution to your business problems. It would give me much pleasure to conduct a wedding service for your daughter here in my little church.'

The Jewish trader nodded and walked slowly from the hut without a word to Jacobus Albrecht. Aaron felt very old, a feeling accentuated by his sense of failure. He would speak to Hannah, but he was aware of the almost intolerable burden he would be placing upon her. He would be asking her to choose between her own happiness and her father's ruin.

Hugo Walder was very worried about Victoria Speke. Sam had returned to Otjimkandje, and the missionary had examined his daughter for the second time. In the silence of the Herero hut her breathing rasped like a coarse-toothed saw.

'I'll be quite honest with you, Sam. If we were lower down towards the coast where they get the sea mists, or the north where there are the marshlands, I'd say she had lung fever; but I can't believe she would get that up here, or at Sesebe. But she has something seriously wrong with her chest.'

'What do you suggest I should do?'

Sam Speke doted on his little girl. Victoria had brought more happiness into his life than he had ever dreamed possible when he was sailing the oceans of the world.

'I just don't know, Sam,' Hugo Walder admitted. 'I have neither the skill nor the knowledge to treat her. I think you should take her to see a doctor at the Cape, but it would cost money.'

'Money isn't important. Victoria's health is all I care about. I'll go back to Sesebe now and find out when the next boat for the Cape is expected a Whalefish Bay. I'll take Mary and Victoria down there on it.'

'Good. Then I will write a letter of introduction to a very good doctor friend of mine in Cape Town. I am sure he will know what to do to help her.'

Mary, Sam's Herero wife, had been listening to her husband and the German missionary talking but had said nothing. She had already made plans of her own. She would see the man who had always treated her when she had been sick as a child — the man who was called to treat everyone in Otjimkandje, from the newest-born child to Chief Tjamuene. Victoria would receive a visit from the Herero tribal doctor. He would make her well.

Daniel awoke from a late-afternoon sleep to hear the sound of voices and someone sobbing. He knew his mother and father were spending the day at the wedding feast of the oldest son of a village elder. He had thought he and Hannah were alone in the house.

Swinging his feet to the floor, he stood up slowly. His health was much improved now and he spent much of the day out of bed. He considered his afternoon rest to be little more than a concession to Hannah, to keep her in Otjimkandje for as long as possible.

He went quietly towards Hannah's room. The door was partly open, and he had almost reached it when he heard Aaron's voice coming from inside.

'My child, it is a hard decision to make, I know, but it would be a good marriage for you. Jacobus Albrecht is a clever trader — far more successful than your old father.'

Daniel felt as though a chill wind had blown into the house.

'He's not clever. He's ruthless and dishonest. You're not.'

'You may be right, Hannah; but perhaps a man has to be all those things if he is to succeed. That doesn't alter the fact that he's asked for your hand in marriage. You know it isn't the first time. He's wanted to marry you for two years.'

'But I don't want to marry him.'

There was a short pause before Aaron spoke again.

'I owe Jacobus Albrecht a sum of money. It's not great, but it's more than I have or can hope to raise quickly. If it's not paid by the day after tomorrow, he'll take everything I own. The store – everything!'

'Unless I say I'll marry him?'

'He wants more than a promise, Hannah. He expects me to take you to him and go on to the new missionary at Winterhoek to be married right away.'

Hannah began to cry again. 'I don't have any choice, do I? I'm going to have to marry him or see you lose everything you've worked so hard for. I've got to marry him. . . .'

Daniel had heard enough. The thought of Hannah marrying Jacobus Albrecht after the things he had said about her in the Miners' Inn made his skin creep.

Back in his room Daniel dressed hurriedly, ignoring the throbbing pain in his chest. He had fought Jacobus Albrecht once over something that mattered far less then than it did now. He was not going to stand back and do nothing when Hannah's whole future happiness was at stake. There had to be another fight; but this time Jacobus Albrecht would not have the advantage, and the result would be decisive. Daniel picked up his gun from the corner of his room and began to load it carefully.

Had he listened at Hannah's door for a few moments longer Daniel would have heard something to change his whole course of action.

Through her tears Hannah repeated, 'I've got to marry him.'

'No. You don't *have* to marry him.'

Hannah looked up at her father and her misery hurt him more deeply than Jacobus Albrecht ever could. He took her by the shoulders and drew her to him.

'You are more important than anything else I have or have ever had.' He gave a short laugh. 'After all, what will I be giving up? A business that is in debt. Something that will never make a penny piece profit for as long as Jonker is chief of the Afrikaners. No, Hannah. You will not marry Jacobus Albrecht. No ill-mannered Boer is going to take my daughter for his wife.'

Hannah pushed herself away from him. 'But your store? You can't give that up. It's our home. What will we do?'

Aaron shrugged, then managed a smile. 'We'll do what I should have done years ago—move away from this uncivilised place. We'll go somewhere else, to where the standards of our fathers are accepted, where I can work for less profit but with much less risk.

'You know, I have just discovered what a relief your decision is to me. I would never have slept easy in my bed knowing that Jacobus Albrecht would take over my business if I died—and as for having him for a son-in-law . . . !'

Hannah knew he was only trying to make her feel better and she loved him for it.

'You are not fit enough to go hunting.'

Kasupi intercepted the armed Daniel as he made his way to the pens to get his horse.

'Oh, yes, I am.' Daniel ignored the throbbing of his ribs. This was the farthest he had walked since before the fight.

'Where are we going?'

'Mind your own business. I'm hunting alone.'

'No, you are not. I am coming with you, whether you like it or not.'

Kasupi made sure he would not be left behind by catching and saddling his own horse before helping Daniel to throw the saddle on his own unexercised and frisky horse.

'Do you know where Jacobus Albrecht is now?' Daniel asked the Herero.

'Probably at Sesebe. His wagons are there. Why do you ask?'

Daniel made no reply and, climbing on to his horse, set off at a trot. He had not travelled half a mile before the pain from his barely knitted ribs had him gritting his teeth to hide it from his travelling companion.

'We will go hungry if we have to make our meals from the game to be found along this road, Daniel.'

'I'm not hunting for food today.'

'Oh? You rise from a sickbed to hunt for pleasure?'

'No. I hunt for the same reason the Herero hunt the lion that has tasted human flesh—because it is necessary.'

Kasupi was puzzled, 'You seek a lion? There has not been one near Otjimkandje—or Sesebe—for many years.'

'Not a lion, Kasupi. I'm going to kill Jacobus Albrecht.'

Kasupi began a smile, thinking Daniel was joking with him. Then he looked at his friend's face and saw it was not a joke. He gasped in horror. 'You can't kill him, Daniel. It would bring big trouble to everyone – especially to you and your family.'

'Rather that than allow him to marry Hannah.'

Now Kasupi began to understand. He did not know what had prompted this sudden decision to kill the Boer, but if Hannah was at the core of it he knew he would not be able to turn Daniel from his purpose. He had known even before his friend had taken such a beating in defence of her good name that the trader's daughter would one day have a great influence over Daniel's life. He had been aware of Daniel's feelings for her before Daniel himself had known. But Kasupi could not allow Jacobus Albrecht to be killed because of Daniel's love for a girl. This thing had to be stopped before the two men met.

Once again Kasupi thought of Sam Speke.

Without another word he shook out the reins of his horse and kicked the willing animal into a gallop. Realising his friend's intention, Daniel gave chase, but his ribs would not accept the extra strain placed upon them and he was forced to slow his horse to a steadier pace.

Once again Sam Speke's intervention proved speedy and effective, and he stood in the path of Daniel as he slowed his horse to enter Sesebe.

'Out of my way, Sam. I'm here for Jacobus Albrecht. I won't need your help this time.'

'You'll be beyond all help if you go through with this stupidity.'

Daniel's face was white and drawn, and Sam could see he was in great pain. Daniel was not as strong as he had believed, and the ride from Otjimkandje had exhausted him. But he was still very determined.

'Stupid or not, Jacobus Albrecht is not going to marry Hannah.'

'At least we'll agree on that,' said the burly ex-seaman as he reached out and took a hold on the bridle of Daniel's horse. 'Now, what's all this about?'

'Aaron owes Jacobus money. Jacobus says that unless Aaron

agrees to let him marry Hannah he'll seize everything Aaron owns and leave him with nothing. Aaron's persuaded Hannah to agree to the marriage.'

'That doesn't sound like Aaron to me. He thinks far too much of his daughter to give her away to a man like Albrecht.'

'I heard it with my own ears, Sam. It will happen unless I kill Jacobus.'

'Will it? We'll see about that. How much does Aaron owe?'

'I don't know.'

'It doesn't matter much; there's more than one way of dealing with a man like Jacobus Albrecht — and shooting him is well down the list. You get off that horse and come inside. We've got some talking to do.'

'Don't try to trick me, Sam. I'm not going to allow Jacobus Albrecht to have Hannah.'

In spite of his bold words Daniel swayed in the saddle. There was agonising pain in his chest, and he felt sick.

'I'm on your side, Daniel,' declared Sam Speke. 'But you go after him in that condition and he'll kill you and still be alive to marry Hannah.'

He called to the Herero. 'Kasupi. Hold this horse while I help Daniel down and get him inside. Then go and watch the Miners' Inn. Let me know if Albrecht makes a move to leave. We'll have business with him shortly.'

Daniel would have fallen from the horse had Sam not been there to catch him and help him into the store. Leading him to his own room, he lowered him into a wide-armed hide chair and Daniel leaned back with a groan of relief.

Sam Speke grinned at him. 'What did I tell you? If Jacobus Albrecht was to walk in front of your gun right now, you wouldn't have the strength to pull the trigger.'

The ex-seaman was right. Daniel knew it.

'Here, get some of this down you. You've a job to do yet and you'll need some strength for it.'

Sam Speke reached down a bottle from a shelf and, pouring half a tumbler of brandy, handed it to Daniel.

It was growing dark outside, and Sam lit a lamp that stood on a table in the centre of the room, then drew the curtains together. He went to the bed in the corner of the room and reached beneath it to pull out a leather-bound trunk. It was fitted with a stout lock, and Sam produced the key on a cord from about his neck.

The heavy lid creaked as it swung open, and inside Daniel saw clothes and an accumulation of treasures the ex-seaman had acquired since arriving in Africa. Delving into the bottom of the trunk, Sam came up with a weighty leather bag that had a drawstring neck. Untying the cord, Sam tipped the bag upside down, and four smaller canvas bags dropped heavily on to the table.

Sam took one of them and balanced it in the palm of his hand for a few seconds, reliving the memories that were a part of bygone years. Then he walked across to Daniel and dropped the bag into his lap.

'Here. I've been saving this against the time you would need it. I think that time has arrived.'

Daniel untied the cord wound about the neck of the bag and reached inside. His hand came out clutching a fistful of gold coins and there were more left inside the bag.

Daniel was surprised and not a little puzzled. 'I can't take this, Sam. Why, it's a fortune!'

Sam nodded. 'Yes, it's a fortune right enough. But you're taking it because it belongs to you.' He pushed aside two of the remaining bags. 'Just as these belong to your ma and pa.'

'But they've never said anything to me about this.' Daniel was utterly bemused.

'It wouldn't surprise me if the whole thing had slipped from their minds,' said Sam, smiling. 'Money has never meant a great deal to either of them — not nearly as much as it did to poor Isaiah Dacket.'

Briefly Sam Speke told Daniel the story of the Bushmen and the two skeletons and the events leading to Isaiah Dacket's violent death.

'So there you have it,' he concluded. 'It should have been shared five ways but for Isaiah's greed. As it is there's four of us to have a part of the gold each. We earned it, Daniel. There was many a time in those mountains when I believed none of us would live to enjoy spending it.'

Daniel looked as though he was about to ask another question, and Sam Speke hurriedly interrupted him. 'Now be quick and swallow that brandy. I'm looking forward to seeing Jacobus Albrecht's face when you walk into the Miners' Inn and settle Aaron's account for him.'

Kasupi moved out from the shadows at the side of the Miners' Inn when they arrived, and Sam saw he had the gun he had taken from Daniel's saddle holster. Whether he had it to prevent Daniel from using the gun or to stop the Boer trader from leaving the inn Sam did not know.

'Albrecht is still in there. His table is in the far corner. There are two others with him.'

Daniel nodded. He had to concentrate on walking. His knees threatened to give way with every step he took. With Sam Speke at his side he pushed through the door and into the inn. It was not as busy as usual. At this hour the miners were being served their evening meal in the large cookhouse next door.

Daniel saw Jacobus Albrecht immediately. The Boer trader saw him at the same time and his expression froze. All talk in the room died down as the two stared at each other. Then Daniel began to walk across the room. The Boer stood up and pushed his chair back. He watched Daniel but addressed himself to Sam Speke.

'If you've come here to cause trouble, Sam, you'd best turn around and go back out through that door right now.' He drew back his coat to expose a new American-made Colt Navy percussion revolver tucked inside his belt. It was the first one seen in Sesebe, and its six pre-loaded cartridges made it a formidable weapon.

'Any trouble will be of your making,' said Daniel. 'We're here on business. I've come to settle Aaron's debt for him.'

Jacobus Albrecht was startled. Daniel saw it, and it gave him much satisfaction.

'If you've got business to discuss, I'll be going,' said one of the men at the table hurriedly. He stood up to go, and the third man at the table stood up with him.

'Sit down,' growled Sam. 'This is business we'd prefer to have witnesses to.'

The Boer trader flushed angrily at the insinuation of dishonesty, and his two companions sat down again.

'How much does Aaron owe you?' asked Daniel, embarrassed

because he could not keep his gaze from wandering to Jacobus Albrecht's smashed nose.

'We didn't work it out in money,' said the trader. 'I supplied him with beads, knives and trade goods.'

'I don't suppose you expected to be paid back in the same,' retorted Daniel. 'How much is owed to you – in gold?'

'About eighty guineas.'

'Eighty guineas?' Sam Speke exploded into anger. 'For eighty guineas you'd rob a man of his daughter or his livelihood?'

'I didn't beg Aaron to get into debt with me.' Jacobus Albrecht was aware of the indignant comments from the few men in the room. 'This is business. Had I borrowed from Aaron he'd have done the same to me.'

'I doubt that,' said Sam, looking at the Boer in disgust. To Daniel he said, 'You've got Portuguese Johannas there, each of them worth five guineas. You're the one who can count. Give him as many as necessary to pay Aaron's debt and let's get out of here. I feel in need of some air.'

Daniel opened the bag and counted out sixteen coins, placing them on the table in two golden piles. Pushing them across the table to the trader, he said, 'That's Aaron's debt paid in full. You can make out a receipt and leave it with Mr Andrews. I'll pick it up tomorrow.'

Drawing the string closed around the opening of the still-heavy bag. Daniel tucked it inside his shirt and, turning his back on the Boer trader, walked from the room.

He made it to the dirt road outside the inn before his legs gave way on him and he fell. Kasupi caught him before he hit the ground and the Herero and Sam Speke helped him back to the store.

The ex-seaman made light of his weakness. 'It's all right, Daniel. It doesn't matter now. What you just did to Jacobus Albrecht hurt him more than any violence.'

'Thanks to you, Sam. I'm still not sure you were telling the truth about that money and that I was meant to have a share of it.'

'I found the money, so the decision was mine to make,' replied Sam Speke. 'But unless I'm mistaken there's your father coming from Otjimkandje. You'll be able to ask him.'

There was more than one horse being galloped recklessly in the darkness on the road from the Herero village. The first horse slowed as it came into Sesebe and turned towards the Miners' Inn.

'Josh, is that you?'

The horse came to a halt, and the hoofbeats of at least two more drew nearer.

'Sam?' It was Josh.

'We're over here by the store. Daniel's with us.'

Josh mouthed something that was lost in the blowing of his horse and, jumping to the ground, he led the animal towards them.

'Daniel? What the hell are you playing at? You've had us all worried half to death.'

Sam Speke pushed open the door of the store, and in the light Josh saw that Daniel was being supported by the others. His anger immediately turned to concern for his son.

'Are you all right? What's happened?'

'He's more than all right, Josh. Come into the store and we'll talk. Who is that with you?'

The other horses were entering Sesebe.

'Aaron and Hannah. They came running to find me with some story of Daniel disappearing from the house and taking his gun with him.'

The other riders had headed for the light of the store, and now a tall slim figure leaped from one of the horses and ran towards them, seeing only Daniel.

'Daniel, are you hurt again? What have you done?'

Had Kasupi not still had a hold on Daniel, Hannah's rush would have bowled him over.

'Father and I were talking and I became very upset. Then I found you had gone and taken your gun with you. I thought you might have heard what we were saying and come here to find Jacobus Albrecht.'

'I did — and I found him.'

The night ride had brought a high colour to Hannah's cheeks. Now the blood drained away, and she turned deathly pale.

'You . . . you found him?' Her eyes were deep dark caverns in the darkness.

'Yes.'

'What ... what happened? Is he ... ?'

'I think we'd better go inside,' said Sam Speke. 'This is no place to hold such a conversation.'

'No!' Hannah looked terrified. 'I must know. Is Jacobus Albrecht ... ? Is he dead?'

'He's not dead—but he's a very unhappy man,' said Sam Speke. 'Now, come inside and Daniel will tell you everything.'

The tension in Hannah and Aaron seeped away. Aaron sagged visibly. 'I don't know whether I should be pleased for Daniel or sorry for myself,' he said.

'You've got reason to be pleased for everyone except Albrecht,' said Sam Speke. 'But if you don't get inside and let me close this door we'll have all the mosquitoes in Sesebe inside your store.'

'You go in. I'll see you in a while. If Jacobus Albrecht is here, I want to see him. I have some unfinished business to attend to. Where is he?' asked Josh.

'Now, Josh ...,' Sam turned to him. 'Any business with Albrecht has already been settled—by Daniel and me.'

'The trader has left Sesebe,' said Kasupi quietly.

The others looked at Kasupi for an explanation.

'His horse was tethered at the back of the Miners' Inn. It has gone, and I heard it being ridden towards Winterhoek a few minutes ago.'

'There, that's settled. We'll go inside.' Sam Speke ushered them all into the store.

Daniel was helped by Kasupi and Hannah. When he was lowered into a chair the pain in his chest caused him to cough violently for a minute or two.

'Now, may we please have the story?' pleaded Aaron when Daniel had recovered his breath. 'Why should I be so pleased when a man is still alive who has threatened to take either my daughter or my business from me? I wish someone would tell me.'

'He won't be taking anything,' said Sam Speke. 'Your debt has been paid by Daniel.'

'Paid by Daniel?' The words came from Aaron, but the same question was evident on the faces of the others.

'Yes, thanks to Sam.'

Daniel told his story. When it had ended Josh said, 'That was your gold, Sam. Yours alone. You found it....'

Sam Speke held up a hand to silence him.

'I found it only because I was the one who went into the gully to check out the Bushman's story. It could as easily have been any one of us. I told you at the time the gold belonged to all of us. There can be no going back on that even after all these years. We went through a lot together during those first weeks. Daniel suffered as much as anyone else. There's a share for you and Miriam when the day comes that you have need of it.'

'Argue about the money later if you must,' said Aaron. 'Right now I want to have something made quite clear to me. Daniel —you paid Jacobus Albrecht eighty guineas to settle my debt?'

'I gave it to him so he would have no claim against you or Hannah.'

The Jewish trader did not miss the look that passed between Daniel and his daughter.

'I see! I see! Well, young man. . . .' He leaned forward and tapped Daniel on the knee. 'You know what you did tonight?'

'I did what needed to be done, that's all.'

'Oh no! You did much more than that. You bought yourself a half-share in a trading business. "Aaron & Daniel, Traders". Or do you think it should be something more formal? "Copping & Retallick", perhaps?'

'You don't owe me anything, Aaron. It was Sam who gave me the money and the idea.'

'Sam is an honest man. There are so few of them I am always grateful to have one for a friend. But please don't say I owe nothing to you, Daniel. That would be foolish, and a fool for a partner I can do without. To you I owe everything. Rather than allow Hannah to marry that ill-mannered Boer animal I'd have given him everything else I owned—and he would have taken it from me. You fought Jacobus for what he said about Hannah and now you've settled my debt with him. Oi! Boy, you're practically family! What else can I do but make you a partner, eh? Tell me that?'

'That's very generous, Aaron,' said Josh. 'But there's no need—'

'Josh, I respect your opinion,' interrupted Aaron. 'But please let my partner speak for himself. This is not such a one-sided arrangement. He's spent his money for me, and I could use his skills for the trading trips I have planned to Lake Ngami. I'm no hunter and I can tell east and west only at sunrise and sunset. I *need* him. What do you say, Daniel? Do we have a partnership?'

He held out his hand and, hardly able to contain his delight, Daniel nodded his head and clasped the hand of the Jewish trader.

'We have a partnership, Aaron.'

'Now we have something to celebrate,' shouted Aaron. 'Sam —come and help me to carry in some brandy.'

'I'd better be getting back to Otjimkandje,' said Josh. 'Miriam will be worrying herself silly.'

'You can go in a minute. First you must have a drink. Come with Sam and me and choose your brandy. I've got three different types in the back of the store.'

Kasupi had not been Daniel's friend for many years without knowing when his absence would be appreciated. 'I'll take the horses around the back for some water,' he said.

When Daniel and Hannah were alone in the room she came to stand to one side of him, her finger tracing imaginary patterns on the arm of his chair.

'I thought I'd die when I realised you must have heard some of the things that were said back in your house—about me marrying Jacobus Albrecht.'

'It made me pretty upset,' admitted Daniel.

'When I found your gun was missing, too, I thought you'd come here to find him and kill him.'

'I would have done it, too, but for Sam.'

Daniel watched her finger on the chair. It came to rest against his bare arm.

'I wouldn't have married him, you know.'

'Wouldn't you?'

'No. I'd have killed myself rather than let him have me.' Daniel said nothing, and her hand gripped his arm. 'I mean it, Daniel.'

He looked up and saw the fierce passion of her expression.

'I believe you.'

Her lower lip trembled as she said, 'Thank you, Daniel.'

Something of her uncontrollable emotion passed to Daniel, and words would not come to him. Clumsily he pulled at her arm, and she dropped to her knees beside him. The next moment he was kissing her passionately, and she was responding violently.

Then her cheek rested against his, and he felt the dampness of tears as she said in a choked whisper, 'I love you, Daniel. I do love you so very, very much.'

He had no time to reply. The noise of laughter and footsteps came from the passageway outside the room, and Hannah just had time to retreat to the darker shadows in the far corner of the room before her father and the others returned.

CHAPTER NINE

It was a few days before Daniel was fit enough to make the return journey to Otjimkandje. Aaron and Hannah stayed in Sesebe. So, too, did Kasupi. The Herero expected Jacobus Albrecht to return and slept little until he heard that the trader was on his way to Whalefish Bay.

Aaron took advantage of Daniel's stay to plan his next trip to Lake Ngami. First he would go to Whalefish Bay himself, to buy the trade goods he would need. He would pay for them with Herero cattle driven from Otjimkandje by Tjamuene's men. It surprised Daniel that the Herero were willing to part with so many of their stock, but Aaron satisfied his curiosity by telling him it was part of a trading agreement he had negotiated long before with Mutjise. The future Herero chief realised, Aaron said, that in their isolated situation trade was important if they intended to break Jonker's stranglehold on their people.

Jacobus Albrecht would not trade with them; neither did the Herero want anything to do with the Boer. They wanted their own trader. Aaron and his new partner satisfied that need.

Aaron felt it wise at this early stage of the partnership to say nothing about the guns he had already supplied to Mutjise.

Hannah made no secret of her pleasure at having Daniel remain at Sesebe for a few more days, and her devotion to him was apparent to everyone who saw them together.

Miriam came to Sesebe the day after Daniel's ride, to satisfy herself that he was as well as Josh had said. She saw how the relationship of the two young people had suddenly blossomed and taxed Daniel with it.

'That girl thinks the world of you, Daniel.'

'Yes, I know.'

Miriam waited in vain for him to amplify his brief acknowledgement.

'Well? Is that all you've got to say about the situation? A lovely young girl like that is so fond of you she hides it from no one, and all you can say is, "Yes, I know"! What am I supposed to presume from that?'

'What do you want to presume, Ma?'

Daniel found it difficult to keep a straight face at his mother's exasperation. He knew it sprang not only from the hope that he would marry Hannah, but also from his mother's fondness for Aaron's daughter and a wish to prevent her from being hurt.

'I don't want to presume anything,' snapped Miriam. 'I just don't want you trifling with that girl's feelings, that's all.'

'Ma, I came to Sesebe to kill a man to save her from being hurt. I'd do the same thing again if it needed to be done. Does that sound as though I'm trifling with her feelings?'

Miriam looked at her son and saw he was in deadly earnest.

'Does Hannah know how you feel?'

'I haven't put it into words but I think she knows.'

'Tell her and be *sure* she does,' said Miriam. Standing up to go, she looked down at Daniel with a mixture of sadness and pride. 'It doesn't seem so long ago that you were a helpless little boy. You've grown up taking after your father, and I can't pay you a greater compliment than that, Daniel.'

Miriam hurried from the room before Daniel could say anything in reply, and a few moments later Hannah hurried into the room.

'What's happened? Have you and your mother had an argument? She just went out of the house as though she was about to burst into tears.'

'No, we haven't had an argument. In fact she's very happy. I expect it's the thought of losing her only son, that's all.'

'Losing a son? Why, Daniel, where are you going? I thought. . . .'

Her dismay was so evident that Daniel reached for her hand. 'Slow down, Hannah. I'm not going anywhere. I meant that Ma knows she'll be losing me to you before very long and a man has to make his own home when he marries.'

Realisation of what he had said dawned slowly and wonderfully for Hannah.

'You mean it, Daniel? You really do want me to marry you?'

'Yes, I want it very much. Will you marry me?'

'Will I? Oh, Daniel! What an idiotic question! Of course I will. Oh, I love you so much!'

256

Daniel tried without success to disentangle himself from Hannah when he heard Aaron coming along the passageway towards the room.

Over Hannah's shoulder Daniel saw the Jewish trader's eyebrows nearly disappear into his thick black hair.

'Please don't let me interrupt anything,' he said when Hannah finally backed away from Daniel. 'I just found a new gun I'd forgotten about. I thought my partner might like to try it on our first trip together.'

The gun was a new percussion musket with a long rifled barrel, but Hannah was not in the mood to admire guns.

'Father, Daniel has just said he'd like to marry me.'

Aaron's smile broke through his beard.

'Congratulations, my boy.' He pumped Daniel's hand, his eyes twinkling happily. 'You've just proved to me you're a businessman my own father would have been proud to know. First you buy half my business at a bargain price and then you offer to marry my daughter so that when I die you have the lot. What a businessman, to be sure.'

'Does that mean you'll let me marry Daniel?'

'If I say no, he'll set up a trading business in opposition and ruin me. What else can I do but say yes?'

'Oh, Father! I'm so happy, I really am.' Now it was Aaron's turn to be hugged.

A few minutes later Josh came into the store with Miriam to say they were about to leave for Otjimkandje, and Aaron broke the news to them.

'The two children think they are grown-up already,' he said. 'They have just told me they want to get married.'

Hannah looked apprehensively at Miriam. They had spent a lot of time together at Otjimkandje, and she knew how much Daniel meant to his mother.

'I've been wondering why they've been so long about it,' she said. 'I was three years younger than Hannah when I first realised I wanted to marry Daniel's father.'

The mention of the marriage of his parents jolted Daniel back into the reality of their situation. Josh noticed it, but Aaron was too happy to think of anything but another reason for a celebration.

'We can't have too many weeks like this one,' he stated as he came into the room bearing the indispensable brandy bottles. 'There will be no profits left. Isn't Sam back yet? He should be part of this celebration too.'

Sam Speke lived in Sesebe during the week, returning to Otjimkandje to spend Sunday with Mary and the ailing Victoria, but upon her arrival in the mining town Miriam had sought out the ex-seaman and told him that Victoria's cough had worsened and she thought he should discuss her condition with Hugo Walder.

Sam was very worried. Victoria weighed no more than a normal child of half her age, and her already weak body would have difficulty in coping with any additional burden.

When a wagon-driver returned from Whalefish Bay with the news that a passenger-ship bound for the Cape Colony was due at the end of the next month, only a few weeks away, Sam decided to return to Otjimkandje immediately and have Mary and the child prepare for the journey to Whalefish Bay.

A passenger-vessel was a rare visitor to the little port and would have a doctor aboard to attend to Victoria on the journey. It also meant the little girl would be away from Otjimkandje during the rainy season, a time when she seemed to suffer more than at any other time of the year.

Sam Speke's unexpected arrival in the Herero village caused much consternation among the crowd of villagers squatting about his hut. When they saw him many of the women scrambled to their feet and fled.

Thoroughly alarmed, the ex-seaman leaped from his horse and ran to the hut, fearing the worst. He flung open the door and walked into a dramatic scene that had been enacted in Herero houses for centuries when persistent sickness was present.

The cow-dung fire in the centre of the hut had been built up with the addition of the green wood of a sacred tree, and the whole room was filled with dense acrid smoke that stung Sam's eyes and momentarily took his breath away.

An old man, his face hidden behind a hideous mask, was communing with the spirits of the villagers' ancestors, urging the good spirits to chase away their evil companions who had taken over the sick body of Victoria.

The old 'holy' man was accompanied by a great many assistants and followers, their painted faces and bodies heavily greased with rancid animal fat. The smell inside the small hut was appalling.

Sam saw his daughter lying on the skin of a lion close to the fire. She appeared to be either drugged or in a deep trance. The old man in the mask knelt beside her, his bony hands first squeezing her thin body then sliding back over her skin as though drawing out some invisible matter from within. As he worked his companions and assistants sat cross-legged about the fire, keeping up a low monotonous chant that brought the hair rising on the back of the ex-seaman's neck. It sounded to him for all the world like a death chant.

'What the hell's going on in here?'

Sam Speke's anger exploded as he forced his way across the crowded hut towards his daughter. The men he touched on the way stopped chanting immediately, but the others carried on as though they were unaware of his presence.

He was intercepted before he reached Victoria by Mary, who stood red-eyed beside the fire.

'Don't stop him, my husband. He is a very holy man. He will make Victoria well again.'

'With all this smoke and stink she'll probably choke. She needs plenty of air and a real doctor, not all this witchcraft. Get out of my way, Mary.'

Pushing his wife roughly away, he forced his way to his daughter's side, knocking over the last two squatting men and towering over the old man in the mask.

'You – get out! And take all these others with you.'

He shook the shoulder of the 'holy' man roughly. The old man rocked back on his heels and looked up at Sam.

'Your daughter is very sick.'

'I don't need you and your ceremony to tell me that.'

'She is sick because you are not of our people and are bringing her up to ways that do not please our fathers.'

'She is learning the ways of both your fathers and mine. She will have two paths to choose from and when the time comes it will be her choice. She will take the path that is best for her.'

The old man closed his eyes for a long time. When he opened them again he said, 'The choice will be hers to make but she will make it not for herself but for another.' He looked up at the glowering ex-seaman. 'She will get well now.'

He got to his feet slowly and with difficulty; he had seen more seasons than any other man or woman in the village, and the coming rains were already attacking the joints of his body. He hobbled to the door of the hut and his followers filed out after him. Not one of them looked back at Sam.

When the last of them had gone Sam Speke picked up the frail form of his daughter and carried her to the door. He spoke over his shoulder to Mary, who crouched by the fire sobbing noisily.

'Mary, get a grip on yourself! Put out that fire and let's get some air in here. It's a wonder Victoria hasn't choked to death.'

Mary did as she was told, talking all the time between violent shuddering sobs. 'I did what I believed to be right for Victoria. . . . She has been getting worse. . . . You were not here to give me advice. . . . I spoke to Tjamuene, and he said this was the way.'

It was no use telling Mary that Tjamuene was an old man who no longer knew what was best for any of his people and who fell back on tradition as a substitute for wisdom. Tjamuene was the chief of the Herero. Mary had asked his advice, and it had been given. Not to accept it was unthinkable. She had followed the way of her people and done what was necessary.

'Well, it doesn't seem to have done Victoria any harm,' Sam admitted. She slept quietly and easily without the rasping breathing that had so upset him for many months.

He moved across to Mary and put an arm about her. 'You did what you thought was best. I'm sorry I was angry, but I'm worried about Victoria too. I came to tell you there's a ship to the Cape in a few weeks. We'll be on it, and let's hope the doctors there can do something for her.'

His words did not make Mary feel better. She was relieved that her husband was not angry with her, but the thought of travelling to the Cape Colony terrified her. She had never before travelled any farther than from Otjimkandje to Sesebe.

*

After his humiliation at the hands of Daniel, Jacobus Albrecht returned to Winterhoek to feed his anger with brandy, away from the eyes of others.

He had enjoyed a two-day drinking bout when William Thackeray paid him a visit. The missionary had completed his church, and Jonker ensured that his Sunday services were well attended. If a great many of his congregation were less than sober, it could not be helped. He was a missionary in a strange new land, among primitive people. He had to prove to Jonker that his way was the best; then he could apply pressure to bring about the changes that were necessary.

That did not mean William Thackeray would sit back and do nothing until then. Jonker's missionary had a full programme planned.

He called on Jacobus Albrecht in mid-morning when the trader had just left his bed, three days' growth of beard shading his face.

The Boer opened the door of his hut and reeled back from the glare of the sun.

'Agh, it's you! Come in, man, if you must.'

William Thackeray stepped into the room, wrinkling his nose in distaste at the wide variety of unsavoury smells that hung on the stale air inside the unventilated hut.

Jacobus Albrecht drew back the rough sacking curtains, then crossed to the table and swept a variety of dirty plates and mugs into a wooden bucket.

'I understand there is to be no wedding,' the missionary said.

'Wedding?' It took some moments for the words to sink in. 'You mean with Hannah?' He scowled. 'No, there'll be no wedding, but that's not the end of it. Nobody makes Jacobus Albrecht look a fool.'

Memory returning to him, he crossed to the bed in the corner of the room and heaved back the heap of bedclothes to reveal a naked black back.

'Hey, you! Get up. The party's over. Go home now.' He gave the exposed rump a slap that sounded like a whipcrack in the room.

A naked Afrikaner girl sat up, grumbling irritably.

'You hear me? Get up and go home, you Kaffir slut. I've got company.'

Only half-awake, and with a throbbing head, the girl swung her feet to the floor. Standing up with a groan, she tottered unsteadily towards the door.

'Hey! You—whatever your name is. Take your bloody clothes with you.'

Her 'clothes' consisted of a ragged dress and nothing else. Jacobus Albrecht screwed it into a ball and threw it at her. She caught it, staggered slightly and, tucking it beneath her arm, stepped naked from the hut into the blinding sunlight.

The Boer trader reached down a full flagon of cheap brandy from a shelf above the bed, found a nearly clean mug from beneath it and half-filled it with brandy.

'You want some of this?'

William Thackeray shook his head. Watching the trader as he swallowed the brandy and belched noisily, he wondered how a man could allow himself to sink so low and to live in such squalor when he had both the money and resources to make a good home for himself. But he allowed none of his thoughts to show. He needed this uncouth Boer to help him.

'Have you come here for anything special, or is this just a friendly visit?'

'I came here to sympathise with you,' replied the missionary. 'Any man who looked forward to marriage and is disappointed should have someone to commiserate with him.'

The Boer trader did not understand a great many of the words William Thackeray used when speaking but he was able to grasp the gist of his talk.

'A man doesn't need more than a few bottles of this when he's down,' he said, waving the flagon in front of the missionary. 'You ought to drink some of it yourself. It might take your mind off saving the souls of Jonker and his people for a while. I'm damned if I know why you bother anyway. If I was God, I'd do my best to keep a lot of them away from heaven—or wherever it is you're trying to send them.'

'Well, you and I don't agree about everything, do we, Jacobus? For instance, if someone had stopped my wedding, I'd be thinking up ways of getting back what I'd lost and not be skulking miles away drowning my sorrows.'

'I'm not skulking! You choose your words more carefully, Preacher. You'll bleed as easily as any other man. Don't forget that.'

'I came here to sympathise with you,' replied the missionary. 'Not to start up a quarrel. We're on the same side, you and I. But we'll neither of us get very far while Hugo Walder maintains such a strong influence over the Herero.'

'That's one of *your* problems,' stated the trader, pouring himself another half-mug of brandy.

'That's not true; it affects us both,' argued William Thackeray. 'Hugo Walder gains his strength from those who support him – the Retallicks, Sam Speke and Aaron. Prise them out and he'll fall. Then you'll have Aaron's trade and his daughter – if that's what you want – and Chief Jonker will be rid of the Herero.'

'How about you?' Jacobus Albrecht asked suspiciously. 'What do you get out of it?'

'I'll send to Cape Town asking for another of our missionaries to be sent here,' replied William Thackeray. 'If the Herero are still around, he can be missionary to them; if not, to whichever tribe Chief Jonker decides to settle in Otjimkandje.'

'Nothing for yourself but everything for the Church,' mocked the trader. 'Such piety doesn't sit well with you, Preacher. You're too ambitious. There's more in it than you've said. What is it?'

William Thackeray flushed but held back his anger. 'Nothing that will affect you. But we'll get nowhere until you stop supporting Hugo Walder's friends. A start would be to dismiss Josh Retallick from the Sesebe mine.'

'You don't like him, do you?' Jacobus Albrecht's bloodshot eyes watched the missionary speculatively over the rim of the mug. 'I wonder why.'

William Thackeray had regained his composure now. 'I knew him before either of us came to this country,' he admitted. 'But, then, Joshua Retallick was known to a great many people. He was so well known that if you were able to persuade some of your trading friends to deliver him to the British authorities in Cape Town their gratitude would go much farther than covering your expenses.'

The Boer trader lowered his mug. 'You mean he's a wanted man? What's he done?'

William Thackeray smiled enigmatically and shook his head. 'I'm saying nothing, Jacobus. It's better that way for the moment. But if you can get him to Cape Town and turn him over to the authorities I promise you the repercussions will be far-reaching. They might even be strong enough to have Hugo Walder recalled for harbouring him.'

The thin missionary got to his feet slowly and grimaced as though the movement had brought him pain.

'Think about what I've said, Jacobus. Our future could lie in your hands. Don't throw it away.'

A few days later Harold Andrews sent for Josh. He was apologetic to the point of embarrassment, but it did not soften the impact of his words. Josh was asked to leave the employ of Andrews and Albrecht.

'I'm sorry about it, Josh,' said the uncomfortable mine-owner. 'The mine is paying its way but it's not making a fortune. If it was up to me alone, I'd keep you on, but Jacobus is my partner and he says we've got to cut costs now there's another trading company working in direct opposition to us. He can't afford a mine-manager.'

'It's strange the opposition didn't worry Jacobus when he invited Aaron to Sesebe,' said Josh sarcastically. 'I wonder what could have brought about this sudden change of mind.'

'We both know the answer to that, Josh,' said Harold Andrews. 'But there's little I can do. I don't know how long the ore is going to last here, and mining is a much chancier business than trading. I can't risk having Jacobus pull out, taking most of the trading contacts with him.'

'You don't have to give me lengthy explanations. I've been expecting this. Now perhaps I'll have time to do some of the things I've been thinking about – going down to Whalefish Bay to see Sam and his family off, for instance.' He looked at the mine-owner, but Harold Andrews would not meet his eyes. 'I wish I could promise that things will work out as well for you, Harold. They won't. I've worked this mine for some years now; it's been my living – and would have been for a few more years – but without a good captain you'll have lost the copper seam in six months. I doubt whether you'll be able to pay the men's wages for long enough to find it again. I wish you well.'

Ignoring the mine-owner's hand, Josh turned and walked from the office.

Josh had not been merely trying to frighten Harold Andrews. At the moment the mine was taking ore from two shallow seams, each with only a short run. The time to be looking for more ore was now — and it needed an expert. The shallow seams might resume their run some distance away, possibly at an acute angle from the original seam. On the other hand, it might prove necessary to go deeper for the ore. This would be disastrous to inexperienced men. There was water in the mine already, and the rainy season was upon them. It would raise the level even higher.

The year of 1860 had been an evenful one. As it drew to a close Josh forecast that the Sesebe mine would not know another Christmas.

This did not necessarily mean the ore-ships would have to stop calling at Whalefish Bay. If a way could be found to prevent interference from Chief Jonker, Josh would persuade Aaron to join him in the purchase of wagons and equipment from the Sesebe mine when it ceased operations. They could then work the copper ore deposit he had discovered on their trip to Lake Ngami.

CHAPTER TEN

The rains did not last long that season. The last two weeks in December were very wet, but then the wind swung away to the south and the clouds disappeared overnight, leaving the year 1861 to arrive hot and sunny.

Using more of Daniel's money, Aaron had been able to have one wagonload of trade goods sent to Sesebe from Whalefish Bay. It was not much but there would be more soon. For now it would have to suffice.

Aaron had made arrangements with the Bechuana chief to meet him at a water-hole halfway between Lake Ngami and Otjimkandje and he did not intend letting him down. He and Daniel set off with their wagons during the rains, worried that the weather would slow them down. They had promised Sam Speke they would be in Whalefish Bay in time to see him and his family on to the boat.

The Bechuanas were waiting at the meeting-place with a fine load of ivory for them. This was the farthest north Daniel had been and he was very impressed with the country and its wealth of animal life. Hunting food was no problem, and he also managed to shoot a fine cheetah. One of the Hereros accompanying them cured the skin for him, and Daniel thought it would make a fine present for Hannah.

The vegetation hereabouts was also exceptional, with a wealth of new growth everywhere. The tall grass stood man-high, and there were hundreds of brilliant-hued flowers, but it was the trees that Daniel found of most interest. They were the giant baobab trees, with a circumference often equal to the length of a wagon. Their stunted leafless branches gave Daniel the impression that the Great Creator had made a mistake and stuck the trees into the earth upside down.

Certainly, the country here was not as harsh as that about Otjimkandje. Daniel became so enthusiastic that Aaron had to remind him he was seeing it during the rains. In the dry months it was almost as desolate as the lands with which Daniel was more familiar — as he would see for himself on future trips to Lake Ngami.

They travelled direct from the water-hole to Whalefish Bay and when the rains ended were able to make excellent time. By keeping well to the north of Jonker's territory they encountered no unforeseen setbacks and arrived in Whalefish Bay ahead of Sam Speke and the others.

Aaron was well pleased to see the ship belonging to his friend Captain Klopper riding at anchor in the bay. It meant he would be able to get rid of his ivory immediately, thus eliminating the risk of having Jonker pay him a surprise late visit. It also meant he could be sure of obtaining a fair price for his goods.

Leaving Daniel with the wagons, Aaron went in search of the captain. Whalefish Bay had grown in recent years. It was no longer possible to locate anyone by standing on a hillock and shouting his name. There were now stores and houses, offices and inns. Aaron started with the latter and was successful at the second one he tried.

'I didn't expect to find you here, my friend,' said Aaron as the two men shook hands. 'Have you given up carrying the more rewarding items of trade and settled for the hard-won profits to be gained from general cargo?'

'For the present, yes,' replied the ship's captain. 'They are expecting some ships at the Cape bringing troops for Natal. All the English frigates are at sea, each anxious to be the first to sight them. They are buzzing up and down the coast like bees around a hive. Unless I was prepared to risk losing my ship and spending the remainder of my days in prison I had to load trade goods. So, here I am with a ship full of trinkets I'll be lucky to sell for much more than my crew's pay.'

'Then this must be your lucky day,' said the Jew. 'I've just returned from trading with the Bechuana and I've got two wagons with the best quality ivory you've ever clapped eyes on. I tell you, Cap'n Klopper, it breaks my heart to have to part with it.'

The captain warmed to Aaron's sales talk. He was well pleased at meeting the Jew. He would return to the Cape with a better cargo than he had anticipated.

'You'll be wanting more than ordinary trade goods for prime

ivory, I reckon?'

'Of course. But you and I are old friends, Cap'n Klopper. We trust each other. You'll pay for half the ivory with the goods you're carrying now. The other half will be paid for with our "special" merchandise, landed in the usual place.'

'When will you be there?'

'How long is it before the troopships are expected and the frigates return to running errands for the Cape Governor?'

'The troopships are expected any day. I should think it will be possible to make a delivery two months from today.'

'Good! Then we have a deal, Cap'n Klopper. If I am not at my cabin, bury the merchandise immediately behind the hut and sail away. With so many newcomers in Whalefish Bay it must soon burst at the seams. When it does people will spill out along the coast. It would be a great pity if inquisitive eyes saw you riding at anchor below the hut and spoiled a good business arrangement.'

'I'll be careful,' promised the ship's captain.

'Excellent! Now, if it's all the same to you, I'd like to complete the trade before dark. I would hate Jonker to ride in and rob me now we've made our deal.'

'I've got four men waiting in a boat inshore. I'll get them working on it. They're waiting to take a special passenger on board for Jacobus Albrecht.'

Aaron was rising from the table when Captain Klopper spoke the Boer trader's name. He promptly sat down again.

'Albrecht? You're doing business with him?'

'I haven't until now,' said the captain. 'He's promised to pay well and I have been told there will be more when I get the passenger to the Cape — although I must admit I don't like the sound of it.'

'Why not? It's not a long trip to the Cape given the right winds. A passenger will not inconvenience you for long.'

'Not if he's a willing passenger,' replied the captain. 'This one's not. He's to be turned over to the Cape Government when I get there.'

Aaron became increasingly interested. There was little love between Boers and British Government. Why should Albrecht be helping them?

268

'What's the name of this passenger?'

'The agreement's between Albrecht and me,' said Captain Klopper. 'I wouldn't tell him of any business you and I did.'

'I hope not,' snorted Aaron. 'For your sake as much as my own. Jacobus Albrecht is no friend of mine and he's up to no good. What's the name of the passenger?'

'Retallick.' Captain Klopper saw the old Jew's jaw drop open in amazement. 'You know him?'

Aaron nodded vigorously and his mouth snapped shut. 'Daniel Retallick is my new partner. I owed Albrecht some money and he gave me an ultimatum: either I gave him Hannah or he would take everything I owned. Daniel Retallick gave him the money to settle my debt. I owe him more than the money, Cap'n Klopper.'

Captain Klopper had been doing business with Aaron for many years and had watched Hannah grow from a tiny child to a beautiful girl. He had felt sorry for the motherless girl living in the harsh unloving world of the Skeleton Coast and when she was smaller had brought her many presents from the Cape. He had no love for any man who meant her harm. Jacobus Albrecht had just made another enemy.

'I'll do no business with any man who would try to take Hannah in that way,' he declared angrily. 'But the name of the passenger Albrecht wanted me to take was Josh Retallick, not Daniel.'

'Daniel's father? Why would the Cape Government want him? He's lived up here for almost fifteen years. Are you sure it wasn't Daniel?'

'I'm certain,' said the captain. 'Not that it makes any difference which one it was to be. I'll do none of Albrecht's dirty work for him. Bring your ivory down to the beach, Aaron. I'll get it on board and return with your trade goods, then I'll weigh anchor.'

'I'll be down at the boat in a few minutes,' said Aaron. 'And thank you for your information, Cap'n Klopper. The Retallicks have been very good to Hannah and me.'

'Then you'd better warn him quickly of what's afoot. Albrecht said he'd have him here for me tonight.'

Aaron ran all the way back to where he had left Daniel with

the wagons. He arrived so out of breath he could hardly get the story out to Daniel.

'Why should he think the Cape Government would be interested in your father?' he ended. 'He's a good man.'

Daniel had listened in tight-lipped silence. Now he said, 'You'd better ask Pa the answer to that yourself. I'll go to meet him and make sure he gets here safely. Kasupi will come with me. Will you loan him your gun?'

The Jewish trader handed the weapon to the Herero as the two friends saddled their horses. Kasupi flung an order at his fellow-tribesmen who had been escorting the wagons on the journey from Lake Ngami and half of the Hereros took their spears from the wagon, eager for a chance to do battle.

'Your father and the others should not be far along the road,' Kasupi explained. 'My warriors will follow us on foot as fast as they can. It is possible Jacobus Albrecht will use Afrikaners to help him to get your father. Our numbers will make them think twice before attacking.'

Daniel nodded acknowledgement of the sense of Kasupi's words. As he swung his horse around Aaron called to him, 'When you meet up with them let Sam, Mary and the child come on here and I'll see them settled in to await their ship. You and your father laager up with Kasupi's warriors. I'll join you with Sam's wagon as soon as Captain Klopper brings the trade goods ashore. Then we'll all return to Otjimkandje together.'

At about the time Captain Klopper was imparting his information to Aaron, William Thackeray was riding in to Otjimkandje.

He rode alone and as his horse picked its way between the huts he could not fail to make comparisons between the orderliness and general cleanliness of the Herero village and the dirt and untidiness of Winterhoek.

He made his way towards the cross on the church that rose high above the mud and straw huts about it. He found Hugo Walder inside hammering at the leg of a bench that had become loose.

The German missionary wiped the perspiration from his hand before greeting his English counterpart.

'You find me in a most unusual situation,' Hugo Walder said. 'I have not had to work with my hands for very many years — not since I began building this church myself. Not that I am complaining; it makes me feel very close to our Lord to think the humble thoughts of a carpenter. No, it is simply that Sam Speke and Josh Retallick have for many years done all the work for me. Now they are at Whalefish Bay.'

'I wish I had men like them at Winterhoek,' said William Thackeray. 'Chief Jonker's men are willing enough most of the time but they are workers in mud and cob only. I have no carpenters or metalworkers.' He was looking at a lectern made of fine scroll metalwork.

'Yes, that is quite beautiful,' agreed Hugo Walder. 'Josh made it when he set up his first forge in Otjimkandje.'

'You have a lovely little church here,' said William Thackeray wistfully. 'This is the first time I have been cool since I left England.'

'The church has thick walls and a double roof,' explained the German missionary. 'One must use every means at one's disposal to make life bearable in Africa. Otherwise this country will defeat even the most dedicated man.' Hugo Walder looked critically at Chief Jonker's missionary. 'You have been working too hard. You have lost much weight since we last met.'

'I haven't been too well,' admitted the Wesleyan Missionary. 'But I've recovered now.'

'H'm!' Hugo Walder did not commit himself to a reply. 'Come into my hut. I have cool water there. The trick is to bury it in wet sand in the shade and keep it damped down.'

'If you don't mind, I would rather stay here and feed my soul on the peace and coolness for a while,' said William Thackeray.

'Then I will bring water to you.'

'You'll find a satchel of mail on my horse,' said William Thackeray as he lowered himself gratefully to a seat on one of the wooden benches used by the Herero congregation. 'That's why I am here. A rider from Whalefish Bay brought me a satchel of letters and it wasn't until he had gone I saw a great many of them were for you.'

'I am obliged to you,' said Hugo Walder. 'Now rest while I fetch water.'

But the old missionary did not go directly to his hut. Instead he went to find Miriam.

She was alone in the house, Hannah having gone with Sam and Mary to Whalefish Bay, ostensibly to help with young Victoria. She had fooled no one. Daniel would be there, and it meant the young couple would be able to share each other's company on the ten-day return journey to Otjimkandje. Miriam did not mind; it was exactly what she might have done – and would now, given the opportunity. Even after all these years, when Josh was away Miriam missed him with all the unreasonable longings of a young girl.

Through her kitchen window Miriam saw the German missionary hurrying towards the house, and his haste was so uncharacteristic of the man that she went to the door to meet him.

He saw the concern on her face and immediately apologised.

'I'm sorry, my dear Miriam. I didn't mean to alarm you. I merely came to warn you – to tell you – that Jonker's missionary has arrived to pay me a visit. I thought you should know in case he calls on you.'

Miriam told herself that the constricted feeling in her chest was not fear. Ever since she had first heard of William Thackeray's arrival in Winterhoek she had known the day had to come when she would be forced to meet him again, to face him and talk to him, to hear him remind her of things that had remained with him as memories but which she had long since forgotten. Her life had been filled with so much since those far-off years in Cornwall. She could only hope his life had been the same; but he would hardly have come to Winterhoek had his years in England been filled with happiness and fulfilment.

'Where is he?' Miriam loosed the apron from about her waist and from habit smoothed her long hair back from her forehead.

'He's in the church. I came to fetch him water. He's hot and tired from the ride. I fear he's not a strong man – certainly not strong enough for Africa.'

'William Thackeray has never needed strength of body, Hugo. He finds others to do his work for him. He's very good at that. I'll take him water.'

'Are you sure? Is it wise?'

'I'll take it – and thank you for the warning.'

Miriam kept her water-jugs cool in a box made from sea-stone carried from the coast near Whalefish Bay. She removed one of them, took a cup from a hook on the dresser and made her way to the church. Hugo Walder watched her go, wondering whether he had been right to tell her. Jonker's missionary might have returned to Winterhoek without troubling her – but Hugo's instincts told him otherwise.

William Thackeray was sitting where Hugo Walder had left him, facing the altar, his back to the door.

Miriam was wearing soft shoes, and they made no sound on the packed-earth floor of thechurch . She paused inside the doorway, waiting for her eyes to adjust to the shadows. For some moments she looked at the back of the man with whom she had shared four years of her life. The grey of age had lightened the colour of his hair, and it was untidily long at the back of his neck. In Cornwall he had always been excessively fussy about his appearance. She could see, too, that he had lost a great deal of weight. Never a heavy man, his shoulder bones now protruded from his shirt like the shoulders of a cow with rinderpest.

William Thackeray turned around slowly, although she had not made a sound. When he looked at her Miriam knew that Hugo Walder had not exaggerated. William Thackeray was a very sick man.

'Miriam!' The missionary stood up, and there was an air of great expectancy about him. This was an important moment in his life, the fulfilment of many years of effort. Miriam knew in that moment that his coming here was no mere coincidence.

'I've brought you the water Hugo promised.'

'So he told you I was here.' William Thackeray smiled wryly. The moment of fulfilment had passed, unfulfilled, and he was aware of its passing.

'Hugo has been a good friend for a great many years.'

'You needn't have come to me here, Miriam. I had no intention of leaving Otjimkandje without paying a call upon you.'

'I'd rather we met in God's house with Him as a witness than in Josh's house with none.'

'It was in God's house we were married, Miriam. He was a witness to that, too.'

'Then He must have known what a mockery it was,' said

Miriam softly, 'with love for Josh in my heart and his son in my belly.'

William Thackeray winced as though she had struck him a physical blow.

'I didn't force you to marry me, Miriam. But what kind of talk is this? I haven't come here to open old wounds. It is not my intention to hurt you in any way.'

'You've never needed force to get your own way, William. Trickery and the ability to seize an advantage have always been your way. As for hurting me, and mine, you did that the day you landed at Whalefish Bay. We had a good life here at Otjim-kandje. Your coming has put an end to that.'

'It needn't, Miriam. I can still be a friend. You can never have too many friends in a harsh uncertain country like this.'

'You had your chance to prove friendship to Josh many years ago. He was on trial for a crime he didn't commit. Your evidence could have cleared him. Do you know, William, had you stood up in that court and told half of what you knew you would never have lost me. I never loved you — that you knew. But I once respected you, and respect kept me with you. When it went I had nothing but contempt and loathing in my heart for you. I couldn't live with that eating me away.

'Yes, this is a harsh and uncertain country, but I'll live and die here — for Josh. Here he is a free man and living a full life. That's unselfish unambitious love, William — something you'll never understand and so will never have. I don't know what you hoped to gain by coming here, but go back. Leave Josh and me and Daniel in peace. You do that and you'll take with you at least part of the respect I once had for you.' Miriam placed the water-jug down on a bench. 'Here's your water. Leave the jug when you've drunk your fill. Hugo will bring it back to me.'

She turned and walked out of the mission church without a backward glance. Miriam had feared this meeting, had lain awake for hours at night worrying about it. Now it was behind her, and had anyone asked what she had felt when she stood before the man who was still her legal husband she would have replied in one word.

Pity.

William Thackeray was no longer the man who had inspired

the miners of Cornwall and fused their enthusiasm into a single union, the preacher men would walk miles to hear, who had once drawn a crowd of three thousand and had them roaring agreement with his every word. Jonker's missionary was a man whose soul had been eaten away by bitterness and whose body was racked by ill-health. Yet, though Miriam had no love left for William Thackeray, she wished he had been able to know a happiness similiar to the one she shared with Josh.

Hugo Walder went into his church an hour later and found the Wesleyan preacher slumped on the stool where he had left him. He was so still the German missionary thought he was ill, but as he approached William Thackeray raised his head. His eyes were those of a weary and disillusioned man.

'Are you all right?' asked Hugo with some concern.

'Yes. I'm sorry if I alarmed you. It is so quiet in here I have been thinking — and praying.'

'Ah!' Hugo Walder gave William Thackeray one of his warm smiles. 'I understand.' He looked around the little church with affection. 'I know in our preaching we are wont to say that God is everywhere — and so he is, of course — yet I always feel closer to Him in here. Here is His peace, His compassion, His inspiration.' Hugo Walder struggled to find the words he wanted but concluded by saying simply, 'He is here.'

'I believe you, Father, but I have kept you from your duties for long enough. It is time I returned to Winterhoek.'

'Nonsense! The Afrikaners did without a missionary for many years; they can do without one for a few hours. I am having a meal prepared for you, and there is a bottle of good wine hidden away somewhere. Come, we will share it and you can tell me all about your church and how that scoundrel Jonker is treating you.'

Daniel and Kasupi met up with Sam Speke's party five miles outside Whalefish Bay. Hannah could hardly contain her excitement at the meeting, but one look at Daniel's face told her that romance would have to wait. There were other things on his mind. He drew Josh to one side and gave him Aaron's warning.

'Is he quite sure of this?'

'Yes. It's too dangerous for you to go on to Whalefish Bay.'

'He wouldn't dare do anything there.'

'Pa! Be sensible. Who'd stop him once he explained why he was doing it?'

Sam Speke jumped from his wagon and came over to them.

'Is something happening I should know about?'

'No,' said Josh. 'Everything is all right.'

'Everything is *not* all right,' contradicted Daniel. 'Jacobus Albrecht is planning to get Pa aboard a boat in Whalefish Bay and have him taken prisoner to Cape Town. He's already made all the arrangements with the captain.'

'It would take more than Jacobus Albrecht to put me on to a ship bound for the Cape,' declared Josh.

'I doubt he'd attempt such a thing alone,' said Sam Speke. 'Daniel's right, Josh. You can't go on to Whalefish Bay. Mary and I will go on with Victoria. You get back to Otjimkandje right away. You owe it to Miriam not to risk being taken to the Cape Colony.'

'Aaron said he'd meet you and arrange a place to stay,' said Daniel. 'We'll wait here for him. We've brought in some ivory from the Bechuana and he's loading trade goods.'

At that moment the Herero warriors rounded a bend in the road half a mile away, trotting in loose formation. Seeing the wagon they let out loud cries and breaking formation ran forward brandishing their spears above their heads.

'What the hell is this?' exclaimed Sam Speke. 'Quick, get to the wagon.'

'It's all right,' grinned Kasupi. 'They are my warriors who are coming to guard us. They will stay until the others arrive with Aaron.' He looked at Josh. 'No man will harm you until every one of my warriors lies dead.'

Kasupi did not know why Jacobus Albrecht should want to capture Josh, he did not particularly want to know. It was sufficient that Daniel's father was in danger. Besides, this made his Hereros feel like men, not skulking away from Jonker and his Afrikaners but standing in the open with sharp spears in their hands — warriors, prepared to die a warrior's death, facing an enemy. It was such a good feeling Kasupi half-hoped the Boer trader would have Afrikaners with him and dare to attack.

'It looks to me as though Daniel and Kasupi have full command of the situation, Josh,' said Sam Speke. 'You'd better take your orders from them.'

'They've done well enough.' Josh acknowledged the sense of the precautions that had been taken. 'All right, Sam. I'll say goodbye to you here. Take care of yourself and bring that beautiful daughter of yours back again fit and well.'

While Josh said goodbye to Mary and Victoria, Hannah asked Daniel what was happening. He told her only that Jacobus Albrecht was trying to put his father on a ship bound for Cape Town, against his will.

Hannah was completely baffled by the whole thing.

'Why? I mean, what does he hope to gain from doing such a thing? And why does he want to get him to the Cape?'

'It's a long story, Hannah. We've got a lot of time on the journey back to Otjimkandje ahead of us. I'll tell you all about it then. In the meantime you go on to Whalefish Bay with Victoria.'

'Let me stay with you here and you can tell me about it right away.'

'No. I want you to go to Whalefish Bay first. There could be fighting here if Jacobus Albrecht arrives with his friends.'

'If he does, you could use another gun. I'm as good a shot as any man.'

'I know you are, Hannah,' Daniel acknowledged, 'but Victoria needs you. The sight of all the buildings at Whalefish Bay will terrify her. Get her settled quickly and return with your father. You should be back here by morning.'

Hannah pouted but made no further argument, and when Daniel leaned forward from his horse and kissed her she was as happy as any girl in the whole of Africa. He had never before kissed her in front of others. It was by way of being a public declaration that she belonged to him, just one step from being married.

When the wagons creaked away and the waving from both parties ceased, Kasupi suggested they should make camp on some rising ground a short distance from the road. It would give them a good view of the surrounding countryside and make a useful defensive position should it become necessary.

Once they moved to the high ground Kasupi proved that in

spite of all the years he had spent as Daniel's guardian, when his apparently idle and self-indulgent ways had brought censure from the elders of the tribe, he was a chief's son. He gave orders to the warriors as though he were an experienced general, and they obeyed him without question.

He sent out single warriors to vantage-points about the camp, to report the approach of any unknown party, set guards in between and rode from one place to another keeping his men alert and ready. He reminded them they were Herero warriors and might be fighting an enemy at any moment.

'I think Kasupi is enjoying this,' commented Josh. 'And I must admit he seems to know what he's doing. Jonker will need to tread carefully when Mutjise takes over leadership of the Herero and Kasupi is given more responsibility.'

Daniel found it difficult to understand how Josh could act so calmly when his whole future freedom was in jeopardy. When he put his thoughts into words Josh smiled. 'It's a tribute to you and Kasupi. Jacobus Albrecht won't risk anything while I'm defended in such strength. He'll most probably abandon the whole idea when he realises we know about it. I expect he was hoping to get me away without anyone here knowing. People in Whalefish Bay might allow him to take me, but it wouldn't increase his popularity around Sesebe and Otjimkandje.'

'I can't understand why he should want to have you sent to the Cape. He has a grudge against Sam, Aaron and me, but you've done him no harm. Why make you suffer?'

'At a guess I would say William Thackeray put him up to it. He has always had the cunning to achieve his own ends by using someone else to do his work and have them believe he is doing them a favour. I've no doubt he persuaded Jacobus that he would be hurting all of you by getting me out of the way — even Hugo. It wouldn't do the mission any good if word got to the Cape that Otjimkandje had been sheltering an escaped convict for all these years. Yes, Hugo might even be recalled for something like that, and it would open the way for the Afrikaners to destroy Otjimkandje and lay claim to all of the Hereroland. Then Jonker would be the most powerful chief in this part of the world for sure. He would control all mineral rights, and the Cape Government could find themselves negotiating with him for permission to use Whalefish Bay. That would make his missionary a very influential man.

'Oh, yes, this sounds just like the William Thackeray I used to know. His planning is in this. No doubt he convinced Jacobus Albrecht that he'd stand to gain all the Herero cattle Jonker would take.' He grinned wryly at Daniel. 'I almost feel sorry for Chief Jonker. He has no idea what sort of man he has living in Winterhoek.'

'Is William Thackeray really that bad, Pa?'

Daniel's life had been spent among primitive and sometimes cruel people, but they were usually kind and generous to their own. Because of this Daniel had grown to near-manhood naïve in the ways of other men. Jacobus Albrecht had given him his first real taste of what other men were like in the world beyond the Herero. Now there was William Thackeray.

'Yes, Daniel. I'm afraid he is. He is also a very clever man. His words do more harm than the guns of others. Mind you, he can be charming at times – and that makes him even more dangerous. I still believed him to be my friend when he was planning to involve me in his schemes. This plan to get me to the Cape is just a beginning. There will be more trouble before William Thackeray is through.'

One of the Hereros called to them, and they looked up to see Kasupi galloping back to the camp.

Leaping to the ground he said, 'Jacobus Albrecht and four white men ride along the road from Whalefish Bay.'

'What shall we do?' Daniel asked, looking at his father.

'Nothing, unless he makes a move to attack us, but I doubt if he'll do that now.'

'I have told two of my warriors to watch them wherever they go,' said Kasupi. 'The others are returning here.'

It was a few minutes before the five white men could be seen by those in the camp. The Boer trader was immediately recognisable, but the others were not known to the men from Otjimkandje.

The five were almost level with the camp before the sunlight glinting on metal spear-heads gave away its position. The riders stopped for perhaps a full minute, their horses milling about in confusion. Then, maintaining a respectful distance, they circled around the waiting men before stopping for another brief conference. Four riders suddenly wheeled about and headed back towards Whalefish Bay. Seconds later Jacobus Albrecht dug his heels into his horse's belly and galloped after them.

'I think we've seen the last of them,' declared Josh. 'They didn't fancy facing Herero spears, Kasupi.'

'No.' The chief's son sounded disappointed. 'But I will keep guards out until Aaron returns with the rest of my men.'

The transfer of goods from the ship to the waiting wagons took longer than anticipated. A stiff onshore breeze blew up, and Captain Klopper called off his plans to work after dark and deferred the off-loading until first light, much to the chagrin of the impatient Hannah.

Aaron sent one of the Hereros to find Josh to tell him what was happening and he and Hannah prepared to bed down beneath their wagon as they had on many occasions before.

'This is just like the old days,' Aaron said to his daughter as he finished his meal of salt beef and leaned back against the wagon-wheel and gazed up at the stars. 'But things are constantly changing down here. Only up there do they remain the same.'

Hannah made no reply; she was too busy with her own thoughts.

'Do you love him so very much, Hannah?'

'Who?' Hannah was startled. Her father might have been reading her mind.

'Who?' Aaron repeated. 'Are there so many young men out here who have asked you to marry them that you can't remember which of them you have travelled all these miles to be with?'

Hannah began to protest she had come to Whalefish Bay to help Mary look after Victoria, but Aaron interrupted her.

'Hannah, my child, you are talking to your father! Do you think that after all these years I don't know your every look and mood, the things that make you sad and the all too few things that have happened to make you happy? You have been the whole reason for my life for many years now. Nothing is as important to me as your happiness. Are you quite sure you love Daniel?'

'Yes, I love him.'

She averted her eyes from her father's face. After all their years together with no one else the admission suddenly felt like a betrayal.

'Do you believe he feels the same way about you?'

'I think he does.'

Aaron looked at his daughter with a smile that was both warm and gentle.

'Yes, I think he does, too. It is good. Daniel is young and has much to learn but he is a good boy. He will be a son to be proud of, a strength in my old age. I am very happy for you, Hannah. It is a great relief to me to know that should anything happen to me you will have Daniel to look after you.'

'Oh father!' Hannah scrambled to his side of the fire and buried her face in his rough cloth jacket, hugging him tight. 'You've become a part of this land. You'll go on for ever.'

'Nothing is for ever, my child' — Aaron lightly patted his daughter's back — 'so be sure to empty the cup of life as it is filled for you. Love especially is too precious a gift to waste even a single drop.'

Aaron and his wagons reached Josh and the others shortly before noon the following day, having seen no sign of Jacobus Albrecht.

There was little likelihood of his trying to carry out his plan now. Before leaving, Aaron had seen Captain Klopper's ship weigh anchor and shake out her sails, nosing out into the long Atlantic rollers, leaning on the wind as it turned south.

Jacobus Albrecht's opportunity had passed.

CHAPTER ELEVEN

The ten-day journey to Otjimkandje in early February in the year 1861 was everything Hannah had hoped it would be. At night after the evening meal she would sit by the fire, leaning against Daniel, sleepy and happy. Then, later, she would lie in her bed beneath the wagon close enough to call softly to Daniel and know he would hear her. In her thoughts he lay alongside her, touching her, holding her and making love to her.

On the fourth night of the journey they outspanned the wagons close to a water-hole at the foot of one of the impressive mountain 'islands' that rose suddenly and dramatically in a dozen places along the road to Otjimkandje.

After they had eaten, the moon rose red and bloated over the horizon and Daniel announced he and Hannah intended climbing the slope to get a view of the surrounding countryside by moonlight.

'Take a gun with you,' called Aaron as they were about to leave. 'This is leopard country.'

Hannah pulled a face, but she took Daniel's rifle from the wagon and handed it to him before they set off hand in hand up the steep rocky slope.

'What it is to be young and in love,' sighed Aaron. 'The joy and the pain of it all.'

'You can't have had very much of the joy of love,' said Josh. 'It's been just you and Hannah for many years now, hasn't it?'

'Yes.'

Aaron said nothing for a long time; then, 'I have had much joy watching Hannah grow up through my own eyes and also seeing her as I think her mother might have done. She has grown into a fine young lady. Her mother would be proud of her. Now she has found a fine young man for herself and my joy is almost complete.'

'They make a handsome couple,' Josh agreed.

'Yet there will always be the sadness too,' mused the trader. 'Every time I look at Hannah I see her dear mother. I wish she might have been spared to see Hannah now.'

He took out a handkerchief and blew his nose noisily. 'It isn't only young men who feel joy and pain – though they think it is. I was not a young man when I met Sofia, Hannah's mother. She was the daughter of a good family in a small town in Russia, near the Black Sea. I was studying law. I was not good enough for her, and her family never missed an opportunity to remind me. But I wanted Sofia and she wanted me, so one day we ran away together.' Aaron gave a short laugh. 'For most young people running away is a brief adventure. They cross a border, are married – and return to face the secret admiration of their families and friends. It was not so with Sofia and me. We were married in Bucharest but did not return home. Instead we went on through Europe to the Netherlands and from there took ship to the Cape Colonies. That is where Hannah was born.'

Aaron paused and pushed a log of wood farther into the heart of the fire. 'Four years later Sofia died. I was trading by that time and doing quite well. But I could not stay in a place where every street, every friend, was a constant reminder to me of Sofia. So Hannah and I trekked northwards, always northwards, and along the way I traded with the English, the Boers, the Bechuana, Nama, Orlam, Witbooi, with Jonker – and now with Kasupi's people.'

A sleepy Kasupi grinned at him from across the fire.

'Yet through all this you brought up Hannah to be a lovely girl.'

'Some credit I will take for her schooling. Her beauty was a gift from her mother.'

'And now Daniel is going to take her from you.'

'Take? Take? Never! I *give* her to him. We are partners now, Daniel and me. Everything we share. I have had Hannah's childhood all to myself. He is given a woman. It is as it should be. Like I said, Daniel is a good boy. You and Miriam can be proud of him – just as I am. For Hannah I could not have wished a better husband. For me, I feared she might one day have chosen worse. So we are all happy.'

Daniel and Hannah climbed the slopes of the mountain until they looked down upon the fires of their camp twinkling far below them. The moon had cleared the horizon and left its red glow behind. A plump silver pumpkin, it hung in the sky sharing its magic glow with the whole world.

It showed Daniel and Hannah to a large flat rock, and without waiting to regain their breath after the climb they kissed until Hannah pushed Daniel away and lay gasping in his arms.

'Do you love me, Daniel?'

The moon had heard it all before and continued its ponderous course across the sky, sweeping the stars before it.

'I love you very much.'

Their lips met again, and Hannah clung to him as though frightened he might run away from her.

'When will we be married, Daniel?'

'I thought we could make it September. Soon after your seventeenth birthday.'

'But that's ages away! Why must we wait so long?'

'We have to build a house and get furniture and things up from the Cape.'

'Such things don't matter. Anyway, we could get them made in Sesebe.'

'Anything made there would be shoddy now that Sam is away. I want us to have the best house in the whole of southwest Africa.'

'Daniel, I don't think I can wait that long for you.' Hannah's voice was hoarse with longing. 'I lie awake at night imagining you are loving me. Daniel, I want you now.'

Hannah had not been brought up among other women. Aaron had been able to teach her many things, but an awareness of modesty was not one of them. She spoke of her feelings openly and honestly because she knew no other way.

Her words burned into Daniel and his body responded immediately. Hannah felt the contraction of his stomach muscles, the tension. Instinctively she knew the reason. She turned in towards him and the next moment they were lying side by side on the rock, their bodies straining hard against each other.

Her mouth moved beneath his as they kissed, and his hand found the gap where her shirt had pulled away from her denim trousers. Moving inside, it touched soft skin and followed the line of her slim body up to the warmth of her armpit. She squirmed in his grasp, and his hand closed about the firm breast that was more mature than that of a young girl but was not yet the breast of a woman.

Hannah moaned and her mouth kissed his cheek, his eyes and his ears. 'I love you! Oh, Daniel, I love you!'

She plucked at his rough shirt and then her hands were on his warm body, stroking and gripping, pulling him to her.

He released her breast and as she half-rolled away from him his hand slipped down from her ribs and caressed her hard flat stomach. She breathed in, and his hand pushed down farther, inside the waistband of her trousers, his fingers moving on until they discovered a new warmth that sent Hannah writhing into a new world of lover's ecstasy.

Daniel, too, was floating away into heady sensuousness until an alien sound broke in upon him, shattering all romance in an instant. He realised then that he had heard the sound a few moments before but had rejected it without thought.

This time there could be no ignoring the asthmatic cough that came from somewhere very close. Daniel hurriedly pulled his hand away from Hannah, and the top button of her trousers went spinning into the night.

'What's the matter?'

'Sh!' Daniel put his left hand over her mouth while the other hand reached behind him for the gun he had propped against the rock on which they lay. His fingers found the cold metal barrel and closed about it. As he drew the gun up to him he whispered, 'Stay perfectly still. It's a leopard, and I'm not sure where it is.'

Bringing the gun across Hannah's body he eased back the hammer with his thumb until it clicked into the cocked position. Then he waited and watched.

For long minutes the only sound was Hannah's carefully controlled breathing and a Herero warrior calling to one of his companions in the camp far below them. Perspiration ran from Daniel's forehead and into his eyes. He hastily wiped it away with the back of his hand. Moving his head, he searched the shadows on either side of the rock. A leopard was a powerful and fearless killer. The night and the shadows were its friends; it could charge silently and launch itself in a tremendous twenty-foot leap before they even saw it.

The creature had all the advantages. All Daniel had was a gun with a single shot. There would be no second chance. If the leopard attacked, Daniel had to see it coming.

Hannah was fully aware of their danger. She lay absolutely still so as not to distract Daniel, all her romantic ideas forgotten.

The leopard gave away its new position by coughing once more. This time the sound came from behind Daniel. The animal was circling, choosing its moment to attack. Slowly and silently Daniel rolled away from Hannah to face into the darkness.

Suddenly he thought he saw a movement in the shadows thirty feet from them. The next moment he was certain. The leopard was making for some rocks on the slope just above them. Had they brought both their guns Daniel would have risked making a shot now. With one gun he dared not miss.

There was another flat rock twelve feet away on the slope above them. The leopard must have got their scent and did not appear to fear humans. Daniel guessed it would launch its attack from the flat rock. It was a calculated guess that Daniel hoped would prove correct. It *had* to be correct.

He moved again to give himself the best shot possible and had hardly settled into his new position when the big cat's head was silhouetted against the sky above the other flat rock.

Daniel had no time to congratulate himself on a good guess. The leopard knew exactly where his intended victims were and his attack came fast and frighteningly silent.

It took all Daniel's nerve to wait the fraction of a second until the leopard had launched itself clear of the rock and was in the air, forelegs extended towards him. Not until then did Daniel fire, aiming for the animal's heart.

The next few seconds were ones of utter confusion. The report of the gun mingled with the angry screams of the big cat and the smoke from the black powder as two hundred pounds of leopard crashed against Daniel and sent him somersaulting backwards from the rock, the sweet-sour smell of leopard in his nostrils.

He crashed to the ground with the breath knocked from him, not knowing quite what had happened. Then, to his great relief, he heard Hannah's alarmed voice calling to him.

'Daniel! Where are you? Are you all right?'

'I'm here and just a bit breathless, that's all—and you?'

'Not a scratch!'

Daniel rose to his feet and tripped over the leopard. It was lying full length on the ground between him and the rock on which they had been lying.

'Oh, Daniel, I was frightened!' Hannah trembled against him and he gave her a reassuring squeeze, aware that her fear had been for him and not for herself.

The shot had been heard in the camp at the base of the mountain and men were rushing up the slope towards them, waving blazing torches and shouting. Among their voices Daniel recognised his father and Aaron calling to them.

'Up here! We're all right. Bring the torches over here.'

One of the Hereros was the first to arrive and his long-drawn-out 'Aaah!' of admiration as he looked down at the body of the leopard would have satisfied the most vain hunter. Soon the whole party arrived at the scene to admire Daniel's kill.

'You were lucky to have hit him in this light,' commented Josh.

'There was no luck about it,' said Hannah indignantly. 'It was hunting us, and Daniel had to wait until it attacked before he could shoot.'

'It looks to me as though he almost waited too long,' said Aaron seriously. He touched the front of Hannah's shirt. In the torchlight Daniel could see two large patches of blood that must have fallen on her as the mortally wounded leopard passed over her head. It had died in mid-air from a shot that had passed clean through its heart.

Daniel and Hannah were never far from each other for the remainder of the journey but never again came as close to consummating their love—or as close to death—as they did on the slopes of 'The Mountain of the Leopard' as it was always known to the Herero tribe from that night on.

The wagons arrived at Sesebe to find a messenger from Otjim-kandje awaiting them. He told Kasupi that he must go to the Herero village immediately. His father, Chief Tjamuene, was dying. Custom decreed that every one of his sons should be with him when his spirit left his body for the world beyond life.

Josh and Daniel went on to Otjimkandje with Kasupi, the Herero wagon escort travelling more slowly on the road behind them. Aaron promised that he, too, would come to Otjimkandje as soon as his wagon had been unloaded. He would not be allowed to see the old chief, but it would be known he had come to be close at the end. It was a very important gesture of respect. Failure to make the journey to Otjimkandje would be taken as an insult by Tjamuene's successor and would not easily be forgiven.

The Herero village was in a state of turmoil. Tjamuene had been their chief for almost fifty years. Most of his people had been born, lived a full life and died without knowing any other chief. The fact that for many years he had been little more than Chief Jonker's vassal made little difference to his status in the eyes of his own people. They still lived in the village where they had been born. They still owned cattle. They were the only Herero village left in the whole of this land they had once called their own. Chief Tjamuene's death would mean the end of an era. For the Herero people the future now held only uncertainty.

The general disruption of village life meant that Miriam's news of William Thackeray's visit did not disturb Josh as much as it might otherwise have done, and Miriam deliberately played the visit down. Jonker's missionary had come to see Hugo Walder. She had met him in the church and spoken to him there. That was all.

The visit had more effect upon Daniel. He bitterly resented William Thackeray's intrusion into his life. He would have liked to forget that the preacher had ever had a place in the lives of his mother and father. But that was not possible; his coming had brought too much unhappiness and uncertainty. There was the attempt to take Josh to the Cape Colony — an incident about which Daniel had been sworn to secrecy, since Josh did not want Miriam worrying about him whenever he left Otjimkandje. Daniel felt a simmering anger for William Thackeray begin to burn deep within him.

Late that evening Kasupi came to the house to say that Chief Tjamuene wished to speak to Josh and Daniel. He escorted them into the chief's kraal, pushing a way through aged head-men and the wailing women of the household.

Hugo Walder was with Chief Tjamuene, and candles burned at the head and foot of the skin bed on which he lay. Mutjise was also present, as were the most senior of the headmen.

Chief Tjamuene of the Herero did not look ill, only very, very tired. He turned his head towards Josh and Daniel as they came to him and managed to raise a weak hand for Josh to take.

'I am passing on, my friend,' he said, the words coming from his throat with little breath to give them strength.

'Your life has been good for your people, Tjamuene,' Josh replied.

'You, too, have served my people,' Tjamuene said and motioned for Mutjise to come close.

'This man is a friend of the Herero for all time,' the dying chief said to his eldest son. 'Be sure that all of our people and their sons who have yet to be born know of this.'

'It will be as though you were still chief for them,' agreed Mutjise.

The old chief closed his eyes. They were shut for so long Josh thought he slept, but as he was about to move quietly away Tjamuene spoke again.

'Bring Kasupi to me.'

The younger son stepped forward and, opening his eyes, Tjamuene looked upon him with affection and reached out for his hand.

'He has been a good friend to your son?' he asked Josh.

'Kasupi has been like a brother to my son and a good friend to my family. He is beyond praise.'

The old chief nodded weakly, well pleased.

'Now the time has come for him and my son to go their own ways,' said Josh unexpectedly and the old chief's eyes took on a sudden alertness as he looked at him.

'Kasupi is a leader, a man for warriors to follow. Mutjise will have need of such a brother. I give him back to the Herero. Even so, he will stay in my thoughts for all time.'

Kasupi tried hard not to show his pleasure at Josh's words. He had given Kasupi his freedom. Had these words not been said to Chief Tjamuene he would have been bound to serve

Daniel for the remainder of his life. Much as he loved his friend, Kasupi had many times longed for such freedom. Now he looked down at his father.

'So be it. Serve your brother well.' Chief Tjamuene released the hand of his son and his eyes closed again. This time Hugo Walder signalled for Josh and Daniel to leave the hut.

The old Herero chief's life died with the sun, and his people mourned loudly throughout the night.

The next few days were spent arranging his funeral feast and many of his best cattle were slaughtered, their carcases beginning the slow process of cooking and their skulls being boiled clean to adorn the grave of the late Chief Tjamuene.

His funeral feast was attended by the chiefs of all the tribes within a radius of a hundred miles. Only Chief Jonker of the Afrikaners was absent. Aaron, Josh and Daniel were there with Hugo Walder, and Harold Andrews came from Sesebe to represent the mining company.

The rites lasted for two days and two nights, many of the participants staying awake for the whole forty-eight hours. Others crawled away to seek a few hours' sleep and then returned hoping their absence had not been noticed.

On the third day the ceremonies ended, and those men who had been closest to Tjamuene in life took his body from his kraal and buried him well away from the village. They were gone for a long time, for a chief's grave had to be marked by a mound of stones, and as he had been a great chief who had ruled his tribe for many years his burial mound needed to be of sufficient size to reflect this earthly status.

It was not until ten days after Chief Tjamuene's death that Otjimkandje returned to a normal routine and the Herero settled down to life under the chieftainship of Mutjise.

CHAPTER TWELVE

The mine at Sesebe ceased operations in May 1861, five months after Josh left the company. Had he stayed it might have been worked for a while longer. He would have brought in the engine from Andrews' previous copper mine to pump out water and gone deeper, but Harold Andrews made the decision to close with considerable relief. Chief Jonker was becoming more difficult with every day that passed. The Afrikaner chief had raised his levy on each wagonload of ore sent to the coast and brought the cost of the ore dangerously close to an uneconomical level.

When Andrews had protested Jonker had said that the mine was not producing enough ore because the Herero workers were lazy. His men waylaid them one Monday morning when they were on their way to Sesebe from Otjimkandje and beat them savagely in an effort to persuade them to work harder. The result had been that Mutjise ordered all the Herero workers back to their own village and no work was carried out at the mine for a whole week. Not until Harold Andrews had gone to the new Herero chief and pleaded with him had Mutjise allowed work to resume.

The Hereros went back to work; but the word was spread around that the Hereros were returning only because it had been agreed between their chief and the mine-owner, and had nothing to do with the threats of the Afrikaner chief.

Mutjise had his own reasons for making his contempt of Jonker common knowledge. The Herero's defeats at the hands of the Afrikaners had been due entirely to the weapons used in past battles. The Herero had fought with spears, the Afrikaners with guns, and the one-sided prohibition placed upon the trade in guns had helped Jonker to maintain his superiority over the Herero.

Mutjise knew the time had come for the proud Herero race led by his own warriors to shake off Jonker's sovereignty. The wagons of the trader Aaron had made more than one journey to the little hut by the sea, returning in the dark of night to

Chief Mutjise's kraal.

It became common for small bands of warriors to steal away before dawn on hunting trips far from the village. At first they returned with little to show for their hunting, but they became gradually more successful. If a man who ate the meat they brought broke his teeth on a lead musket-ball, nothing was ever said about it. If a woman found one in her cooking-pot, she was told it must have been shot by Kasupi, who owned a gun given to him by his friend Daniel.

Such a tense and unnatural state of affairs could not last for long. There was much resentment and ill-will on both sides. The Europeans could sense it and, though only Aaron knew the reason for the new confidence of the Herero, it was apparent to everyone that serious trouble lay ahead.

Hugo Walder preached the peace of the Lord at his Sunday services, but he knew as well as anybody that just as it needed two sides to make a war it would be necessary to persuade the same two opposing factors to work for peace. He was confident that Mutjise's people would never start a war, but he had no such confidence in Jonker's Afrikaners.

The German missionary decided it was time to return William Thackeray's visit.

He set off for Winterhoek early one morning in the middle of the year. Winter in this part of the world was no more than a slight relaxation of the burning heat, but the morning felt almost cool as he set off from the village that had been his home for so many years. His boyhood home in Germany in the wooded valley of the Rhine, with its rain and snow, was no longer real to him. Snow was no more than a dreamlike memory.

The missionary could not see himself ever returning to Europe. Home had become the familiar little church in the Herero village. He even spoke the Herero language more fluently than his native tongue now. He stopped his horse and looked back at the neat village, the round mud huts with their thatched roofs and thin threads of smoke rising from early fires. From the pens a thickening cloud of dust rose as the cattle became restless for food. It was a village awakening, a scene he had witnessed on hundreds of occasions.

Rising above the village, unobscured by smoke or dust and

proudly recording his modest success, was the cross of his church, Hugo Walder's achievement. He had brought Christianity to Otjimkandje and the Herero.

He enjoyed the ride to Winterhoek, his good mood lasting until he topped the ridge and looked down into the beautiful valley where Jonker had his untidy township.

There was surprisingly little life to be seen, only a few women and naked children. Most of the huts appeared to be deserted, the smoke of cooking-fires rising from only a dozen places.

Hugo Walder was puzzled; something here was not right. But he would not find the answers to his questions up here on the ridge. Flicking the reins, he urged his horse down the slope to Winterhoek.

The deserted air of the township extended to the mission church. The doors were closed and a thin layer of blown dust lay on the stone step in front of them. Neither did there seem to be anyone inside the mission hut. Curtains were drawn across the single window, and he could hear no movement inside when he listened outside the door.

The German missionary knocked twice and was about to leave when he thought he heard a faint sound from within. He tried the door and it opened beneath his hand. He pushed the door open wide, and the unhealthy smell of sickness rushed out past him to attack the clean sunlit day.

Hugo Walder strode into the hut and drew the curtains back as far as they would go. In the light that now filled the hut he saw the pale and emaciated figure of William Thackeray lying back in a rumpled and untidy bed.

'What in heaven's name are you doing lying here in this mess? How long have you been like this?'

William Thackeray could do little more than wave a weak hand towards the water-jug that stood on a nearby table.

The jug was a quarter full but the water smelled foul. Hugo Walder went outside and unhooked a water-bottle from his horse. Bringing it inside the hut, he poured the contents into a mug and took it to William Thackeray.

He lifted the Wesleyan missionary to a sitting position. His body was so thin and fragile that Hugo Walder felt obliged to handle him as gently as he would a small baby. Jonker's missionary drank the water as though it was the first he had tasted in days, choking over it and dribbling it helplessly down his chin.

'How long have you been in this condition?' Hugo Walder repeated when the other man had drunk his fill and lay back against his pillows, gasping for breath.

'I don't know. I've had a fever. It's been a long time.'

'Has none of Jonker's people been near you in that time?'

Hugo Walder was angry. The chief of even the most primitive tribe accepted a duty to care for a missionary when he came to live with them.

'Jonker has moved most of his tribe to another village about twenty miles away. He says it is unhealthy here.'

'Nonsense! This is one of the best spots anywhere in this country — though I am not saying it would not have been unhealthy for Jonker had I found him here today.'

William Thackeray winced as a pain caught him. 'I wish I had your energy, Hugo. I fear I have been a failure as a missionary. I should never have come to Africa.'

'You are a sick man. You will feel different when you are better.'

William Thackeray shook his head wearily. 'No. Chief Jonker stopped attending my church. When I asked him why he said I had brought no luck to his people. Since I came here nothing has gone right for him. Jonker lost what few cattle he owned through some cattle disease soon after the mine at Sesebe closed. Now Jonker has nothing to trade, and Jacobus Albrecht won't supply him with any more brandy until it can be paid for.'

'Where is Albrecht?'

'I don't know. I think he went with Jonker.'

William Thackeray lay back into his pillows. 'This is a judgement upon me, Hugo. I used God as an excuse to come here, to pursue personal ambition. It was not even an honourable ambition. I wished ill to a fellow-man, and now the illness has fallen upon me. It is His judgement.'

'It is your weak condition filling your mind with foolish thoughts,' said the German missionary as he pulled back the bedclothes and tidied William Thackeray's bed around his emaciated body. 'I will make you comfortable and then go and find someone in this place to bring you some food.'

'You are being very kind,' said William Thackeray. 'But it is a waste of your time. I am dying, Hugo. I know it and so do you. Leave me here to die alone. It is no less than I deserve.'

Hugo Walder had seen dying men before and knew William Thackeray had spoken the truth, but he would not leave a fellow-missionary alone to die in such miserable squalor. He finished tidying the bed.

'There! At least you have a little comfort. Now I go to find some food.'

He went to the nearest hut from which smoke was rising. An old woman sat in the shade outside the door, waving a desultory hand as the flies landed on her leathery wrinkled face in a vain search for moisture.

'I want food for Chief Jonker's missionary. What do you have?'

The eyes that were turned upon him held nothing but flat defeat.

'Who would hunt for an old woman who has no sons?'

The old crone nodded towards a hut from which a younger woman emerged, only to hurry back inside when she saw Hugo Walder. 'That is the one who should be taking food to the sick white man. Instead she sits and sulks because Jonker took her new husband from her to travel with him.'

'Thank you, mother. A blessing on your house.'

Hugo Walder went to the hut of the younger woman and called in through the open doorway. 'You in there. Come out! I want to talk to you.'

'I am busy. I have no time to talk.' There was fear in the voice.

'Come out here this instant. If I have to fetch you, I will take you straight to Chief Jonker.'

The trembling girl emerged from the hut, her naked bosom rising and falling rapidly. She was terrified of what was going to happen to her.

'Chief Jonker told you to feed and tend his missionary. Why have you not carried out his orders?'

'The missionary frightened me.' The Afrikaner girl burst into tears. 'In his sickness he threw himself about on his bed and said many strange things to me. There is a bad spirit in him.'

'He is Chief Jonker's missionary and he is very sick. You should be looking after him.'

'My man told me Chief Jonker is not pleased with him. He would be happy if his missionary was not alive when he returned.'

'Then listen to me, and hear me well. If the missionary dies because you have not fed him, I will bring such trouble upon Chief Jonker that he will kill both you and your man because of it. I am going back to the missionary now. You will bring him water and meat broth very quickly. Then you will clean his hut. When that is done I will ride back to Otjimkandje while you stay with him until my return. Is that understood?' The unhappy girl nodded. 'I hope so, for your sake. Now, hurry with that food and water. If you are slow, you will feel my anger as well as that of Chief Jonker.'

Hugo Walder returned to William Thackeray and found him lying just as he had left him. The Wesleyan missionary opened his eyes as his bearded colleague leaned over the bed.

'I thought you had returned to Otjimkandje.'

'I went only far enough to arrange for food and water to be brought to you. I will be leaving soon to arrange for a wagon to take you to my house, but someone will stay with you while I am gone.'

'No, I don't want that. I don't want to leave Winterhoek.'

The vehemence of his statement set William Thackeray to coughing so violently that Hugo Walder hurried to his side and held him tightly until he stopped. The Wesleyan missionary had a handkerchief clutched in his hand and he held it to his mouth as he coughed. When he finished he quickly tucked the handkerchief beneath his pillows, but not before Hugo Walder had seen the dark-red blood glistening upon it. William Thackeray was in an advanced state of lung disease. It was Hugo Walder's opinion that he had also contracted malaria. There could be no doubt that he was dying. It was a miracle he had managed to survive for so long.

'I can't leave you here with only an unreliable girl to look after you.'

'Hugo, please don't try to spare my feelings. You know I am going to die. I am aware of it myself. I have not been in Winterhoek for very long, but I have rebuilt the church here and done my best. Given time I would have grown to know and love it as you do your own church at Otjimkandje. It is all I have in the world that is familiar to me. Please allow me the selfish privilege of dying here and being the first man to have a Christian burial in the churchyard. Don't deny me that, Hugo.'

The German missionary could say nothing. He had heard William Thackeray's dying wish and felt obliged to respect it.

'There is one other thing you can do, Hugo. Bring Miriam here to see me before I die.'

William Thackeray looked up at the other man and anticipated his objections.

'I know she will not want to come. Plead with her for me. It is of great importance to us both. You must return with her, too, Hugo. I want you here. . . .'

The sick man's voice faded away and his eyelids drooped closed. His arm was dangling down at the side of the bed. It was frail and fleshless, no fatter than a man's two fingers. As Hugo lifted it and tucked it inside the bedclothes the Wesleyan preacher's lips moved in a faint whisper: 'Bring her here, Hugo. Please bring Miriam here.'

The frightened Afrikaner woman brought food within the hour. There was meat and maize porridge as well as broth. The German missionary took only the broth and fed it to William Thackeray himself.

Although he managed to get most of the food down, the effort left the sick man in a state of complete exhaustion. When Hugo Walder was sure he slept he ordered the woman to clean up the hut and stay there until he returned. She began to protest, but the missionary held up his hand and silenced her.

'It does not matter if I do not return for a whole week. You will stay here with him. You understand?'

The Afrikaner woman understood. She might not be a willing nurse, but she would not leave Chief Jonker's missionary.

On the return journey to Otjimkandje, Hugo Walder wondered how he might persuade Miriam to go with him to Winterhoek. It would not be easy, of that he was certain. He hoped he would find Josh at the house. It might be easier to reason with him.

But Josh was not at Otjimkandje. He had gone with Aaron to

the copper deposit he had found to the north of the Herero village. It was possible that at some time in the future it might be worked. Josh was carrying out a full survey of the extent and grade of the ore. He and Aaron would be away for some days.

Daniel was with Miriam, fretting because he would rather have been with Hannah at Sesebe. She was remaining there because Sam Speke was expected back from the Cape Colony any day now. He would be calling at Sesebe first, unaware of the events which had closed down the mine and left Aaron's store the sole occupied building in the mining village. Hannah should be perfectly safe inside the massively built store. It would defy a besieging army that was not equipped with cannon.

'Come in, Hugo,' called Miriam when he knocked on the door of the house. 'I've been expecting you. I called to see you this morning but you must have left early.'

'Yes, I went to visit William Thackeray at Winterhoek. I have just returned from there.'

'Oh!' Miriam's mouth snapped shut like a trap.

'He is a very sick man.'

'Africa doesn't agree with everyone. He should go home to England.'

'William Thackeray will never see England again.' Miriam's dark eyes met his and they widened. 'He is a dying man.'

'Then you'd best pray for him, Hugo. He'll have a lot to answer for when he meets the Lord.'

'I do not think you meant that to be as cruel as it sounded.'

'And why not? What do I owe William Thackeray but unhappiness?'

Miriam defied Hugo Walder's steady gaze for ten seconds, then she surrendered. 'No, you're quite right, Hugo. He's the one who's had nothing but unhappiness. I've had Josh and Daniel. I feel nothing but pity for him.'

'Enough pity to go and visit him?'

'Visit William Thackeray? Oh, no, Hugo! That's asking too much.'

'He wants to see you, Miriam, and I would come with you, of course. The desire to see you together with his wish to be buried next to the church at Winterhoek are probably the last requests he will ever make.'

Miriam opened her mouth to refuse again but she changed her mind.

'I'll think about it.'

Hugo Walder shook his head. 'There is no time for thinking. We must leave immediately. I will be surprised if he lives to see tomorrow's sunrise.'

Miriam searched the missionary's face for a sign that he was exaggerating the seriousness of William Thackeray's illness. She saw no deceit there.

The missionary received support from an unexpected quarter.

Daniel said, 'I'd like to meet William Thackeray before he dies.'

'You? Why?' Miriam rounded on him. 'He's nothing to you. Why should you want to meet him?'

'Is it so unreasonable, Ma? I was born with his name. But there's another reason, too.'

He knew he had to choose his words carefully, so as not to hurt her.

'You're right when you say he means nothing to me. I've got you and Pa right here. Whatever my name was when I was born I'm Daniel Retallick now and it's a name I'm proud of. But I'd still like to meet William Thackeray. I'd like to know whether he spent all these years trying to find us because he hated Pa or because he loved you, and why he's come here to try to part you. I've never met that sort of man before.'

'I doubt whether you'll find any of the answers in the man who lies dying at Winterhoek, Daniel,' said Hugo Walder sadly. 'There is very little of the physical man left. But he is a dying man and he has much on his mind. It is possible he hopes for forgiveness before he leaves this world. I don't know. I only know it will make me very sad if I have to return to Winterhoek alone.'

'What about Chief Jonker?' asked Miriam. 'Will he be there?'

'Jonker has moved his people to another village. William Thackeray is dying in a near-deserted township, believing himself to be a complete failure, his whole life wasted. When I found him no other human had been near him for days.'

Although she fought hard against the feeling, Miriam could not prevent pity from welling up inside her. Although she tried

hard to ignore them, there had been times when William
Thackeray had been kind and considerate, especially in the
days when she was a barefooted illiterate girl attending his
chapel school.

'Well, what are we waiting for? If we don't hurry, we won't
be there until morning. I can't ride a horse, so you'd better
harness the horses to a small wagon. Oxen would take far too
long to get there.'

After a flurry of activity they all set off in a wagon that sent
every bump up through the spine of the three travellers; but
Miriam insisted they continue as fast as was possible, and they
reached the church at Winterhoek soon after the setting sun
had erased the long shadow of the mission cross from the hut
where the dying preacher lay.

The Afrikaner girl was sitting in the darkness inside the hut,
close to the door. She had made some attempt to tidy the room,
but her heart had not been in the task and she had made a poor
job of it. The truth was that she had not expected Hugo Walder
to return and the prospect of staying with the white missionary
until he died terrified her. When Hugo Walder lit some candles
and motioned for her to leave she fled gratefully.

Miriam was appalled by the lack of material comforts in the
hut. There were only the bare essentials of life to be seen. Then
she reminded herself that the man in the bed had been ill for a
long time. It was probable the Afrikaner woman and her friends
had stolen everything else. To the women it would be a matter
of simple logic. The missionary was dying and would have no
further use for his belongings. It was better to take them now
and be sure of them.

Yet the poverty of the room did not shock Miriam nearly as
much as the sight of the man lying there. His sunken eyes were
closed and the skin on his face drawn so tightly across the bones
of his face that it was like looking at a skull. She had seen much
sickness and suffering since coming to Africa but she had never
before seen anyone who looked like this — and still lived.

A spasm of pain crossed the taut face and the deep-sunken
eyes flickered open. William Thackeray looked first at Hugo
Walder and then at the others with no sign of recognition. At
that moment Hugo Walder thought he had made a wasted

journey to fetch Miriam from Otjimkandje. It looked as though the Wesleyan missionary was delirious.

Then William Thackeray's confusion cleared and he looked up at the German missionary. 'You've come back. Did you . . . ?'

He turned his head on the pillow and saw Miriam. He tried to speak, but his laboured breathing overtook the words and for a full minute it was the only sound to be heard in the hut.

'Miriam! Thank you for coming.'

William Thackeray's eyes took in Daniel. 'So this is your son – the child I once held in my arms and loved as my own.' It was not possible to know whether the sudden pain that showed on his face was the result of remembering the past or had its origins in his present low physical state. 'You're every inch your father's son, Daniel. You'll grow up to be a fine Retallick.'

Miriam suddenly warmed towards this dying man. She was unable to feel anything more intimate for him than that. For the same reason she could feel no animosity towards him. This emaciated figure was no one she knew or had known. He was a dying stranger, entitled to her pity.

Yet William Thackeray had just said something that stirred memories of the preacher she had first met, the kind and considerate man she had once thought him to be. William Thackeray had just cast away any future doubts that Daniel might have felt about his parentage. Confirmed, as no one else could, that Daniel was indeed Josh's son.

'Sh! Don't try to speak. You need rest.' Miriam moved forward and fussed with his bedclothes, moved instinctively to do battle with untidiness.

'I must speak. There's so little time . . . so little time.'

William Thackeray fought a battle with his breathing again. When he had won he pointed to an old chest of drawers against the far wall.

'Top drawer . . . papers . . . fetch them for me, Hugo.'

The German missionary moved across the room as William Thackeray ran his tongue about his dry thin lips.

Daniel filled a mug with water and carried it to the bed. He held it to the missionary's lips while Miriam lifted the sick man higher in the bed with frightening ease.

'Thank you.' William Thackeray nodded the water away, and

Daniel removed the mug from the lips of this man he had been prepared to hate but for whom he had nothing but pity.

There were a number of sheets of thick paper in the drawer, each page filled with neat handwriting that must have called for great concentration on the part of the sick missionary.

'Read it, Hugo. Aloud, please.'

Hugo Walder began to read, and from the very first line he had the full attention of Miriam and Daniel. William Thackeray leaned back on his pillows and listened with closed eyes.

What William Thackeray had written was a complete confession of his part in the Cornish riot for which Josh had been convicted. He told how he had sent a messenger to Josh in order to get him to the town where the riot was being staged. How Josh had gone there believing he would be able to prevent the disturbance. He mentioned names and meetings and implicated an officer who had been instrumental in having Josh arrested.

In short, the document went much farther than any evidence William Thackeray might have given before the Court of Assize which had found Josh guilty. There William Thackeray would have given only evidence enough to clear Josh of guilt. This document detailed his own responsibility for all that had gone on in that Cornish port – and much more beside.

When Hugo Walder finished reading the Wesleyan missionary said, without opening his eyes, 'There is a quill and ink in the same drawer, Hugo. I wish you to witness my signature.'

Without comment, the excited German missionary witnessed the document, adding the date and the information that the confession had been made by William Thackeray in the full knowledge of his imminent death.

'Does that win back a little of the respect you once had for me, Miriam?' The question came out as a feeble whisper.

'Yes, William.' Miriam swallowed the bitterness she felt. William Thackeray could have said something many years before.

'And your forgiveness?'

Miriam remained silent, and William Thackeray moved his head a fraction and opened his eyes to look at her.

'Will you at least try to forgive me?' he pleaded.

'I'll try.'

All the tension drained from William Thackeray's body.

'Then I'll leave you and your family in peace, Miriam. That's what you asked for.'

The dying missionary's eyes closed once more and his lips hardly moved as he whispered, 'We could have conquered the world, you and I, Miriam – and it would have been yours, all of it.'

William Thackeray never spoke again. He appeared to sleep, his breathing shallow but even. Then, half an hour later, Hugo Walder took William Thackeray's wrist to find a pulse and there was none.

'Poor William' was all Miriam could think of to say about him.

'What will you do with his confession?' asked the German missionary.

'What is there to be done? It comes fifteen years too late. Had he spoken when we were all in Cornwall our lives would have been very different. Now . . . ?' Miriam shrugged. 'Keep it until we return to Otjimkandje, Hugo.'

'All right, but the last well-intentioned task of a dying man should not be carried out in vain.'

Hugo Walder stepped to the door and looked out at the bright moonlight. 'You should have no difficulty in making your way back to Otjimkandje. I will stay here and bury William Thackeray in the morning.'

'We'll all stay here,' said Miriam. 'Whatever he did the past is over now. He's a man who has died in loneliness and has need of our prayers.'

'Then Daniel and I will carry him to his church now,' said the German missionary. 'He would have liked that. The rebuilding of it was the only thing William Thackeray believed he had successfully done for God. His soul will find peace there.'

CHAPTER THIRTEEN

Chief Jonker learned of the death of his missionary four days later when a boy sent from Winterhoek arrived at his new village. The messenger found him with Jacobus Albrecht, drinking brandy grudgingly given from the Boer's own fast-dwindling stock.

'Where is the body of the missionary now?' asked the Afrikaner chief.

'Buried in the ground by the stone hut with a cross,' replied the boy. 'The Little Father from Otjimkandje put him there. He was with your missionary when he died. So, too, were the white woman and her son.'

To Chief Jonker this spelled treachery. He had known his missionary wanted the white woman from Otjimkandje for himself. He also knew Jacobus Albrecht had taken part in an unsuccessful move to get her husband out of the land. Jonker believed that when this had failed William Thackeray had turned to the Little Father from Otjimkandje for help.

'The Little Father should not have gone to Winterhoek without first asking my permission,' he declared sulkily. For the fate of his missionary Jonker cared nothing. He had brought with him none of the authority of the Cape government Jonker had hoped for. Neither had his presence increased the Afrikaner chief's influence with the British administration. The missionary had been too filled with his own ambitions. He had promised Jonker that the chief's aims would be achieved as his own were fulfilled, but Jonker was prepared to take second place to no man and he was no longer of an age when he could afford to wait.

'Why not ride to Otjimkandje and tell Hugo Walder not to interfere with your Afrikaners, chief?' suggested Jacobus Albrecht.

Jonker glared at the trader. He had no wish to try to force a showdown with the German missionary. He was no match for him in a verbal battle. There was a time when he might have put up a good fight, but these days his thoughts took longer to change into words.

'When I wish to speak to the Little Father I will send for him to come to me.'

Jacobus Albrecht splashed more brandy into his mug and gave a short laugh.

'By that time he might be too high and mighty to come to you, Jonker. He might think the Herero are better than the Afrikaners. . . .' The trader saw a dangerous look appear on Jonker's face. 'I'm not saying they *are* better than your people,' he hastily added. 'I'm just saying what he might think. After all, the Herero still have plenty of cattle. Good big healthy cattle.'

The Boer trader did not have to spell out the comparison. The Afrikaners were left with a mere handful of scrawny unhealthy stock. But the Afrikaner chief would not let this man sitting across the table from him criticise the weakness of his tribe.

'Perhaps I should send you to Otjimkandje to fetch the white man, Retallick, to explain what has made them so rich,' he said. 'Or would you prefer to speak to the wagonmaker about it?'

Jonker laughed uproariously as Jacobus Albrecht's hand went instinctively to his misshapen nose.

'I'll settle my own debts,' the trader growled. 'That doesn't alter the fact that the Herero have more cattle than they know what to do with, while you don't have enough for trading.'

He divided the last of the brandy between the two mugs. 'I'm not going to be able to order any more of this until I've got something to trade with.'

'You order more brandy,' demanded the Afrikaner chief. 'I will give you cattle for trade. Get me powder, too, and new guns — good ones.'

'Now, that's getting pretty ambitious, Jonker. You know guns and powder aren't allowed in here. Oh, I can get them! But it will cost plenty of cattle.'

'There will be plenty of cattle.'

Chief Jonker drowned the last of the brandy, savouring the feel of its fire passing down his throat.

'Since the death of his father Mutjise has not been to see me to offer the friendship of the Herero people. Neither have I been asked to approve his selection as the new chief of the Otjimkandje Herero. I will have to go to him and show my displeasure. It is going to take many cattle to buy the protection of Chief Jonker of the Afrikaners once more.'

'Do you think he'll give them to you, Jonker?'

'Does a man have to ask to take what is rightfully his?'

'That's more like it, chief. Let me know when you're going for the cattle. We'll drive them straight to Whalefish Bay and ship them out. It will be too late for any argument about who owns them then!'

Josh and Aaron returned from the site of the copper deposits well pleased with their findings. Josh had carried out exhaustive tests and ascertained it was a very high-grade ore and far more extensive than the ore at Sesebe. It would make a good profit — but first he had to find a way to obtain Chief Jonker's agreement before he could work it without undue interference. The Afrikaner chief would want his share from the profit by way of 'tribute'. This was acceptable if his demands were reasonable, but Josh did not want to repeat the experience of Sesebe. He wanted to leave no loophole for Chief Jonker to bring in someone else to work the ore at a later date.

Josh and Aaron decided that for the moment they would say nothing to the Afrikaner chief of their find. Instead, they would begin work on the mine in secret, stockpiling the ore until such time as they might safely transport it to the coast.

The two men stayed in Otjimkandje only long enough to collect two wagonloads of mining-tools and gather together some of the men who had worked on Andrews' mine, before returning to their find.

Josh's reactions to William Thackeray's death-bed confession were even more confused than Miriam's had been. At first he was overjoyed, convinced he could take it to the Cape government and enjoy the ending of his forced exile. Miriam brought him sharply down to earth.

Before Josh could be a free man he would have to be granted a pardon by Queen Victoria, setting aside his conviction. It could only be accomplished in England and would take time.

Meanwhile he would be imprisoned in the Cape Colony.

There was no absolute guarantee a pardon would be granted. It it were refused, or the ship carrying it from England were lost, Josh would be condemned to spending the rest of his life in prison.

It was far too great a risk to take and Josh, bitterly disappointed, had to agree. Even after all these years the terrible memories of life on board a prison hulk were enough to cause him to break out in a cold sweat.

Ever since he had left the Assize Court in Bodmin as a convicted man Josh had dreamed of clearing his name and living his life free from fear of capture. Now he had to face the realisation that he might never achieve that end unless he was prepared to place the freedom he already had at risk.

It was a view not shared by Hugo Walder. He kept William Thackeray's confession and the day after Josh and Aaron departed for their new copper mine the missionary set off on a journey of his own to the Cape Colony, expecting to meet Sam Speke and his family along the road to Whalefish Bay.

Chief Jonker and a hundred of his armed warriors chose that very night to pay the promised visit to the new chief of the Herero. Jacobus Albrecht had been informed of his plans and had managed to find enough brandy to send the Afrikaner warriors on their way fortified with all the courage that brandy and superior weapons could bestow upon a fighting man.

Jonker wanted to surprise Mutjise and his people but there was no way an army of half-drunken men and a hundred horses could travel in complete silence. Hannah heard them pass by the shuttered and barred store in Sesebe.

It was doubtful whether Chief Jonker knew she was there, or would have cared if he had. One woman would not be able to stop a hundred armed warriors.

Hannah had other ideas. When the horsemen had passed by she unbarred the door and went to the hut at the back of the store where one of Aaron's Herero employees cowered in terror with his family. In answer to her questions he could only keep repeating that Jonker and all his warrors were on their way to destroy Otjimkandje.

'Then you must go and warn them,' said Hannah. 'You have

family there?'

The frightened man nodded. He had a father, mother and brothers in the village.

'Then get hold of yourself. Unless you want them all slaughtered in their sleep you will have to go and warn them. Take my horse and ride as fast as you can. You must get to Otjimkandje before Jonker's men. First warn the Retallicks, then Mutjise. Go quickly, now.'

Hannah physically pushed the man from the hut and made sure he mounted the horse and set off before she returned to the store.

Hannah had underestimated the Afrikaner chief. Jonker had been on many raids, and his army did not ride to do battle without outriders to guard against surprise attack. One of these flank outriders caught the terrified Herero from Sesebe and dragged him before Jonker.

'Where have you come from? Where were you going?'

The Herero's eyeballs rolled white in the darkness of his face but he said nothing.

'He was riding towards Otjimkandje,' said the man who had captured him. 'He probably came from Sesebe.'

'You did well,' said Jonker to his warrior. 'He will warn no one now. Kill him.'

The Herero's eyes rolled again and he began to speak. The words broke off in noisy gurgling as his captor pulled back his head and slit his throat with one slash of a sharp-bladed knife. The incident over, Chief Jonker resumed his advance upon Otjimkandje.

The village came awake to a frightening cacophony of noise as Jonker's men charged into the outskirts of the village not far from the mission church. The screams of the Herero women mingled with the shouts of Jonker's men and the firing of their guns.

The noise woke Daniel, and leaping from his bed he ran from the room, bumping into Miriam outside the door.

'It sounds like an attack on the village,' he said. 'It must be Jonker's men. Grab the old gun over the fireplace and get over to the church. I'll bring my own gun and some more ammunition.'

'What about the others – the villagers?'

'If they've got any sense, they'll make for the church, too. It's the only building we have any real chance of defending. Hurry now, Ma.'

Daniel grabbed all the powder and shot he could find and carried it to the church. As he had thought, many of the villagers were already there, but he saw immediately they were the women, children and old men only. None of the warriors was there.

Thinking the men of Otjimkandje must be trying to stem the Afrikaners' advance armed only with their spears, Daniel saw that Miriam had a loaded musket, then left the church. He made his way towards the shouts of the Afrikaners, the way illuminated by blazing thatch roofs deliberately fired by Jonker's men.

The attacking warriors were in no hurry to press home their attack, content to loot as they advanced. They were noisily firing their guns as they came, but there seemed to be little actual fighting taking place as so far the Afrikaners had met with no resistance.

Then, as Daniel knelt in the shadow of a hut watching the Afrikaners advancing towards him and trying to think of some way to stop them, he was joined by some of the missing Herero warriors. Others could be seen moving up into a rough line across the village, cutting off the approaching Afrikaners.

'I am happy to see you with us, Daniel.'

Kasupi spoke from the shadows beside him.

'We will remember you were ready to fight with us, but this is the night of the Otjimkandje Herero. Tonight we became warriors one more. Got to the church and take care of our women and children.'

A nearby roof erupted in a fountain of flames, and Daniel saw that every Herero warrior carried a gun and handled it as though familiar with its working.

'Go now, my friend. This is our fight. We have waited for it for too many years.'

Daniel knew better than to argue with Kasupi. The fact that the Herero were well armed and had kept it a secret meant that they were prepared for such an attack as this. He would only get in their way if he stayed.

Just before he entered the church he heard Kasupi shout an order to his men and the Herero warriors fired their first volley at Jonker's men. It was followed by another only a few seconds later.

Daniel smiled grimly and slipped inside the crowded stone church. Jonker had stuck his nose into a hornets' nest tonight. The stings would be painful indeed.

Outside in the flame-broken darkness the Herero divided into two parties, one led by Kasupi, the other by their chief Mutjise. They formed two straight lines, right across the village. One line would move forward until they were close enough to see the Afrikaner looters and open fire. Then the second line would move ahead of them while the others reloaded.

It was an orderly and thoroughly well-organised operation. Swiftly and efficiently they swept the Afrikaners from the village ahead of them, inflicting heavy casualties. Behind the musket-carrying warriors came others with assegais to despatch the Afrikaner wounded.

Jonker himself was lucky to escape with his life. Going forward on his horse after the first volley hit his men, he was caught in the second and had his horse shot from beneath him.

But there was no shortage of Afrikaner horses. By the time Jonker's men realised what was happening and turned to flee many of their number lay spilling their blood in the dusty spaces of Otjimkandje.

The Herero had won a great victory of vengeance. For the loss of three women and a baby they had killed thirty of Jonker's men and captured forty guns and eighteen horses.

What was more important was that tonight the Herero had broken Jonker's iron grip on their people. Never again would he and his tribe dare to claim sovereignty over the Herero.

It was more than two hours since Hannah had sent the messenger to Otjimkandje. His mission was urgent and he had a fast horse. He should have been there in half that time.

She wondered what would happen. Mutjise and his warriors would defend the village, of that she was sure; but it was possible that Daniel would try to get Miriam out and bring her to Sesebe before the fighting started. If all had gone well, they might arrive at any time.

When the knock came Hannah had no hesitation. Running to the door, she unbarred it and flung it open.

'Daniel . . . !'

But it was not Daniel. The man standing in the doorway was Jacobus Albrecht.

Hannah tried to slam the door shut, but the big Boer was too quick for her. He put his boot in the doorway and prevented it from closing. Hannah was terrified but she did not lose her head. She stamped hard on his toe. Jacobus Albrecht swore, then put his shoulder to the door, knocking it open and sending Hannah staggering back along the passageway.

Turning, she ran to her room. This time she reached it before the Boer and shut and bolted the door hurriedly. She turned to pick up her gun but to her dismay remembered she had left it just inside the door to the storeroom.

Hannah ran to the window above her bed. There was a glass window opening inwards with a stout shutter outside. She opened the glass window as Jacobus Albrecht lifted the latch on the door and found it bolted against him.

The Boer put his weight against the door and it gave slightly. This was not made of thick timber as was the front door. Taking a pace backwards, the Boer trader gave the door a hefty kick with the heel of his boot and the door burst open, taking the bolt staple clean out of the door-frame.

Hannah had opened the glass window but the shutter had two large bolts, both of them stiff and heavy, and she could not slide them open in time.

Standing on her bed, she turned to face Jacobus Albrecht as he came across the room at her. His smile had just begun when Hannah kicked out at his face. The Boer jerked his head to one side, but the kick landed, splitting his lower lip.

'You bitch!'

Hannah kicked again, but this time Jacobus was ready for her. He caught her foot between his two hands and twisted. Hannah overbalanced and fell backwards on to the bed. Releasing his hold on her foot, Jacobus Albrecht dropped to the bed on top of her.

'That's better. Now, you just behave and you'll enjoy it.

You're going to learn what it's like to lay with a real man instead of a young boy.'

The Boer trader smelled of brandy but he was not drunk. Hannah pummelled at his body, then tried to scratch his face, but he caught both her wrists and taking her arms above her head held both her wrists in his huge left hand while his right fumbled at her trousers, ripping and pulling as Hannah bucked and struggled beneath him.

The Boer's face came down close to hers and Hannah butted him, her forehead cracking hard against his disfigured nose. It hurt. Bringing up his right hand, Jacobus Albrecht struck her hard on the side of the jaw.

Everything went blank for Hannah. It seemed to her it could only have been for a matter of seconds, but it must have been longer than that because she regained consciousness aware of Jacobus Albrecht's body undulating on top of her, crushing her chest and making breathing difficult.

Then she felt the Boer inside her, hurting. She moaned and bit back a sob as her body began to move in time with the movements of the man above her. She wanted to stop it but could not. She hated herself and him but still her body would not stay still. The moans that escaped from her throat had nothing to do with the pain inside her. That was something she was no longer aware of.

The Boer began gasping as, head back, he drove farther into her and her moans became shouts, half-screams.

Then an animal grunt came from Jacobus Albrecht and his body shuddered to a stop. He released his grip on her wrists and her arms dropped down to his body, sliding from his back to his waist — and to his belt.

Her left hand touched metal. It was the Boer trader's American revolver, held in its holster by a short leather strap that came undone when she slid a finger beneath it.

The Boer's convulsions ended, he lay with his full weight upon her. Hannah, too, was still now, her body her own once more.

Raising himself to one elbow, the Boer looked down at her face and grinned.

'There, didn't I tell you you'd enjoy it? Where did you learn to do it like that, eh? It wasn't from the Retallick brat, that's for sure.'

Too late Jacobus Albrecht saw the expression upon Hannah's face. He grabbed down for his gun and heard the click of the hammer being thumbed back as Hannah pushed the barrel up into his stomach and pulled the trigger.

The .36 calibre bullet tore up through the Boer's stomach and blasted a hole in his heart big enough to take a pocket watch.

Hannah pushed with all her strength and the body of the big Boer rolled away from her and fell to the floor.

She sat up retching, the gun still in her hand. Jacobus Albrecht lay on his back on the floor, his mouth open, leaking blood, his eyes staring up at something he would never see.

His trousers were still undone, and looking at his exposed body Hannah remembered how her own body had responded to his. She had given herself to him.

'Oh God! What have I done? Daniel! Daniel!'

She never had to think about her next action. It was something that had to be done. Something evil inside her that had to be destroyed.

Lifting the gun slowly as though in a dream, Hannah put the cold steel barrel to her temple and pulled the trigger.

CHAPTER FOURTEEN

Sam Speke met Hugo Walder on the road and told him there was a vessel at anchor at Whalefish Bay, awaiting the arrival of a high government official from the Cape Colony who was on a brief and well-protected visit to this unclaimed territory.

In return, Hugo Walder was able to tell Sam Speke of the closing of the mine at Sesebe and of the deaths of Chief Tjamuene and William Thackeray.

It left Sam with plenty to think about as he drove the slow ox-wagon on towards Sesebe.

His trip to the Cape had been entirely successful. Even before the ship had reached the Cape, Victoria had shown signs of improvement. The doctors in the capital of the expanding colony examined the girl and declared that, although her lungs showed signs of weakness, she was now well on the road to recovery. They thought it probable that the dust of the copper workings in the dry desert soil of Sesebe had done much to irritate her lungs. If she stayed away from such conditions, there was no reason why she should not make a complete recovery.

As the wagon neared Sesebe, Sam Speke looked at the deserted buildings on the horizon. There was nothing here to irritate Victoria's lungs now. He wondered how the closure was affecting Aaron's business.

Of a sudden he felt he was nearing home and he cracked the long whip over the backs of the stolid oxen in a vain attempt to goad them to greater speed.

Sesebe was indeed a deserted town. It seemed unnatural to be arriving at midday without a sound coming from the Miners' Inn, but the door to Aaron's store stood open and Sam Speke hauled the oxen to a halt in front of it and handed Mary and Victoria down to the ground.

'Hello! Is anyone there? Aaron? Hannah?'

Nobody came to the door, and Sam Speke frowned. Anyone in the store should have heard the creaking of the ox-wagon from a quarter of a mile away. There had to be someone inside;

they would not have gone away leaving the front door open.

He walked into the store and along the passageway. Mary and Victoria behind him.

There was no one in the storeroom, and then Sam Speke saw the door to Hannah's room standing half-open. He pushed on it and his nose wrinkled at the dry acrid smell of a burnt-out lamp-wick. He had taken one pace into the room when he stopped suddenly. The light from the sunlit passageway sliced through the doorway and fell upon the wide-eyed face of Jacobus Albrecht staring up from the floor. Beyond him Hannah lay contorted in death upon the bed, a vast dark stain on the bed cover around her head.

Sam Speke slammed the door shut and turned quickly. 'Mary, get Victoria outside quickly!'

Mary Speke did not ask her husband what he had seen. The look of horror on his face was sufficient. She stopped Victoria from coming any farther and hurried her back along the passageway to the warm sunshine outside.

Sam Speke waited until his wife and daughter were out of the store before he opened the door to the room of death again.

There were candles in the room and he lit them. The disarray of Albrecht's clothing and the gun held in Hannah's stiff fingers were enough to tell Sam Speke the whole story. He prised the gun from her hand, the task made no easier by the tears that welled up and clouded his eyes.

'You poor child. You poor dear child.'

Sam Speke straightened Hannah on the bed as best he could and covered her body with a sheet he took from a cupboard in the room.

He dragged the body of Jacobus Albrecht from the room and into the passageway outside. Looking down at the flattened nose, he regretted that he had not killed the Boer trader instead of merely disfiguring him.

Going out of the house, he found Mary waiting at the wagon with Victoria. In a choked voice he told her what had happened.

Mary made no attempt to hold back her tears.

'Poor Hannah — and poor Daniel!' was all she was able to say for some time. When she regained some measure of self-control she was able to tell her husband that there was no one else in the mining village. There were signs that the hut behind the store had been occupied until very recently and that the occupants had left in a great hurry, but apart from themselves there was neither human nor animal left alive in Sesebe.

'Take the wagon out of sight beyond the end house,' said Sam Speke. 'There's something I must do before I leave.'

'Are you going to bury Hannah here?'

'No. The decision on that belongs to her father. Just take the wagon out of sight and I'll be with you in a few minutes.'

When his self-appointed task was complete, Sam Speke rejoined his wife and daughter and wheeling the oxen back on to the track he pointed them towards Otjimkandje.

Twenty minutes out of Sesebe he met up with the last person he wanted to see. Daniel was cantering his horse towards the mining 'ghost' town and he was in a happy and talkative mood.

'Sam! Mary! It's good to see you again—and Victoria! You look a different girl.' He leaned forward from the saddle and gave her a kiss. 'It's wonderful to see you looking well again.'

Before Sam Speke could interrupt his chatter he said, 'You arrived a day too late, Sam. You missed a great battle. Jonker and his Afrikaners attacked Otjimkandje last night, but somehow Mutjise had got hold of a whole lot of guns. Our Herero gave the Afrikaners the hiding of their lives. They taught them a lesson they'll never forget. I'm on my way to tell Hannah about it now. Did you see her? She'll be—'

'Daniel!' Sam Speke could not allow him to chatter on any longer. 'Listen to me.'

For the first time Daniel saw the strained expressions on the faces of the others.

'Daniel, we've just come from Sesebe. Something happened there last night, too.'

'To Hannah?'

'Yes . . . to Hannah. She's dead, Daniel.'

'Dead?' Daniel was so stunned he was unable to accept what Sam Speke had said to him. 'Dead? But . . . how, Sam? Not Jonker? I'll kill him . . . I swear I'll kill him.'

'It wasn't Jonker. Here, Daniel. Get down off that horse and we'll take a walk.'

In a daze, Daniel swung down off his horse and walked beside Sam Speke, away from the wagon. Sam told him what he had found, leaving out as many of the details as he could.

'I left Hannah lying on the bed. I didn't know what Aaron would want to be done.'

'Aaron's not in Otjimkandje. He's two days' ride away at the new copper mine with Pa.'

'Then I'll send a wagon back to bring her to Otjimkandje. We'll bury Hannah near Hugo's church.'

'Where's Albrecht's body?' Daniel asked fiercely.

'I pitched it into the copper workings. I didn't want to have anything to do with a burial for him.'

Daniel nodded his agreement, still numb with shock at the news of Hannah's death. 'You go on to Otjimkandje, Sam. Tell Ma what's happened and ask Mutjise to send a rider for Aaron, then get a wagon back to Sesebe.'

'Where will you be?'

'I'm going on to Sesebe.'

Sam Speke put a hand on his arm. 'Don't, Daniel. Nothing you do will bring her back to life. Remember her as she was, not as she is now.'

'I'll always remember her as she was, Sam. But I've got to go to her. We were to be married this year, and as Aaron's not here it's up to me to be with her until she's taken to Hugo's church.'

Sam Speke let his hand drop away. 'It doesn't make a deal of sense to me, Daniel – but I doubt if I'd feel any different if she was mine. Go and do what you need to. I'll have a wagon back as quickly as I can.'

Kasupi led forty mounted Herero warriors to Sesebe to escort his friend and the body of Hannah back to Otjimkandje. On the way they found the body of the messenger sent to warn the villagers. His body was placed on the wagon alongside Hannah.

Hannah was buried in the mission churchyard three days later. Aaron, upon his arrival, had declared he would rather she be laid to rest in a place where she was among friends than adhere to the rites of a religion he had long since given up practising.

As the coffin made by Sam Speke was lowered into the ground the Jewish trader stood a lonely figure at the graveside. In the absence of Hugo Walder, Josh said a few prayers, and the brief service was attended by Mutjise, Kasupi and many of the villagers who had been looking forward to attending the wedding feast of Daniel and Hannah later in the year.

Daniel, too, stood alone, isolated by his grief. Of all those at the graveside only Miriam knew how deeply Hannah's death had affected him. He would never speak of it to anyone, but the deep sense of loss was something that would return to haunt many lonely camp-fires.

Josh would not allow Aaron to return to Sesebe and be alone there with memories of Hannah. He insisted that the trader remain at Otjimkandje.

Later that evening Sam Speke came to the Retallick house and the talk turned to what the future now held for all of them.

Aaron was the first to state his views and he spoke in a flat voice full of despair, far removed from his usual extravert self.

'For me, I am ready to give up. Everything I did was for Hannah. Now she is gone, so what is there to work for—me?' He shrugged. 'I could open a shop in Cape Town and make a living in comfort.'

'Don't make any decision yet, Aaron,' said Josh. 'This has hit you hard, and we all grieve with you, but you're needed in this country. We need you—every one of us. If you give up now, progress will be set back thirty years.'

'Progress?' Aaron was bitter. 'You can call it progress when the tribes use my guns to raid and kill each other? When a white man attacks a girl in her own home and causes her to take her life?' His voice broke as he cried, 'My God! If that is progress, it is better we leave this country alone and take our progress back with us.'

Aaron broke down and wept, and there was nothing anyone could do to comfort him.

The long uncomfortable silence that followed was ended by Josh.

'The tribes were fighting long before we got here, Aaron. Jonker brought his first guns up to this country with him from the south to terrorise all the other tribes. What you've done is to give Mutjise's people a chance to fight back and end Jonker's reign of terror. Neither is there anything that can be done about the Jacobus Albrechts of this world. If anyone is to blame for allowing him to roam free, it's me. I should have killed him after he gave Daniel such a beating. Fortunately there are few men like him, but they are to be found wherever there are men and women.'

'I know! I know!' Aaron spoke in an emotion-choked voice. 'Tell it to me next month — or next week — and I might understand. But not today. Not today.'

'Come back to the copper mine with me for a while,' said Josh. 'Help me to build a few huts and get people working there. We'll be able to make it a full-time operation now. I doubt if Jonker will try to stop it after his defeat.'

'Do you intend staying there?' asked Sam Speke.

'For a while. We don't know how the Cape government will react to this battle between the Afrikaners and the Herero. They might decide to send troops up here and find out what it's all about. I'd rather not be here if they do come.'

Sam Speke snorted. 'There's little fear of that. Half of them in the Cape don't even know of Whalefish Bay! Otjimkandje could be on the moon for all they know — or care.'

'All the same, I think I'll go to the new mine for a while,' said Josh. 'Miriam and I have already talked it over.'

'But what about this confession made by Jonker's preacher? Hugo was very excited about it when he told me. You shouldn't have to hide anymore.'

'I wish I had as much faith in it as Hugo. Whatever William Thackeray wrote doesn't alter the fact that I'm a convicted felon. If I stay out of the way, I can be sure there'll be no trouble for me. I prefer it to be that way.'

'How about you, Daniel?' asked Miriam. Her son's withdrawn unhappiness worried her. 'You haven't said anything yet. Do you have any plans?'

'Yes. I'd like to get away from Otjimkandje.'

There were too many things around the Herero village to remind him at this time of Hannah. He wanted to forget everything about her until he could remember her as she had been and not as a corpse with the side of her head blown away. Sam

Speke had been right; Daniel should not have gone to the store.

'Do you have any idea where you want to go?' asked Josh.

Daniel looked at Hannah's father and recognised that the bearded Jew's sorrow was as deep as his own and his heart went out to him.

'That depends upon Aaron. If he decides to carry on trading, I'll move up to Lake Ngami and stay there for a while — perhaps build a permanent trading store among the Bechuana and encourage them to make use of it.'

Everyone in the room looked to the Jewish trader, who said nothing for some moments. Then he shrugged his shoulders. 'All right. For Hannah's sake I'll carry on as Daniel's partner — but only if Sam comes in with us and takes full charge of the store at Sesebe. I don't want to have to return there for a long time.'

'That will suit me fine,' said Sam Speke. 'The mining has stopped, so there's nothing to make Victoria ill again. All the stuff for wagon-making is there, and you'll be needing plenty of transport if you're going to trade between Whalefish Bay and Lake Ngami. The new mine will keep me pretty busy, too, I expect.'

'There are all of Andrews' old wagons to work on,' said Josh. 'When you were away there was no one here able to do a repair job that would last. We'll need wagons fairly soon to carry timbers to the mine to build new huts. As Miriam and I will be spending a lot of time there I'd like to build something substantial for us.'

'Doesn't this copper mine have a name?' asked Sam Speke.

'The Herero say there used to be many rhino there,' said Daniel. 'They called it "the place of the rhino", or "Ongava".'

'That's a good name for a mine,' said Josh. 'May the Ongava mine prosper in a peaceful land.'

And so the decisions were made. Hannah was dead and nothing would ever be quite the same again, but they would go on. The Ongava mine would be worked and would make money, but not in a peaceful land. The life they had all known until now was over. Otjimkandje would no longer be the hub of their very existence and the last bastion of the Herero.

The news of Jonker's first defeat travelled fast. Soon those Hereros who had fled far to the north to escape his tyrannical rule began to flock back to their homeland.

At the same time other Europeans were already beginning their exploratory treks to the unknown corners of the land that was soon to be known as South-West Africa.

CHAPTER FIFTEEN

Daniel threw himself wholeheartedly into the task of establishing a trading post at Lake Ngami. He arrived there at the end of 1861, taking with him all the store goods from Sesebe in five wagons driven by Herero wagoners.

Aaron had gone in the opposite direction. Mutjise had paid him in full for the guns he had bought, and the trader was supervising the cattle drive to Whalefish Bay.

Daniel found it a long gruelling haul to Lake Ngami and he established two smaller posts between the two main points of trade. Here he would keep small supplies of goods for local tribesmen and food for his wagoners. He did not think it was good policy to let the small local tribesmen see wagonloads of goods passing through their territory without allowing them a share of the trade. Daniel knew that if he wanted to maintain regular trade he needed friends. The harsh country and long distances involved were enemies enough.

The Bechuana chief at Lake Ngami was happy to have Daniel build a trading post at his village, but he would not allow the Herero to work there. Relations between the two tribes had recently been strained by a pair of unscrupulous Portuguese traders working southwards from Angola. They had brought with them a large party of northern Herero and camped near a Bechuana village not far away. Trading was good and the Portuguese could have seen a handsome profit by honest dealing, but that was not enough for them. At the end of the day the Herero turned on their Bechuana hosts, murdered the men and departed with all the trade goods and the Bechuana women.

'It is not that I expect your Herero to do the same,' explained the Bechuana chief. 'But the deed weighs heavily upon my people. Trouble is easier to prevent than to stop.'

Tolotebe, the Bechuana chief, spoke perfect English and was a well-educated man. His father had held a disputed chieftainship and in order to safeguard his son's life and ensure his succession had sent him as a four-year-old child many weeks' journey to the south, to the mission station at Kuruman. There he had lived with the Moffat family and learned the language and high principles of the exceptional Scots missionary.

Tolotebe had gained something more. By a strange quirk of circumstance the missionary had formed a warm and enduring friendship with one of the bloodiest and most powerful chiefs in the whole of the African continent – Mzilikazi, chief of the warlike Matabele Zulus.

Breaking away from the main Zulu nation, Mzilikazi had fought his way northwards to settle his people on the far side of the Limpopo River, close enough for his foraging warriors to have caused trouble to the Bechuana, despite the wide desert that separated them.

Thanks to Tolotebe's association with Moffat, the fighting impis of Mzilikazi's army did not sweep through his country like hungry locusts. Instead, peaceful emissaries passed between the two tribal chiefs and trade links were established.

Daniel learned of this trade one day when he saw a group of unfamiliar natives in the Bechuana village. Tall, well-built and very black they were almost naked but carried themselves with such an air of dignity that it fell hardly short of arrogance. Each of the men was armed with a spear such as Daniel had never before seen. It was not the throwing spear of the Herero or the Bechuana, but a short broad-bladed assegai designed for close combat.

When he asked one of the men working on the store who they were he was told they were men of the mighty Matabele.

That night Daniel met two of their leaders across the fire outside Tolotebe's hut. He had been invited to discuss trade with them. The men wanted to know what items would bring most profit to the Matabele and to tell Daniel what they expected to receive in return.

'It is a far journey to our lands,' said one. 'It is better that only the things that will bring much in return are carried.'

'Then I'd say you'd do well to bring ostrich feathers,' said Daniel. 'I would prefer ivory, but for the amount your men could carry over a long distance feathers would be easier.'

'We will bring both,' promised the spokesman.

'Why not let me come to you?' asked Daniel. 'Two of my

wagons can carry as much as fifty men.'

'No.' The Matabele's tone signified that this was not a matter open to discussion. 'Mzilikazi wants none of the white man's wagons to come among his people. He says they do not bring more prosperity – only more trouble.'

'Then take me to him and let him hear my words. I might be able to make him change his mind.'

'Mzilikazi's mind is his alone. Only Mzilikazi can change it.' The Matabele stood up, and his companion rose with him. 'Tolotebe will tell you of the goods we need. You will bring them here and we will have elephant tusks and ostrich feathers for you.'

'I seem to have offended them,' said Daniel as the two men walked away from the fire. 'I'm sorry. I didn't mean to.'

'Only young men are so easily offended,' smiled Tolotebe. 'Had you offended the Matabele they would not trade with you. They were merely telling you to choose your words more carefully, that was all.'

Daniel grinned in return. 'Thank you, Tolotebe. I stand corrected. But I would very much like to meet Mzilikazi. Would some of your people guide me to him?'

'No.' Tolotebe's face lost its humour. 'Mzilikazi and I are friends, but it is not wise to presume on such a friendship. There can be no help for you from the Bechuana for such a journey.'

Although it seemed he could expect no help to be forthcoming from anyone, Daniel had been impressed by the men he had seen and was determined to make the journey to the land of the Matabele.

With this aim in mind he took to hunting and exploring the land far to the east of Lake Ngami. He travelled at least a hundred miles and was shown the few water-holes known to the Bechuana hunters accompanying him. Then he pushed still farther into the burning desert that the Bechuanas called the 'land of the little people'. Bushman country.

It became increasingly apparent that, in order to reach Matabeleland, Daniel would have to go northwards, skirting Lake Ngami before swinging westwards across the desert region. It would be a dangerous expedition, especially as he would have to rely upon his own resources and scant knowledge of the Kalahari desert region.

The solution to this problem arrived in a dramatic manner in mid-1862. Daniel and his party of half a dozen Bechuanas had killed a zebra in broken bush country on the edge of the desert, and two of the hunters were skinning the animal, when another of the tribesmen came to him.

'There is a little man out there.' He extended an arm that vaguely took in the whole landscape of sand and coarse brown grass. 'He wishes to speak to you.'

'A Bushman wants to talk to me?'

'Those were his words.'

'Why didn't you bring him here to me?'

'He would not come and he says he will speak only to you.'

'All right. Cut me off a fore-quarter of the zebra to take with me. I expect he wants food.'

Daniel mounted his horse, and one of the Bechuanas slung the large joint of meat up in front of him.

'Now, where did you see this Bushman?'

The direction was as vague as before. 'You go that way. You will find him.'

Daniel moved off slowly, balancing the meat on the saddle before him.

He covered two hundred yards before a thin figure rose from the ground before him. Daniel reined in his horse and spoke in the Bushman language. 'Your message was given to me. I have come and I have brought food.'

'You have had good hunting. Xhube's people have fed from your hand before today.'

Daniel looked more closely at the Bushman. 'I remember. It was almost four years ago in Hereroland.'

'It was the land of my people long before the Herero came,' corrected the Bushman. 'And I have not come for food, though it is very welcome. I have some of your people. They are very sick.'

'My people?' Daniel was surprised. He knew of no Europeans in this part of the country.

'Three of them. They came from that way.' He pointed to the north. 'We watched them for two days. They walked first to the sun and then away from it. They do not know where they are.'

'Are all three of them sick?'

'Yes. One of the children and the man are very bad.'

'*One* of the children? You mean you found two children and a man wandering out here?'

'Yes.'

'Then you'd better take me to them quickly.'

The Bushman turned and trotted away, and Daniel rode slowly after him. The Bushman's camp was a mile distant, hidden in a small depression where water seeped into a sandy hole dug three feet in the ground.

The Europeans were all under one small grass shelter, and Daniel was appalled at their condition. The man's clothes were ragged and torn, and he wore no shoes. The children turned out to be two girls who could have been no more than four and six years of age. The younger had shoes, but the older girl was in as desperate a state as the man. The hair of both children was bleached to a washed-out gold colour by the sun, and their skin was burned brown.

Two of the little Bushmen took the meat from Daniel with difficulty as his horse shied away from the smell of the rancid fat with which the Bushmen had rubbed their bodies.

As Daniel hooked his reins over a low bush and kneeled on the ground beside the ragged trio the youngest girl struggled to a sitting position, ignoring Daniel's order to 'lie still'.

'I want a drink.'

Daniel's water-bottle was looped on the pommel of his saddle and he called to Xhube to fetch it for him.

He held the bottle to the girl's mouth, and she drank noisily and much too fast, choking herself. Daniel had to pummel her back to check her coughing, and then she lay on the ground exhausted. The sound had brought movement from the man, who now began to thresh about on the ground, mumbling unintelligibly. Daniel tried to quieten him and force water between his parched lips, but the man would not take it and continued to mumble incoherently about someone he called 'Isabella'.

Daniel wiped off the perspiration that soaked the delirious white man before turning to the conscious white girl again.

'Is your name Isabella?'

'No, I'm Anne. Auntie Isabella's dead. Mummy's dead.' She prodded the other little girl. 'Nell's asleep.'

Nell was so still that Daniel was afraid she might be dead. He checked her pulse and was relieved to find her still alive, though her breathing was feeble and shallow.

'Xhube?' he called to the Bushman. 'Get one of your women to cut up some of the meat into small pieces and boil it. I want to get some food inside these people. They need nourishment.'

The ribs of the sick man protruding from beneath his unhealthy skin confirmed Daniel's words.

While he waited for the meat to be prepared, Daniel sat the man up in the crook of his arm and managed to get him to swallow a couple of sips of water. Then Daniel did the same for the elder girl, though it was with a great deal more difficulty. A few minutes later a Bushman woman came along with an evil-smelling poultice which she laid on the foreheads of the man and the girl named Nell.

'That will help to take away the fever,' explained Xhube.

Daniel had heard too much of the legendary medical skills of the Bushmen to cast doubt on the statement.

When the meat had been boiled to the point of disintegration Daniel fed the three patients with some of the hot meat-juice. The younger girl insisted she was able to eat by herself, and after she had swallowed enough to satisfy a grown man Daniel took the rest away from her.

'She, too, was very sick when we found her,' said Xhube. 'But the man was carrying her and she had more strength than the others.'

He pointed to the other girl. 'This one is still very sick. She will be lucky if she ever leaves the desert.'

'Well, we won't give up yet.'

When the three wanderers had been fed Daniel rode back to the Bechuanas and sent two of them off to Lake Ngami with instructions to bring out a wagon to meet him. Until then he would move the man on a litter. The girls could be carried in the arms of the Bechuana hunters.

Daniel spent the night at the Bushman camp, feeding the man and Nell once more before night fell. He fancied that the man was not quite so feverish during the night, and little Anne slept soundly now her belly was full, but there was little change in the condition of Nell.

Then, in the cool of the dawn, Daniel felt the brow of the man and knew the fever had left him. As Daniel took his hand away the sick man's eyes flickered open and he looked up at Daniel, his initial shock giving way to disbelief.

'It's all right,' Daniel reassured him. 'You're safe now. There's nothing to worry about.'

The man's eyes suddenly opened. 'The others? Where are they?'

'Don't worry about anything. Nell and Anne are right here beside you. They're both sleeping.'

'Nell? Anne?' There was puzzlement on his face for a few moments, and then all the animation drained away and he closed his eyes as though in great pain. 'Yes, Nell and Anne. We are all that are left. Just the three of us.'

'There were more? How many? Where are they now?'

The man opened his eyes again, and the pain in them made Daniel wince.

'There were eleven of us. Eleven. Three men and our families taking the word of the Lord to the natives. My wife and our baby – and the others.' He closed his eyes, but tears forced their way from the wrinkled corners of them. 'Now they're dead. All of them. Isabella, Mary – every one of them.' He opened his eyes and looked past Daniel.

'The natives didn't want us. Their chief said so. We trekked all the way to the Zambezi River to bring them the Word, and they didn't want us. They made us leave. The babies were dying, but they wouldn't listen. They made us leave.'

'Sh! Try to rest now.'

Mention of the Zambezi River had startled Daniel. It was a great river about two hundred and fifty miles to the north-west. Daniel had never before met anyone who had seen it. He tried to quieten the sick man; but he rambled on as the fever returned, and the disjointed wanderings of his mind told a terrible story of suffering and death.

'The wagon's gone, Isabella. We can't get it back. The river's too deep. . . . Cover the baby's face; the flies are here again. Clouds of them. They're trying to eat us. . . . No, Isabella, you must put the baby down. God's taken her for His own. God's taken her. He's taken Lizzie and Roger. . . . He's taking us all. He doesn't want us to be here. He doesn't want these people for his own. . . .'

His voice trailed away, and Daniel stood up, shaken. His own sorrow was as nothing when compared with what this man had suffered. He thought the sick man slept until he saw another tear trickle from between the closed eyelids and course down his face.

Daniel turned away to leave the man to his terrible delirious ramblings when, without opening his eyes, the man asked, 'What's your name?'

'Retallick. Daniel Retallick.'

'Thank you for your kindness, Daniel. I am Charles Deacon. The children are Nell and Anne Gilmore. Where are we?'

'You are in the northern Kalahari. Tomorrow we'll be setting off for Lake Ngami. I have a trading store in a Bechuana village there.'

'Bechuana?' Charles Deacon's face came alive again. 'Then I was nearly to Kuruman. I had nearly made it.'

Kuruman was Robert Moffat's mission station more than five hundred miles to the south, but Daniel did not spoil Charles Deacon's brief moment of joy at his supposed achievement.

'Get word to Kuruman. Tell them what happened. They should be told Nell and Anne are safe.'

'Do the girls have anyone there?'

'No, not now. Mother, father, brother . . . they all died at the Zambezi.'

Daniel looked across to the two sleeping orphans, then back to the haggard man who had fled with them from so much tragedy.

'You must sleep now. We'll soon have you back at Kuruman.'

'Thank you. It has been a very long nightmare.'

When Daniel next checked Charles Deacon slept as soundly as the two girls he had brought from the far Zambezi River.

Daniel decided to let the man sleep as long as he was able, and later that morning he sat and talked with the Bushman leader, Xhube.

'What would you have done with these people had I not

arrived here?' he asked.

'I knew you were coming,' he said in a matter-of-fact voice.

'You knew? How could you?'

The Bushman grinned. 'I knew,' he repeated.

It would be useless to question him further. Daniel never doubted that the little Bushman was telling the truth. He was equally sure that Xhube could not have explained it had he wanted to. He knew, that was all.

'You have come a long way to hunt when there is much game to be found near Ngami.' Xhube called the lake by the Bushman name meaning 'Bitter Water'.

Daniel smiled at the Bushman's shrewd observation.

'You are right. I seek more than animals to hunt.'

Xhube waited politely for Daniel to explain.

'I wish to know the country well so I may journey safely to the land of Mzilikazi and the Matabele.'

'You hunt with the Bechuana. They know the way. Why not ask them to take you?'

'I have. They fear Mzilikazi too much. They say he will not be pleased if they take a white man to him.'

'They do well to fear him,' said Xhube. 'But the way is not hard — for a Bushman.'

'You know the way to the land of the Matabele?'

Xhube nodded.

'Then, will you guide me? If I can get to Mzilikazi and persuade him to allow me to trade direct with him, I promise you your family will never be short of food again. I will leave small stores for you along the way.'

Xhube looked into his face to see if he spoke the truth. He was satisfied with what he saw there.

'Yes, I will guide you across our lands to where there is running water. But you must find Mzilikazi yourself. He is not a friend of my people.'

'I could not ask for more.'

Daniel was elated. After all his efforts of the last months the way was now clear for him to travel to Matabeleland. He dismissed the thought that it might prove dangerous. Reports of the ways of great chiefs were always exaggerated to legendary proportions.

'When do you wish to go?' asked Xhube.

'As soon as I have taken the man and the children to Lake Ngami and they are fit to continue their journey.'

'When you are ready return to this place,' said the Bushman. 'If we are not here, wait. We will come for you. But it is better that we leave before the rains begin.'

The Bushmen were relieved to see the sick white people leave. They had feared they might die in their camp. Such an event would have forced them to leave for ever one of their most important water-holes. It was part of their tradition that no one might stay in a place of death. It said much for them that they had even risked it happening and not left the sick trio to die in the hot sand of the Kalahari.

On the second morning after Daniel had left the Bushmen the older girl's fever broke and she stared wide-eyed at Daniel and his Bechuana companions. So frightened was she of the Bechuanas in particular that Daniel took her on his horse with him.

Her young sister was far less concerned and she chattered ceaselessly to everyone. The hunters from the Lake Ngami village vied with each other for the pleasure of carrying her.

Charles Deacon's condition was not so satisfactory. His fever had returned and he threw himself about with such force that Daniel was unable to feed him and had to tie him to the rough litter the Bechuanas had made for him.

By the third day Daniel was really concerned about the sick missionary. He was delirious for most of the time and his condition slowed down their progress. Daniel applied poultices of herbs given to him by the Bushman women, but they had little effect. Not until the sun was sinking over the horizon that day did the sick man become rational, but he was so weak that he could hardly swallow the water that Daniel held up to his mouth.

It was now that Daniel had to make a difficult decision. He could either stay out here in the killing heat in the hope that Charles Deacon might improve with rest after a few days, or he must move forward as fast as he could to try to reach more hospitable country in time to save the man's life.

Daniel decided to go on. The two girls influenced this decision. They were still so weak that the heat exhausted them very quickly. If either of them developed a fever again, he doubted whether they would have the strength to overcome it.

He explained his decision to Charles Deacon in the darkness. The sick missionary accepted it in the same stoic manner he had shown throughout the whole of his brief and terrible experience of Africa.

'I put my earthly body in your hands, Daniel. My spiritual being I gave to God long ago. I can't hope to understand why I have been chosen to undergo the trials of the last weeks. Perhaps if I live I may one day know it was not in vain. If I die, I shall join those I loved above all others on this earth.'

His words made it easier for Daniel when Charles Deacon joined his loved ones at dawn the following day after an all-night march. He was buried in a shallow unmarked grave of sand, the exact spot forgotten by all except the warm Kalahari wind, never knowing that the news of the appalling losses suffered by his party would be carried in the mission and church magazines of the world. The sacrifices of Charles Deacon, his family and friends inspired many others to lift their own missionary efforts to new heights.

Later that day they were met by a wagon from Lake Ngami being driven by Aaron with Josh acting as an outrider and a dozen Bechuanas providing an escort. One of them was the warrior who had jogged a hundred miles through heat and foot-burning sand to bring help.

'Some trade goods arrived at Whalefish Bay when we were both there,' said Josh, explaining their presence. 'Aaron and I decided to come up here to see how you were getting on.'

He looked at Nell, whom he had taken from Daniel's arms. 'I didn't expect you to be trading for pretty little girls. But we were told there was a man with them.'

'There was — and a very brave man,' replied Daniel. 'He lost his own family yet managed to bring these two back to safety all the way from the Zambezi River. He died at sun-up this morning.'

'It was a miracle you found them,' commented Aaron, looking out over the vast wastes of the northern Kalahari.

'I didn't find them,' explained Daniel. 'They have to thank a little Bushman for that.'

'So even the Bushmen are different here. Elsewhere they run and hide from strangers.'

'The leader of this group is rather special. I met him first about four years ago when I was out hunting with Kasupi. He and his people came originally from the coast. I gave him meat, and he has a good memory. He's an honest and intelligent little man.'

'I'm not arguing with you,' said Josh. 'You should know better than to think you have to justify your friendship with a Bushman to me. I've always thought it sad that they should be such a persecuted people.'

'I'm sorry,' said Daniel. 'I've got so used to defending myself whenever I talk about Bushmen it's become a habit. This one is going to guide me as far as Matabeleland as soon as I've seen Nell and Anne safely on their way.'

'On their way to where?' asked Aaron, looking at the two little girls, who were waiting for beds to be made up for them in the wagon. 'I think a week at Lake Ngami will build up their strength. But what shall we do with them then? Do they have any family in Africa?'

'I doubt it. Charles Deacon told me their parents and brother died with the others at the Zambezi River. But he said they were known at the Kuruman Mission.'

'What sort of a party was this, for God's sake?' Josh asked. 'They obviously knew nothing about looking after themselves. What were they doing going that far north in the first place?'

'You've already answered that,' replied Daniel. 'They were at the Zambezi River "for God's sake". They were missionaries with their families. Eleven of them set off. Nell and Anne are the only survivors.'

'Well, now Hugo is back I'll ask him to write to the Cape and call for a full enquiry into such a foolhardy trek. In the meantime these two mites can stay with your mother and me at Ongava.' Josh smiled. 'I can imagine the look on her face when I return with two little girls. That reminds me. I'm to tell you it's time you paid a visit home.'

'I will – after I've been to see Mzilikazi. But you said Hugo had returned. What happened about Thackeray's confession? Are you a free man again?'

Josh dropped his glance to the ground. He did not want Daniel to see his eyes. 'Yes, I'm a free man – just as long as I stay in this land.'

'You mean you've been refused a pardon?'

'No, not in so many words. Hugo says a pardon might take years to come through.' He grimaced helplessly. 'I think he's trying to let me down lightly. I believe he, too, realises it's hopeless.' Josh's manner suddenly became brisk. 'However, there are more important things to think about. Let's settle these children down in the wagons.'

There would be no more talk of a pardon. It had been a brief flare-up of hope, no more. Only Miriam would ever know the deep and bitter disappointment within Josh.

Once back at Lake Ngami, Daniel was kept busy with his preparations for the journey to Matabeleland. He was uncertain of his welcome there, so would not take a wagon. Instead he loaded a selection of the best trade goods on to two pack-oxen and chose a good horse for himself. When he was almost ready, Josh announced that he would travel with him as far as the Bushman meeting-place. Aaron would stay with the two children until his return. The bluff Jewish trader was finding their presence a painful mixture of stirred memories, both happy and sad. The happiness was in rediscovering the joy of having a curious and guileless child take his hand as they walked together. The sadness was remembering that Hannah had done the same thing many years before.

Josh and Daniel had a pleasant trek to the meeting-place. Trek-oxen cannot be hurried, and the slow journey together gave Josh time to learn more about his son now he was a man. He missed him, as did Miriam. Their permanent home was now at Ongava, but Miriam was not as happy there as she had been in Otjimkandje.

Yet things had changed in the Herero village too. When they had lived in fear of the Afrikaners the Herero looked to the Europeans as more than friends. They were all that stood between themselves and a powerful enemy. Now the Herero had beaten the Afrikaners and found a new pride, a proud independence. They relied upon no one but themselves.

Although nothing in their relationship had changed outwardly, Miriam felt that they – and Hugo Walder – were not welcome in Otjimkandje but were tolerated because of past links with the tribe.

Hugo agreed with her and said their presence was a reminder of the days when the Herero were a subservient people. It was not a comfortable memory for Mutjise's people to live with. The missionary hoped the attitude of the Herero would change as they became more used to their new status.

Josh doubted whether there could be such a simple solution. Mutjise was an ambitious chief who had been effective ruler of the Herero for years before his father's death and he was impatient with the old ways of his people. Now he was their official chief and had won for them a great victory in battle. Other Herero were returning to their homeland, and Mutjise wanted to be paramount chief of all the Herero. Some of the others would not be happy with his ambitions. There would be more fighting, but Josh believed Mutjise would win in the end.

The Otjimkandje chief was also fortunate in having a brilliant general in his younger brother, Kasupi. Once the Herero had been united Josh believed Mutjise would use his brother's qualities to extend his influence still farther. He would not be satisfied until he dominated all the neighbouring tribes – including Jonker's Afrikaners. It made the future uncertain for everyone in the country.

But for the moment it lay in the future, and Josh and Daniel plodded their slow way across the Kalahari.

The Bushmen were not at the meeting-place, but there was water and good hunting nearby and they passed two days pleasantly until Xhube and his people arrived.

Josh picked out the family leader immediately, although there were many more lines on the Bushman's face now.

Daniel began to introduce Josh to the Bushmen, but Xhube stopped him.

'We have met before, your father and my people. It was many, many years ago. When you were no older than my grandchild there.'

Xhube pointed to a shy pot-bellied child who peered at them

from behind the legs of its mother.

'It was a meeting that brought you much sorrow,' said Josh. 'I do not look back with pride on what happened then.'

For the first time Daniel realised that this was the same Bushman who had helped his parents and Sam after the shipwreck. It had happened so far from here that he had never associated the incident with these Bushmen of the Kalahari.

'There have been greater and lesser sorrows in the years since then,' said Xhube, the pain of his persecuted people in his eyes. 'The thing that happened then was not of your making. We were friends, you and I.'

'I owe you much,' said Josh with great feeling. 'Had it not been for you we might have turned back to the coast and I doubt if we would have survived to be here today.'

'The seasons have gone well with you,' declared Xhube. 'Is it the same with your woman and the other white man?' His expressive hands moulded a shape in the air that immediately told Daniel the Bushman was enquiring after Sam Speke.

'They are well. And your people?'

'There are few of us left' — Josh could see less than a third of the original number Xhube had once led — 'but we live. We have travelled far, and the good things have not always stayed with us. Now we have this land.'

Xhube indicated the semi-desert land about them. 'This is good land for us. No one else wants it. Cattle will not live here, and there are not so many animals that others wish to come here to hunt. Yet there is enough to keep us alive. We have water — and some seasons the rains come.' The little Bushman smiled. 'Who could ask for more from life?'

'Perhaps I can bring you and your people a few good years,' said Daniel. 'With regular supplies of food from my trading wagons your tribe will grow strong once more.'

'I hear what you say and am happy,' replied Xhube. 'Because it is said in friendship it is as welcome as the rain, but white men have come into our lands before and they have moved on. The tall tribes have been here, too. They fought with each other, then they also went away. One day you will go from here. Only the Bushman and the desert stay. All around us there is much change. We are told of this by Bushmen who have heard it from brothers. While there is nothing here for other people to want my family will survive. Our needs are few.'

Daniel thought it was little enough to ask from life, but what the Bushmen received would probably be even less. Men like Jacobus Albrecht were trekking steadily northwards, not passing through but looking for places to settle. They would find the scales of survival finely balanced. The Bushman needed little to keep him alive. That 'little' might be the difference between life and death to a settler — or so he would probably claim. Until the little Bushman was accepted as something more than an animal he had no chance of being allowed to live his simple life.

The men talked until well into the night. Josh and Daniel had brought food, but it was a quieter, wearier camp than the ones Josh remembered from years before. There was no dancing and no singing. For all Xhube's expressed confidence in the future Josh thought the Bushmen had lost their zest for life, had accepted the inevitability of their fate.

Daniel and the Bushmen set off soon after first light the next morning.

'Take care of my son, Xhube,' said Josh. 'You will find him a good hunter, but to his mother he is still her only child.'

'He will be as my own son,' replied the Bushman, touching hands with Josh.

Josh knew that Xhube's words meant he would lay down his own life for Daniel if necessary.

He watched them move off in single file and merge with the sun-flooded skyline. He hoped such a dramatic sacrifice would not be necessary, but the Matabele occupied lands that were far distant and remote. Mzilikazi was their absolute ruler, a chief of a type as yet unknown in this part of Africa.

CHAPTER SIXTEEN

Aaron remained at Lake Ngami to run the trading store in Daniel's absence, and Josh took the two young Gilmore girls to Miriam in Ongava.

It was a lively trip. Both girls had recovered from their long ordeal, and the curiosity of Anne in particular was insatiable. She wanted to know everything about what was going on around her and displayed a keen and searching intelligence.

Nell Gilmore was much quieter than her sister. The death of her parents had been more real for her than for the younger Anne. Both girls completely captured the heart of Josh by the end of the trip, and they were no less successful with Miriam.

'What will we do with them, Josh?' asked Miriam when the two girls had been tucked up in the room they had built for Daniel, a room that had not previously been used.

'We'll have to send word to the mission at Kuruman, telling them we have the girls here.'

'And then . . . ?'

Josh knew what Miriam wanted him to say, but he avoided committing himself for as long as possible.

'We'll have to be guided by what they say at Kuruman.'

'Josh Retallick, you are the most exasperating man I have ever known! Your own son rescues two young girls miles out in a desert, their parents dead and no one in this world to care for them. Aren't you going to suggest we keep the girls with us? And if you say "No" I'll call you a liar. You've spent weeks with them on the way from Lake Ngami, and I've seen the way you look at them. They've been delivered into our hands, and we've love enough for both of them.'

Josh grinned. 'Does it matter whether I suggest it or not? Mind you, I don't know what Kuruman will think of the idea. We haven't a lot to offer two young girls out here.'

'You mean they would have had more on the Zambezi River? With everyone dying off like flies around them?' Miriam snorted indignantly. 'No, Josh. We won't *ask* whether we can keep them here with us. We'll *tell* them.'

Josh said no more. Hugo Walder could write to the missionary, Moffat, at Kuruman and suggest it would be better for the girls to remain with them in Hereroland. He hoped Moffat would agree with the arrangement. Nothing short of armed intervention would persuade Miriam to give up the two young girls now.

They took the two girls with them to Otjimkandje and found Hugo Walder with two younger men – one of them little more that Daniel's age. They were new missionaries, sent to replace the man who had spent so many years caring for the Herero people.

'My society has recalled me to Cape Town,' Hugo Walder said, making a determined effort to hide the sadness in his voice. 'I suppose I should feel flattered that they have sent two men to continue my work, but I will miss my little church and my people.'

He introduced the newcomers as Theodore Wohlfarth and Wilhelm Doelker, both German. Neither of the two new missionaries was fluent in English. Their society, for reasons best known to itself, had taught them only Dutch and basic Herero. This lack of communication made them appear to Miriam to be more shy and consequently younger than they probably were.

'They've arrived at an opportune time to learn the hazards of missionary work,' said Josh grimly. He lifted the two girls from the wagon. 'Meet Nell and Anne Gilmore. They are the only survivors of a missionary party of eleven who set off to the Zambezi River.'

The younger of the new missionaries looked closely at the two young girls, then spoke rapidly to Hugo Walder in German. Hugo Walder replied briefly, and Wilhelm Doelker nodded his head.

Hugo Walder turned back to Josh and Miriam. 'Wilhelm says he recognises these children. They arrived in Cape Town with their parents only eight months ago and immediately went up-country to Kuruman.'

'Then they must have headed north within weeks of their arrived there,' commented Josh. 'I hope your two young men heed the warning, Hugo. This land doesn't give a second chance to those who are not fully prepared for all its moods.'

'I have told them,' replied Hugo Walder. 'For their own sakes I hope they have listened.'

Josh brought up the subject of the girls remaining with him and Miriam, and the old missionary promised to write to Moffat.

The news of Hugo Walder's departure had taken much of the pleasure of the visit away for Miriam. When she climbed down from the wagon she stood on tiptoe and kissed the big bearded missionary, much to his delight and the surprise of his young colleagues.

'Oh, Hugo, what are we going to do without you? Can't you persuade your society to allow you to stay at Otjimkandje?'

'No, that would be self-indulgent. I go wherever I can best serve God. My society believes I am needed in Cape Town. Perhaps it is right.' He nodded towards the two children. 'At least if I am there I might be able to prevent another such tragedy as they have survived. I could ensure that all missionaries understood what to expect in a strange new land.'

'There is one last favour I would like from you before you go,' said Josh quietly.

'Of course, my friend. What is it?'

'Marry Miriam and me in your church here in Otjimkandje. I thought about it soon after William Thackeray died, but it didn't matter very much then. Now you are leaving I would like us to be married here where we have found so much happiness; and it should be by you who have been our greatest friend.'

Miriam slipped her hand in Josh's and squeezed it happily.

'It could be important, Hugo,' she said. 'We want to keep Nell and Anne with us and we could hardly ask you to recommend us to Kuruman knowing we were not married.'

'That would not have stopped me,' said Hugo Walder firmly. 'You are as married as any two people I have ever known. But I am glad you wish it to be recorded in the house of God. It will give me great pleasure.'

Josh and Miriam were married the next evening in the mission church of Otjimkandje, with only Sam Speke and Mary to witness the ceremony. There was nothing unusual in it for Mary. Among her people it was often not possible for a young man to raise the bridal price at the time when passion decreed he should live with the partner of his choice. It often happened that there were one or more children of the union before it became official. Besides, she and Sam had lived together before they were married.

Many miles from Otjimkandje, life was not progressing smoothly for Daniel. The unpredictable rainy season was due, and with the long hot year drawing to a close there was little water to be found in the vast spaces of the desert country. For this reason Xhube had taken Daniel far to the north, to where there was the muddy trickle of a river. Once they had located it they turned eastward for the land of the Matabele.

Unfortunately, the drawbacks of this route soon made themselves known. He and the Bushmen now had all the water they needed – but they were plagued by great swarms of mosquitoes and tsetse flies.

Daniel soon learned to button his shirt up to the neck and fasten his sleeves at the wrist, but there was no way of protecting his face and hands.

By the second day of travelling along the river-bank Daniel's face was an ugly mass of swollen stings, his eyelids puffy and throbbing, and the backs of his hands driving him mad with their constant itching.

Then disaster struck. Both oxen died within hours of each other and, apart from a few items he gave to the Bushmen and the little that his horse could carry, the trade goods, presents for Mzilikazi, had to be abandoned.

But worse was to follow. Daniel's horse had come in for its share of tsetse stings and it began to walk stiff-legged, its head hanging low, not bothering to shake off the flies that gathered in clusters about its eyes. Daniel walked the horse behind the Bushmen, stooping frequently to allow the dejected animal to drink from the river.

Towards sunset the condition of the horse had worsened. For the last hour it had staggered along on legs as elastic as those of a drunken man.

Daniel was so distressed by his horse's sickness that when it next paused for a drink at the water's edge he paid more attention to the animal than to his surroundings. He was within ten feet of an expanse of river-grass that rose tall and green, half-in, half-out of the water. Concealed by the grass, submerged except for the tip of its snout and two yellow-and-black pebble-sized eyes, was a fifteen-foot-long crocodile, its pale soft-leather belly pressed against the mud of the river-bed.

It was this mud that helped to deaden the advance of the ugly creature. It moved slowly forward with the exaggerated stealth of a chameleon, hard reptilian eyes never off its target. The crocodile covered the last few feet in a headlong rush of surging water, expelled air from the gross body erupting noisily from between long yellow-toothed jaws.

The horse was too ill and lethargic to move back from this violent headlong attack and with a sideways twist of its jaws the crocodile grasped the foreleg of the unfortunate horse and toppled it into the river on its side.

Daniel managed to grab his gun from the saddle holster, but before he could unhook the pouch containing powder and shot, the feebly struggling horse was dragged further out into the river.

The Bushmen came running back to the scene and noisily and enthusiastically jabbed at the huge crocodile with their ineffective spears. The powerful amphibian was goaded to a near-frenzy. Its heavy tail swung to one side and bowled over one of the more daring of the Bushmen. Fortunately for the little man Daniel saw him fall and was able to drag him half-conscious from the water before the sluggish current could carry him away.

Their efforts were all in vain. The crocodile had carried the horse to deeper water now, sheer weight dragging the sick horse down to its death.

'Get back! Get back! It has a mate.'

A sharp-eyed Bushman had seen the brief flurry of disturbed water as the eyes and nostrils of another crocodile momentarily broke surface some yards downstream.

Hurriedly everyone splashed their way out of the waters of the river, and within seconds there was nothing to show for the life-and-death struggle of the horse but the disconsolate group standing on the river-bank.

Looking at the faces of his companions, Daniel saw nothing but unhappiness and defeat. The Bushmen blamed themselves for the mishap. They had undertaken to guide him safely to Matabeleland and now they had allowed him to lose his most precious possession, his horse.

Daniel waited until Xhube looked at him and he managed to produce a weak smile for the Bushman leader.

'We are fortunate. It might be one of us at the bottom of the river now.' Daniel shuddered at the thought. 'Shall we move on away from the river? I don't fancy making camp here tonight.'

When the Bushmen saw that Daniel did not appear to be unduly upset about the accident they cheered up and followed him up the incline away from the river.

They made camp near the top of a low hill. Daniel had his gun but no powder or shot. Without them he felt dejected and vulnerable.

The next morning Daniel had more than powder and shot to worry about. He woke in a burning fever with his teeth chattering together and the feeling that he was floating upwards to meet the sun.

Daniel had malaria.

The Bushmen recognised the illness immediately but stood around helplessly, unsure what to do. They had left their women behind in the Kalahari, not wishing to risk them in a strange land, and it was the women who knew the things that had to be done when a man had bad fever.

They only knew they had to bring Daniel's temperature down. Their method was primitive but effective. Carrying Daniel down the slope closer to the river they scooped a shallow grave in the sandy soil and put him in it, covering his body with a thin layer of sand until only his head was showing above ground. Then for the remainder of the day they brought water from the river to keep the sand moist and his body cool.

Daniel came out of the fever for a brief while at dusk, and Xhube fed him with fish caught from the river and baked in mud in the heart of their fire.

'I'm a trouble to you, Xhube,' gasped Daniel when he had eaten as much as he could take. 'First my horse and now me.

You'll be sorry you offered to bring me on this journey.'

'Save your strength for eating,' said the Bushman leader. 'You have eaten a fish so small it would not satisfy a bigger fish.'

'Give me the bigger fish tomorrow, Xhube. I'll be better then.'

But Daniel was not better, and fever still had a tight grip on him. Xhube was worried. He had seen his own people die from just such a fever as this and he knew white men were not as strong as Bushmen.

His companions did nothing to ease his mind. They were not happy so close to the river. They feared the crocodiles and the spirits who possessed their ungainly bodies. Such spirits were not kindly disposed towards the little men from the great desert country. Xhube's men did not want to stay. They wanted to return to the Kalahari – without Daniel.

When they put it to Xhube he refused to consider it. 'No. We have said we would take him to the land of the Matabele. I have told his father his life is my life. I will not leave him.'

'But this is not a good place for us,' argued one of his warriors. 'He will die here and we may die with him.'

'That is true,' agreed Xhube. 'And so tomorrow we will go on.'

'But the way ahead is hard. The land of the Matabele is far.'

'All these things are true,' said Xhube. 'We will have to move fast and rest only a little. The white man is very sick, so he must be carried.'

He looked at each face in turn. 'We will carry him to the land of the Matabele.'

One after another the Bushmen dropped their eyes before their chief's look and Xhube knew he had won. He was still their leader and they would do as he told them.

Xhube drove his men to the edge of exhaustion – which meant they travelled twice as far each day as any other man would have deemed possible. Their stamina was truly incredible and during the few hours' sleep Xhube allowed them they lay on the ground like dead men. Apart from this brief daily rest they stopped only when Daniel had one of his infrequent lucid periods. Then the Bushman chief would ply him with as much food and water as he could force down his throat.

It was difficult to assess whether Daniel's condition was improving. One hour he would be in a raging fever, tossing his body around, his mind assailed by delirious fantasies, the next he would sleep peacefully, undisturbed by the jogging of the improvised stretcher being carried by the uncomplaining little men.

Then came a day when it became necessary to cross the meandering river. Once more Xhube's men expressed their fears to him. On the far side of the river was Matabele country. Not their hunting-grounds only, but also their kraals and grazing-lands. They were liable to encounter groups of warriors in training and patrolling impis. The Bushmen felt they had come far enough.

Xhube understood their fears and sympathised with them, but he had made a promise to Josh and he meant to keep his word.

'We will cross the river tomorrow,' he said. 'Then we will move as Bushmen. We will not be seen by the Matabele. When we sight one of their kraals we will take him' – he pointed to Daniel – 'and leave him outside a hut before dawn. They will find him and care for him. I will have kept my word and we will return to our land.'

He looked about him at the tired faces of his men and smiled. 'Do not fear, we will all see the desert again. This I know.'

After this there could be no further argument. Xhube was a man of visions. They came to a selected few of their people. They were not to be questioned or doubted. Like the sun, the wind and the origins of the world they defied all explanation. But, like the sun, the wind and the world, they were real.

Nevertheless, the faith of the little Bushmen underwent a severe test the next morning. They awoke with the sun to find themselves inside a circle of Matabele warriors. The big black men squatted silently and menacingly, the blades of their broad stabbing assegais glinting ominously red in the light of the early sun. As the Bushmen rose from their shallow scraped sleeping-holes the Matabele stood up, their glistening well-muscled bodies towering above the little desert people.

The leader of the Matabele impi pointed his spear at Daniel, who was in the throes of one of his delirious dreams.

'Who is this white man? Why have you brought him here, so far from your hunting-places?'

'He is a trader on his way to see the great chief Mzilikazi. He fell sick along the way. We are hurrying to get him to the kraal of your people.'

The tall Matabele warrior frowned. He was Muvandi, one of Mzilikazi's ablest and most trusted indunas or generals. He had been returning from an expedition undertaken to punish a wayward subjugated tribe when his path had crossed the tracks of the Bushmen. Sending the main body of his men home, he had followed the tracks to this place.

Only the presence of the white man had stopped him from slaughtering the Bushmen immediately. Now he was uncertain. His standing with the Matabele chief gave him the power of life or death over any other tribe, but he would not dare to risk offending Mzilikazi by killing a man who was on his way to see him.

'Is Mzilikazi expecting the white man?'

'Why else would he ask me to bring him to your land? Since he became sick we have travelled night and day. It would not be good if he died and the great chief Mzilikazi was unhappy because of it.'

Xhube was well aware of the original intentions of the Matabele induna. The Bushman's guile was the only shield he possessed against the assegais of the most powerful warrior nation Africa knew.

'Your unhappiness will be even greater if the white man is not expected,' said Muvandi menacingly. 'Mzilikazi does not like the shadow of a white man to fall on his lands. Come, we have a full day's journey to his kraal.'

Muvandi forced the pace almost as hard as Xhube, but it was the Matabele induna who called for the brief rest periods.

They passed several small villages along the way but had not come within sight of Mzilikazi's kraal by nightfall. With the onset of darkness they were forced to slow their pace, but Muvandi kept them moving.

Not until more than half the night had gone did Xhube smell the smoke that lingered from a thousand cooking-fires. It hung on the air like the night itself, covering the land. There was no escape from it. When they travelled for another half an hour before reaching the first of the quiet bee-hive huts Xhube knew this must be a kraal such as none of his people had ever seen.

Muvandi and his men threaded their way between the huts until they entered the maze that was Mzilikazi's own inner kraal. Here the induna led them to an empty hut with a hard cattle-dung floor.

'Mzilikazi sleeps' he said. 'I will speak to him in the morning. I will send for one of our healers to attend the white man. Do not try to leave. I have warriors outside.'

The Matabele healer arrived within minutes, disgruntled at being called from his sleep and insulted at having to share a hut with a party of Bushmen who rubbed themselves with animal fat and never washed. The healer wrinkled his nose at their offensive odour, but he was here at Muvandi's command and knew better than to complain. Without attempting to hide his distaste he went about the business of doctoring Daniel.

After the jostling he had received on the long journey the rest did Daniel as much good as the ministrations of the reluctant healer. By morning his fever had subsided and he slept fitfully as incantations were said over him and a variety of medicaments applied to his aching body.

Xhube, on the other hand, was becoming increasingly nervous as time went by without anything happening. He wondered whether the Matabele chief was thinking up a new and particularly unpleasant fate for the Bushmen.

It was mid-morning before a commotion outside the hut brought the little hunters to their feet. Seconds afterwards the light coming in through the doorway was abruptly blocked by the huge figure of a man. Six feet four inches tall, he must have weighed at least two hundred and sixty pounds. Entwined in his tight black hair was the warrior ring of the Matabele fighting man, and a leopard skin flung over one shoulder proclaimed his royal status. Mzilikazi had come visiting.

The Matabele healer flung himself to the ground in abasement, and Xhube and his men hurriedly followed suit to pay homage to the absolute ruler of ten thousand people, conqueror of a vast land.

The huge chief ignored the grovelling of the men in the hut.

Closely followed by Muvandi he stooped over Daniel, who lay on his improvised stretcher.

'This man is nothing to me,' he boomed in a deep voice. 'Let those who brought him here be put to death.'

With this brief pronouncement Mzilikazi turned to leave.

'If someone is to be punished for my presence here, then let it be me, not the Bushmen.'

Daniel's voice was weak, but it was sufficient to halt the Matabele chief. He looked back at the sick white man.

'You would die in place of these who are as nothing?'

'Willingly. I owe them my life — as they once saved the lives of my father and mother. If someone must die, it should be me.'

'Why have you come to my kraal?'

'To seek trade. I have exchanged goods with your warriors at Lake Ngami. I liked what they brought. They were pleased with my trade goods.'

'There are many men, English, Boers and Portuguese, who would like to trade with Mzilikazi. I have refused them. Why, then, should I allow you to trade here?'

The effort of talking was draining the strength from Daniel at a time when he needed to use all the persuasive powers he possessed.

'Because I am an honest man' was all he could think of to say.

Mzilikazi looked at him for a long moment, then gave a deep-throated chuckle. 'Then you are not as other traders. We will speak more of this when you are well.

'You hear me?' he spoke sternly to the grovelling healer. 'You will make him well and bring him to me.'

To Muvandi he said, 'Send someone to take the little men across the river. They may return to their desert.'

Having given life to the Bushmen and threatened death to the healer, Mzilikazi, the all-powerful, took the daylight away from the hut once more — and was gone.

CHAPTER SEVENTEEN

Xhube left Mzilikazi's kraal that same morning, in the company of a small impi. The Matabele warriors were not pleased at being given the task of ensuring the safe conduct of the little men through their lands. Their duty was not made easier when they met another impi returning from a foray into the land of the Manyika tribe. They were forced to endure gibes of 'goat-herders', and worse. The homeward-bound impi also made elaborate moves to get up-wind of the small party. The Matabele were a scrupulously clean people and the Bushmen's habits offended the nostrils of Mzilikazi's warriors.

Daniel was sorry to have his little friends leave him. They had saved his life as surely as he had secured their freedom. But he knew he was likely to see them again. They would be waiting for him on his return journey to Lake Ngami.

Mzilikazi's healer spared no effort to safeguard his own life by nursing his charge back to health. Even so, it was eleven days before Daniel was well enough to walk from the hut by himself. He wandered slowly about the kraal, an object of curiosity to the children. Warriors and women pretended not to notice him.

The village was as well ordered as Otjimkandje but on a vastly larger scale. Daniel was further impressed when his ever-attendant healer told him this was the kraal of only one of Mzilikazi's regiments. There were others of similar size dotted over the whole of Mzilikazi's land.

A few days later Mzilikazi sent for Daniel. The Matabele chief was holding court in a huge area in the centre of the village surrounded by members of his household. His armed personal bodyguard were in close proximity, standing between the chief and his people.

Mzilikazi sat on a throne of cow hides in the shade of a wide-branched tree, his leopard skin draped carelessly across one shoulder. Out here in the sunlight Daniel could see the grey hair of the warrior chief. Mzilikazi was an old man but he was still enormous and regally impressive.

As Daniel was led up to the chief he saw the way the indunas and headmen called before Mzilikazi behaved. They first saluted him with a cry of 'Bayete!' which meant 'Greetings, great one,' then fell on their knees at a respectful distance to state their case.

Sometimes Mzilikazi would make a brief reply. On other occasions he would dismiss a request with a peremptory movement of his hand.

All around the square were women and children, gathered to take advantage of an opportunity to gaze upon their great and feared chief.

Mzilikazi greeted Daniel with an affable wave and motioned him to a seat beside him in the shade.

'You are better, trader?' The chief's manner was friendly and courteous.

'Thank you, yes,' Daniel replied. 'I have been well looked after.'

'Good!' Mzilikazi nodded approvingly at the healer, who backed away with a feeling of huge relief, his knees weak beneath him.

'Have you ever seen a kraal the size of this one in the lands of the Bechuana?'

'No,' replied Daniel truthfully. 'Nor in the lands of the Herero, or the Afrikaner, or the Bergdama.'

Mzilikazi's eyebrows met across the bridge of his wide nose.

'You have travelled to many places and met many people. Could none of these tribes give you elephant teeth and the things you seek?'

'Yes, but there is fighting between the tribes in Hereroland. War is not good for trade.'

The big chief chuckled. 'You are the first man who has sought the Matabele to find peace, trader. But you have been living with the Bechuana. They are at war with no one.'

'No, and I have a store there still, but I wanted to come out and find new trade.'

'Yet you bring no present of trade goods with you?'

'I brought them,' said Daniel. 'But the last of them is inside a crocodile's belly now.'

He told Mzilikazi how he had lost his oxen and then his

horse, and added, 'But when I next come to trade I'll bring a wagon with the best in my store—'

'*If* you come again,' corrected Mzilikazi. He had negotiated with white men before. They had a clever way of twisting a man's words to their own advantage. It was necessary with them to be sure that each word had the same meaning for both parties.

Daniel understood this. 'All right, *if* you agree to allow me to trade with your people, perhaps you would permit me to build a store. I will pay you rent for the land, of course.'

Mzilikazi smiled. 'The land is like the sky and the waters of the river. A man cannot take a handful and say "This is mine". It belongs to no one—and to everyone. The Matabele fought for the right to live here. Because I won that right I can say this man will stay and that man must go. That is all. So how can you pay me for land that is not mine to give? If I say you may stay, you will give me presents because you are grateful. But I have not yet decided. Sit with me now and see how Mzilikazi rules his children.'

Daniel would have liked to continue the discussion on trading, to settle the issue there and then, but he knew better than to make any attempt to force the chief's hand.

He sat in silence, listening to Mzilikazi's people bring their troubles before their chief. In the main they were minor disputes. Mzilikazi's opinion was sought over a disputed bride-price. A man's calf had strayed into another's herd and ownership was disputed. A warrior from one of the bachelor impis sought permission to marry; the request was refused, the Matabele chief considering that the man had not yet proved himself a man in battle. Until he had blooded his spear he would not be man enough for a Matabele girl beneath a marriage blanket.

Then came more serious complaints. A wife was alleged to have been unfaithful to her husband. She and the lover were brought to kneel before their chief. She knelt with downcast eyes, but the young man was unrepentant, his eyes fixed on a point beyond Mzilikazi's left shoulder while the woman's husband gave his evidence in a tremulous voice. The husband was old and withered, and Daniel found his sympathies lying with the young adulterers.

Mzilikazi listened carefully to the evidence. The couple had been caught in the act of making love. There could be no doubting their guilt. Nevertheless, the chief asked them whether the husband's evidence was true. The wife began to cry, and the young man's eyes went to her before he looked at Mzilikazi's face for the first time.

'It is true.'

Mzilikazi acknowledged the young man's honesty in the briefest inclination of his head before making a quick signal to his bodyguard. Four of them moved forward, and the girl began screaming and sobbing loudly as two of the warriors pinioned her arms and dragged her away.

The young man rose to his feet and walked calmly away between the other two armed men.

'It is a pity,' said Mzilikazi. 'I have just lost a good warrior.'

Only then did Daniel realise he had witnessed the Matabele chief sentencing two of his subjects to death. They would be taken to a spot beyond the village and speared by their guards.

Yet this double execution paled into insignificance when compared with what followed.

A group of twenty-five mature and experienced warriors came from the crowd and kneeled before Mzilikazi. Their cry of 'Bayete' rang out loud and clear above the buzz of the crowd's interest.

'You have been away a long time, Nyamatakah,' said Mzilikazi to their induna. 'The news you bring back to me is good?'

'It is good,' said Nyamatakah. 'We found the village of Chiweshe and punished him for raiding his neighbours. He and all his warriors were killed, as you ordered.'

'And how many of your warriors did you lose?'

The induna held up all the fingers of one hand and one finger of the other. 'They died as men.'

Mzilikazi accepted the news with apparent satisfaction.

'Your families have been without you for too long,' he said. 'Tell them to step forward. I would see them.'

Eagerly, the wives and children stepped into the clearing, happy at the honour bestowed upon them.

'Closer!' boomed their chief. 'Come closer.'

The women and children moved forward to kneel beside

their husbands and fathers.

'And the families of those who died,' said the Matabele chief. 'Let them come forward and kneel in a place apart from the others.'

A smaller group of women and children moved forward. They did not smile.

When they were settled, Mzilikazi turned his attention back to the induna.

'You will have brought me back many cattle, Nyamatakah?'

The induna shook his head sadly. 'Chiweshe and his people were poor. He did not deserve to be a chief. His cattle were few and old. A man could lay his fingers beneath their ribs.'

Mzilikazi leaned towards him, his eyes glittering angrily. 'Then it could not have been Chiweshe's cattle you left to graze in the valley of the Umniati River with those of Chiweshe's herd-boys you allowed to live?'

Nyamatakah mouthed like a fish, but it was a full minute before words came.

'I know nothing of this.'

'Then it seems I must help your memory,' said the Matabele chief as his bodyguard moved to surround the warriors and their families.

'Take Nyamatakah's wife to the stake.'

The induna started to his feet, but the broad flat blades of the assegais held by the bodyguard beat him to his knees again.

Others from the bodyguard were dragging a young woman from among the families. They carried her screaming to a four-foot-high stake driven into the ground nearby, the top of it sharpened to a point. As Daniel watched in incredulous horror the warriors lifted the screaming woman high into the air and brought her body down upon the stake. The point quite literally cut off her scream.

As the men of the bodyguard stood back Nyamatakah's wife crouched before the assembled crowd, knees bent and arms dangling, but her body was held as erect as a Matabele warrior by the stake. She was quite dead.

Daniel's stomach contracted violently and for a second he thought his malaria-wrecked body would let him down and cause him to faint in front of the assembled Matabele people.

Mzilikazi was talking again.

'How is your memory now, Nyamatakah? Do you remember Chiweshe's cattle?'

Still the induna hesitated and the angry chief called, 'Fetch out Nyamatakah's young son.'

'No!' The erring induna leaped to his feet, but the crossed assegai-handles of the bodyguard prevented him from running forward to throw himself at the feet of the chief. 'It is true! I took Chiweshe's cattle and hid them in the valley of the Umniati River.'

'I know it is true,' said Mzilikazi. 'But I wanted to hear it from your lips. Now I will speak. The wives and children of every one of you will die on the stakes on the execution hill, and you will watch them. Then it will be your turn to die also. All your goods and cattle will be shared between the families of those who were killed in the attack on Chiweshe's village.'

There was a long despairing moan from the doomed families. It stopped when Mzilikazi held up his hand.

'Nyamatakah's impi did not lose six men by Chiweshe's hand. His men were not Matabele! They ran from battle. It became a hunt for our warriors. No, Nyamatakah, my six men died because they were loyal to me and had not agreed to steal Chiweshe's cattle. They died by the spears of their brothers.'

Mzilikazi spoke to the induna of his bodyguard. 'Before these men die remove their warrior rings. They are not Matabele fighting men. I cast them out from my tribe. Kill them and feed their bodies to the dogs.'

Only at this sentence did the condemned men show any signs of emotion, but they were quickly escorted away, one man between two warriors of the bodyguard. Their families, herded like goats, were taken to the execution hill.

Daniel turned from watching them to see that the chief's eyes were upon him.

'You are shocked, trader. You do not agree with the sentence I have just passed?'

Daniel shook his head, not trusting himself to speak until he had more control of himself.

'It's not the way of my people. Human life is valued by us.'

'Good! Then my people are safe from you and yours. You

will not come across the river to hunt my people as do the Boers. To kill them with guns and steal their cattle. That is not your way?'

There was a bitterness in his voice that Daniel was quick to recognise and felt able to match.

'I, too, have suffered at the hands of the Boers. I hunt only animals, not men or women.'

'Then we can trade. Build a hut here and make it ready for your trade goods. You will stay with my people until the rains have ended and it is easier to travel. My warriors will then go with you along the road to Lake Ngami.'

The thought of remaining so long as a guest of this harsh and cruel man did not appeal to Daniel, but he knew that if he wished to trade with the Matabele he had no alternative.

Mzilikazi saw his hesitation and knew the reason for it.

'You will be safe here,' he said. 'Safer than one of my warriors would be among white men. You have seen me punishing my people today. It gives me no pleasure. But many years ago I and my people were Zulus ruled by the great Shaka. I was sent on just such a raid as Nyamatakah. I, too, kept the cattle to myself, but those cattle were numbered as the stars in the sky and I had with me many warriors. We fought our way to this land where we live feared by all men. If Nyamatakah had tried to do the same with the few warriors he took with him, he would one day have met with a stronger army and been beaten. The news would have travelled far; but it would not be said, "Nyamatakah has been beaten in battle." Men would say, "Mzilikazi's warriors have been beaten in battle." Then others would try to do the same, and my people would know no peace. Think about it and you will understand my ways more clearly, trader.'

It was then that Daniel realised that Mzilikazi was more than a warrior chief. His reputation for being a great leader was justified. Even so, Daniel could not forget the cruelty he had just witnessed.

'Was it necessary for the families of these men to die with them?'

'Yes, for two reasons. Among their families were fine sons who would have grown up to be warriors — perhaps great

355

warriors. They would never forget it was Mzilikazi who killed their fathers. One day, perhaps not until my son ruled the Matabele, they would think themselves strong enough to turn on their chief.'

'And the second reason?'

'Ah! That one is not so deep, trader. It was necessary to make an example of them. My warriors are brave men. They learn to fight and to kill and are not afraid of death – for themselves. But they would not wish to bring it upon their families.' Mzilikazi rested a large hand on Daniel's shoulder. 'A people are only as strong as their laws, trader. The Matabele are a mighty people. Their laws must be strong enough to be obeyed. The first of these laws is that all men must obey their chief. The punishment for breaking that law must be greater than for any other.'

He dropped his hand and Daniel had a quick flash of intuition that the great Matabele chief who was always surrounded by advisers, indunas and headmen yet remained a lonely man.

'You are still young, trader. I do not expect you to understand everything about my people. But build your hut, stay with us a while and learn our ways. Afterwards I do not think you will be happy living among any others.'

CHAPTER EIGHTEEN

Chief Jonker saw the arrival of the rains, then he took to his bed and died within a few days. It was the end of a legend. He and his Afrikaners had been the scourge of South-West Africa for a quarter of a century, until his defeat by Mutjise.

Unlike Tjamuene, Jonker left no strong son to take his place and his passing left a vacuum that only bitter strife would fill.

For all the years of his leadership the Afrikaner tribe had occupied the best valleys and grazing-land, denying access to all other tribes. Now Jonker was dead, and even while he lay breathing his last the other tribes were closing in like jackals around a corpse to seize pieces of the land the lion of the Afrikaners had won and held.

Waiting for someone to take the initiative, the tribes and sub-tribes held their guns and spears in readiness: Herero, Nama, Topnaar, Veldshoendraer – and many more. The holocaust of war was about to descend upon the land, and for a decade progress would mark time.

Josh had seen it coming for a long time as had many others. Sam Speke brought two wagons loaded with trade goods from Whalefish Bay to Sesebe and on his own authority added another loaded with powder and shot. He spoke seriously to Kasupi about the situation and could see the unquenchable war-lust burning in the young Herero's eyes.

The one-time sailor believed that when the rains ceased and powder could be kept dry the Herero would spearhead an attack on the tribe that had terrorised the country for so long. Ignoring Mary's protests that no harm would come to them, he loaded everything from the Sesebe store on the ox-wagons and with his wife and Victoria set out for the new mine at Ongava.

Their arrival stopped all work there until Sam Speke and his Herero drivers were able to assure the miners that war had not already broken out.

'I just couldn't think what else to do, Josh,' said the burly storekeeper as they all sat down to a meal together. 'War is coming soon and it will affect every one of us. I've had no news from Aaron or Daniel for months and don't know what their thoughts are about keeping a store fully stocked in the midst of a land torn by war. I doubt if they have even heard of Jonker's death and the troubles facing us here. I thought the best thing to do was pull out and take everything to their new store at Lake Ngami.'

'It makes sense, Sam, and I'm sure they'll be able to use the stores,' Josh agreed. 'I know no more than you about things at Lake Ngami. The last news I had was a fortnight ago. An Ovambo tribesman was passing through and he said Aaron was worried about Daniel. It has been many months since he left to visit Mzilikazi and there has been no word of him. Aaron is staying at the Lake, expecting Daniel to arrive with every day that comes.'

'Daniel will come back safely. Kasupi says he can out-think and out-shoot any man who's been born of woman.'

It was Victoria who spoke. She entered the hut with a Gilmore girl clutching each of her hands and cast her opinion into the conversation.

'Did he, now?'

Miriam looked at Sam Speke's daughter with great interest. It was the first time she could remember Victoria speaking without first being asked a direct question. The fifteen-year-old had blossomed into a striking young lady since her health had been restored to her. She was far removed from the spindly underweight sickly child who had caused such concern to her father.

Victoria was one of those fortunate girls who inherit the best of both parents. She had the grace and ready smile of her mother and the honest gaze and quickness to learn of her father. Her skin colour, too, was inherited from them both. It was a beautiful golden colour, slightly paler than the skin of a Bushman.

'Since when have you been the confidante of the leader of Mutjise's army?' asked Miriam.

Victoria's smile was contagious, and Miriam found herself smiling with her.

'Since he started telling me all about Daniel. Kasupi says if Daniel would lead half the Herero warriors they could overrun

358

Ovambaland and Damaraland and own all the land between the Kalahari and the sea.'

'I wouldn't know about that, Victoria. But I'm worried about him now.'

Miriam turned to Josh. 'Why don't we all go to Lake Ngami with Sam?'

The idea took Josh by surprise, but after he had thought about it for a few moments he realised the suggestion made much sense. The threat of war hung over the mine as it did the rest of the country. During recent weeks nearly half of Josh's work-force had drifted away to become warriors again. Josh did not blame them. A Herero man had to look to his future in the same way as anyone else.

The warriors who followed Kasupi strutted the villages of the Herero, fierce pride lifting their heads high. A man wanted to be with them. There were more battles to be fought, great victories to be won. When the warriors returned to talk of their exploits about the camp-fires there could be only scorn for those who had remained behind. When full-scale war began there would be no men left to work Ongava.

'Why not?' Josh said to Miriam. 'At the rate my miners are leaving the mine will have to close in a few weeks anyway.'

Miriam hugged him in relief and Josh smiled above her head at Sam Speke.

'Stay with us here for a couple of days while I wind things up, Sam. Then we'll all set off together. No doubt Mutjise and Kasupi will be pleased to have our miners helping to fight their battles and will keep the other tribes away from the mine. I'll send a horseman to Whalefish Bay to pass the word that there will be no ore arriving there for a while.'

He held Miriam away from him. 'You'll need to pack all your valuables and take them with us. Leave nothing behind that can't be replaced should it be stolen.'

Later, after Josh had told his mine-workers what he intended doing, he went into the bedroom of the hut to find Miriam close to tears.

'What's the matter? What's happened?'

Miriam clung to him and rubbed her face fiercely against the front of his coarse shirt.

'Nothing. I'm just being silly, but packing everything seems so final — more final than the move from Otjimkandje. Do you think we'll ever return?'

Josh kissed the top of her head gently. 'Who knows? War can change so many things, Miriam — and war is coming.'

Miriam nodded vigorously. 'I know — and it's all so unnecessary. With Jonker dead everyone could live in peace now. Nobody needs any more land than he has at the moment.'

'Ambition doesn't end because one man dies. Jonker has left a legacy that will lure a great many men to their deaths.'

Miriam pushed herself away from Josh. 'Then I'd better get on with this packing. After hearing what Kasupi is saying about Daniel it's better we go to Lake Ngami before he returns and comes to visit us. The farther Daniel stays from Hereroland the better. I didn't bring him up to become a Herero war-chief.'

It was as though their departure from Ongava was the signal the country had been waiting for. Full-scale hostilities broke out almost immediately. Kasupi led his men on a raid to Winterhoek, which had once more become the capital of the Afrikaners. In a fierce and bloody battle the Herero wreaked a terrible revenge on the children of Jonker. When they rode back to Otjimkandje they left two-thirds of the Afrikaner fighting force and a quarter of their women and children staining the dust of Winterhoek with their life's blood.

Within a week it was the turn of Otjimkandje to be attacked by a force of Namas under a chief from the south. When this battle was over the Herero had even more cause for celebration. They not only broke up the attack and inflicted heavy casualties, but also killed the Nama chief and captured his three sons. The two eldest were promptly put to death, but the youngest, hardly more than a boy, was released after he had promised allegiance to Mutjise.

It was the time of the Herero.

Aaron extended a delighted welcome to the travellers from Hereroland, although he thought some disaster must have overcome Mutjise and his people for them all to have left Hereroland. When Josh explained their reasons for descending upon him with all their own — and Aaron's — possessions the trader agreed it was the wisest course to have taken.

'You should have brought the two new missionaries with you,' he declared. 'But they will be safe in Mutjise's village. That one will lead his people to great things, you wait and see.'

'And so he might,' said Miriam. 'But he'll find it difficult to protect the missionaries. Mary says they rode off as calm as you like, saying they felt Hugo Walder had spent too much time in Otjimkandje and neglected the remainder of Hereroland.'

'Don't they realise that if it hadn't been for Hugo there would have been no Otjimkandje — and no Hereroland?'

'They don't want to know,' said Josh. 'They are young men out to make their own names. There's little room in their hearts to give credit to another. And on the subject of young men — have you heard how Daniel is getting on in Matabeleland?'

Much of the pleasure that came from meeting old friends left Aaron's face and he was uncharacteristically lost for words.

'What is it?' Miriam immediately feared the worst. 'Has something happened to him?'

'I don't know,' Aaron replied unhappily. 'I've heard a rumour that he was taken ill whilst on his way to Matabeleland, but I can't run down the source of the rumour and I can't find out any more. I've tried.' The old trader spread his hands apologetically. 'Tolotebe won't allow any of his men to take me to Mzilikazi, and I can't find the Bushmen. I've spent days in the desert looking for them.'

'I'll go out there myself tomorrow,' said Josh. 'The Bushmen are wary of strangers but they know me.'

'I'll come with you,' said Sam Speke.

'Then be sure to return with Daniel or some news of him,' said Miriam. 'Or you'll have me out there searching with you.'

It was a busy time unloading trade goods and personal belongings and settling the seven new arrivals in an establishment that normally catered for a maximum of two men.

Fortunately, the Bechuana chief proved particularly helpful by providing two large huts for the newcomers. Aaron had already told him they came to Lake Ngami to search for Daniel. Tolotebe was unhappy about his inability to help them in this respect but he did not dare send uninvited messengers to Mzilikazi's land. They would be killed long before they reached the Matabele chief and might cause an impi to be sent against Tolotebe's people to remind him that visitors were not welcome north of the Limpopo River.

There was another reason. Tolotebe had been the first to hear the rumours from the desert country that a dying Daniel had been left with the Matabele. It did not make sense to stir up trouble looking for a man who was already dead.

Josh and Sam set off at dawn to begin their search for the elusive little Bushmen. The rains had only recently ended and the 'desert' was a canvas liberally splashed with the bright colours of flowers and the remarkably rapid-growing grasses. It made the task of the two searchers much harder. There were small catchments of water to be found all over the land, much of it caught in rock-pools buried just beneath the surface in remote places known only to the Bushmen. It might be months before Xhube had to fall back on his traditional water-holes.

Intending to be out for only three days, the two men continued their fruitless search for a full week before they were forced to acknowledge defeat. Xhube was either making the most of the opportunity to hunt new territory or he was deliberately avoiding Josh.

The two men returned to Tolotebe's village depressed by their failure — to find their efforts had been unnecessary. A party of four of Mzilikazi's warriors had arrived from Matabeleland, having cut straight across the flowering desert. They were an advance party sent on by Daniel and carried a note from him. He was well and instructed Aaron to send to Sesebe for more stores as he was following with many tusks and ostrich feathers as well as a few fine animal skins.

The atmosphere had changed dramatically. Now there was nothing to do but to relax and wait for Daniel to arrive. It was a full year since Miriam had last seen him.

While they waited news came to them that the situation in South-West Africa had deteriorated still further. They learned that the Afrikaners had carried out a raid on the harbour settlement of Whalefish Bay. Meeting with little resistance, they had helped themselves to whatever they wanted and set fire to a couple of buildings.

362

A few days after this they had news of a more serious incident.

The bodies of the two young Otjimkandje missionaries were found twenty miles from the Herero village. They had been hacked to death and robbed of everything they had with them and their naked and mutilated bodies left beside the track. No tribe would admit responsibility for their murder and, although Mutjise sent parties of armed men scouring the countryside, they learned nothing.

Now there was no missionary at Otjimkandje, and Hugo Walder's work of more than twenty years might never have been.

Not until late April did Daniel arrive at Lake Ngami. He had with him a large party of bearers 'recruited' by the Matabele from neighbouring tribes.

Miriam hugged her son to her, observing that he was much thinner than when he had left and had the hollow-eyed look of a man who carried malaria in his blood. The illness was something he would carry with him for ever, but Miriam would work hard to put some meat back on his ribs.

Daniel was surprised and pleased to have all his family and friends at Lake Ngami to witness the success of his trading mission to the land of the legendary Mzilikazi. He was delighted, too, that Nell and Anne were now part of the Retallick family and he gave a specially warm greeting to Victoria. He completely won her heart by treating her as a young woman and not as a child.

Daniel found it difficult to look at her in any other way. Her figure told its own story and her expressive brown eyes were as bold and guileless as Hannah's had once been.

The simile brought with it a brief moment of painful memory, but it quickly passed and Daniel was able to smile when he told Sam Speke loudly, 'You've got a beautiful young lady for a daughter, Sam. Don't go accepting any offers of marriage for her until I've put in my bid.'

Sam Speke was only half-joking when he replied, 'One day you'll be reminded of that offer, Daniel. It was made before witnesses.'

They all found much to talk about during the days ahead. There was almost a year's news to exchange, and this in a country where the arrival of an unscheduled ship five hundred miles away provided days of speculation.

Daniel told them of his illness and the loyalty of the Bushmen, and Miriam gave up a silent prayer for the little Bushman and his family. It was a ritual she had performed on many occasions in earlier years.

Josh was aware of many gaps in Daniel's story, but he said nothing until all the women had gone to bed and the men remained seated around the fire outside the store drinking brandy and smoking pipes as they breathed in the woodsmoke-scented night air.

'You've had an interesting trek, son, and been lucky with your friendships – but you've told us very little about Mzilikazi himself.'

Daniel had seen his father's look when he had not taken one of his earlier stories through to a logical conclusion. To have done so would have meant bringing in details of one of the many executions he had witnessed. Yet, although he had expected to be questioned about Mzilikazi, he was not sure he had any answers to give.

He watched the smoke that was being sucked upwards from the fire dancing with the light warm breeze from the desert.

'I suppose there are many reasons for not talking about Mzilikazi,' he said thoughtfully. 'And I didn't want to speak in front of Ma or Mary about some of the things I've seen him do. He's a cruel man, more cruel than any man I've ever known.'

Daniel told them of the execution of the men of the impi and their families and of the methods employed.

Sam Speke had been listening so intently he had allowed his pipe to go out. He sucked on it and pulled a wry face as he took in a mouthful of bitter ash. Spitting it to the ground, he said, 'The man sounds mad. What sort of people are the Matabele that they allow such a man to rule them?'

'They are a wonderful people.' Daniel leaned forward, attracting the full attention of the others with the forcefulness of his words. 'The Matabele are honest, courageous and have incredible discipline. What's more, Mzilikazi is everything a good chief ought to be. It may not seem that way to you after hearing of some of the things he does, but his ways are right for his people. His punishments appear cruel to you and me – but only the guilty are punished. If there is any doubt about the guilt of anyone brought before him, they are set free. His people would follow him anywhere, even to certain death. That's what they think of him.'

He paused and looked around at the faces of his father, Aaron and Sam chiselled into deep shadowed facets by the glow from the dying fire.

'If I haven't said very much about Mzilikazi himself, it's because I'm not certain of my own feelings for him. It appals me to see the number of executions he orders, yet I have a tremendous respect for him both as a chief and as a man.'

'Will you go back to Matabelleland?' queried Josh.

'Oh yes.' The answer came without hesitation. 'I've a large hut there for trade and there's good business to be done with the Matabele.'

Aaron's teeth glinted momentarily in the firelight. He had made a trader of this young man already.

'That's not the only reason, though,' added Daniel. 'I've promised Mzilikazi I will go back and I wouldn't break my word to him. Perhaps that's also why he's such a great chief. I would never consider breaking my word to him, and I'm just as confident he will honour his promises to me.'

'And what promises has he made?' asked Aaron.

'That I can trade freely with the Matabele tribe and that my life will be as sacred as his own while I am in any lands over which he has jurisdiction.'

'Then you've done well, Daniel.' Josh knocked the bowl of his pipe gently against a log, pitching the pellet of ash and damp tobacco into the fire. 'You've not only come to a satisfactory business arrangement, but you've also found yourself a powerful friend at the same time.'

As Daniel lay down on the floor of his hut and pulled the blanket up to his chin he knew his father was right. Josh had put into words what Daniel had found so hard to accept until now.

Mzilikazi had become his friend.

CHAPTER NINETEEN

The stories of the ferocity of the conflict in Hereroland grew with every visitor who arrived at Lake Ngami from the south-west. They came from the members of various tribes, some non-participants in the battles being fought, others refugees from the fighting. Tolotebe fed the latter and allowed them a brief time to rest but always sent them on their way again after a day or two. To harbour anyone from a warring tribe might have been construed as involvement by other combatants, and the Bechuana chief wanted no part in this war.

Each traveller told his own story, but they all agreed on one thing. The hub of the war was Otjimkandje, and Mutjise and his Herero warriors had not lost a single battle.

Communications between Whalefish Bay and the interior had ceased after the first raid on the small trading port. Even the hardy Boers, who had for years brought goods overland from their Free State, now turned their wagons around well short of Hereroland. Aaron and Daniel had good reason to thank Sam for his initiative in bringing the wagons from Sesebe. They alone continued trading and were never short of food to eat.

When there was a long lull in the fighting they intended sending the goods they had collected to Whalefish Bay, but they would need to ask for a Herero escort to take them there.

Before that happened word reached Lake Ngami that Hugo Walder had returned to Otjimkandje to investigate the deaths of the two missionaries. He sent a message to Josh that as soon as he had completed his unpleasant task he would come to Lake Ngami.

As Hugo Walder was mounted and his messenger had travelled on foot he arrived a mere twenty-four hours after his letter. He had more grey hairs and looked very tired, but he was as indomitable as ever.

'Why did you come all the way up here and make me chase halfway across Africa to find you?'

Miriam kissed his bearded cheek affectionately. 'Had we known you were coming we would never have left Otjimkandje. But why did the Cape authorities send you? Have they realised after all these years that it was only your influence that kept the peace in Hereroland?'

'In Cape Town? My dear Miriam, they know nothing about Hereroland – or Damaraland, or Namaland, or any other land if it comes to that. They think we give tea-parties every week-end for chiefs and their wives.' He snorted. 'Do you know what one of the ladies gave me as a present when she knew I was returning here?' Without waiting for a reply he said, 'Boot polish! Can you imagine that? I am ordered here to investigate the murder of two missionaries and someone thinks I should have boot polish! They live in a different world in the Cape Colony.'

Josh smiled sympathetically; it was difficult to imagine the German preacher living among such people. Hugo Walder was a natural missionary and was at home only with the tribes who lived far from civilisation. He was wasted in Cape Town.

'Have you learned anything about the deaths of Wohlfarth or Doelker?'

'No, and I doubt if I will now. It was most probably an Afrikaner raiding party – there was one in the area at the time – but we will never know for certain. They were young fools to have left Otjimkandje at such a time, but death is a high price to pay for foolishness.'

'True,' said Miriam. 'Yet there are some who would say it is foolish for an unarmed man to ride hundreds of miles in such an uncertain land just to visit old friends.'

'Ach! Then such people would be wrong,' declared Hugo Walder. 'I have something here that I would have ridden a thousand miles to deliver personally.'

The missionary had a small pouch slung over his shoulder. Undoing it tantalisingly slowly, he drew out a large envelope sealed with a large red wax seal and handed it to Josh.

The name written in bold black script on the envelope was 'Joshua Retallick, Esquire'. There was no address. Turning the envelope over, Josh saw that the seal was that of the Governor of the Cape Colony.

'What is it?'

Hugo Walder gave a sigh of mock exasperation. 'The only way to find out is to open the envelope.'

Josh took a skinning-knife from his belt and carefully slit the end of the envelope. From inside he drew out a parchment document with another seal attached to it by two red ribbons. The document dropped open, and Josh immediately saw the bold signature, 'Victoria R.'

He began to read, and those watching saw his eyes widen and his jaw drop loose.

'Josh . . . ? It isn't . . . ?'

Josh nodded humbly to Miriam. 'Yes. It's a royal pardon. It sets aside my conviction.'

'Oh, Josh, I'm so happy! After all these years they've accepted your innocence. You're a free man once more.'

Miriam and Josh clung to one another for a few moments and Josh accepted the congratulations of Daniel and Sam Speke. Then he looked to Hugo Walder for an explanation.

The German preacher appeared slightly embarrassed. 'It was granted a long time ago,' he said. 'But no one had thought of sending it out to the Cape Colony from England. We would not have it now if I had not asked the Governor himself to make some enquiries about it.'

'And there would be no pardon at all but for your efforts. Bless you, Hugo.'

Miriam hugged him, and Hugo Walder beamed happily.

'What can I say?' asked Josh huskily. 'After all these years I didn't think it mattered to me anymore. I was wrong. It matters more than you'll ever know, Hugo. There will no longer have to be a part of my mind closed off to everyone, a need to be careful what I tell about my past to strangers. It means more than I can put into words, Hugo.'

'Then thank me by saying a prayer for the man who made it possible,' said Hugo Walder. 'He will have had much against him when he stood before the Lord.'

'I'll say one for a wonderful friend, too,' said Miriam. 'We've been very lucky, you and I, Josh.'

Josh nodded happily, trying to resist the urge to open out the Royal Pardon and read it again.

'What will you do now?' Sam Speke posed the question.

'Do?' The full impact of the pardon suddenly hit Josh. 'I . . . I don't know. It will need thinking about.'

Josh had made quite a lot of money during his years in Africa. He and Miriam could go anywhere. Return to England even. He looked to where the two young Gilmore sisters were playing together not far away. He and Miriam could take them to England, give them a good education and a new start in life, far from the dark memories of Africa.

'I just don't know,' he repeated. 'I don't know.'

Josh and Miriam slept very little that night. Hugo Walder had opened new doors for them at the very time when events in Hereroland had squeezed them into an unfamiliar corner of Africa.

They lay side by side in the small round hut, Josh's arm about Miriam's shoulders. Above them in the thatch an upside-down lizard scratched its way in search of insects. Somewhere nearby a cricket rasped its tuneless melody, and outside the drums of the Bechuana still attacked the night.

'Would you like to return to Cornwall, Miriam?'

She turned to face him. 'It's something I've thought about many times, but before the girls came to us I could think of no reason for going. There's no one left alive there I want to see again. How about you?'

Josh thought hard about the high Cornish moor, the bushes and grass, the greenness of everything. He thought of his mother and father in their little granite-grey cottage on the slopes of the tor.

'I would like to see the family again.' They had been away for a long time, but things changed slowly in Cornwall. He would find work again as a mine-engineer if he needed to.

'They would love the girls,' Miriam said. 'But what about Daniel? Do you think he would come with us?'

'It would be unfair to expect it of him. He has his future here. He'll do well. Would you go to England without him?'

Miriam thought hard about it. Her immediate reaction was to say she would not leave their only son, but she realised it was a mother's instinct and an unreasonable one. Daniel would return to the Matabele. Even if she and Daniel stayed in Africa she might not see him for years at a time. Meanwhile, massive strides were being made in world-wide travel. Hugo had told them of the steam-driven ships he had seen in Table Bay at the Cape, ships that belched black smoke like floating engine houses and made the voyage from England in thirty-five days. Daniel and Aaron were good partners. They were well on their way to becoming wealthy men. There was no reason why Daniel should not come to visit them in Cornwall.

None of this sound logic would fill the emptiness she would know having Daniel living two continents away from her. But Miriam knew what her answer to Josh must be. It would have been easier to say had Hannah lived to exercise a cautionary influence upon Daniel. Then suddenly she thought of the young Victoria. This time it was her intuition as a woman and not as a mother that told Miriam that one day the young girl would become the biggest single influence upon Daniel's life.

'Yes, I would go to Cornwall and leave Daniel here. I think he'll be in good hands.'

Josh rose on one elbow to look down at Miriam in the dim light shining through the glassless window.

'Then we'll go? We'll go – home?'

'Yes.'

Josh and Miriam told Daniel and the others of their decision the following morning.

'Your mother would be happier if you came with us – and so would I,' said Josh. 'I can't think of any one thing that would make me happier than to have us return to Cornwall as a complete family.'

'I can't come,' said Daniel. 'I must go back to Mzilikazi. But I'll think of you often and be very happy knowing you are both safe there, far from the wars of Hereroland. It will give me less to worry about.'

'I wish I were able to say the same about you,' declared Miriam.

Daniel smiled. 'I'll be under the protection of Mzilikazi, Ma. Can you think of anyone better able to take care of me?'

'Yes, a good wife,' said Miriam firmly.

'How about you, Sam?' asked Josh. 'Will you return to England with us?'

Sam looked at Mary and Victoria before answering.

'There's nothing for me in England that I haven't already got here, Josh. It wouldn't be fair to ask Mary to start learning new English ways.'

He did not bother to add that during their visit to the Cape Colony with their sick daughter he and Mary had been ostracised by the European community because theirs was a marriage between the two differing races. He would not take Mary and Victoria back to England and risk their becoming objects of curiosity.

'I'm glad you've made that decision, Sam,' said Daniel. 'I was hoping you'd come to Matabeleland with me for a year or so – bringing Mary and Victoria with you, of course.'

Daniel saw the doubt on the burly ex-seaman's face. 'I've already discussed it with Mzilikazi. He's fascinated by the trek-wagons he's seen belonging to the Boers. I told him I would willingly give him one of mine but that you could make him a new one – made especially for him. He talked about nothing else for days. When I left he was already having a hut built for the three of you.'

'Do you think we'll be safe, Daniel? I'm not worried for myself, but what about Mary and Victoria?'

Miriam was looking at Victoria. The young girl was willing her father to agree to go with Daniel.

'You will be going at Mzilikazi's invitation, Sam. I know of no better guarantee than that. Oh, I know I spoke about Mzilikazi's harsh justice, but he's a man of his word. You'll all be better protected than you will be this side of the Kalahari.'

'Go, Sam,' this from Aaron. 'I'll stay here and look after your possessions. By the time you decide to return things might have quietened down in Hereroland and we can shift our store from Sesebe to Otjimkandje. That might suit you well enough.'

Sam Speke knew it would suit Mary very well. She was never completely at ease away from her own people. But Victoria . . .? He turned to his daughter and caught her expression as she looked at Daniel. At that moment he saw as clearly as Miriam where the interests of his daughter lay.

'All right, we'll come with you, Daniel.'

Miriam had not shifted her gaze from Victoria during all the talk. Now the young girl returned her look, and Miriam smiled. Victoria's expression was one of triumphant confidence. She knew what she wanted. She would be spending a lot of time with Daniel in the months ahead, and with her looks and determination she could afford to be confident.

'Then everything is settled,' said Hugo Walder. 'I can look forward to having delightful company on my return journey to Cape Town.'

He smiled at Miriam. 'I only wish I was more observant, then perhaps I could prepare you for the latest fashions at the Cape. I believe women set great store by such things.'

'Well, here's one who doesn't,' said Miriam, her chin going up defiantly. 'My clothes will be clean and well mended, just the way they've always been. We'll not waste good money on frills and the like because everyone else is wearing them.'

Josh smiled to himself. Miriam had changed little since she was a barefoot girl. Her attitude towards what other people thought of her dress had been the same then. Nevertheless, she would be as excited as a child at Christmas when she had the opportunity of looking around the stores at the Cape. It would give him a great deal of pleasure to buy her all the things she was claiming not to want.

'When were you thinking of leaving?' asked Hugo Walder.

'We don't have to think about that yet,' said Miriam alarmed at the thought of an early parting with Daniel. 'Let's all relax and enjoy ourselves together while we can.'

Nobody argued with her. It was pleasant to have nothing to do but fish in the bitter waters of the lake and hunt the animals that came there to drink.

But they had enjoyed only a few days of relaxation when a Bechuana herd-boy ran into the village shouting that an armed Matabele impi was advancing upon the village from the north. The Bechuana hastily gathered up their belongings and fled into the desert to the south while the Europeans gathered up their guns to prepare for the worst.

The impi soon came in view but they were marching in a relaxed manner, not advancing in the 'head and horns' formation they used for attack. As the warriors drew closer Daniel saw they were men of Mzilikazi's own formidable bodyguard, led by the induna Muvandi. These were the foremost warriors in the Matabele army, each pledged to give his life willingly for the chief. Mzilikazi would not waste such warriors on a raid. This was not a war-party.

Daniel put aside his gun and went out to meet Muvandi. Those watching saw the induna advance and salute Daniel with a raised hand. Even at a distance of three hundred yards they saw the smile of the induna.

Daniel brought Muvandi back to meet the others, the induna greeted each of them courteously and to Hugo Walder he said, 'Even in my country we have heard of "The Little Father". Mzilikazi will be pleased to know I have given you his greetings.'

'Muvandi has come to escort us back to Matabeleland,' Daniel said to Sam Speke. 'Mzilikazi heard of the troubles in Hereroland and was afraid it might affect us here. Muvandi was sent to fetch us. He would like us to leave tomorrow.'

'Tomorrow?' Miriam echoed. 'But that means this will be our last day together.'

'For a while,' Daniel said gently. 'You've been telling me yourself that England is only a month away by sea. We'll write and if I haven't come to visit you in three years' time, then you must come back here again to see me.'

'Three years!' Miriam whispered. She managed to make it sound a lifetime. 'So much can happen in that time.'

'Ma, this is supposed to be a happy time,' Daniel reminded her. 'After all the years of hardship you've both suffered Pa's name has been cleared. You can return home with your heads held high. I'm staying here because I've got a trading agreement with the most powerful chief in the whole of this part of Africa. Things could hardly be better.'

'I know.' Miriam shook her head vigorously. 'It's a mother's privilege to worry, that's all.'

Josh put an arm about her shoulders and spoke to Daniel. 'She's all right, son. Wait until we get back to Cornwall. There won't be a single household on the moor that doesn't know Daniel Retallick is trading with Mzilikazi.'

He rubbed his chin ruefully. 'Mind you, unless things have changed an awful lot since I was last there they won't have heard of Mzilikazi, and if he's got nothing to do with the price of gin or corn they won't care a lot, either.'

'It isn't necessary to go to England to find such an attitude,' said Hugo Walder. 'I'll introduce you to people in the Cape Colony who are exactly the same.'

They were up until late that evening, the men working hard to pack the wagons for the journey to Matabeleland and Miriam and the Gilmore children helping first Mary and Victoria with their packing and then drifting from wagon to wagon talking. Miriam resisted the urge to stay close enough to Daniel to reach out a hand and touch him whenever she thought of their imminent parting.

The next morning the farewells were exaggeratedly subdued, everyone deliberately playing down the occasion for their own particular reason.

Only when the final ox was inspanned did Miriam's feelings threaten to overflow in choked tears. To the young Victoria she said quietly, 'Daniel is a good man, Victoria. He'll make you a good husband one day. Take care of him.'

She was gone before Victoria could reply and she clung to Daniel for long minutes, pressing her face into his shoulder, fighting to control the emotions that threatened her self-control.

Finally it was Daniel himself who gently held her away from him.

'Take care of yourself, Ma. I'll be thinking of you and happy to know you and Pa will be back in England. Write to me through Hugo. He'll make sure I get your letters.'

He kissed her quickly and she stood away from him, hands clenched tightly at her sides.

The parting between father and son was easier. They gripped hands and looked at each other in a silence that said more than words. It was a look that spoke of love and mutual respect. They were each of them men to be reckoned with.

Both parties set off at the same time and they waved until distance and the heat of the day distorted the wagons and hid them from view in a shimmering haze as they disappeared into a new future.

374

They were pioneers. Each in his own way had given something new to the land they were now leaving.

To the west went those who were leaving the frontiers of Africa, the life they had known gone for ever! Josh and Miriam, returning to England to take up life again in a land they had known long before; the young Gilmore girls, memories of their terrible suffering already fading; Hugo Walder, the first white man to live among the tribes of Hereroland and teach them the faith of his order, a man who by his integrity and dedicated example had brought much honour to his calling.

To the east went those who would push the frontiers still farther into the vast unknown continent. To Daniel and Victoria the future held excitement and fulfilment. Africa was their home. They had known no other. Sam and Mary had forged a link between the old and the new with love and respect. It was a way that would be accepted by neither side for generations to come, but it was a beginning.

Watching both parties leave was Aaron, the trader. His thick long beard and chosen calling were representative of a people who had managed to keep their unique identity for two thousand years without the encouragement of a homeland. To the Herero he had given guns to bring them back from the brink of extinction. To Africa he had given his wife and daughter.

EPILOGUE

The steam clipper *Great Britain* bound from Melbourne, Australia, via Cape Town nosed into Liverpool dock on 25 May 1864. Listed among her passengers were 'Joshua Retallick, esq.' and wife'.

Six thousand miles away in the northern Kalahari, Pieter van der Stel and his small party of Boer trekkers were in trouble. They had been seventeen days without finding fresh water, and during the heat of the afternoon three of the oxen pulling their two wagons had dropped dead.

Pieter van der Stel was lost. The party had left the Orange Free State more than twelve months before, lured northwards by the promise of land and unlimited opportunity in the Portuguese west-coast colony of Angola.

From isolated farms and villages hundreds of Boers had been doing the same thing. Fiercely independent and resentful of the inexorable advance of British influence and control from Cape Town they moved northwards and eastwards in search of a new land, free from the laws and petty disciplines of the British.

Such was the background of Pieter van der Stel, his brother Jan and their wives and thirteen children. There had been fifteen children when they set off, but Pieter van der Stel had lost two. One, a girl of three, had fallen from the wagon-seat and been crushed by the wheel of the big canvas-topped wagon. The other, a baby born on the long trek, had simply wasted away and died because the milk of its underfed mother contained no nourishment.

They were both laid in the ground with all the formality that the prayer-book had to offer. Pieter van der Stel was a Christian man. His children had Christian burials, their bodies lain to rest in Christian coffins of rough-planed wood. A large bundle of the cheap planks dangled from the rear of each wagon, brought especially for such a grim purpose, a constant reminder of the hardships expected along the way.

376

But this was the hardest time of the whole trek. Today their situation was desperate. They had used the last drop of water, and the oxen were staggering.

Pieter van der Stel had altered course for Lake Ngami a week before and he expected to sight the water at any moment. He was blissfully unaware that the lake was still fifty miles away, and on his present course he would pass its northernmost extremity without ever sighting water.

Xhube knew it. He also knew of the Boers' desperate plight. He and his tiny family group had watched them for two days, Xhube being torn between instinctive shyness and the thought of his special relationship with Daniel.

'Today their oxen die. Tomorrow it will be their turn,' said the troubled Bushman leader.

'Death walks close beside all of us,' replied the aged Hwexa, the oldest member of Xhube's tribe. 'When he takes our hand there is no one may break his grip—not even you, Xhube.'

'I remember a time when our people lay in the sun and the skin of their bellies touched their backbones. It was a white man who saved us then.'

'He is a friend and the son of a friend. There are few such men for our people, Xhube.'

'You speak the truth. But can I look a friend in the face as a man and say I watched his people die and did nothing?'

Xhube rose to his feet, his mind made up. 'No, Hwexa. Tell the women to bring water. I will go and speak to the white men.'

Pieter van der Stel saw Xhube and his three hunters coming across the hot sand towards him. Behind the Bushman chief came Hwexa and the four women carrying water-filled eggshells and moving more slowly.

'Jannie,' the Boer called to his brother. 'Come here and bring your gun. Tell the boys to have their guns handy, too. Some Bushmen are coming. Do nothing until I tell you.'

Xhube's resolution faltered when he saw the big Boer and his brother walking out to meet him carrying their muskets in front of their bodies. Behind them, sheltered by the two wagons, he glimpsed a number of younger men, similarly armed.

His hunters had also seen and were unhappy.

'It will be all right,' explained Xhube. 'They must take care because they do not know us.'

His words lacked conviction. Xhube was beginning to think he might have erred in coming to the assistance of these white men, but he could have done no less.

However, there was no need to risk all his small tribe. He told his hunters to stay where they were and wait for the women.

They stopped about forty yards from the advancing Boers, and Xhube went on alone. He felt very vulnerable as he walked towards the Boers and was constantly aware of the musket-barrels which protruded from behind the two wagons.

He and the Boers met in the open desert, the Boers towering over the little Bushman.

Xhube smiled his greeting. 'You are tall and we have seen you from afar. We have water and you have none. What we have is yours. I will guide you to the bitter water and show you fresh water along the way.'

Xhube's words were accompanied by gestures, first to his people who waited patiently behind him and then to the wagons.

'What's he saying?' Jan van der Stel asked his brother.

'I don't know. I think he's asking us to give him and his people food, or something.'

'Hell, man! What does he take us for? Can't he see we're desperate for water?'

Xhube realised the Boers did not understand him and he turned, walking a few paces towards the waiting hunters and women.

'Come, bring the water.'

His soft call went unheard as a sharp-eyed boy behind one of the wagons called, 'Pa! Those Bushman women have water.'

The loud shout frightened Xhube's women and one of them turned away and began running.

'Stop! Bring the water here.' Xhube's cry was louder, more urgent.

It was too late. The tragic misunderstanding between the two parties had to run its inevitable course. Peiter van der Stel threw his gun up to his shoulder and shouted, 'Shoot the women first! We want that water.'

He fired, and one of the fleeing women crashed to the ground. She fell upon one of the two ostrich eggs she had been carrying and the water from it diluted her blood as it seeped into the hot sand of the Kalahari. The other egg fell on the soft sand, the water held in by the plug of dried grass.

Xhube ran to prevent Jan van der Stel from firing, but before he could reach him a musket-ball from one of the guns behind the wagons tore its way through his chest and bowled him over.

Muskets were crashing, and all the women were down now. The desperate Bushmen strung arrows in their tiny bows and ran at the two Boers as they reloaded their weapons with experienced swiftness.

One of the arrows found its mark in the neck of Jan van der Stel, but it was not poisoned as the Bushmen had not been prepared for hunting. The arrow was no more painful than the sting of a large bush-wasp, and the Boer shot dead the Bushman who had fired it at him.

The massacre was over in less than two minutes, and the two Boer women and the children were soon gathering up the precious water-filled eggs.

'Pa! This one's still alive.'

One of the van der Stel boys leaned over Xhube. Pieter van der Stel strode to where the Bushman lay on his back, blood bubbling from the hole in his chest and dribbling from the side of his mouth.

The Boer raised his gun to bring the butt down and finish the dying man. He found himself looking into the unwavering eyes of the Bushman and unexpectedly lowered the gun.

'Agh! Leave him. He's as good as dead already.' Pieter van der Stel ushered his family back to the wagons where he and his brother doled out the water sparingly to humans and oxen.

No trace was ever found of the van der Stel trekkers. The two families, their oxen and wagons found their last resting-place in the Kalahari desert of Xhube's people, the exact spot known only to the wind, the sand and the silent elusive Bushman from whom the desert keeps no secrets.

Xhube lived long enough to crawl to a rock and claw himself to a sitting position with his back to it. He watched the Boers leave and the sun overtake them, and when he died his shadow stretched as far as that of the tallest man who had ever walked the land.

HISTORICAL BACKGROUND

This book has as its setting the South West Africa of the 1840s and 1850s and whilst the majority of events and characters are ficitious, the tribes and the lands they occupied were, and are, very real.

The first man to make his home there was the Bushman. He had no need to make tribal boundaries, the whole of the land was his. There *were* no other tribes. For thousands of years he wandered at will and it was this very freedom that was to prove his downfall. When other tribes invaded he was unable to adapt to their ways. Their cattle grazed the land therefore he hunted them as he had always hunted grazing animals. Their crops grew from the land therefore they must be his also. When the newcomers sought him out to kill him the Bushman had no tribal structure to call upon for help. He was an individual and the numbers of the strangers defeated him. The Bushman, a natural victim, lost his place and became a diminutive enigma.

The Herero tribesman had his boundaries, but they were wide. He himself said, 'Wherever Herero cattle have grazed, there is Hereroland.' By the early years of the 19th century he was firmly established in an area of 100,000 square miles, from Rehoboth to Grootfontein, and from Gobabis to the sea. His was the power of numbers and he possessed the arrogance of a ruling race. His cattle raised dust to the sky from horizon to horizon. The sun shone to warm *his* back, the rains fell to water *his* stock.

But then, in 1823, the tribesmen of Jonker Afrikaner invaded the land. One of the Orlam tribes, the Afrikaners had moved northwards from the Cape over a period of many years, settling for a while on the Orange River, ruled by their chief, Jager Afrikaner. When Jager died he left his younger sons without an inheritance. One of them gathered together all the wildest elements of his late father's tribe and led them northwards to carve out a territory of his own. That son was Jonker. Armed with guns, his followers fell upon the Hereros, stripping them of everything they owned. He built himself an empire about the hills of modern-day Windhoek and stamped his name indelibly upon the history of his adopted land.

There were many tribes, many chiefs, but only Jonker rose above the fiction I was able to weave about the others. For as long as he lived, he ruled absolutely. When he died at Okahandja in 1861 it was the end of an important chapter in history. The strength went from his Afrikaner tribe and Jonker's empire fell apart. If I have bent his image in order to tell my story — I apologise to his memory.

But my story is set in a harsh, scorched and uncertain land, and in the difficult days of the mid-19th century. Jonker lived there. So too did the Herero and the Bushman. Their lives have been documented by the historian. They, together with the characters of my story, truly reaped a Harvest of the Sun.

E.V.T.

Nicholas Monsarrat
The Master Mariner
book 1 **Running Proud** £1.50

'He will not die: he will wander the wild waters until all the seas run dry . . .'

The flawed courage of one man imperilled Admiral Drake's masterstroke on the day the English fireships sailed against the Armada in the Calais Roads. That coward was Matthew Lawe, Drake's coxswain, cursed from that day to sail the seas for all time to purge his guilt – through centuries of wind, wave and warfare . . . with the doomed Hudson to the Arctic, to the sunbleached Main with Morgan the pirate, as clerk to Pepys at the Admiralty, with Cook to bloodstained Hawaii and with Nelson at Cape Trafalgar.

'A rich, rare and noble feast' THE TIMES

'The cruel sea and the valiant men who sailed on it through all the generations' DAILY MAIL

Frederick Nolan
Carver's Kingdom £1.25

The story of Theo Carver, merchant adventurer, seeker of fortune, builder of empires . . . of his brother, the coldblooded Ezra, ruthless manipulator of money and men, infamous as 'The Back Bay Bastard' . . . and of Sarah Hutchinson who survived a doomed marriage to become the greatest actress of her generation.

'A meaty read . . . plenty of skulduggery, murder, rape and lynching' SUNDAY TELEGRAPH

Sir Arthur Quiller-Couch and Daphne du Maurier
Castle Dor £1

A spellbinding love story and a superb evocation of the romance of Cornwall. *Castle Dor* is a book with unique and fascinating origins. The unfinished last novel of the celebrated 'Q', Sir Arthur's daughter passed the manuscript to her friend Daphne du Maurier, whose storytelling skills were perfectly suited to the old master's tale.

The result is a magical recreation of the legend of Tristan and Iseult transplanted to nineteenth-century Cornwall.

'A novel in the spellbinding du Maurier tradition' MANCHESTER EVENING NEWS

Lauren Elder with Shirley Streshinsky
And I Alone Survived 90p

Not since *Alive*! has there been a survival story like this one.

Lauren Elder set out in a light aircraft with the pilot and his girlfriend on a joyride, skyborne sightseeing over the splendour of the Sierra Navada range. When the plane hit the mountain, the joyride turned into a nightmare. After a night of sub-zero temperatures, Laura, the only survivor, faced a fearsome 8000-foot climb down to safety . . .

'Vividly recreates a nightmare ordeal' YORKSHIRE POST

Pat Seed MBE
One Day At a Time 95p

Intensely moving, heartrending, finally inspiring – the victim of cancer who transformed tragedy into triumph tells her story.

Pat Seed, housewife, mother of two, working journalist, learned she had cancer and had to learn to live one day at a time. She had a goal : to raise a million pounds to buy Manchester's Christie Hospital a CAT scanner, the machine that can diagnose cancer early enough to save life.

This is the story of how she raised that money, and of the thousands – from schoolchildren to stars of the entertainment world – who helped.

'Spoken direct to the hopes, fears and hearts of millions'
JEAN ROOK

You can buy these and other Pan Books from booksellers and newsagents; or direct from the following address:
Pan Books, Sales Office, Cavaye Place, London SW10 9PG
Send purchase price plus 20p for the first book and 10p for each additional book, to allow for postage and packing
Prices quoted are applicable in the UK

While every effort is made to keep prices low, it is sometimes necessary to increase prices at short notice. Pan Books reserve the right to show on covers and charge new retail prices which may differ from those advertised in the text or elsewhere